THE KEEPER

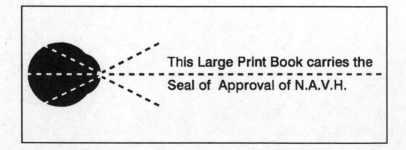

This Large Print Book carries the
Seal of Approval of N.A.V.H.

THE KEEPER

JOHN LESCROART

THORNDIKE PRESS

A part of Gale, Cengage Learning

GALE
CENGAGE Learning·

Farmington Hills, Mich • San Francisco • New York • Waterville, Maine
Meriden, Conn • Mason, Ohio • Chicago

LIBRARY OF CONGRESS CATALOGING-IN-PUBLICATION DATA

Lescroart, John T.
  The keeper / by John Lescroart. — Large print edition.
    pages cm. — (Thorndike Press large print basic)
  ISBN 978-1-4104-6792-8 (hardcover) — ISBN 1-4104-6792-9 (hardcover)
  1. Missing persons—Fiction. 2. Large type books. I. Title.
PS3562.E78K44 2014b
813'.54—dc23   2014010164

Published in 2014 by arrangement with Atria Books, a division of Simon & Schuster, Inc.

Printed in the United States of America
1 2 3 4 5 6 7 18 17 16 15 14

Once again
To Lisa Marie Sawyer,
My endless love

"Woman's virtue is man's greatest invention."

— Cornelia Otis Skinner

1

At seven-fifteen on the Monday morning after Thanksgiving, Dismas Hardy sat at his dining room table, the *San Francisco Chronicle* spread out before him. He reached for his mug of coffee, took an all but unconscious sip, put it back down.

His wife, Frannie, coming in from the kitchen behind him, put her hands on his shoulders, then kissed the top of his head. "Are you all right?"

"Fine."

"You sure?"

"Why wouldn't I be?"

"I don't know. You're sighing just about every ten seconds."

"It's a new breathing technique I'm working on."

"I'd say you've got it down."

"Every ten seconds?"

"Give or take." In her bathrobe, fresh from a shower, she pulled out a chair and sat as

Hardy sighed again. "Like right there," she said. "You're also not zipping through the paper the way you always do."

Hardy looked down, turned a page. "Am, too." He sat back. "Okay, so the kids stay here for five days, and the whole time I'm aware of how much space they're taking up and the energy it takes to keep up with them, and by yesterday I am really, really ready for them to get back to their school lives and out of here. And now this morning I wake up and they're not here and I wish they were. How does this make any sense?"

"You miss them, that's all."

"Yeah, but when they're here . . ."

"They're great."

"Of course," Hardy said. "Perfect in every way, as we've raised them to be. But I barely get used to seeing them and they're gone again. Then I want them back."

"Kids," she said. "Can't live with them. Can't kill them. Meanwhile, do you think you can spare me a piece of the paper?"

Hardy sighed again. Reaching up, he tore off a corner the size of a postage stamp and slid it across to her.

"Thank you," she said. "Now could you please spare me a section of the newspaper? Any section would be fine."

"You said 'piece.'"

"I know I did. That was an egregious error, and I deserved what I got." Striking quickly, she pulled the front section over to her. "How have I tolerated living with you all these years?"

"That whole 'never a dull moment' thing?"

"That must be it." She scanned the headlines, turned the page, and after a minute or two gave a quick gasp.

Hardy looked over. "What?"

But she was reading and didn't respond. Her hand went to her mouth.

"Fran?"

Now she looked up, puzzled and pensive. "Katie Chase," she said. "One of my clients. It says here she's gone missing."

"When?"

"Looks like Wednesday night." Frannie kept scanning. "Her husband, Hal, went to pick up his brother at the airport, and when he came back, she was gone."

"Gone how?"

"I don't know. That's all it says here, missing from her house."

"Any signs of a struggle?"

"I don't know. It doesn't say." She looked across at him. "She's got two kids, Diz. One and three. That's part of why she was seeing me."

11

"What's the other part? No, wait, let me guess. Her marriage." Then he shook his head. "But the husband's got an alibi."

"It's not an alibi, Dismas. It wasn't him. I'm sure it wasn't him."

"No? Why do you say that? Do you know him?"

Frannie lifted then lowered her shoulders. "They have their problems. This just in: Raising kids isn't easy. You said it yourself. Hal was at the airport. Maybe somebody snatched her. Maybe she ran away."

"And left her kids?"

"Maybe they weren't there. Maybe Hal took them with him to the airport."

"Because toddlers are so much fun to be with? Especially at an airport. No, they were home with her."

"So what happened to them?"

"They're still home," Hardy said. "They're fine. If they weren't, that article would have said something about it. It's only her. She either left on her own or somebody took her. And sorry, but nobody kidnaps adults."

"Either way . . ."

Hardy finished her thought. "Either way, I admit, it's not good. And speaking of other things not good, you should read 'CityTalk' " — a popular daily column in the paper — "third overdose in the jail in

12

the last three months."

"Overdose in the jail? How do you get drugs into the jail?"

"I'm going to rule out the Tooth Fairy."

2

JaMorris "Jambo" Monroe and Abby Foley wound up pairing off in Homicide because of softball. JaMorris played two years of varsity at Cal and, after finally reconciling himself to the fact that he wouldn't get drafted to play pro ball, went to the Police Academy in San Francisco.

Last summer he turned thirty-five and felt the need to come back to an approximation of the game he loved. He joined the Hammerheads and played the whole season with eight other guys and one woman: the catcher (the catcher!), Abby. He'd been blown away not only to have a woman on the team — it wasn't a coed league, strictly speaking — but also to find out that she was a great athlete, almost forty years old and a full inspector with the Homicide detail. After the season — they'd batted two and three in the lineup and had clicked as people — she'd lobbied to get him assigned there, too.

Because of some department shake-ups (a former lieutenant who retired, an inspector who moved up), it had worked out.

Now, partnered for three months, they were sitting in the office of the new Homicide lieutenant, Devin Juhle, discussing an assignment that Abby wanted some clarity on. "I don't know why this isn't Missing Persons, Dev. She is simply missing, is she not?"

Juhle nodded equably. "She is."

"You see my quandary?"

"Of course. In my earlier days, when I wondered about things, that might have been something I would have wondered about."

"It's just that —"

"I know." Juhle stopped her. "If we don't have a dead person, how can it be a homicide? Maybe it's because it's the wife of a sheriff's deputy. Maybe somebody knows somebody at City Hall. Ours is not to reason why."

"That's what I was thinking," Abby said.

"And thinking is a good thing." Juhle spread his hands on his desk. "We encourage thinking and the questions it raises. In this case, fortunately, we have an answer to the main question."

"The husband," JaMorris said.

15

Juhle nodded with approval at his newest inspector. "The husband. Hal. Missing Persons thinks he ought to be at least a person of interest. His alibi is squishy as hell."

"What is it?" JaMorris asked. "The alibi."

"He went to the airport to pick up his brother. But he says he left at seven-thirty for an eight-fifty flight. It's a half-hour drive. Then the plane got delayed — that checks — so he pulled off and had a beer in South City, but he paid cash. Nobody remembers him where he says he stopped. So, all in all, squishy."

"Anything else?" Abby asked.

"Well, the wife was seeing a marriage counselor — Hal admits this — about some issues between them."

"Just the wife was seeing the counselor?" JaMorris asked. "Not him, too?"

"No. Just her. And another thing," Juhle said. "Small but provocative. Blood in the kitchen."

"Blood is good," Abby said. "A lot?"

"Drops. Just enough for DNA. Hers. The point is, Missing Persons thinks it's all coming back to Homicide eventually, so we might as well get in on the ground floor."

"Anything else in the realm of physical evidence?" Abby asked.

"Not yet, no. But a couple of other things just the same. First, when Hal and his brother got home, the wife was gone, but the kids were still in their beds, asleep. I have a hard time seeing her walking out and leaving the kids behind. Better odds that something happened to her, right? Second, one of the neighbors heard some arguing — maybe fighting, maybe struggling — down on the street."

Abby let out a small sigh. "And how long has it been?"

"Since Wednesday night." Juhle put on a perky face. "So she's officially missing since last night." Absent signs of struggle or violence, because of the large number of random runaways, it took three days in San Francisco for a person who couldn't be found to become a true missing person to the police.

"Yeah, on that subject again," JaMorris said, "just one more time. Why are we taking on a missing person? Everybody in town who goes missing is going to have a relative who thinks it's a murder and goes after Homicide for not doing their job."

"I appreciate your concern, Jambo. But here's the deal. They tell me. I tell you. And I'm telling you we're on this one."

Abby stepped in. "So, in reality, she's been

17

missing for four days." Everyone knew that the window on solving a homicide closed down dramatically after two days, and after four, the evidence trail tended to be very cold. But Abby understood that there was no point in arguing further. It was going to be their assignment, taking time away from their other, possibly solvable homicides. "How do you want us to handle this?"

"Talk to the husband, of course," Juhle said. "Start there."

"Is he being cooperative?" JaMorris asked.

"He's the very soul of cooperation."

With a defeated sigh, Abby reached out and lifted the case file from the surface of Juhle's desk. Opening it, she asked as she scanned, "Where are we off to?"

"That's the easy part," Juhle said. "Hal's just next door. At the jail."

"He's already arrested?" JaMorris asked.

"No," Juhle said. "He works there."

3

The dartboard in Dismas Hardy's office was designed to look like an upscale cherrywood cabinet. Behind its dark polished wooden doors was a professional-quality board on a green baize backdrop — Hardy never, ever missed the board entirely. Not exactly camouflaged, but subtle, was a cherrywood throwing line built into his light hardwood floor.

Now he stood at that line and threw a dart that landed in the center of the 4, his target. He was playing his third round of Twenty Down today, and so far this round, he hadn't missed. His coat hung over the chair behind his desk, his collar and tie were loose, and he knew that he was in the zone, locked. He had one more dart this round. Taking very little time so that he wouldn't think and screw it all up, he hefted his little tungsten beauty with its custom-made blue flights and let fly.

Nailed it. The 3. One round away from perfection.

He had come close once before, when the telephone rang and distracted him as he was setting up to throw, so now he hesitated a moment before going to the board to re-trieve his last round. He knew he could walk over to his desk and take the phone off the hook. But by his own internal rules, that would be cheating. He could call Phyllis out in the lobby and tell her to hold his calls for exactly one minute, although she might — no, she would — ask him why and ruin his concentration. Or he could ignore the phone altogether, keep his head out of it, get his darts right now, and throw the god-damn things.

Finally, giving these options no more than the split second they were worth, he moved forward, retrieved his round from the board, walked back to the baseline, turned in a measured and unhurried fashion, lifted his first dart, aimed, and threw.

2.

Second to last dart.

1.

No thought. Don't think. Don't fucking think. Throw it throw it throw it.

Bull's-eye!

"Yes!" Hardy threw up his hands in a

touchdown gesture. "Thank you, thank you, thank you," he said aloud, pumping his fist. "Yes!"

After three quick knocks, his office door opened, and Phyllis was standing there with a look of alarm. "Is everything all right? I heard you calling out."

"I'm great. I'm at a peak moment." Hardy, beaming, his arms again halfway raised, motioned her inside. "Check this out." He gestured to the dartboard. "I ask you, is that a thing of beauty? A last-round two-one bull's-eye. Twenty down and no misses! First time ever. Is that awesome or what?"

His receptionist/secretary shot a nervous glance over at the board, then back at her boss. "Very nice," she said with some uncertainty, "but I really think I should get back to the phones."

She had barely started back toward her workstation when a man in a uniform appeared behind her, tapping on the open door. "Excuse me," he said. "I don't know if I'm in the right office. I'm trying to find a lawyer named Dismas Hardy."

Hal Chase wasn't aware that he'd made a rational decision to come to Hardy's offices. All he knew was that after his interview with the two Homicide cops, he had to get out of

21

the jail, like now, or he might crack. He needed to take a walk, clear his head. It was way early for lunch, but he didn't care. By now, all of his coworkers knew Katie was gone — no one would call him on anything. He passed through the lobby without a word on the way out, and the guys behind the counter just watched him go.

He turned uptown but didn't consciously know it. Cruel and relentless, his brain kept replaying scenes of good times he had shared with Katie; in the early years, it seemed they'd never had anything else: the blessed couple, the golden couple, the pair all their friends envied.

Where had those two people gone?

The enormous old seal lay sleeping in his usual spot right down by the water, on the ramp by the Santa Catalina ferry landing. Katie in her Dolphin shorts and the sexy tank top, as lovely as any swimsuit model with her long tan legs, her shoulder-length hair blowing in her face in the breeze, was urging Hal to get nearer to the seal for the picture.

"I get any closer, he's going to bite me."

"Is my big brave boyfriend afraid of a little old seal?"

"That little old seal weighs about half a ton."

"Chicken."

"How about if I take your picture with him? You can sit on his lap."

"Seals don't have laps. At least Ben doesn't."

"That's just your excuse. I think you must be the chicken."

"Come on. Look at him. He's so cute. A couple more steps, and I get a classic picture. We're making a memory here."

Hal hesitated another moment and finally said, "Only because I love you." He moved a step closer down the ramp.

The apparently sleeping seal suddenly lurched at him with an earsplitting angry cry. Which Hal pretty much matched with his own scream as he jumped out of his skin and ran back up the ramp to Katie, the seal hot on his heels, not nearly as slow as they might have supposed.

When they stopped running, all the way up by the ticket window (although the seal had called off the chase after only a few yards), they were breathless, holding each other.

And laughing, laughing, laughing.

Holding hands over the table after their pizza dinner at Giorgio's, which was one of the few places they could afford in San Francisco. "Something seems wrong," Hal said.

"No, not really."

" 'Not really' really means 'yes really.' "

Katie sighed. "It's not that big a thing. The important thing is we're getting married."

"But . . . ?"

"But . . ." She took a small breath. "I've tried to get used to it, but I don't really like the 'obey' part. 'Love and honor' I'm good with, but . . . I don't want to have a fight about it. I mean, if it's important to you."

"That you obey me? I've never thought of asking you to obey me. How weird would that be? We decide things together. That's who we are. That's who we're going to be after we're married."

"It would really be okay with you? To leave out 'obey'?"

"I wouldn't even notice it. Now that we're talking about it, I don't think I'd even want it at all. I'm a little embarrassed that I didn't think of it first. How about 'love, honor, and cherish'? That's got a nice rhythm, and it's how I feel."

"Cherish," she said. Her hand went to her mouth. Her eyes glistened in the pizzeria's dim light. Nodding, she pushed her chair back, stood up, and came around to kiss him right in front of God and everybody. "I love you so much," she whispered. "You are so who I belong with."

When Katie was pregnant with their first child, Ellen, she and Hal had nicknamed her Zy, for

24

zygote. Every night before they went to sleep, he kissed Katie's stomach, and if that didn't lead to something else, he would say, keeping his mouth close, "Hi, Zy. Your daddy loves you."

Now newborn Ellen lay swaddled on Katie's stomach outside the delivery room. Twenty-five hours of labor with Hal by her side every minute of it, and then at last the delivery of the healthy child. Hal looked down on her tiny face, her eyes scrunched closed. He touched her cheek. Leaning over, he gently kissed his exhausted wife. Then he looked down at the baby. "Hi, Zy," he said.

Thirty minutes old, the baby opened her eyes — only for a second or two, but it was there, a definite moment of recognition — and she smiled at him.

Hal broke down and sobbed.

4

Although he already had an idea of the answer, Hardy asked what he could do for Mr. Chase.

"My wife disappeared from our home last Wednesday night, while I was at the airport picking up my brother. I was cooperating with Missing Persons every way I knew how, until this morning, when a team of hard-ass inspectors — Homicide, not Missing Persons — took over, obviously thinking I had something to do with her disappearance."

Over in the corner by the windows, Chase had taken one of the chairs in the more informal of the two seating areas in Hardy's office. So far, he had left untouched the cup of coffee Phyllis had brought in; it sat on the table in front of him. He held himself with his hands clenched on his thighs, his back ramrod-stiff, his feet planted flat on the floor. His hazel eyes were shot with red, bruised-looking underneath. "I'm sorry to barge in without an appointment," he said, "but I didn't know I was coming here until I got to your front door."

"Walk-ins are always welcome." Hardy gave him his professional smile. "Did somebody refer you to me?"

"Not in so many words. You may know, though, that my wife, Katie, was — is — a client of your wife's. In one of your last trials, Katie had put together who you were. All of a sudden this morning, I think I might need a lawyer. So here I am."

"Your wife's missing. Is there some evidence indicating that you had anything to do with that?"

"No. They say they found a few drops of her blood in the kitchen, but she was prepping the Thanksgiving stuff that night and probably cut herself. Big deal. Being more or less in law enforcement myself, I knew what they were thinking. These were not good cops wanting to help me find my wife. All they were interested in was me as a suspect, what I was doing when she disappeared."

"You were at the airport?"

"Correct. Picking up my brother. Half brother. Warren."

"And these inspectors you spoke to, they had a problem with your alibi?"

"Alibi. Jesus Christ. It's not an alibi. It's where I was. They didn't know why I left my house when I did. An hour and twenty minutes for a half-hour drive? I tell them, 'Guys. It's the day before Thanksgiving, the biggest travel day in the world. Of course I went down early.' I figured traffic would be hell, although as it turned out, it wasn't. But who knew? I was checking my cell, and it turned out the flight was delayed, so I pulled off in South City and had a beer to kill some time."

"And they weren't buying?"

Hal wagged his head from side to side. "It's like they were starting from the position that Katie was dead. And that I killed her. Okay, if we got home and she was dead on the floor, I could see where they're coming from. I know it's always the spouse. I get it. I'm a cop. It always is the spouse. But that's if she's dead, and she's not. Thank God. Not that we know of, anyway. She's missing, and nobody who knows how to go about it is trying to find her."

Hardy took all of this in, fighting his own skepticism. He'd been in the law business a long time himself, and his experience told him that in cases like this, the spouse was most often in the middle of it one way or another. Hardy felt, on the one hand, that

Hal was smart to get hooked up with a lawyer as soon as he began to feel that he was a suspect; on the other, the fact that he'd decided he needed a lawyer this early on was in itself somewhat — perhaps illogically — disconcerting. There must be something more to the picture if, without any physical evidence, the police were already considering Hal a suspect.

"I might be able to put you in touch with people who could help with trying to find her," Hardy said. "Meanwhile, your job is to fully cooperate with the police, but through me. If they want to ask you specific questions about you and your wife, or the timing on the night she went missing, or anything that sounds to you like they're considering you as a suspect, you direct them to me. Your main concern is that you've got a missing wife and want to know what they're doing to find her. You're not willing to concede that she's dead, and you sure as hell didn't kill her." He sat back. "That's where you are right now. If the inspectors come again, get back to me. No more talking to them directly, and never without me. When they talked to you earlier, did you tell them anything other than your concern about your wife's disappearance?"

"Not really. I saw where they wanted to

go and cut off the interview."

"When you say 'not really,' do you mean no, you told them nothing? Or you got into it a little?"

At Hardy's questions, Hal's lips went tight, and he cast his eyes upward as though praying for patience. "They asked me how our marriage was, if we were having problems, and I told them what I'd told the Missing Persons cops. Katie was seeing your wife about some issues . . ."

"Yours? Hers?"

A shrug. "Both, I'd say. We were working on it. The kids were wearing us down. Even if we were doing that, what did it have to do with Katie being gone? Then they pressed it. 'So there was something wrong between you two?' Which was when I told them I was done talking with them."

Because Katie was Frannie's client, Hardy knew the marriage had problems, but what relationship didn't? Eventually, he would probably find out all he'd ever want to know about the Chases and their life together. Meanwhile, Hal's wife was missing, and Hardy thought that somebody should spend some time looking into that instead of trying to prove that this worried and exhausted husband must have been involved.

5

Ten minutes after Hal Chase had left, Hardy was on the phone with Abe Glitsky. "You're an ex-cop," Hardy was saying. "You've investigated hundreds of murders. I know you could figure out a way I could kill her where I wouldn't get caught."

"You want to kill Phyllis because she didn't appreciate your dart game?"

"No, that's not the only reason. As you know, I've wanted to kill her for years on general principle. Today was the last straw. Really."

"I don't know. It seems a little harsh."

"Hey. It's not like I want to hurt her. Just eliminate her with something quick and painless."

"And untraceable."

"Ideally, yes."

"I'll give it some thought. But what are you really calling about?"

"I told you, my perfect round. I had to

tell somebody who'd appreciate it. Share the excitement."

"Oh, okay. Whoopee."

"That sounded a little sarcastic."

"Not at all. I'm happy for you. Thrilled, in fact. You've made my day. A perfect round of darts. Yesirree. Now we're talking."

"I was going to ask if you wanted to go to lunch and celebrate. Sam's. On me."

"Now we're talking."

It was a cool day of perfect sunshine and no wind. Hardy walked the six or so blocks from his office and got to the restaurant early, then decided that goddammit, even if nobody else cared, he had thrown that perfect round and he was going to celebrate. After he ordered his martini, he told Dan Sillin, his favorite bartender, about his moment of glory, and at last got the rise he'd been hoping for — and a drink on the house.

He took his first sip; the door opened, and there was Abe.

In truth, Hardy was concerned about his best friend. Never the most upbeat of humans, Glitsky had been pressured to leave the Police Department a few months earlier, and it had shaken him up. For nearly forty years, he'd been a cop, most recently head of Homicide. At one point, he'd served as deputy chief of detectives. He was a police officer through and through, and now he was hanging out by himself most days, reading and reading some more at his upper duplex in the suburban Avenues while his two young kids went to school and his wife, Treya, worked full-time as the secretary to San Francisco's district attorney.

Glitsky cut an imposing figure. A former tight end in college football, he was six-two and about two-twenty. His father was white and Jewish, and his mother had been African-American, so he was milk chocolate with piercing blue eyes and buzz-cut gray hair. He had a prominent nose and a scar that ran at an angle through his lips, top to bottom. His default expression was a frown, and most people found him, frankly, scary. It was a reaction that, as a cop, he had cultivated.

Now he was showing off his version of a smile, a slight uptick of the corners of his mouth. Without a word of greeting, he pointed at Hardy's cocktail and made a show of checking his watch. "Talk about getting an early start," he said. Glitsky rarely touched alcohol.

"It's a special day," Hardy replied.

Dan Sillin leaned in over the bar. "He shot

a perfect darts game."

"I heard," Glitsky deadpanned. "It's all they're talking about out in the Avenues."

Sam's offered booths for private dining; tables that seated between two and ten diners could be closed off behind curtains. In their small booth, Glitsky was waxing eloquent about one of the books he was currently reading, Edmund de Waal's *The Hare with Amber Eyes.*

". . . about this collection of Japanese netsuke."

"Wait," Hardy said. "Is there another kind?"

"Kind of what?"

"Netsuke. Ones that aren't Japanese, I mean. You don't hear much about, say, Ethiopian netsuke. By the way, what is a net-skey?"

"It's a small art object carved out of ivory or wood. It's spelled like net-su-kay, but it's net-skey."

"Got it. And you're reading about these things why?"

"They're interesting. Fascinating, even. But the book's really about this guy's family, the author's, who used to be as rich as the Rothschilds, and how, being Jews, they lost it all in Germany. Except for this col-

34

lection of netsuke. Having a drop or two of Jewish blood myself, I feel some resonance."

"I can imagine."

"Anyway, that's what I've been up to. Mostly reading."

"Are you getting bored?"

Glitsky put down his fork. "Funny you should ask." He paused, let out a breath. "Besides reading, yesterday I watched three episodes of *Friends* in a row. It looks like Ross and Rachel might be getting together again." He held up a hand. "I know. You don't have to say it. Any reasonable alternative suggestions about how to pass the time gladly accepted. And don't say golf or fishing. Or darts."

"Have you thought about going to work for Wes?" This was Wes Farrell, San Francisco's district attorney and a friend to both men. The DA's office had its own staff of inspectors to assist in cases the office was prosecuting.

Glitsky nodded. "That was my first thought, and I asked, but he's got budget problems. If somebody leaves, he says he'll do his best to try to bring me on, but adding staff is a luxury he can't afford right now."

Hardy said, "Well, if you want to get out of the house, I could probably find a job or two to keep you busy, pay you enough to keep you off food stamps."

Glitsky cocked his head, unable to disguise his interest. "What about Wyatt Hunt?" For the past few years, Hunt had handled all of Hardy's investigative work.

"He's on his honeymoon. Through New Year's."

"That's some serious time off."

"Tell me about it. I need to talk to him about his work ethic, but I don't think he cares. He says if you're going all the way to Australia, you might as well stay long enough to make it worthwhile. In any event, he's gone, and my practice soldiers on."

Glitsky sipped at his iced tea. "It's tempting, but I don't have a PI license."

"I won't tell if you won't."

"And you've got real work?"

"I could probably keep you busy a few days. And there's one client who could be big — I've got a feeling his case might heat up. Hal Chase."

Without missing a beat, Glitsky said, "The missing wife."

"That's her. I see you're keeping your hand in."

"He kill her?"

"He says no."

"What else is new? Have they charged him?"

"Not as of an hour ago. But it's on their minds. Homicide talked to him this morning. He came to see me afterward."

"Homicide is on it? How can that be? We don't know she's dead."

Hardy shrugged. "We all know what's going on in the jail. Our sheriff's an asshole, and his department is corrupt. Maybe SFPD thinks this investigation will get them into his organization. Normally, I would call my friend Abe Glitsky and ask him, but he's all hung up on *Friends* just now."

Abe ignored that. "What exactly would you want me to do?"

"Hal wants the focus to be on finding his wife, not his wife's killer."

"Good luck with that." Glitsky chewed ice. "What else is he going to say?"

"I got the impression that he really didn't expect the Homicide guys yet. He thought everybody was on the same bus he was, looking for his wife."

"He thought that, huh?"

Hardy shrugged. "He could be faking me out, but I'm somewhat cynical by nature, and I believed him. At least about whether Missing Persons should be on this."

"What do you see as my role in this?"

"I don't know, exactly. See if you can find her?"

Glitsky's mouth twitched. "With all the vast resources at my disposal?"

"Not to get your head all swelled up, but you are a seasoned investigator. So investigate. Homicide already thinks it's Hal, or maybe it's Hal. If you don't find the wife, at least find an alternative suspect."

Glitsky chuckled. "Really? What about the Homicide guys I'll be shadowing?"

"Be subtle. Do it right, they won't even know you're there."

"Uh-huh."

"Could happen."

"World peace could happen, too. I'm not holding my breath."

Hardy sat back. "Hey, if you're not interested, give me a call when you find out if Rachel and Joey get back together."

"Ross," Glitsky said. "Not Joey. Ross." He tipped up his glass. "You mind if I think about it?"

"I'd be disappointed if you didn't."

6

Not that it was a tough decision, given his options, but by the time Glitsky left Hardy at the Sutter Street office, he'd made up his mind to look into the Katie Chase disappearance.

Having ridden the Muni downtown, he was on foot and took the opportunity to get some exercise and walk over to the Hall of Justice. At the metal detector by the front door, an officer he didn't know greeted him by name and former rank and waved him through. Apparently, though it had been several months, word of his retirement hadn't reached everyone in the building.

Glitsky turned left and walked down the long hallway on the main floor. Aside from housing the offices of the district attorney and the county sheriff, the Superior Court and its attendant departments, the Homicide detail, and one wing of the jail, the monolithic seven-story Hall of Justice was also home to Southern Station and the administrative hub of the city's Police Department. Glitsky strolled into Missing Persons as if he owned the place, picked his way through the desks in the main room, nodded at a few familiar faces, and finally knocked on the open door to Lyle Wiedeman's office.

Trim and ridiculously handsome, the affable Wiedeman was alone at his desk, glasses on, studying a file. At Abe's knock, he looked up and broke a smile. "Lieutenant," he said, rising and extending his hand. "Been awhile."

"It has."

"What brings you down to our little piece of paradise? Grab a chair."

"I'm just getting my feet wet in the freelancing waters. If I spend another day at home alone, I'll become a full-fledged menace. A lawyer I know offered me some part-time work, and I took it."

"I hear you," Wiedeman said. "I'm down to my last three months myself. I've got no clue what I'll do day to day. My son suggested I set up the old Lionel train set down in the basement. I shot him."

"Good for you."

"So who's the lawyer?"

"Dismas Hardy."

"He's got you trying to locate a witness?"

"Not so much that," Glitsky said. "Katie Chase."

Wiedeman's eyes lost a couple of degrees of warmth. "Her husband was here not two hours ago. Doesn't think we're doing enough, which is how I'd play it myself."

"You think he's playing it?"

"If he doesn't confess, it's pretty much his only move. The captains had a meeting and passed it upstairs to Homicide. That takes me out of it. Nothing personal."

"No, of course not. I just thought you might have formed an opinion."

Wiedeman shifted in his chair. "Let's say I didn't fight the decision."

"So you think she's dead?"

"Think, schmink. Her blood was in the kitchen. She was seeing a marriage counselor. She hasn't used a credit card or phone in four days, going on five. She didn't leave her babies at home and just walk out, and there's been no ransom contact." Wiedeman settled back in his chair, speaking with more resignation than passion. "It might not be the husband, okay, but he looks like as good a bet as any, and it's a slam dunk somebody has killed her."

"I imagine you said this to Hal."

"Pretty much word for word."

41

"How'd he take it?"

"It seemed to take the piss right out of him, to tell you the truth."

"What do you mean?"

"I mean, he came in here ready to do battle with somebody because Homicide thought he was a suspect. If it was an act, it was a good one."

"What?"

"Well, he came across as nowhere near ready to believe his wife is dead. He maintained that she's just missing and we should be concentrating on finding her. But after I laid out the facts, like I just did with you, he saw the situation for what it was. It wasn't even about him. It was about her being not just gone but really dead. Somebody, therefore, must have killed her. If he's one of the suspects, that's too bad, but can he blame us for thinking it? I asked him, was there any other scenario he'd like to offer where she might be alive?"

"Did he have one?"

"No. He was on the verge of tears, but you and I both know that he wouldn't be the first killer to shed real tears in remorse over what he'd done."

Glitsky hadn't been in the building since the previous April, when his job had ended.

Now he took the elevator up a couple of floors and walked down another long hallway, this one empty. His footsteps echoed under the dim fluorescent glow until he came to a floor-to-ceiling glass partition whose double doors opened to the lobby of the district attorney's offices. Past those doors, he turned left and walked over to the reception window, where he told the clerk he had an appointment with Treya Glitsky. In a flagrant dereliction of protocol, the clerk said, "Sure, Abe," and buzzed him right through.

His wife's door was open; she was at her computer, in profile, concentrating. Out in the hall, Glitsky hung back a couple of steps and, leaning against the wall with his arms crossed, spent a few seconds watching her.

Treya was a big woman who carried not an ounce of fat. Her father and mother were both African-American, but one of her great-grandmothers had been Japanese, and her face carried a hint of an Asiatic cast — slightly exotic, classically structured, with a sudden and startling beauty. In repose, or when immersed in her work, as she was now, she projected a serenity that hit Glitsky like a drug.

After eleven years of marriage, he was still utterly smitten.

Moving up to the door, Glitsky knocked. Her fingers stopped over the keyboard as she turned, her eyes lighting up. Just as quickly, her face clouded and her eyebrows came together in concern. "Are the kids — ?"

Glitsky held up a hand. "Everybody's fine. I just thought I'd drop by and say hi. Believe it or not, I was in the neighborhood."

Treya stood, came around her desk, and gave him a quick hug. "Not that this isn't a nice surprise, but what in the world are you doing in this godforsaken neck of the woods?" After he gave her the short version, she frowned and said, "Dismas really needs you to do this?"

"I think there was a bit of charity involved. Plus, Wyatt Hunt is out of town."

"What about Wyatt's staff? Don't they find missing people all the time?"

"I think so. But for whatever reason, Diz asked me." She gave him a look that was ambiguous enough to force him to ask, "What? Not a good idea?"

"You're a big boy. You can decide that for yourself. Evidently, you already have."

"But what?"

She drew a breath. "But I was just getting used to the fact that you weren't going to be living anymore in the regular company

44

of murderers. Or people who know murderers. Or witnesses to murder. Any one of whom, I need hardly tell you, might be a murderer himself. Or herself. I didn't think you'd really miss being around those people."

"I'm not missing those people. We don't even know there was a murder yet, Trey. Diz wants me to try to find where the wife has gotten to."

"If it turns out she was killed, then what? You'll identify the murderer, right?"

"It may not go that far. If she turns up dead, as far as I know, the job's over."

"Unless you're on to something that might clear Diz's client."

"Maybe that. If he even gets charged."

"In other words, you'd be at cross-purposes with Homicide."

"Again, not necessarily, although it's possible, I suppose." Glitsky backed away a step. "Call me clairvoyant," he said, "but I'm sensing you don't want me to do this. In which case, I won't. I'll call Diz right now and bail. He'll find somebody else, if he really needs the work done."

"Of course he needs the work done. He's got a client. The client needs his help. Diz didn't ask you to help him because he felt sorry for you."

45

"You weren't there. I was pretty pathetic."

"You asked him for work?"

"Well, no. But he picked up that I was maybe slightly bored from day to day."

Treya touched his face. "Or, just sayin', he knows you're a world-class investigator and he really could use your help."

Glitsky broke a smile. "Okay, maybe a little of that. And you know, warts and all, I always loved the work."

"The work, yes; the job, you might remember, not always."

"More often than not, though. At least I felt I was doing something important. Instead of like now, when I'm waiting around for the next major life milestone after retirement, which I'm told tends to be death."

If Abe thought Treya was unhappy with his decision to look into Katie Chase's disappearance — and she was — he didn't want to even casually run his freelancing by the personnel of the Homicide detail. If he wound up covering some of the same investigative ground as the inspectors assigned to the case, they'd find out soon enough and could deal with it as they saw fit. Glitsky didn't want to have another discussion — or argument — before he'd even begun.

So instead of going up another two floors, he went downstairs and out the back door, then into the admitting lobby of the jail, a separate oval building that adjoined the main rectangular edifice of the hall. The deputy behind the counter — his name tag read CREELEY — greeted him cordially and with no sign that he'd gotten the memo about Glitsky's retirement. "Lieutenant," Creeley said, "what can I do for you?"

"I wonder if I could have a word with Hal Chase. Is he still on duty?"

"He's Mr. Popularity today, isn't he?" Creeley checked his watch. "Shifts change over in about fifteen, if you want to wait. I'll get word to him."

Glitsky thanked the deputy, decided to take a walk around the back parking lot to stretch his legs, and returned to the admitting desk to find Hal Chase — name tags were a wonderful invention — by the counter, his face a mask of worry.

Glitsky introduced himself without a handshake, and Chase barely whispered, "So you found her?"

"Why do you say that?"

Chase's temper flared. "Because you're Abe Glitsky out of Homicide, and you wouldn't be hassling me again after I told your inspectors to pound sand this morning

47

unless you knew Katie was actually dead."

"Easy," Glitsky said. "I'm not hassling you. I don't know if your wife is dead. I'm not in Homicide anymore. I'm working with Dismas Hardy." As he watched the gears shift in Chase's head, Abe explained, "I retired six months ago. The word doesn't seem to have gotten out too well."

Hal's shoulders fell with relief. "I heard your name and I thought . . ."

"I get it. But really, I'm retired. Hardy told me you wanted somebody working on finding your wife, not finding evidence that you killed her. It looks like I'm your man."

Chase nodded, then another thought seemed to strike. "Is Hardy paying you? Because I'm tapped out after the retainer I gave him."

"That's covered. Hardy can afford it." Glitsky shrugged. "The guy's a little unorthodox, but for a lawyer, he's actually got a heart. Plus, he seems to be about the only one who's inclined to give you a chance."

"That I didn't kill her, you mean."

"Yep."

"How about you?"

"I've got an open mind. With your permission, I'd like to get ahold of some facts and see where they lead. I'm not going on any assumptions. I was just over in Missing

Persons and got their opinion, which you already know."

"Katie's dead."

"Right. But I'm not starting there. I hope your wife is still alive. I'm going to assume that. If there are other possibilities that might have driven her to leave, or somebody to have taken her, I want to find out what they were. You want to help me with that?"

"I want to find her, whatever it takes."

"That's a good answer. Are you on your way home now?"

"That was my plan."

"If you don't mind, I'll ride out with you."

7

"Tell me about the night," Glitsky said as Hal pulled his Subaru out into traffic. "Wednesday, wasn't it?"

Though Hal's sideways look telegraphed what Glitsky read as impatience, he sighed in resignation and started in. "There wasn't any drama before. It was just a regular night, except with me going down to pick up Warren. My brother. Half brother. He was coming up from L.A. for the holiday."

"What did you have for dinner?"

"What does that matter?"

"I'm not sure it does," Glitsky said, "but when I was at Missing Persons, the lieutenant said there was blood in the kitchen. I just wonder if your wife was cutting something you were going to be eating."

"I don't remember that. I don't think it happened before I left. I saw the blood when I got back, of course, and left it where it was. It wasn't like a flood of it. A few drops on the counter by the sink, a couple more on the floor. I don't think the blood means anything. We had spaghetti and salad, so she might have been slicing tomatoes or bread and cut herself by accident."

"And she didn't wipe it up?"

"I don't know. Maybe one of the kids started crying. In which case, she would have dropped everything and come running."

Glitsky noted the change of tone, the first negative thing about Katie that he'd heard out of Hal, namely that she might be a little fanatical about her duties as a mother. Maybe this was part of why she'd been seeing Frannie Hardy.

"Okay," Glitsky said. "Let's leave the blood. Tell me about the kids. Two, right?"

"Will and Ellen. What about them?"

"They must have been asleep when Katie went missing."

"That's my assumption. We put them down early when we can. Our goal is seven o'clock, so we can get a little time as adults. Wednesday, they were both in bed when I left, and still sleeping when we got back."

"Where are they now?"

"At the house. My stepmother, Ruth, is staying with them. Warren's here, too. They're holding down the fort."

Glitsky sat back and watched the city roll by for a few blocks. The sun was low in the sky in front of them, but the day remained cold, clear, and windless as they made their way across Arguello and down into the Avenues. "So you left for the airport when?" he asked.

"Seven-thirty or so. The Homicide cops don't know why I left so early for an eight-fifty pickup, but hey, the day before Thanksgiving, I thought I'd be late, even leaving when I did."

"And then what?"

"Then I picked up Warren —"

"Before that. Did you park at the airport and wait?"

"No. When I saw there wasn't any traffic, I checked my cell for flight information and found out it would be another hour before he got in —"

"You could have done that before you left."

"Right. I know that. Should have, in fact. But I didn't. I didn't think of it. To tell you the truth, I was looking forward to getting out of the house and having some company around to lighten things up. Katie and I had a lot we weren't talking about. Anyway, when I realized Warren was going to be late, I stopped by the Hungry Hunter down in

South City and had a beer and watched ESPN."

"Did you talk to anybody?"

"I sat at the bar and ordered from the bartender. I paid cash, and I'm not a regular. We didn't have any conversation. He might remember me, but I don't know why he would. The place was jumping. I was one guy out of a barful. Even if he could ID me positively, there's most of an hour unaccounted for. I realize that as alibis go, this one isn't much, but that's what I did."

Glitsky looked across at Hal. It occurred to him that, if anything, the weakness of the alibi spoke to its plausibility. If Hal were going to construct a story, he would have made sure the bartender remembered him. He would have established the time of his arrival at the bar. He would have made it seem impossible that he could have killed his wife. And he hadn't done any of those things. "So," Glitsky said, "then you picked up your brother?"

"That's the whole story, Lieutenant."

"Abe," Glitsky said. "I'm not a cop, and I'm on your side, remember. Okay, so then you get home. When you drive up, do you notice anything suspicious?"

"Nothing. I know Katie's car is in the garage, so I pull into the driveway. The light outside the front door is on, and so are some inside lights, like they were when I left. So Warren grabs his stuff and we go in the front door and first I think Katie must be in with the kids, so we wait a couple of minutes, staying quiet so we don't wake anybody up, then I go into the kids' room and she's not there. It's totally bizarre. I mean, you come home and your kids are sleeping and your wife is gone. It takes a while to kick in."

"What did you do?"

"Whatever I could think of. I tried her cell. No answer. Tried again. Texted her. And the whole time I'm with Warren, just stumped. It doesn't seem real. I mean, where is she? Is this some kind of sick joke? There's no way she's not there. Finally, I go upstairs. I go out in the backyard. I check the garage, and her car's there. I leave Warren at the house in case the kids wake up, and I go knock on the neighbors' doors, see if anybody's seen anything. It starts to sink in. I mean, really." He turned to face Glitsky. "You know?"

"I can't imagine."

"I didn't kill her. I truly did not."

After a pause, Glitsky asked, "You think she might have just up and left? I mean, left the kids upstairs sleeping?"

Hal drove in silence for most of a block before he shook his head. "Never," he said. "Never ever ever ever." Letting out a sigh, he went on. "Here's the thing, Lieutenant. Having kids has been incredibly tough on her. At the same time, they're the most important things in her life. That's probably why raising them has been so hard. She cares so goddamn much about every part of it. If she was giving up so much of the rest of her life, she was going to be the absolute best at it. And they in turn were going to be perfect children. And then she felt guilty about how much she resented what they'd done to her life, how much of it they were taking up, and she hated herself for that. It was complicated, to say the least. But would she have walked out on them? Honestly, I can't imagine it."

"All right. What about you and her? Did you have problems?"

Hal shrugged. "Who doesn't?"

"Maybe they were more serious than you thought."

"No, I thought they were serious. We don't have enough money, she's too protective of the kids, I'm not sensitive enough with them, I yell, she doesn't. She doesn't like my job or the people I work with. We were getting pretty bad at just talking to each other, and that wasn't good. So, yeah, some problems. But that's the thing. We never had any kind of physical fight. I never hurt her. I never would hurt her. And really, what I said, she wouldn't leave the kids.

"That was one of her main things. We couldn't even get a babysitter and go out on a date. Even with Ruth living half a mile away, ready to watch them at any time. But Ruth wasn't good enough. Nobody else was good enough. Bottom line, she didn't leave the kids sleeping and walk out of the house under her own power. Somebody took her and forced her." He looked over again at Glitsky. "You're not saying much."

"Nothing very comforting is springing to mind."

8

The house was a small stand-alone two-story on Stanyan Street in the Upper Haight-Ashbury District. Hal parked in the driveway in front of the garage door, and he and Glitsky walked up the sidewalk to the stairway leading to the porch. The front door featured a stained-glass half-moon window that glared in the rays of the setting sun.

Chase knocked twice, lightly, at the door. Footsteps sounded from inside, and then the door swung open and they were looking at an attractive fortysomething woman holding a swaddled baby up against her shoulder. Accepting a quick buss from her stepson, Ruth Chase pulled the door all the way open, while from behind her, another child came running up: "Daddy, Daddy, Daddy!"

Hal Chase leaned down to grab up his daughter and press her to him, raining a flurry of kisses onto her face. "How's my very, very favorite girl?"

More kisses as the greetings continued to play out. Hal Chase might be an insensitive guy who yelled a lot, Abe thought, but his daughter gave every indication that she loved him absolutely.

Five minutes later, Ruth had settled Will into a playpen in the living room. Effectively out of earshot, Ellen sat at her own little table across the kitchen, drawing with crayons. Hal and Warren drank coffee from mugs while Glitsky, across the dining room table from the brothers, waited for the tea that Ruth was brewing in the kitchen.

If the half brothers shared genes, they weren't much in evidence. Hal was medium to stocky, with thick dark hair and ruddy coloring. Warren, perhaps a dozen years younger, was tall and lean, with wispy blond hair that he wore almost to his shoulders. He sported some grungy facial hair, a UCLA sweatshirt, well-worn jeans, and flip-flops — to Glitsky's mind, the typical college look.

Hal was finishing up the explanation of who Glitsky was and why he was there when Warren cut him off. "You mean to tell me the actual Missing Persons police aren't looking into where she's gone? What's that about?"

"It's about them thinking she's been" — Hal looked over at his daughter, engrossed in her drawing, and lowered his voice — "done away with. And," he added, "apparently, they think I had something to do with it."

"They can't really think that." Ruth, carrying a tray with a teapot and cookies, stopped in the doorway. "When did all this happen? Nobody was saying anything like that over the weekend."

"Maybe not, but they were thinking it. This morning, a couple of Homicide cops came to see me at work. It was obvious I was a suspect, and they thought Katie . . ." Again, he looked over to his daughter, who was paying them no mind, then he shrugged at the adults. "It was obvious what they thought."

"So you went to a lawyer?" Ruth asked.

Hal nodded. "It seemed like a good idea. If they were going to be questioning me, I wanted some advice on what I should say."

"How about the truth?" Ruth asked.

"Sometimes they can twist the truth and make it sound pretty bad."

"But getting a lawyer, isn't that going to make you look guilty no matter what?" Warren asked. "I mean, you don't need a lawyer unless you've done something."

"No. Sometimes you need a lawyer before anything happens. If only to keep it from happening."

Ruth crossed to the table, placed a cup and saucer in front of Glitsky, and poured. "The bottom line is that no one's looking for Katie?"

"They say they are," Hal said. "But they're looking for her body."

"That's just wrong," Ruth said. She turned to Glitsky. "That's why you're here, right?"

"I hope I can help find out where she is," Glitsky said, trying to keep everything low-key. "Basically, I'm investigating her disappearance. If she doesn't use a credit card and we don't hear from her or whoever took her, I can't —"

"What do you mean, whoever took her?" Warren asked. "You think somebody kidnapped her?"

Glitsky put his cup into its saucer and held his hand out, palm down. "Easy," he said softly to Warren. "Your brother and I talked on the way out here. He doesn't think she would have left on her own, not with the kids asleep in the next room. Do you think it's possible she did?"

Warren, flustered, met eyes around the table. "She could have had some sort of breakdown, couldn't she?"

"Possibly," Glitsky said. "She also could have slipped and banged her head and woken up and wandered outside. Neither very likely."

"You were saying," Ruth put in, "that if she doesn't use a credit card or get in touch with us . . . ?"

"Then there's no trail," Glitsky said. "And without a trail, finding her is going to be problematic."

Ruth asked, "What are you looking for?"

"A reason," Glitsky replied. "Something that makes sense, that leads somewhere, possibly to where she is now."

"You mean, in her life?" Ruth asked. "What could that be? I mean, she was, is, a stay-at-home mother of infants. I don't say that disparagingly. I raised two boys, and it can be a noble calling. Are you saying she might have been involved in something that got her in trouble? That seems a stretch."

"It might be," Glitsky agreed. "If there's a rational answer at all."

"What if it was a random crazy person?" Warren asked. "He saw Hal leave, and he looked through the window and saw Katie here alone and knocked at the door and had a weapon . . ."

Glitsky nodded. "Entirely possible. I don't

have any idea. I've barely begun with this."
He sipped his tea. "At least I'm not trying
to build a case against Hal. I'm trying to
find out what happened to Katie and why.
I'm not working with the police. Really. If
there's an answer to be found, wherever it
leads, I'll try to run it down. That's what
I'm here for."

"If there's an answer . . ." Hal said. "What
if there isn't?"

"Let's not go there," Glitsky said. "Not
for a while, anyway."

9

At about the same moment, JaMorris and Abby knocked at the front door of the Dunne home on Guerrero Street in the Mission District. It was a three-story structure on its own lot that gave the impression of having been the project of several shabbily genteel architects over its thirty years of life. Odd angles jutted from corners and roofs; the entire second floor seemed to float behind plate-glass windows; a fountain splashed over perennial reeds into a koi pond in the half-covered courtyard that doubled as the welcoming lobby on the first floor.

Exposing a fairly common vein in San Francisco's über-liberal culture, some past owners (or perhaps the Dunnes themselves) had spent serious money in an effort to render the home aggressively proletarian.

The detectives, negotiating around the bicycles parked along the walls, followed the head of the household down the hallway that ran inside along the courtyard, and came to a large family room at the back of the house, where three women sat on stools in front of a bar, turned to face their incoming visitors. Each had a full glass of white wine at her elbow, and all of their eyes showed signs of tears.

With an air of exhaustion, Curt Dunne stopped just inside the door and said with some formality, "These are Inspectors Monroe and Foley. Inspectors, my wife, Carli — Katie's mother — and my daughters, Barbara and Sherrie. My son, Daniel, couldn't get off work, but he told me he'd be glad to talk to you by appointment; I believe you have his numbers."

"We do, thank you." JaMorris turned to the women. "Thank you all for agreeing to sit down with us this afternoon. I know it's been, and continues to be, a tremendously difficult time."

He silently ceded the floor to Abby, who picked up where he left off. "As you know, it's been nearly five full days since Katie's gone missing, and in that time we haven't heard from any third parties, such as kidnappers demanding a ransom. We haven't gotten any messages from Katie, and we don't have a record of her having accessed her credit cards or used her cell phone." She paused. "Given all of these realities, we are forced to consider the possibility that Katie was the victim of foul play, perhaps even — I know you've all considered this — murder."

At the word, Carli Dunne brought her hand to her mouth. Curt crossed over to stand directly behind her, his arm along the bar. The younger women, in tandem, reached for their wine.

JaMorris pulled up a stool from near the wall, sat down, and picked up the narrative. "This means that we're shifting the object of our investigation somewhat. It's not that we're not doing everything we can to locate Katie or some sign of where she could be, but if she was murdered, our next order of business is to identify a suspect whom we might profitably question to see whether we can move along this investigation and get to the bottom of what happened to Katie."

"Since you are among the people who know her best and love her" — Abby, taking over, was careful to keep references to Katie in the present tense — "we thought an interview might help to get us off on the right foot. Now we understand, as you made clear to our colleagues last week, that you've always been on reasonably good terms with

Hal, and that you're all going through this tragic time together, but —"

Suddenly, Curt Dunne blurted out, "No buts. Let's forget all that. Hal was the last one to see her alive. He had almost three hours between when he left the house and got home with his brother. Which is more than enough time to have done whatever he decided to do and —"

"Curt!" His wife put her hand down on his arm. "Wait! We can't just . . ."

"The hell we can't. We can call a spade a spade. Can you give me any other plausible scenario? Who the hell even knew he would be gone at exactly that time?"

JaMorris threw a glance at his partner. "So I'm gathering that you, at least, Mr. Dunne, think Hal might have played a role in Katie's disappearance? Missing Persons didn't mention anything about your suspicions. They said you were all coming from basically the same place, which was wondering what could have happened. Has something changed since last week?"

Curt Dunne didn't wait for a consensus. "You're damned straight something's changed. It's become obvious that Katie didn't just walk out on her own. None of us can imagine she would have abandoned the kids, not even for a couple of minutes. And once that's clear, who does that leave?"

"Well, sir," Abby said, "it leaves the whole universe, unless you've got some specific reason to think it was Hal."

The woman nearest the inspectors spoke up. "We never really thought about Hal until we started talking about him. I mean, it's just not something we'd ever considered. We'd always assumed that they got along the way most of us did."

"I'm sorry," Abby said. "Your name again?"

"Barbara. Barbara Payson." She spelled her last name.

"And what did you start talking about?"

"You know, stuff between them that we didn't think was very important before. Stuff Katie had told us."

"Like what?"

"Well," Barbara said, "you know she was seeing a family counselor. Hal wouldn't go with her. He thought it was a waste of money and didn't believe they needed counseling. But their fights were getting more serious, and she was worried about them."

"Physical fights?"

"No. She never said that he hit her."

The other sister, Sherrie, said abruptly, "She wouldn't have said if he did."

"How do you know that?" JaMorris asked.

"That's who she was," Sherrie replied. "She was the oldest of us and . . ."

Carli joined the discussion. "She definitely would have left him if he'd been abusing her. But I don't like how we're demonizing Hal because she was going to counseling and he wouldn't go."

"Was there any talk of them breaking up?" Abby asked. "Did she talk about divorcing him?"

"I never heard that," Barbara said.

Sherrie added, "We really didn't acknowledge they were in trouble until . . . until this thing. And now she's gone, and we may never know."

"Still, do any of you have a specific reason for suspecting Hal?"

"They could have had a real fight that night," Curt said. "I mean where he actually hit her. And then he had to get rid of her so there wouldn't be any sign of it. That could have been why he did it. To cover it up."

"Although you are not aware of any evidence of a physical fight between them. Am I right?" Abby asked.

Curt answered, "He could have gotten rid of any evidence. Straightened things up."

"That's all conjecture, dear," Carli said.

"You know it is. Whether he hit her, whether they were fighting. We don't know."

"We do, Mom," Sherrie said. "At least arguing."

"Okay, so they were going through a rough spell, maybe, but with two young children, is that really so unusual? She wanted or needed help dealing with what was bothering her, and he was too proud to go along with her. That could have been all this is. We all talked to Hal last week. We know he's truly devastated. I looked in his eyes, and he was in agony. He wasn't faking that. I don't think we should accuse him of anything unless we find out something that he definitely did."

"That's good advice," JaMorris said. "Anything you do find, whether it's about Hal or anybody else, please come to us first. We know the newspapers have been bothering you, and it wouldn't be productive to have them put Hal on trial in the press."

Curt wasn't ready to give it up. "Let's not forget that he could have simply woken up that morning and done what he did with no new reason. He could have gotten to the end of whatever he was going through and decided to act."

"Yes," Abby said, "that could have happened. But usually, there's a reason of some kind, and without any hint of what that might have been, we're in the dark. More important, we don't have grounds to charge anyone."

"I'm telling you, it's him," Curt said. "Hal. No one else fits."

Abby nodded. "We're going to keep looking and hope we turn up something in the line of motive or evidence. If it's any consolation, at the moment, he certainly remains a person of interest."

10

"Prejudice," Glitsky said, "is a powerful thing."

"What makes you say that?" They'd just finished doing the dishes, and Treya was drying her hands.

"Because I am in the grip of it."

"Ahh. And who are you being prejudiced against?"

"Hal Chase. Husband of missing, probably now-dead person Katie Chase."

"You think he had something to do with it?"

"That's the thing. It's not a thought, although in ways it's much stronger. It's like an automatic default. Woman disappears from her home with no sign of struggle, my very first reaction is to look at the husband. So I look at the husband — any husband — and what do I see? I see a guy who probably killed his wife."

She put the towel down. "After hanging

out with him all afternoon, do you still think that?"

"As I said, I don't think it, not rationally. I just feel it. And I know I'm not supposed to. But my gut keeps pointing in the same direction it always points. Meanwhile, my brain is trying to come up with plausible alternatives."

"Such as?"

"Such as a random snatch, some guy walking along the street who decides to abduct a woman out of her house, but this guy can't be walking down the street, because then what does he carry the woman away in if he's not in a vehicle of some kind, so that means he's got a car or something and drove up while Hal was driving away, but then how would he know that Hal wasn't just driving to the store for a six-pack and wouldn't be back in five minutes?"

She smiled at him. "That might be the longest sentence of your life. And what you're describing probably didn't happen."

"Right. I agree. But somebody came by, apparently, who knew when Hal would be gone and used that time to grab Katie and take her away. Which leads to the question: Why take her away? If they were going to kill her, why not kill her in the house? Whereas, if it was Hal, he's got a reason to take her away, which is that without a body, it's probably not going to get charged as a murder."

"Wouldn't that be true of anybody?"

"Yeah, but look at the hassle. Taking the body somewhere, then hiding it, and meanwhile, you're left with traces of the victim in your car and maybe on your person. Alternatively, you could shoot her in the house, and in that case it goes down as a B and E that went wrong, and every criminal in San Francisco will be suspect. Which brings us back around to Hal, who's Diz's prospective client and who I'm supposed to believe is innocent, although I'm having somewhat of a hard time with that because it's not what I feel."

"So I see."

"Prejudice."

"There you go. So you're going to stick with this for a while, this investigation?"

"If you're not still going to be mad at me."

"I'm not mad at you. I was just getting used to the idea that you weren't going to be involved in murder cases anymore. For the record, I was comfortable with that."

"Also for the record, this isn't yet a definite murder case, although I must admit it's leaning in that direction. And my prejudice about Hal isn't doing anybody any good. I'm trying to imagine what happened to this woman if it wasn't something to do with her husband."

"Maybe you shouldn't focus on the husband, Abe. Maybe you could go about getting to know her better. Who was Katie?"

Frannie Hardy was sipping her coffee at the dinner table. Putting the cup down, she shook her head and leveled an admiring gaze at her husband. "Sometimes," she said, "you simply astound me."

"Thank you. You mean because I'm already on board with Hal Chase?"

"Not really that, no."

"What, then?"

"The fact that you've been home for about two hours, and we've just had a leisurely and pleasant dinner together, and you have spent nearly every minute of that time talking to me about your perfect game of darts this morning."

"I know. It was groundbreaking."

"Evidently so. Making every single shot from twenty down to and including the bull's-eye without one miss. Not even the bull's-eye."

"Bull's-eye's the killer."

"Of course it is. And you've described it all so perfectly, I feel like I was there, witnessing it all firsthand. The thrill of victory."

"Especially the last round," Hardy said. "Could you believe how I cleared my mind, instead of thinking about it and letting the tension get to me? That's what could have done me in. But no, I just picked those suckers out of the board, walked back to the line, turned, and threw. Bam. Bam! BAM!"

"I think you did mention the mind-meld the first time. Or the second. One of them, anyway."

"And that's not what astounded you?"

"No. Actually, it was nothing about the dart game."

"Do you want me to guess?"

"I don't think you could, so I'll tell you. What astounded me is that my client's husband came to your office this morning and asked you to be his lawyer because he was afraid they were going to charge him with murder, and then you met Abe for lunch and got him on board as your investigator. And all of this was really further down your list of interesting things that happened today than your perfect score in Twenty Down."

Hardy shrugged. "I've had lots of clients, Fran. But never a perfect game. Think about it. What would you rank higher, interest-wise?"

She stared at him. "Amazing."

He nodded. "Thank you."

"Is there anything else you'd like to tell me about the perfect game? Or do you think we might chat for a minute about Hal and his situation?"

"Phyllis didn't seem to fully appreciate it, either," he said. "That woman is a major trial. I asked Abe if he thought he could kill her and get away with it. He didn't think so."

"Really, though, enough. Okay?"

"All right." Hardy reached for the wine bottle and emptied it into his glass. "What do you want to know about Hal?"

"How was he?"

"Depressed and worried. Sleep-deprived. About what you'd expect. Homicide — not Missing Persons — had just come by and interviewed him, and he got the impression they were going to charge him in Katie's death, and he thought he might need a lawyer."

"Why were they going to charge him?"

Hardy shook his head. "They weren't quite there. But they were looking at him basically because he's the spouse. That's always the first stop, as you may know. I told him it was early in the game and he probably didn't have to worry yet, but I'd get going, and I'd get Abe started just in case."

"Where does Abe come in?"

"If Hal does end up arrested, I'm going to need an investigator, since Wyatt's out of town. Better to get in early if it comes to that."

"Do you think it will?"

"I don't know. Coming to me at this stage was a bit unusual, but he seemed legitimately freaked out. Have you ever met him?"

"No. But I feel I know him a little through Katie."

"What do you think?"

"You mean, did they have such serious problems that I thought she might be in physical danger? I'd have to say no. She was just having some troubles with full-time motherhood and deciding to stay at home with the kids instead of working."

"What did she do when she worked?"

"Pharmaceutical sales. She made a fortune."

"What's a fortune?"

"Two hundred, two fifty."

"Thousand dollars? A year? Can I get into pharmaceutical sales?"

"I don't think so. I think you have to be young, female, and pretty."

"Two out of three isn't bad. Young and . . . well, I'm more handsome than pretty, but that ought to count." Hardy sipped wine. "So she was making this kind of money and then just stopped? I can see why they were having problems."

"Diz, it wasn't mostly about their problems with each other. You know I can't go into detail, but it was self-esteem stuff, her place in the world, whether she was a good enough mother, like that."

"No talk of divorce or abuse?"

"No."

Hardy blew out a heavy breath. "So nobody knows," he said.

"Nobody knows what?"

"Anything."

11

Glitsky opened his eyes in the darkness, at once fully awake.

Treya lay on her side next to him, an arm stretched out across his chest. He turned his head enough to read the time on the digital clock on his dresser: 6:14.

He lay still another minute, then carefully lifted her hand and moved it over nearer to her. She stirred but did not awaken. Throwing off the blankets, Glitsky swung out of the bed and went into the adjoining bathroom.

Since school started in September, he'd gotten into the habit of waking up to the alarm at six-thirty, throwing on some sweats, going into the kitchen, and assembling whatever they were having for breakfast. Afterward, he'd kiss Treya goodbye and drop the kids at school, then come home to read the paper. Eventually — say, by ten or eleven o'clock — he'd shave, shower, and throw on some old jeans and a T-shirt for hanging around the house while he read and read and then watched television and read some more.

Today, by the time the alarm went off, he had already shaved and showered. Opening her eyes, Treya saw him standing in front of the dresser in pressed slacks, buttoning up a black dress shirt. "Where are you off to, sailor?" she asked.

"Just getting a jump on the day, that's all. I'll go get the rats moving. How's French toast sound?"

"Perfect. You're making?"

"I am."

"If you want to save that nice shirt, put on an apron."

Glitsky looked over, nodded, and pointed at her. "Good call."

After he left the children at school, Glitsky drove downtown, parked in the Fifth and Mission garage, and walked down a block to the offices of the *San Francisco Chronicle.*

In the almost-deserted basement, a heavy-set, gray-bearded reporter named Jeff Elliot was sitting in his cubicle, staring at his computer. For about twenty years — far exceeding the predicted life span of a man suffering from multiple sclerosis — Elliot had been writing a column on page three called "CityTalk," a staple of San Francisco's media diet. When he'd started out, he was slim, clean-shaven, and baby-faced, and he got around town pretty well with the occasional help of crutches. He'd even been able to drive in his specially rigged car. Now, though the newspaper supplied him with a car and driver, he rarely strayed out in the field. His sources either phoned in their information or came to him. After all of his time on the job, his contacts in the city were second to none. If there was a story to be told, Elliot probably knew something about it.

He and Glitsky had a lot of history. Once Glitsky had been shot making an arrest, and while he was in the emergency room and expected to die, Elliot had written an obituary column praising him as a cop and a person. Word that Abe was going to live arrived just in time to keep the column out of the paper, but it had been typeset and ready to go; Glitsky had a framed copy of it hanging in the hallway of his home.

Now Glitsky knocked on the doorframe, and the reporter pushed himself away from his desk, turning as his wheelchair slid back. His face broke into a welcoming smile. "Look what the wind blows in. Dr. Glitsky."

The men shook hands, and Glitsky sat himself down on the ancient leather armchair next to the cubicle's opening. They caught up on personal stuff — kids and wives all good, life going along — before Elliot said, "I'm thinking this is not purely a social visit. Which in itself is interesting, since, if I'm not mistaken, you're still retired."

"I am, although you seem to be one of the few who know. I stopped by the Hall yesterday, and nobody seemed to realize that I'd been away. I think I could have gone back to my office and set up shop and nobody would have blinked."

"Devin Juhle might have been a little perplexed."

"Okay, him, but nobody else."

"So what were you doing at the Hall? Business?"

Glitsky played it casually. "I'm doing some work for Hardy."

Elliot's steel-wool eyebrows went up. "You're going private?"

"I wouldn't say that. Just a little freelance. I wondered if you might be able to tell me anything that isn't in the public domain about Hal Chase or his wife."

Jeff squinted into the distance for a second, then came back. "The wife who's gone missing?"

"That's her."

"Is she dead?"

"We don't know yet."

"If she is, did he kill her?"

"Homicide seems to think so, but he says not. He came to Hardy. Diz is choosing to believe that there's more here than meets the eye, and he thinks I'm the guy who can sleuth it out. Whatever it is."

"And you think I might know something?"

"You usually do."

"Well, let's see." Elliot closed his eyes and took a deep breath or two. "Nothing in the immediately downloadable brainpan." Holding up a finger, he swung around in his chair. "Hal, right?" He tapped on his keyboard, waited a second or two, then nodded as the screen filled. "Okay, maybe this has nothing to do with his wife, but . . . he still works at the jail?"

"Yep."

"Have you talked to him about what he does there?"

"No. I gather he's your basic guard. What do you have?"

"Same thing, nothing. But any time I see the words 'San Francisco County Sheriff,' my antennae go up. It's not the best-run show on the planet. Maybe you've heard."

Glitsky, of course, knew the general reputation, which was not good. San Francisco was a geographical anomaly in that the physical boundaries included both an incorporated municipality — the city — and a state jurisdictional entity — the county. Thus, two law enforcement agencies — SFPD and the Sheriff's Department — coexisted, cooperated, and sometimes overlapped, but were totally distinct entities. The chief of police was appointed by the mayor. The sheriff of San Francisco County was elected by the voters. With a visiting dignitary or demonstration or riot, the agencies might cooperate, but for the most part, they had separate jobs.

The sheriff supervised the bailiffs who were responsible for the safety and security of the courthouses, the guards who ran the jails, and the jails themselves. The department's only other function was eviction, which had become something of a higher-profile responsibility in recent years, when the number of home foreclosures in the city had gone through the roof. The common perception was that the eviction deputies were not always the souls of sensitivity during these difficult exercises.

SFPD was responsible for all the other law enforcement in San Francisco, including homicides. In the case of a jail death, both agencies had jurisdiction. SFPD would handle any possible criminal implications in the death. The sheriff would run an internal investigation on how someone in custody could have died.

"Here," Elliot continued. "Here's what I mean. The latest, a week and a half ago. 'Inmate Dies Following Arrest.' You read about this?"

"Probably, though I don't remember specifically. It's common enough that I didn't pay much attention."

"Most people don't. Who cares about inmates? But look, it's the sixth inmate death this year and the third in three months. This one was an overdose. And those six deaths don't even count the overdoses where guys didn't die, or serious injuries from other causes. The jail might be the most dangerous neighborhood in town."

"That's what I mean by common enough."

Elliot leaned forward and read from the screen. "Angel Deloria. Forty-seven years old, doing ninety days on a probation violation. No apparent signs of foul play or suicide. Heroin overdose."

"Your point is? What's this got to do with Hal Chase? Or his wife?"

"Maybe nothing. Probably nothing. As I said. But if you want to scratch around Hal Chase, I could pretty much guarantee that if you talk to him about what's going on at the jail, about the culture of the place, you'll get a few surprises. Anything Burt Cushing's involved in probably has dirt sticking to it someplace."

This abrupt segue to the sheriff himself brought Glitsky up short. "Do we know that Hal Chase knows Cushing, other than he's his boss's boss, or something like that?"

"No." Elliot sighed and pushed back his wheelchair again. "It's probably wishful thinking on my part."

"What is?"

"Thinking your guy Chase might be the way to get inside over there, to find out what's really happening."

"And 'over there' is where?"

"The Sheriff's Department. I figure there's got to be a crack in the armor someplace, but three or four years now, I've been waiting and watching and hoping — you should see my files — and nothing ever seems to develop into a real story, which in my soul I believe is a big one. Have you met our good sheriff personally?"

"Couple of times at law enforcement events. If I remember, he gravitated toward the political side. I never had a conversation with him."

"Probably just as well. He's one of those guys, if his lips are moving, he's lying. Anyway, I was thinking that if you've got a legitimate reason to talk to your guy Chase, he might say something about how things are going, in a general way, at the jail and environs. If he did that, and you thought it smelled funny, maybe you could relay some of that back to me."

Glitsky sat back and crossed his legs. "What arc you looking for?"

Elliot pointed at his computer. "Let me show you something. These files I've been keeping." A few keyboard strokes, and he leaned in to read his screen. "Here's last October. Another inmate, Alanos Tussaint, died of blunt force trauma to the head, suffered when he evidently slipped and fell in a holding cell at the jail. In a jail full of people, nobody noticed him on the ground, unconscious, for an hour. Mr. Tussaint's death was investigated and apparently found to be accidental, since there was no follow-up story of any kind, and believe me, I looked."

"What were you looking for?"

"Well, trauma to the head . . . what would you have been looking for?"

"You think he was beaten?"

Elliot shrugged. "Another inmate talked to the SFPD and said some guards were involved. Later, he retracted that accusation. And nothing ever came of it. No prosecutions, no nothing. You want another one?"

"Sure."

"Okay." A few more keystrokes. "Back to August, three heroin ODs in one night, which leads to the question, 'Where are these guys getting super-pure and therefore deadly black tar heroin if they are already locked up in jail?' Do you think it's remotely possible that guards could be smuggling drugs into the population? And if that's the case, can the sheriff really be unaware of it?"

"You think Cushing's part of all this?"

"The short answer is absolutely. Though he runs a very tight ship and nobody's leaking. And that's just stuff around the jail, not even counting the irregularities and problems with the evictions he's in charge of."

"You want to get him," Glitsky said.

"I think he's a corrupt despot and a menace, Abe. But he's got loyal people, I'll give him that. Loyal as only fear can make you. And as you well know, the code of silence among the guards makes the Mafia look like a gossipy quilting bee."

"I've heard that," Glitsky said. "But interesting and provocative as all this is, we've come a long way from Hal Chase and his missing wife."

Elliot broke a chagrined smile. "I know. Sorry. I got wound up. It's just I hear about any little tenuous connection to Cushing, and I start thinking this might be the big break I've been looking for."

"I'll keep an open mind, but except for here, I haven't heard a whisper about Cushing in any of this. If anything pops, I'll let you know."

"You da man, Abe," Elliot said. "And hey, welcome back."

12

Hal Chase eased himself into the comfortable chair that faced the sheriff's desk. As always in the presence of his boss, he was somewhat nervous, and more so now because he had no idea why he'd been summoned. Adam Foster, the boss's chief deputy and a hard-ass of the first order, hadn't given him any hints to ease his mind while he'd waited in the outside office, although he came up with a few possibilities.

Hal had had several interruptions in his workday yesterday, including: extra time off at lunch when he'd gone over and called on Dismas Hardy; the earlier interview with the Homicide people; Abe Glitsky's appearance before his shift was technically finished. Burt Cushing wasn't a big fan of flexibility in work scheduling. You were supposed to be somewhere at a certain time, and by God, that's where he wanted you to be. To keep a jail full of animals at bay, you had to keep order, and a key element of order was punctuality. You were where your comrades expected you to be so that you could be counted on — for backup, for protection, for the power of numbers, and for simple safety.

A relatively short, squat, powerful fireplug of a man, Cushing made up for his stature with an oversize personality. Hal found it difficult to read Cushing's face and, until he knew why he was here, hardly dared to look at it. But he knew its features well: pitted pale cheeks, closely set dark eyes under a low brooding forehead, a brush-cut marine haircut, a cauliflower nose over a thin-lipped mouth that somehow managed to convey warmth with a frequent smile. Hal had heard the voice rumble in anger, had heard it command attention with a low-volume order. But today, when it came, the voice was solicitous and sincere. "How are you holding up, son?" he asked.

"Trying, sir."

"Those Homicide people giving you a bad time?"

Hal nodded. "Pretty much. They think I killed her."

"Pardon me for putting it baldly, but do they know she's dead?"

"I don't think so. Someone would have told me."

"I guess that's true. I pray she's not."

"Thank you, sir."

Cushing paused, then lowered his voice. "She's a terrific person. You know that? A wonderful person."

Hal straightened in his chair. "I wasn't sure you'd have remembered her, sir. It's been a couple of years."

"Yes, well. She's not the kind of person anyone is likely to forget. Even if she hadn't . . ." He stopped and took another tack. "I sometimes feel she saved my daughter's life. That may be an exaggeration, but not much of one."

Hal remembered it well. Cushing's thirteen-year-old daughter, Kayla, had been suffering for months from severe acne, her lovely face starting to scar, perhaps permanently. Kayla had gone to at least three dermatologists and taken several different drugs, all to no avail, when Hal had overheard a conversation between a couple of his sergeants about the sheriff's extreme distress at this seemingly hopeless situation. Hal had suggested a new anti-acne drug that his wife was very enthusiastic about.

It turned out to be a bit of an effort. Only two doctors in the city were prescribing the drug, and neither was accepting new patients, but Katie told Cushing that she could probably get Kayla an appointment and, if the doctor agreed, get her on the drug. Within a month, Kayla's acne was all but gone.

"She was glad to help," Hal said. "That's the way she . . . That's how she is."

"Yes, it is. I remember well." Cushing blew out through his mouth. "Who's watching your kids?"

"My stepmother's standing in until I can get somebody else. She lives close, so it's not much of a burden."

"What about you? Would it be helpful to you to be home with them? At least until you get a more permanent solution?"

Hal drew in a breath and finally said, "It would, sir, yes. But I've been worried about the time off."

Cushing waved a hand. "You've got too many other things to worry about without having that be any kind of a concern. You should go home now. Be with your kids. Let me worry about your time. We'll take care of it. You're on special assignment for as long as you need. Full pay."

13

Abby and JaMorris met with Katie's brother, Daniel Dunne, in his office at the law firm where he worked — Daley Silver Edwards — on the twenty-third floor of Two Embarcadero. As it turned out, Daniel had talked to his parents the night after they'd met with the Homicide inspectors, and he'd decided that he needed to be more proactive. When he'd heard that Homicide had gotten officially involved, he counted it as the beginning of real progress, so he'd called the department and asked the inspectors to come by.

As soon as they'd gotten settled, he started right in. "I understand that my family didn't exactly present a united front with you guys yesterday."

"We don't need a united front," Abby said. "The more input we get, the better."

"My father thought that you favored the girls' opinion."

"Which was what, as you understand it?"

"That Hal was just destroyed by all this and couldn't have had anything to do with it."

JaMorris joined in. "We were interested in your father's opinion, except he had nothing specific to offer, other than, given the timing, Hal was the only reasonable suspect who could have abducted Katie and gotten her out of the house."

"What's wrong with that picture?"

"Nothing," JaMorris said, "except that your father couldn't supply a motive, not even a hypothetical one. And from all we've been hearing, some money issues aside, Hal and Katie were doing pretty good together."

Daniel shook his head. "That's just plain not true," he said. Dragging a hand over his forehead, he leveled his gaze at the two inspectors. "This really pisses me off. You guys know she was going to a counselor, right? Tell me, is that what you usually see with happy couples?"

"Lots of couples go to counseling," Abby said.

"But they didn't go as a couple," Daniel countered. "Katie went by herself. She was trying to save the marriage, and he didn't want any part of it."

"How have we not heard about that yet?"

JaMorris asked.

"Because she didn't talk about it. She was working on it. Katie was a fighter and wasn't about to give up on something she'd put so much effort into."

"Let me ask you," Abby said, "how do you know this when your mother and father and sisters don't seem to?"

Daniel spread his palms. "What can I say? She didn't confide in them. She did in me. We're close. We were close. We are close." Taking a deep breath, he blinked a couple of times, then continued, "Look, she's the big sister, she's Mom's firstborn. She was going to present a good front to them — Mom and Dad — until there was nothing else she could do. She was happily married, goddammit. That was the story. A good mom, a loving wife. As long as she and Hal were living together, making a go of it, the story was that they were happy. Because what if she fixed it all up and things really were good again? She didn't want Mom and the girls to harbor bad feelings about Hal, about how he'd made things tough for her."

The two inspectors shared a look. "So what was the problem?" Abby asked.

After a slight hesitation, Daniel came out with it. "Have you guys heard anything about Patti Orosco?"

JaMorris answered, "No. Who is she?"

"She was Katie's best friend until a couple of years ago, when she started hitting on Hal."

"And?" Abby asked.

"As I understand it," Daniel said, "they're now an item. I mean, I don't know for sure, but I think it's pretty damn likely. He still sees her all the time. Katie knew that. He'd stop by her place coming home from work. He'd disappear for a while on the weekends. Katie could smell her perfume on him, but she never got solid proof. Maybe she didn't want it, I don't know. I told her she ought to hire a private eye, follow the son of a bitch around, that I'd even pay for it, but she didn't want to do it. Still, every time she talked to me, she brought it up."

"She didn't call him on it?" JaMorris asked.

"No."

Abby wanted to know, "Why not?"

"Same thing as with my family," he said. "If she didn't tell them something was wrong, then when things got better, she would have saved everybody a lot of pain, and everything could go back to normal." He ran a finger under an eye, clearly fighting his emotions. "She was just such a stupid believer that if you ignored certain things, even important things, they'd eventually go away. You didn't need to have a confrontation about everything."

"Good luck with that," JaMorris said.

"Tell me about it." Daniel scratched at a speck on the arm of his chair. Then, with apparent reluctance, he went on. "Besides, she felt she couldn't accuse him without coming straight with him herself."

The inspectors waited.

Daniel brought his hands together on the desk. "She had a thing with a guy a few months after Ellen was born. She was going through severe postpartum depression and made a mistake. At least that's how she made it sound to me. But she decided she was going to end it and not mention it to Hal, and sure enough, it all worked out. So now, if he was screwing around, it wasn't like she couldn't understand what he might be going through. If she didn't bring it up, maybe it would all go away, like hers did. Except, in this case, he wanted to get free, and he killed her."

"Over this Patti woman?" Abby asked. "Why would he kill her? Why not just get a divorce?"

"Let me tell you about Katie. She wants to come across as the perfect girl, the perfect woman. But if ever Hal tried to divorce her, I promise you, she would show fangs like you wouldn't believe. She'd go after him with everything she had, not only for betraying her but for exposing that she was the kind of person who would get betrayed. She'd ruin his life and any chance that he could be happy with somebody else. If I know this about Katie, and I'm just her brother, I guarantee you Hal understood it perfectly."

"Okay, she might want to get nasty," JaMorris said, "but what could she actually do?"

Suddenly, Daniel seemed to pull himself up short. Yanking at his tie, he undid the top button on his shirt and ran a finger around the inside of his collar. Letting out a heavy breath, he assayed a fragile smile. "Okay," he said. "I've thought a lot about how much I wanted to tell you, but here it is."

"Whatever you want to tell us," Abby said. "You think she would have been able to make Hal's life miserable?"

"Maybe more than that."

JaMorris chimed back in. "And how does she do that?"

"I don't know any of the details here — names and so on — but you could find them easily enough. A couple of weeks ago, you might remember, there was a stink about this inmate who died in jail. He slipped and fell and banged his head against his cell or something and died. Does that ring a bell?"

Abby resisted the urge to laugh. "Always," she said.

"Yeah, well, this time they had their usual investigation, and another inmate said it wasn't any accident. He saw one of the guards kill him. Hit him on the head, locked him in his cell, and left him to die."

JaMorris picked it up. "The guard was Hal?"

"Evidently not. But Hal told Katie that the inmate was right, one of his coworkers killed the guy. Hal was one of the six guards who all alibied each other. Oh, and did I mention that the inmate witness recanted his testimony? Hal was part of the team who helped persuade him."

"So if Hal filed for divorce," JaMorris said, "Katie would have brought this out?"

"That's my take," Daniel said. "Even if he hadn't gotten arrested, there would have been a full-fledged custody fight, and she would have used that to try and keep the kids. She wouldn't have had to warn him. He would have known she'd take him down. He might do prison time, and you know what prison is like for former guards?"

Abby didn't have to guess. "So your theory is that Hal had decided to leave Katie for this other woman, but he couldn't divorce her because she'd go public with the cover-up that the guards were all part of. So if he wanted out, he had to make sure she didn't talk and couldn't accuse him. Therefore, he had to kill her."

"It's a motive," Daniel said. "My dad didn't have one for you guys. I do. And while we're at this, there's one other thing you ought to know about Patti Orosco."

"What's that?" Abby asked.

"She's filthy rich."

14

To the casual observer, Lou the Greek's restaurant — directly across the street from the Hall of Justice — might appear to have health and hygiene issues. People in the know suspected that the A it received every year from the city's Health Department was the result of either a health inspector with severely poor vision or an influential clientele who didn't want the place to change or get hassled. Nevertheless, if you lingered on the stairway that led down to the door — say, waiting in line — you'd detect an odor that spoke to the presence of some of San Francisco's treasured homeless population, who used the stairway as a windbreak, bedroom, and sometimes toilet.

Lou got in every morning about four hours after closing at two A.M. and before the place opened at six. He rousted the sleepers, hosed everything down, Cloroxed, squeegeed, then opened up for the early-morning drinking crowd.

In spite of all that, but mostly due to proximity to the courts, the place was always jammed at lunchtime. Cops, lawyers, clients, reporters, jurors, witnesses, all of them needed lunch, and Lou's was convenient, cheap, fast, and surprisingly and consistently good. This was all the more unexpected considering that it served only one course every day, the famous Special, which was nearly always an original combination of the ethnic foodstuffs of Lou and his wife, the cook, Chui — Greek and Chinese. So you'd get a lot of lamb and pork dishes, squid and octopus and shrimp, meatballs, noodles, rice, grape leaves, and bao dumplings, seasoned heavily with lemon juice, Mae Ploy, or soy sauce. Often weird but always edible, if not downright tasty.

Its other great advantage was that its popularity tended to produce a noise level comparable to a jet engine's. This made it convenient not only for privileged communications, say between lawyers and their clients, but for other conversations that might otherwise have to take place behind closed doors.

Today, at the front of the line that extended up the stairs and out to the sidewalk, Glitsky stood with Treya and her boss, Wes

Farrell. Abe had stopped by the Hall to see if he could talk to one of the DA's investigators or assistant district attorneys who'd looked into some of the irregularities at the jail, and if somehow he could bring the name Hal Chase subtly into the conversation. Basically, nobody knew nothin'.

Abe was talking to Farrell about it. "It just seems odd that none of these allegations ever got any legs. Jeff Elliot's got files on every incident — every death in custody, OD, or inmate treated for blunt force trauma — that's happened at the jail for the past few years, and none of them has gone anywhere."

"This surprises you?" Farrell asked.

"Slightly. Especially when you look at what happens if somebody starts talking abuse or excessive force with regular cops. The whole world jumps all over them. Particularly, if memory serves, your office jumps all over them."

"True. And you know why that is?"

"You guys hate cops?"

Farrell turned to Glitsky's wife. "Try to keep him away from stand-up." To Abe, he went on, "As you know, that was the wrong answer. We love cops. We have a full and free and respectful working relationship with the Police Department. I am the DA himself, and I have personal friends in the PD. The truth is, our good citizens demand that cops be held to a higher standard than normal people. SFPD operates in the community. They interact with criminals, sure, but also with regular people, many of whom have cell phones with those cool video functions. They operate in an open environment and, when they show up, often don't know what is going on. So they've got a much better opportunity to screw something up and a much better chance that a credible person will be there to see when they do it.

"The sheriff, on the other hand, totally controls the jail, and the inmates are pretty much at his mercy. The only people who are not, by definition, criminals in the jail work for the sheriff, which hardly fosters a transparent environment. So the chances of solving a crime involved in the jail approach zero, and if a guard brutalizes an inmate, nobody's ever going to know. But if we get a righteous case, we try it. I promise you."

"You haven't gotten one? Not even one?"

"Sometimes we get one. But the ones we do get tend to fall into the misdemeanor category, the Sheriff's Department policing itself and making sure that its members adhere to the law and protocol in all cases. The occasional small-fry investigation yields a misdemeanor conviction that allows for plausible deniability on larger matters. Their story is that they investigate every allegation of wrongdoing, and when they find something actionable, then by God they act on it."

"None of the larger cases make it upstairs?"

"Very few, if any. And what do you think that could be about?" Farrell asked as they finally got to the door. "I bet, being an ex–police officer of unrivaled sagacity and experience, you can figure this out."

"You never have witnesses."

Farrell beamed, spread his arms, and again turned to Treya. "And there it is," he said. "But now let me ask you one."

"Shoot."

"Why do you care? Are you not done with the daily exertions of your brain about criminal matters?"

"I thought I was. But Diz asked me to look into something for him, and Wyatt Hunt is out of town, so I said yes."

Farrell once was Hardy's law partner, and the news obviously took him by surprise. "You, a cop —"

"Ex-cop."

"Still. You're working for Diz the defense attorney?"

"Part-time."

"It's a work in progress," Treya put in. "He's only just started."

Farrell asked, "You don't feel like you're working for the wrong side? Don't you find that a little weird?"

"Did you find it weird prosecuting people after thirty years as a defense attorney?"

"Actually, yes. I don't know if I'd recommend it for normal people."

"In my case, I'm an investigator, and I'm investigating, that's all. It's not like I'm on one side or another."

Farrell chuckled. "No? Just wait. It will be. So what's the case? Something to do with the jail?"

"Only in the sense that Hardy's client is a guard there. I was down with Jeff Elliot at the *Chronicle* this morning, nosing around about my guy, and next thing you know, Jeff's going off about all the troubles at the jail."

"Connecting them to your client?"

"No. No apparent connection at all."

"Do you think there is?"

Glitsky shook his head. "No reason to. My guy's wife has gone missing, and I'm trying to find out where she went. Unless she's hiding in the jail, the jail's got nothing to do with it."

15

Patti Orosco lived alone in a small but beautifully appointed two-bedroom condominium on the semi-private road running parallel to Polk Street, at the bottom of the escarpment where Chestnut ended at the steps that climbed steeply up to Hyde. From her living room's picture window, San Francisco's western vista extended past the Palace of the Legion of Honor out to the low green hills of the Presidio, over to the Golden Gate Bridge, the bay, and Marin County on the right, Pacific Heights on the left.

After Sheriff Cushing had excused him from work for the foreseeable future, Hal Chase knew that his first duty was to go home and spell Ruth and Warren, who had certainly put in enough time watching his children. Instead, he'd called Patti and driven straight to her place.

Hal hadn't seen her for the past three

weeks, ever since he'd ended their five-month affair. And now, when she opened the door, her beauty brought an involuntary catch to his breath. She was barefoot in running shorts and a 49ers sweatshirt that was unsuccessful in camouflaging the assertive curve of her breasts. Her blond hair touched her shoulders and framed a face that Hal considered perfect. No. Beyond perfect.

They embraced, holding each other tightly for nearly a minute.

"I shouldn't let you in here," she said, but with a sigh, she took a step backward and pulled the door all the way open. When he came in, she closed it behind him, then led the way up the stairs and into the kitchen, where he pulled his familiar stool over to the bar and sat. She boosted herself onto the counter, feet crossed at the ankles, and gave him a searching look. "I . . ." she began. "I am so, so sorry."

He nodded. "It's the worst."

"How are the kids?"

"Ruth's with them for the time being. Will doesn't have any idea, but Ellen . . . I think she's starting to get it."

"She's a smart kid."

"Yeah. Not always the advantage you think it might be."

"No. Probably not." She lowered her eyes,

then raised them and met his gaze. "How are you holding up?"

"Pretty much not. It's all so surreal." He touched her cheek. "Thank you for saying you'd see me."

"How could I not?"

"I could come up with lots of reasons, all of them good."

"None would be good enough."

He hesitated. "You know that the cops think she's dead and that I killed her."

"That's ridiculous."

He shrugged. "They don't think so."

"Well, I do."

"That's good. Because I didn't."

"Of course you didn't."

Hal blew out heavily. "I can't tell you how good it is to hear you say that. When I didn't hear from you . . ."

"I didn't think, under the circumstances, that my calling you would be the best idea."

He held up a hand. "I get it. I really shouldn't have expected you to call. Not after the way it ended with us. But —"

"But it didn't end," she said. "It's nowhere near over." She slid off the counter and put her arms around him. "You don't have to say anything, babe. You don't have to make any decisions about me. I'm always going to be there for you, if that's what you want.

You know that, I hope."

He leaned in to her. "I do know that. But right now . . ."

"Of course," she said. "No pressure." She gave him a quick kiss on the lips. "I still love you, you know."

He nodded. "I'm in bad shape. I don't know what's happening. And I don't know when I'm going to start knowing."

"In your situation, that would be normal, wouldn't you say?"

"Normal? I can't imagine normal ever again."

"That's normal, too," she said.

"Okay." He took a breath. "I'm going to believe you." After hesitating, he said, "You know, it's not impossible that some Homicide inspectors are going to want to talk to you. About you and me."

"How would they ever have heard about you and me?"

"They'll be talking to Katie's friends. Her brother, Daniel. You'll probably get mentioned by somebody." He shifted on his stool, and his eyes met hers. "It would probably be better if they didn't know anything that happened with us."

"You want me to lie to the police?"

"Not necessarily lie. Maybe omit. They're going to be looking for a motive, and if they knew that you and I had a thing going on . . ."

Patti flared. "It wasn't a *thing,* Hal. I was in love with you. I'm still in love with you. And you still love me."

Hal's eyes bored in on a spot on the wall over her shoulder. He let out another breath. "All right."

"All right, what? Yes? No? What?"

He held up a hand. "The fact is, I was getting back with Katie. I'd made that commitment. I wasn't planning to leave Katie to be with you. Maybe I should have been, but I wasn't. That is the real fundamental truth. And if these inspectors come to realize what we had, you and me, they're going to see a reason why I might have wanted Katie out of the way. So it would be better if they didn't know."

Patti sat for a moment in silence. "You know," she said, "if they really decide they're going to look, there's no way they won't find out."

"Maybe, but not if —"

She shook her head. "Hal. Think about it. Phone records, restaurant receipts, snoopy neighbors. Things like this always come out, and then everybody looks worse for lying about it to start with. We should tell them what we had and tell them when it ended and stand firm together."

Hal brought his hands up to his temples, over his forehead, back down to the bar. "The minute I become the unfaithful husband, to the cops and to the world, I'm done. Nothing else is going to matter. Don't you see that?"

"The unfaithful husband is what you are, Hal. That's also a fundamental truth. And if I deny it, then when it comes out, and it will, we're both liars, aren't we? And that makes both of us look guilty, too. Like I was in with you somehow. Like we planned something. It's better to tell them up front and just live with it."

16

Glitsky sat on the couch in Hal's living room while Hal paced back and forth. "I told her she shouldn't say boo about it to the Homicide guys, and I probably shouldn't be telling you about it, either," Hal said.

"No," Glitsky replied. "Telling me is a good thing."

After the client had called and invited him down to his house to talk, Glitsky had bee-lined out to his place on Stanyan. The stepmother and her son were out grocery shopping; the kids were both napping. It was an ideal moment for confessions, and Hal had just dropped the whopper about him and Patti.

"How long did this affair last?" Glitsky asked.

"Five months or so."

"And when did it end?"

"Three weeks ago."

Glitsky grimaced. "Weeks?"

"I know," Hal said. "Terrible timing."

"Maybe better than if it was still going on," Abe replied. "Did Katie know?"

"No. I don't think so, anyway. But she might have suspected. I just don't know." Hal made a face. "For years, Patti was her best friend. I know it sounds awful. I promise, it wasn't like we planned it."

Glitsky shrugged. "It is what it is, Hal. It's not my job to judge you, but Patti was right. It is better to know everything we're dealing with. And we're going to be dealing with this, trust me." He chewed at the inside of his cheek. "Are you sure Katie didn't know? Could she have found out?"

"Why?"

"It occurs to me that if she was feeling betrayed by her husband and her best friend, there's another way she could have disappeared."

Hal worked through the permutations, finally getting to it. "I don't . . ." he began, then, "You're saying she might have killed herself."

Glitsky nodded. "Call a cab and take it out someplace close to the Golden Gate. Walk halfway across. Most jumpers, no one ever sees them again."

Hal brought his hand up to his face.

"Christ. I never thought . . ."

"Was she the kind of person who might have done that?"

Hal didn't have to ponder long. "No. She wouldn't have left the kids. I keep coming back to that. She was a fanatically protective mom. Say whatever else you will about her, the kids were everything. Besides, she left her purse, so how could she have paid for a cab?"

"Cash still works," Glitsky said. "Here to the bridge is under twenty bucks. I'm saying it's someplace we can check that I don't think anybody's looked into. But this theory is premised on the idea that Katie knew about you and Patti. And you say she didn't?"

"All I can tell you is that there was no sign if she did. She never accused me of anything. We never fought about it. Although our personal life had gotten pretty bleak."

"You mean sexually?"

Hal nodded. "It'd been probably a month, maybe more."

"So a little before you and Patti called it off?"

Clearly, this wasn't something Hal wanted to discuss. "Something like that," he said. "I didn't keep track, exactly. But I didn't think it would be forever. I thought we'd get back

116

to the way we were. She was just distant or taken up with the kids most of the time, and I was feeling guilty and didn't want to push her."

"This was when you and Patti were calling it off?"

"Somewhere in there, yes."

Glitsky got to his feet and walked over to the window, where he cracked his back, stretched, and turned around. "This is the second time I've heard you talk about how much Katie protects the kids. She wouldn't get a babysitter, right? Not even Ruth, who lives a half a mile away?"

"She has a problem with Ruth, but it's not only Ruth. She has a problem with everybody. She's the classic gatekeeper. You know the term?"

"Sure."

"Well, she's that in spades. She is convinced nobody else can do the job she's doing with the kids."

"And how do you feel about that?"

"It's a little much, if you want my opinion. Not to criticize her, but it's not her most endearing quality. I can't do anything. I mean, change a diaper, comb hair, put on clothes, make the beds a certain way. Fold the goddamn towels. Forget it. She did it all. You know why? Because I couldn't do it right." Hal looked over at Glitsky. "It pissed me off, to tell you the truth. Not that it's any excuse, but it's one of the things that got me together with Patti."

"How was that?"

"Patti had been over a few days in a row — which used to be pretty common for us — and Katie wanted the kids down by seven exactly, so we could have an 'adult' dinner later. We all went in to help with the bedtime ritual, you know? Getting pajamas on and reading a story and then a lullaby and all that madness. Anyway, Patti and I were getting a little goofy, and I guess we started doing things out of order — out of order! — whatever that meant, and Katie kicked us both out to the kitchen while she calmed the kids down. She was really a bitch about it.

"Patti and I poured some wine, and we were laughing at how kind of crazy all of it was, and next thing you know, Katie comes storming out of the kids' room. We're keeping them up, for Christ's sake! She told us to find our own dinner somewhere if we were having such a good time and couldn't keep quiet enough to let the babies sleep." He shook his head at the memory. "So we went out. Then we went over to Patti's."

"Maybe you don't want to tell the Homicide people that story," Glitsky said.

"Katie was confused and messed up," Hal said, "but I loved her. I thought we could work it out. I wanted to for the sake of the kids, if nothing else. I know that's a cliché, but it's how I felt. It killed me that Patti and I had started up, and while it killed me to break up with her, Katie and I used to be great together, and I thought maybe we could be again."

"But you wouldn't go to counseling with her?"

"No."

"Why not?"

Hal gave Glitsky a cop-to-cop look. "You ever go to counseling?"

"No."

"You think you would?"

"What I'd do isn't the issue. You admit you and Katie were having troubles. She wanted you to go with her. You were involved with another woman. Under those circumstances, you might have thought it was worth a try."

Hal shrugged. "I'm not a counseling kind of guy. Besides, if I'm in counseling, first thing I'll have to do is tell Katie about Patti, and that is simply not happening. That would have been the end of us, and I didn't want that. Besides, I know what Katie's basic problem is."

"You do? What's that?"

"The whole stay-at-home-mom thing."

"What thing is that?"

"She was raised to believe that she could have it all. Great career, lots of money, motherhood, perfect kids, you name it. When she got out of school, she started her career and was great at it. By the time I met her, she was making way more than I was with the sheriff, and she thought she'd keep that up forever. We got married and saved our money and bought this house, and for the first couple of years, everything was easy and fun and we were really happy. We had friends and we went to restaurants and clubs and lived like royalty. It was great.

"Then we had Ellen, and we were both blown away by how much time she took and how much work she was. Still, Katie went back to her job, like she'd planned. We got a nanny who basically cost my entire salary, but we were all right, both money-wise and together. Then Will came along, and every-thing changed."

"What happened?"

"The main thing is Katie decided she had to quit working. She thought that it wasn't fair to be raising kids without at least one of the parents at home. I told her if that was the case, it should be me, since I made so much less. We wouldn't miss my salary as much as we'd miss hers. But she wouldn't do that. She was going to stay home and be there for the kids, and that was all there was to it. And since the kids had become her full-time job, they were going to be her full-time responsibility. She would do everything for them. And nobody else, including me, was going to poach on her turf. What I was making didn't turn out to be nearly enough, and things started sliding from there. On all kinds of levels."

Glitsky's cop instincts were on full alert. He'd just heard Hal confess not only to his own infidelity and estrangement from his wife but to the financial difficulties brought on by her quitting her job. This, in the usual course of events, should have raised Hal's profile as a murder suspect.

But as it had from the beginning of his dealings with Hal, Glitsky's gut was overriding his mind. He felt in his gut, God help him, that his client was telling the truth. Hal's was a common enough human story, and while it wasn't a particularly happy one, it didn't strike Glitsky as the prologue to Hal deciding to take his wife's life.

"It was you who called things off with Patti, right?"

"Yep."

"How'd she take it?"

"Not great. She thought we were going to be together. I thought so, too, for a while. But it felt too wrong. As I've told you."

"You thought you could get back with Katie without telling her about Patti at all?"

"I don't know. I didn't have any idea how everything was going to work itself out. But I was going to give the marriage another chance."

Glitsky had come up to the couch and rested a haunch against the back of it. "Okay. Before today, when was the last time you talked to Patti?"

Hal pondered for a second or two. "When we broke up. I could probably check the exact day; it was something like a month ago. Why?"

"Just checking things. How about Katie?"

"How about her?"

"Might she and Patti have talked?"

"Sure. They were friends forever. If Patti had stopped all communication, that would have been more suspicious than anything else. On the surface, everything was the same. Patti agreed we were going to try to keep it that way."

"But the two of them, they might have talked just before Katie disappeared?"

122

"I don't . . . No, wait. Now that you mention it, Patti was going to come to Thanksgiving dinner with us. She called Katie to say she was down with the flu and wouldn't be able to make it."

"That day? The day before Thanksgiving?"

"Maybe. Or the day before that, I'm not positive. What are you thinking?"

"I'm thinking about people who might have had a reason and an opportunity to kill your wife."

"You're not saying it could have been Patti?"

Glitsky scratched at the side of his face. "Why not?"

"Because it's just . . . She wouldn't ever have done anything like that. I told her it was over between us, and she didn't like it, but she accepted it."

"You just told me it was because you didn't want to break up your family. Is that what you told her?"

"I told her I thought I owed it to Katie not to give up."

"But if Katie were gone, suddenly out of the picture, leaving you free?"

Hal swallowed, then took a breath. "No," he said at last. "That's not possible."

Glitsky put some edge into his voice. "I promise you it's possible. People kill each

123

other over jealousy every day. Now, you've got your recently jilted lover Patti talking to your wife on the day she disappears, possibly discovering exactly when you're driving down to the airport, when she'll be alone. Why couldn't she have done it? Do you know what she was doing that night?"

Hal, mulling it over, shook his head.

"Okay, if it's not you and it's not Patti, maybe you could point at somebody else Katie knows. Because right now, I'm seeing a mom with very little life outside the walls of this house. So you tell me, Hal. Am I missing something?"

17

Frannie Hardy moved up the hallway, past the closed doors to three other offices on her right, past the stairway on her left. At the front of the hall, a window looked down onto Clement Street, and she stopped when she got to it, pushing the white gauze curtains to one side.

A steady stream of pedestrians filled the opposite sidewalk, the majority of them Asians. The storefronts across the street mirrored this demographic. Standing in the window, Frannie had within her field of vision a sushi bar, an acupuncture studio, a Thai and a Chinese restaurant, a fishmonger, a corner grocery with crates of fresh vegetables, two massage parlors, and a store featuring lots of camera equipment and electrical gear.

Frannie normally loved not just her work but going to work, since it wasn't quite a mile from her home and she almost always walked. It was like traveling to another country every day. But today she stood at the front window, frowning. She'd seen two clients in the morning, then she'd gone out for sushi, which she found herself unable to eat. She had sipped at her green tea until it was lukewarm, then, exhausted, had walked back home and lay down for an hour and a half. Finally, her mind empty, she had walked back to her building.

This was the regular hour for Katie Chase's weekly appointment. From the minute Frannie had woken up in the morning, she'd found herself more and more upset. Although she'd talked with Dismas about the disappearance a couple of times, the emphasis had fallen upon the criminal case that might be building against Hal. Katie's true situation was something Frannie and Dismas had never discussed. And now the reality of that situation — that Katie might very well be dead — hit her with a crushing force.

Katie was an educated, vibrant, sensitive woman with whom Frannie felt a strong bond. Her issues had been similar to many Frannie had faced many years ago as a young mother — adequacy, attractiveness, purpose. They had both decided to leave their jobs and become stay-at-home mothers. As of last week, Katie was hanging in with that decision, but Frannie knew it was getting to be a close thing. In spite of the spin she'd given Dismas, the couple had been negotiating some serious shoals. True, Katie hadn't started out seeing Frannie to talk about problems in her relationship with Hal, but as the counseling had gone on, the scope of the conversations had widened. And Hal had begun to feature prominently.

Frannie turned from the hallway window and let herself into her office at the back of the building. It was a small but warm and comfortable room with one window that overlooked the backs of the neighboring structures. Frannie had her own relatively small leather recliner, and her clients could choose between a quilt-covered love seat or another recliner, larger than Frannie's. A fully loaded bookshelf covered half of one wall, and on the bare wall space, she'd hung some fine-art prints — Picasso, Vermeer, Monet — in simple frames.

She crossed to the file cabinet and removed a manila folder that she brought back to her chair. Leaning back, she sighed and said, "Oh, Katie," and then pulled the sheaf of pages, about eighty in all, out onto her lap.

FRANNIE HARDY: So how have things been this week?

KATIE CHASE: About the same, really. But sometimes I don't know why I bother to come in here every week. Other than it's nice to see you. I seem to be going over the same things again and again, and I don't feel I'm making any progress at all. All of this talking and trying to understand myself and what I'm feeling and why I feel it — I'm supposed to be getting better someday, aren't I? Whatever that means.

FH: Don't you feel like you're making progress?

KC: I don't feel particularly better, no. This morning Will got up at four, which meant I got up at four . . .

FH: I thought you were going to talk to Hal about that, about helping you when the kids get up early.

KC: I was going to. But I just . . . can't.

FH: Why not? Katie?

KC: He's got his job. He can't go in to work exhausted. The people there are . . . well, you can't imagine. And not just the guys in the cells. If he's not sharp, he could literally get himself killed. So that leaves the kids to me. They're my job. I can't let anybody else do it. It's what I signed on for, and I can't . . .

FH: It's all right.

KC: Not really. No, it's not. I know I'm a total bitch about it, but it's the only power I've got left with him.

FH: Who's watching them now?

KC: My mother. At least she didn't completely mess me up, so for an hour or so once a week, I guess I can trust that she probably won't ruin them, either.

FH: And you feel like you need power with Hal? Or what? Katie?

KC: I'm sorry.

FH: There's nothing to be sorry about. Here's some Kleenex. If it's too painful, we don't have to . . .

KC: No. It's all right. I'll be all right. I just can't believe Hal and I have come to this. We used to be so in love with each other and have so much fun. I can't believe we're the same two people, me talking about power and control. And Hal, he used to be such a great guy.

FH: He's not anymore?

KC: How could he be, living with me? I barely let him breathe. And part of me knows I'm wrong . . . I'm just punishing us both.

FH: For what?

KC: Well, him, for being who he is. For not

making enough money. For not fighting me hard enough when I'm not the me I know I can be, the best me. For being tired. I know that sounds terrible, blaming him for all that is wrong, so I feel guilty for that, too. I'm just such a complete mess. I'm really so sorry, Fran.

FH: It's all right. You can let it all out. That's why you're here.

KC: I just need a minute.

FH: You've got it. All the time you need.

KC: I should never have had the affair. That's what ruined everything.

FH: Does Hal know about that?

KC: No. I could never tell him. It was just a pure mistake. I didn't even love the guy. I was feeling ugly and useless and trapped by my baby and just . . . Well, I did what I did. There's no turning back from that now. Every day I feel like a liar and a fraud. And then I resent Hal because he's a constant reminder of who I really am. The bad person I really am.

FH: Have you tried to talk to him?

KC: No. Our deal was if one of us was unfaithful, that would be the end.

FH: People say that, but it isn't always true.

KC: I think that for us, it would be.

FH: So you're living all the time with the fear that Hal will leave you?

KC: Not so much that. I don't know that he'll ever find out. It's more that I'm living with the guilt of knowing what I've done. That we're still trying to build this life that's so hard and isn't based on the truth anymore.

FH: That could change, Katie. It really could.

KC: You mean if I told him?

FH: It could be a start. You've got a family now. It's different. Would he leave you over a mistake you made almost three years ago?

KC: I don't know. He might.

FH: But if things continue the way they're going now, and you don't tell him, what kind of chance would you give yourselves? As a couple, I mean.

KC: At this point, almost zero.

FH: So think about it, Katie. What have you got to lose?

18

Glitsky lived on a one-block cul-de-sac north of Lake Boulevard and south of the Presidio. Aside from the occasional neighbor looking, usually in vain, for a parking spot, the road had very little traffic. Over the fall, a few of the grade school children on the street had started coming out in the late afternoon to play on the relatively open expanse of asphalt, at first hopscotch and soccer and then, as more of the local kids showed up, picking up teams for whatever game was on that day. Today was kickball, bases and home plate chalked on the street.

To Glitsky's astonishment, the wildly disparate group of fifteen or more kids seemed to incline naturally toward inclusivity. The ages ranged from Zachary's five to Austin Blake's eleven, and everybody seemed to understand the basic rule that if you showed up and wanted to play, you'd have a place.

Even more amazing was the ethnic and gender mix; it didn't seem a question of anybody's enforced tolerance so much as a complete indifference to skin tones and accents. Glitsky's kids were mostly black (with a little Jewish), but the others ran the gamut from Caucasian and Hispanic to at least three different kinds of Asian and subcontinental Indian.

Every night some parents would wander down to the sidewalk to watch the games, not to organize or supervise but simply to enjoy the spectacle. Two months earlier, enough of the parents had met this way that they decided to throw a block party. It was a beautiful warm September night, the whole block closed off to traffic and the street packed with grills, tables and chairs, and coolers full of drinks and side dishes. Glitsky, who'd lived in his duplex for almost thirty years and who couldn't have picked any of his neighbors out of a lineup a year before, now knew the majority of them by first name. It blew his mind.

Probably only fifteen minutes remained before they'd have to call tonight's game because of darkness. Glitsky was standing chatting idly with Natalie Soames, the mother of twin eight-year-old girls from across the street, and Austin's dad, James

Blake, another recent retiree. Abe's daughter, Rachel, was setting up to kick with runners on second and third.

"I hear this girl's awesome," Glitsky heard from behind him. "Big long-ball threat."

Glitsky looked over his shoulder. Dismas Hardy had managed to walk the entire length of the street and sneak up on him.

Rachel kicked a little blooper to second base, and the kid playing there caught it for the third out. With a minimum of fanfare or confusion, the teams changed positions.

Glitsky turned back to Hardy, introduced him to the neighbors, then said, "You jinxed her. She hasn't made an out all day."

"It'll keep her humble. Is this what I'm paying you the big bucks for?"

"No. I've been out pounding the pavement all day and have lots to report, but I thought I'd wait till after the game, since it's likely you'll want a drink."

"That good, huh?"

"You can be the judge of that."

Dusk had faded to black. Treya had not yet made it home from work. Rachel and Zachary were glued to a barely audible cartoon in the television room behind the kitchen.

Hardy sat at Glitsky's kitchen table with his hands templed at his mouth. When he took them down, he said, "He ended this affair three weeks ago? In the grand scheme of things, that's, like, yesterday, you realize."

"Right. He was going to keep on hiding the whole thing and hope nobody would notice, but then he talked to Patti, and she convinced him that it would be better to admit it, at least in terms of PR."

"He's thinking about PR?"

"It appears so."

Hardy shook his head wearily. "So they could be an item, planning how they're going to handle this thing together?"

"That idea had occurred to me."

"Have you talked to her?"

"Not yet. I thought I'd wait to see if you wanted me to go ahead. As you know, I've been fighting my natural prejudice against husbands all along. Hal's a pretty good guy, and he'd been shaking my faith in that eternal verity up till I heard about this."

"And now?"

Glitsky shrugged. "It's definitely gotten more complicated. Though, for the record, he still appears to be coming forth with the truth, even when it makes him look bad. It doesn't much matter what we think anyway. He either did it or he didn't."

Hardy considered. "So you think he originally came to me . . . why?"

"He's in law enforcement. He knows there's a good chance he'll need a lawyer as things unravel, so he might as well get one on board early. Better to have that covered before they arrest him."

"They won't do that until they find her body. Even with this affair in the mix."

"No? How much you want to bet?"

"You really think so?"

Glitsky nodded. "They'll find a way. Trust me."

19

Wes Farrell attained his eminent position as the district attorney of San Francisco more or less by chance. As a lifelong defense attorney, he had no record as a prosecutor. In fact, his notoriety stemmed mostly from a high-profile case he had won years before, for the defense, getting — unbeknowst to him at the time — a guilty murderer who happened to be his best friend, off with a clean acquittal. Beyond that, he had gained a certain hip cachet as a lovable oddball because of the themed T-shirts he wore every day under his business suit — and showed off regularly to friends, associates, and reporters. Today's shirt read: "Smiling on the outside, berserk on the inside," and it was indicative of, albeit slightly less offensive than, most of the others. More typical in terms of general sensitivity had been yesterday's: "I hate being bipolar. It's awesome!"

When friends had persuaded him to seek the office three years before against a heavily favored rival, he'd gone on the ticket, half as a simple acknowledgment of their belief in him, and half to strike a blow for what he called moderation in the face of a super-lenient prosecutorial culture that had essentially given up on trials in favor of plea bargains and counseling in lieu of the most toothless of punishments. At least, Wes had said, he'd put some bite back into the system. In a Farrell administration, violent criminals would be tried and, if convicted, do prison time. (Almost anywhere else, this would not have been considered a particularly aggressive stance for a prosecutor, but in San Francisco, it was considered right-wing extremism, and his nastiest detractors had labeled him Fascist Farrell.) In any event, fate played into his hands when his front-running opponent died the week before the election, and Farrell was swept to victory by a whopping ninety votes out of three hundred and fifty thousand cast.

But a cultural shift had to start at the top, and in spite of his campaign rhetoric, Wes in his heart was a very long way from being a hard-core law-and-order guy. After a lifetime at the defense bar, his sympathies had always instinctively gone to the accused.

He believed there were reasons, and usually good ones, why people went bad.

But more and more lately, he found himself not caring about that. His job was prosecuting miscreants. Whether or not he understood them or their upbringing played very little if any role in the process.

In his first months as DA, on a very public stage, he had to figure out who he was, what he really believed. What had begun more or less as a parlor game — what if he humored some of his buddies and actually ran for DA? — had turned into the marrow of his existence. Now he was San Francisco's chief prosecutor. He had a job that the people in the city he loved had elected him — albeit narrowly — to do. And gradually (some said glacially), he began to think and act like a DA, to the point where he often found himself in the middle of a prosecutorial moment without having decided to be there.

In the grip of just such a situation, he walked down the hallway when his official workday was done at a little past six o'clock, pausing just outside the front door to the Office of the District Attorney, Bureau of Investigations. Here fourteen inspectors worked under his nominal supervision, although, like most of the DAs who'd served before, he never exerted direct authority over any of these people.

He continued down to the parking lot, backed his tiny Smart car out of his assigned parking spot, and drove over to Waterbar on the Embarcadero. Leaving his car with the valet, he entered the restaurant and saw Frank Dobbins, his chief of investigations, sitting at the end of the bar next to an attractive Hispanic woman. She was probably around thirty years old, with sleek black hair and sparkling brown eyes, and though he would never use the word around any female of any age, the Neanderthal in him couldn't help but notice that she was just plain cute. Low heels, terrific legs, a short plaid skirt, and a sky-blue cashmere sweater.

His casual talk with Abe Glitsky had gnawed at him all day long. The cases of inmates who had died or been injured in custody were perfect examples, he thought, where the district attorney had a moral obligation to investigate and, if warranted, prosecute — even if that meant prosecuting the sheriff himself. Like everyone else in the greater legal community, Farrell had been aware of the rumors and innuendo surrounding Burt Cushing and his troops, but also like everyone else, he'd found it easier to ignore the whole situation.

Cushing operated within his own little

fiefdom. It was well ordered, efficient, and performed several important civic functions. And Cushing kept his nose clean everywhere else, so what would it profit Farrell or anyone else to hassle him? To make waves? Except — and this was the thought that had nagged at Farrell all afternoon — what if it were less about not making waves and more about rooting out criminal behavior within his jurisdiction and punishing those responsible for it?

Wes crossed the room to join Dobbins and the young woman. "Yo, Frank," he said, then turned to the woman. "You must be Ms. Solis-Martinez."

The woman gave him a bright smile and proffered her hand. "Maria T. Solis-Martinez, at your service, but please call me Maria, if you're comfortable with that."

"Maria it is," Farrell said. "And I go by Wes. Have we met before?"

She nodded. "At my preliminary interview six months ago, when I flew up from L.A. We shook hands." She pouted prettily. "You don't remember?" Before Farrell could answer, she touched him on the arm and fetched another smile. "I'm teasing. Of course you don't remember, and you're forgiven. But next time . . ."

"Maria," he said. "Got it, now and forever." But how, Farrell wondered, could Dobbins have reached her so quickly? Wes had talked to his chief investigator about this idea only a few hours ago. "Do you still live in L.A.?" he asked her.

"No. I knew that Frank had me on his short list, and I wanted to get out of L.A. anyway, so I packed up and moved here a couple of months ago. Job or no job. I figured it would happen if it was meant to be." Her bright smile flashed again. "And here I am."

Farrell beamed back at her. "Like magic," he said.

"If I may be so bold . . ." Dobbins leaned in, breaking up the lovefest, and moved things back to business mode. "Maria and I were talking about the job, Wes. She agrees it might be right up her alley, and she's interested, but I told her you could fill her in a little more."

The waiter came over, and Farrell ordered a beer, then turned his attention back to the young woman. "Frank may have already told you that another inmate died in jail the other night. That's the latest in a string of deaths in the jail this year. On top of a large number of overdoses and inmates who appear to have been assaulted. He was number ten this year."

"This year? Was he autopsied?"

"Absolutely. Cause of death was 'natural causes.' His heart simply stopped. It's stressful getting arrested. It could have happened."

"All right." Maria crossed her arms, her brow furrowed. "But here we are, so something must be bothering you."

"This latest guy got my attention, but I'm more immediately concerned with a guy named Alanos Tussaint, who died in jail last month. Poor guy fell down and bumped his head."

"He bumped his head and died? That was a hell of a bump."

"Right. A significant bump. Anyway, it seems there was some question about Mr. Tussaint's death. In the early stages of the investigation, another inmate told the SFPD cops that a guard had gone off on Mr. Tussaint and beaten him to death. The next time the inmate got interrogated, he changed his story, saying he'd gotten it wrong. The guard had hit Mr. Tussaint a couple of times in self-defense, but it wasn't really a beating. And since there were no other witnesses, the case never got off the ground. It obviously wasn't much of a priority. I'll take responsibility for that, since assigning priorities is my job. But the fact remains. Bad stuff is going on at the jail, and it needs to end. We were hoping to bring in somebody from the outside who's unknown around here. Frank thinks that ought to be you."

Maria nodded. "I'm flattered and very interested, but I'm a little concerned how the rest of your office is going to take it."

"How's that?" Farrell asked.

"If I come on, it kind of implies that whoever handled those cases didn't do a thorough job, doesn't it? If somebody like me got ahold of one of these — say Mr. Tussaint — on the rebound, whoever had it first won't be happy. Plus," she added, "if we're going to question our inmate witness again, he's probably already been talked to, or worse, by the guards. That's why he recanted, obviously. They threatened him. So you'll have to get him protected and out of the population, and as soon as you do that, you're in the sheriff's face. All on the off chance that this guy might have seen something he wants to talk about again, something that might get him beaten or even killed." She paused. "I'm just saying that this doesn't strike me as a casual decision. You're opening a big can of worms."

Another round of drinks later, the conversation turned to the overdoses. "Black heroin in the jail," Farrell said. "How do you think it got there?"

"How do you think it got there, sir?" asked Maria.

"There had to be guards involved. But as Frank here will tell you, he's already talked to the sheriff about it. Mr. Cushing, too, was appalled by the evidence of drugs in jail, but he was pretty sure it was some of the defense lawyers or shrinks visiting their clients or patients, since it couldn't be any of his guards, and the family and friends didn't get any physical contact with the inmates. The lawyers and psychiatrists, they hide it anywhere — briefcases, pockets, you name it."

Maria chuckled. "He didn't really say that? Professional people were bringing it in?"

"Sure. They have no respect for the law, those guys. Some of the lawyers — I bet you didn't know this — accept payment from their jailed clients in drugs, then sell it to their other clients out on the street."

"Sure, I'll bet that happens all the time," Maria said with heavy irony. She turned to Wes expectantly. "So . . . what do we do now?"

"Well, if you'll take it," Wes said, "I'm offering you a job as a DA investigator. You have a police background, you speak Spanish, and Frank tells me you're perfect for the job, which he never says about anybody. But this first assignment is going to be absolutely confidential and, frankly, damned dangerous. We want to get you inside the jail to find out what's happening to these people. I want to be sure you're okay going after these guys."

"Are you kidding?" she asked. "It would make my year. We're the good guys, aren't we? If we don't have the guts to take on the bad guys, who will?"

Wes nodded appreciatively and looked over to Dobbins. "That sounds like the right answer to me, Frank. How about you?"

"It's why I called her in," Dobbins replied.

"All right, Maria." Farrell held out his hand. "Welcome aboard."

20

At seven-thirty, when Hal came back into the house after dropping Warren off at the airport, the tenuous truce between Ruth and Ellen that had held since Katie disappeared seemed to have come unraveled. His stepmother was sitting on the living room couch, nursing a glass of clear liquid with ice cubes. She did not get up, merely turned her head and nodded.

"Is everything all right?" Hal asked her.

"Not exactly, no."

"What's wrong?"

"Your daughter. She can be an exasperating little girl, you know that?"

"She's lost her mother, Ruth. I can't blame her if she's having a hard time. And you shouldn't, either. Where is she?"

"Last seen in your bedroom. I closed the door. Don't worry. She's perfectly safe. She just needed a time-out."

"I'm going to go see her."

Ruth lifted her glass. "Please. Help yourself."

His shoulders sagging under the strain, he went down the hallway and knocked, then opened his bedroom door. "Ellen?" He switched on the lights and saw his daughter wedged into a corner on the floor, holding one of the bed's pillows against her. "Hey," he said gently, crossing over to her. "Are you okay? Want to give your dad a hug?"

She shook her head. "Where's Mommy?"

"We don't know. We're looking for her."

"Grandma isn't. She wouldn't tell me where she was."

"She doesn't know where she is, sweetie. Nobody knows. That's the problem."

"Why didn't Grandma just tell me that? That she didn't know. That nobody knows. Why don't they know? Where did she go?"

Hal slowly lowered himself to sit in front of her. "If you give me your pillow, it'll make my lap softer."

She stared him down for a moment, then handed the pillow across and finally crawled into his lap, where she started to cry. "I want Mommy."

He smoothed her hair and let her lean against him and cry herself out. At last, he asked, "Do you think you want to go to sleep?"

She shook her head. "I want to know where Mommy is."

He kissed the top of her head. "We all want that. We just have to keep trying to find her."

"But where? And why would she go away?"

Hal shook his head and rocked her against him, and time stopped while he kept rocking and she settled against him and started to breathe with a deep and easy regularity.

Blessed sleep.

Gradually, he managed to get all the way up without waking her, then carried her into the bedroom she shared with Will. Putting her down in her bed, he covered her and tucked the blankets around her, then leaned down to plant a kiss on her forehead. On the way out, he pulled the door, leaving it a little bit open so that he could hear either of them if they called out or needed him.

It looked as though Ruth hadn't moved an inch, except now her glass was nearly full. She glanced up at Hal. "She wouldn't go to sleep for me," she said.

"She's worried about where Katie is, Ruth. I don't think that's so inappropriate."

"No, I don't suppose so. But she was so willful. I told her it was time for bed and we could talk about all this tomorrow, but now she was tired and she needed to be a big girl and do what I told her."

"She's not used to you, Ruth, that's all."

"And whose fault is that?"

"What does that mean?"

"It means how can they get to know me if I'm never around?"

"Ruth. Come on. You know you are always welcome. You've always been welcome."

She broke into a chilly smile. "You know that's not true, Hal. Maybe welcome to you, but Katie wouldn't let anybody else have any influence on those children. That's the way she was."

" 'Is.' Let's go with 'is' until we know something different."

"I didn't mean anything by that."

"I know." Hal let out a heavy sigh. "I'm going to get a beer. Do you want a refill?"

"No, thanks. I've had one." At his questioning look, she said, "One. Really."

He went to the refrigerator, opened his beer, returned to the living room, and sat down across from her. "I really appreciate all you've done this past week, Ruth. I don't blame you if it's getting tiresome. I've got the time off if you're burning out."

"It's not tiresome, Hal, and I'm nowhere near burning out. These are my grand-children, and I'm just so happy I'm finally getting to spend some time with them. Not that I'm happy about the circumstances. Of course they're heartrending. But then I see the way Katie . . . well, how Ellen got so belligerent so fast when I told her she had to go to sleep. Has she ever not gotten her way? I thought it would do her good to have somebody tell her no."

Hal pulled at his beer. "I don't want to talk about Katie's mothering, Ruth. We didn't always agree about that, but this isn't the time, all right? I think she was getting more flexible; at least I hope she was. And I'm sorry we didn't have you over more often, but we'd stopped seeing many people because a lot of times we weren't having much fun."

Ruth waved him off. "That's all right. I'm a big girl. I just think that maybe I could have helped, and gotten to know my grandchildren a little more in the bargain. But Katie wouldn't let that happen. You know that's true."

"If we find her, that's going to change. Lots of things are going to change."

"I hope so," Ruth said. "That would be very nice."

Wednesday morning, after he dropped his kids at school, Abe Glitsky decided to try to clear up as many of the outstanding uncertainties about Katie's disappearance as he could. As his first stop, he drove out and parked by the Highway Patrol station on the San Francisco side of the Golden Gate Bridge.

Over the course of his career, he'd been out here dozens of times, but the familiarity of the place did little to erase the negative energy he attached to it. Getting out of his car, even wearing his heavy leather fighter jacket, he felt the cold wind cut through him. He found it hard to believe that people chose to come out here by the hundreds, if not thousands, for recreation; even as he wondered about it, a trickle of people was passing him on all sides, wrapped up for the weather, enchanted by the view. Before they got on the bridge proper, all of them had to pass the sign over the telephone hotline that read CRISIS COUNSELING. THERE IS HOPE. MAKE THE CALL.

There might be hope, Glitsky thought, but not enough of it to go around. Although no accurate figure was possible because so many suicides off the bridge went unnoticed, it was generally accepted to be among the most popular places on the planet for people to take their own lives. In spite of the Highway Patrol's success in talking down perhaps eighty percent of the potential jumpers they encountered, the known or suspected suicide rate every year held steady at around thirty, or about one every two weeks.

Glitsky put his hands in his pockets and, into the wind, made his way across the small lot. If he'd learned anything over the past couple of days, it was that his name still carried some weight in legal circles. Sure enough, when he dropped it at the back door, they knew who he was, or used to be, and let him in.

A Highway Patrol officer led him back to a small and crowded room with desks that could sit a total of eight, each with a computer. At the moment, five other Highway Patrol officers filled the space. One glass wall faced the recently redundant tollbooths; another faced video screens showing different live shots of segments of the bridge — people on the walkway, cars in the road going both directions, overhead distance shots from up in the cables, pretty much the entire bridge on videotape all the time.

The sergeant running the operation of the office today was Ted Robbins, from the looks of him an all-business career officer in his mid-forties. If a detective from Homicide was here, there would be only one reason for it, to Robbins's mind, and he got right to it. "You're looking for a jumper."

Glitsky nodded. "A mother of two named Katie Chase. She went missing last Wednesday." He started to give more details but hadn't gotten too far before Robbins was shaking his head, and Glitsky stopped. "What's wrong?" he asked.

"You're saying she was at her home at seven o'clock last Wednesday?"

"Right."

"We don't let pedestrians out after dark."

Though this statement contained the potentially good news that Katie was not dead from suicide off the bridge, it also closed off at least one possibility that would have left Hal Chase in the clear for her murder. Glitsky bit at his cheek in some frustration. "You actually close the gates?"

"That's right."

"And when do you open them again?"

"Basically, first light. I could check the exact time for any given day, but you don't think she waited out here all night and then went out in the morning, do you?"

"No. I don't really see that. Any other way she could have gotten on the bridge without being seen?"

Robbins considered. "Do you think there's a chance she rode out here on a bicycle?"

"What difference would that make?"

"It might not, but bicyclists are allowed after dark. They buzz at the gate, and we get them on the security camera and open up for them."

"Bicyclists are allowed and walkers aren't?" Glitsky asked. "What's that about?"

"You got me," Robbins said. "I don't make the rules. But bikes are allowed."

Glitsky asked, "Would it be all right if I looked at some tapes?"

"DVDs. We back everything up nowadays. You could look, but what would you be hoping to find?"

"Some bicyclist buzzes and you open the gate. It's open for a few seconds behind the biker, isn't it? If people are waiting, they could stroll right through, couldn't they?"

"In theory, it could happen. But I wouldn't bet on it."

"I wouldn't, either, but I'm here, and it couldn't hurt to make sure."

22

Patti Orosco opened her front door to two Homicide inspectors and, under the impression that she'd made an appointment for this visit, invited them in.

Barefoot, Patti was wearing jeans and a blue sweater. She led the way up the stairs and into the living room. When they got there, the view stopped Abby in her tracks. "Wow," she said.

Patti turned and said with an air of apology, "I know. It's kind of ridiculous, isn't it?"

"I wouldn't use that word. If I lived here, I wouldn't get much done. I'd just sit and stare out that window."

As everyone took a seat around the coffee table, Patti said, "I spend some time doing that myself. Probably too much. If I were working, I'd have to go someplace else to get anything done."

"You're not working?" Abby asked.

"I don't. No. I haven't in some time." Patti offered another apologetic smile. "Sometimes I think I'm one of the luckiest people in the world, except for my personal life. But how I really feel is that I'd trade it all, straight up, the money for the other stuff. People don't believe me, but sometimes I think I would."

"Did that cause friction between you and the Chases? The fact that you were wealthy?" Abby asked. "We've heard that they were having trouble with money."

"I think that was part of it, at least recently, after Katie stopped working and her cash flow dried up. In a way, I couldn't blame her if she was jealous about my situation. I mean, what happened to me was so weird."

"And what was that?" JaMorris asked. "What happened to you?"

Patti brushed some hair off her forehead, let a sigh escape. "It's nothing to be embarrassed about, I suppose, but it usually hits people funny."

"Do you want to tell us?"

"When I got out of college, I got a job as a secretary with Bazoom! Nobody remembers them anymore, but back then they were a happening start-up. They gave us the option to take some of our pay in stock.

Anyway, long story short, I took them up on it, and about two years later, say '03 or '04, Sprint bought us out and I made about three million dollars."

JaMorris nodded in appreciation. "That must have been a good day."

"It was completely amazing. But then — for better or worse, depending on where you were — I invested in some other stocks, and everything doubled over the next few years. On top of that, I got freaked out at my exposure in the market and pulled it all out and into cash about two months before the crash. I've been so stupidly lucky, and all I do now is feel guilty about everything." She shook her head. "Oh, but listen to me, the poor little rich girl."

"I love that story," Abby said. "So it really happens."

"It does." Patti brought her hands together. "But where are my manners? Can I offer you anything, or do you want to just get down to it?"

A small silence settled before JaMorris asked, "Down to what, exactly?"

"You know. Me and Hal. What you called me about yesterday."

The two inspectors shared a questioning glance. JaMorris took up the ball. "Sure," he said. "You and Hal."

"All right. Then let's start with I know he didn't kill Katie."

"How do you know that?" Abby asked. "Do you have any solid proof or evidence? Did you see him or talk to him or anything that night?"

"No, but I know he was trying to get back with her and make it all work."

"Get back with her from what?" JaMorris asked.

"Well" — Patti looked quizzically from one inspector to the other — "from us." He had made up his mind that we weren't going to be together anymore, so there was no reason he had to do anything drastic about Katie. Isn't that pretty much what I said yesterday?"

Abby could stand it no longer. "Patti. Who did you talk to yesterday?"

Patti was looking at JaMorris. "It wasn't you?"

"No."

"I thought it was you. You said you'd be by this morning, and then when you guys showed up here . . ." She stood up. "Just a minute." She left the room and came back after a moment with a small notebook. "You're not Abe Glitsky?"

"No, ma'am. I'm JaMorris Monroe. Abe Glitsky used to be head of Homicide. You're saying you talked to him yesterday? About Hal? And Katie's disappearance?"

She nodded. "I told Hal we should tell the truth about us, that hiding it would just make us look bad. So he told Inspector Glitsky, and he called me last night . . ."

"Glitsky called you last night?" JaMorris asked.

Patti nodded. "Yes. He asked if he could come by and talk a little this morning, so when you showed up . . . I mean, you said you were inspectors . . . I just thought . . ." Clearly flustered, she sat down on the edge of her couch. "So who are you guys if you're not working with Glitsky?"

Abby had her ID out. "We're inspectors with the Homicide Department, Patti. We're investigating Katie's disappearance. We came to see you because Daniel Dunne, Katie's brother, told us that you and Hal were probably in a relationship."

"I just told you about that. But wait a minute. Who is Glitsky, then?"

"He's retired," JaMorris said. "You say he's working with Hal?"

"That's what he said."

Abby raised her eyebrows — a question — at her partner, who could only shrug.

Then the doorbell rang.

■ ■ ■ ■

"I can't say it was my finest hour." Glitsky sat in Hardy's office, trying to look relaxed in one of the comfortable chairs by the Sutter Street windows. But he drummed his fingers on the chair's arm and hadn't touched the tea that Hardy had poured for him.

"You had every right to be there," Hardy said. "You were a private citizen paying a call on another private citizen, with whom you had a scheduled appointment. Nothing about that is remotely illegal."

"True enough, but everybody knew I was really investigating Katie's disappearance, and possibly impersonating a law officer in the bargain."

"Did you state or imply to Ms. Orosco that you were a cop?"

"Not in so many words, but she must have gotten the general idea somehow."

"Again, not your problem, and you broke no law."

"I'm not worried about breaking a law. Nobody cares if I'm breaking a law. What they're going to care about is that I'm sniffing around and maybe obstructing what's starting to look like a righteous homicide investigation. I hated that kind of stuff back in the day. I still do, if I think about it."

"Well," Hardy said. "It was only a matter of time."

"Thanks. That's heartening."

"You're welcome." Hardy stood by the windows, looking down at the traffic. Finally, he turned back to Abe. "What's she like, the other woman? Worth killing for?"

"You know I've only got eyes for Treya, so my opinion can't be relied on. But I think most normal males would find her irresistible in the extreme."

Hardy raised his eyebrows. "In the extreme?"

"At least."

"So the answer to 'worth killing for' would be yes."

"If anybody is."

"And yet Hal broke up with her."

"That's what they say."

"Now I'm hearing reservations from you."

Glitsky crossed one leg over the other. "You know when I said she was 'irresistible in the extreme'? I lied. She's about two or three times that. If Foley and Monroe hadn't been there, and in spite of my only having eyes for Treya, I don't know if I would have been able to talk to her without babbling."

163

"I'd like to see you babble."

"Many people would, but few get the chance. Patti Orosco would have gotten a large dose of full-blown babble. Really, she's so beautiful, it's silly — no other word for it. Oh, and she's worth ten million dollars, too. Did I mention that?"

"How did it come up in casual conversation?"

"Hal mentioned it to me last night. To prepare me, I suppose."

"For?"

"For the whole package. He told me that when I met her, I would have a hard time believing he'd let her go. He was right, but he wanted me to know what I was walking into."

Hardy said, "You know what this is starting to remind me of? When he first came in to meet me. Homicide had only just had their first talk with him, but he wanted to prepare me for when they turned up the heat, so I'd be ready."

"There are similarities," Glitsky said. "Strategically."

"I wish I knew what they meant."

"Maybe it's the way Hal handles things. Of course, he tries to leave me with the impression that he knows nothing about Katie's disappearance, and if I'm fore-

164

warned about all the stuff that makes him look bad, suddenly, I'm not surprised. Therefore, I don't jump to conclusions." Glitsky shifted in his chair. "I'm assuming you still want my basic mindset to be that he didn't do it."

Hardy allowed himself the germ of a grin. "Until you find a bit of evidence that says he did."

"I haven't. But on that, I've been trying to imagine other scenarios and have come up with a couple."

"Hit me."

Glitsky reached for his tea, took a sip, and made a face. "This stuff is cold."

"Think of it as iced tea that's gotten warm. What are your scenarios?"

After a rundown of his visit to the Golden Gate Bridge that morning to check on the feasibility of Katie's suicide — in an hour of tapes, fast-forwarded, there hadn't been any sign of a woman sneaking onto the bridge behind an unsuspecting bicyclist on the night in question — Glitsky concluded, "So that took the idea of her suicide, which I think was slim to begin with, pretty much out of the running."

"You really think she might have killed herself?"

"Maybe. If she found out about Hal and

Patti, if life at home with the kids was hell . . ." He shrugged. "I can't rule it out entirely. People have been known to get creative, doing themselves in. She might have walked into the ocean and swum till the current got her. Did Frannie say she was depressed?"

"No. We haven't talked about their sessions, Abe. Privilege."

"My favorite. Would she talk to me?"

Hardy didn't have to think about his reply. "Not unless they find her body, and even then maybe not. You're welcome to try, but I wouldn't hold my breath. Is that all you had with alternative scenarios, possible suicide?"

"Actually, no. Next was checking the lovely Patti Orosco's alibi, which is the primary reason I'd gone by to meet her."

Hardy nodded in appreciation. "Isn't it fun to force your brain out of its ruts? If you'd gone on the assumption that it was Hal, you never would have met Patti, not to mention suspect her of murder. What was she doing on the night in question?"

"She went to the movies by herself. She thinks it was the seven-fifteen showing. *Life of Pi.* She loved it. And no, she did not keep her ticket stub. She also called Katie the day before — covering the phone records that will surely be discovered — and while that gave a plausible excuse why she couldn't make the Thanksgiving dinner, it also would have allowed her to find out, if she didn't already know, exactly when Hal would be leaving to pick up his brother at the airport."

Leaning against his desk, Hardy crossed his arms and let out a small sigh. "You think they were in it together?

Glitsky replied, "I'm under orders not to think it was Hal, remember. Patti didn't need him to be part of it, and if she can avoid suspicion, she comes out smelling like a rose, the sexy rich best friend who stood by Hal in his moment of torment and need. But one thing is certain: Both of their lives are immeasurably better if Katie is out of the picture."

"You really like them for it," Hardy said.

Glitsky's mouth ticked up a quarter of an inch. "I'd be lying if I said I wasn't warming to the idea."

23

Hal didn't want to call his stepmother and beg her to return, not after last night, when he'd essentially kicked her out, saying he could handle the kids on his own. In truth, it had not been only Katie who'd had problems with Ruth, not only Katie who'd wanted to limit the time their children spent in the company of their daddy's stepmother. Ruth was nothing like the maternal, quintessentially grandmotherish Carli Dunne, Katie's mother. Ruth was younger and prettier but far more demanding, and at times she seemed unstable. But then Ruth Chase had had a much harder life than Carli Dunne could have imagined.

Hal's birth mother, Eileen, had died of a cerebral hemorrhage when he was nine years old. Within a year, his father, Pete — like Hal, a San Francisco deputy sheriff — had fallen under Ruth's spell. She was twenty-five years old then and beautiful.

She, too, had lost her first spouse. Widow Ruth and widower Pete had bonded over their shared grief, among other things. Warren had come along a couple years later. But Hal remembered only a few happy family years before tragedy struck again. On a cold and foggy Saturday afternoon, Pete had accidentally killed himself with a lethal cocktail of prescription insomnia medication and alcohol.

Between Pete's pension and the private life insurance they'd taken out — their previous marriages had taught them both the value of such a policy — the Chases had enough to get by, but for Hal, life with his stepmother after his father's death was never the same as it had been before. Hal was, after all, the stepson, not the real son, the way Warren was, and he felt the difference keenly. Ruth favored Warren in almost every way, even as the younger son gradually developed into a rather unremarkable slacker of a teenager and a socially awkward young adult.

For a time after he'd left home, Hal had largely dropped out of Ruth's and Warren's lives. He'd visit on some holidays and call to check in from time to time, but he lived independently. It never occurred to him that anything he did even mattered to Ruth.

But when he got involved with Katie, things took a turn. Katie came from such a tightly knit family that she couldn't accept Hal's estrangement from Ruth and Warren. Family was family, she told him. It was the most important thing. And so they'd reached out, and by the time they got married, Ruth was in a low-key but very real way back in his everyday life.

The sad truth was that this wasn't always pleasant. Ruth drank too much, and apart from the deaths of two husbands, she had other demons that plagued her. One of her uncles had abused her when she was a child; there had been some unpleasantness with one of her high school teachers. Also, because her two men had died, she had been denied the love and security of a normal home life, which she said was all she'd ever wanted. Although she tried to show her nicest side to Hal and Katie, a fundamentally bitter nature seemed always ready to assert itself.

This was a serious but not insurmountable problem until Ellen was born, when Ruth decided that she needed to play an active role in the rearing of her grandchild. Ruth took to stopping by while Katie was at work, often finding fault with the nanny, and passing along her suggestions for improving Ellen's life in a steady stream of well-meaning but intrusive suggestions that neither Katie nor Hal particularly agreed with. After Will was born and Katie started staying home, the gatekeeper in her could no longer coexist with her mother-in-law. Katie had very strong ideas about how to raise her children. It was now her full-time job, and she was going to do it her way, which was the right way. Ruth was welcome to come over, as long as she didn't try to interfere with Katie's absolute authority on all things related to her kids.

Inevitably, the visits became fewer.

Last week, the Thanksgiving invitations to Ruth and Warren had represented an effort to reach out and reconcile with Hal's side of the family after he and Katie realized that Ruth hadn't come by — by invitation or otherwise — in over three months. Katie and Hal didn't feel a lot of affection for Ruth or Warren, but they were still family, and mending a fence by asking them over for Thanksgiving had been the right and good thing to do.

But in the here and now, Hal was going a little nuts with his kids. He had forgotten how much planning and patience and simple energy they took. Will had gotten up for good at six-thirty this morning after the random three A.M. wake-up, when he'd needed to be calmed down and rocked back to sleep.

Hal was somewhat ashamed to realize that he didn't know where Will's diapers were kept anymore, and when he found them, he was shocked to find that Katie had graduated him out of cloth and into Pampers. He finally got them both dressed and at the kitchen table for breakfast; he needed Ellen's help because he didn't know what food they both liked and could eat. He pushed a stroller and held Ellen's hand as they walked down to the nearby playground, but he hadn't dressed either of them warmly enough, so they came home almost immediately, after which he put a video on the tube and got them settled in front of it. Checking the time, he could not believe that it wasn't yet nine o'clock. What were they all supposed to do for the rest of the day? And the day after that?

Leaving them in front of the TV, he walked back into the kitchen and saw the accumulated dishes from last night and this morning. A wave of fatigue washed over him, nearly knocking him over.

He gripped the edges on either side of the sink. His heavy head felt as though it hung by the thinnest of threads. He heard Barney the dinosaur singing, and he brought his hands up, covering his face. A minute ticked away and he did not move an inch.

Now, somehow, it was two o'clock. He'd gotten both of them fed lunch and then down for naps, although who knew how long they would sleep? He honestly felt that he might not survive if he didn't get a nap himself.

He lay on his bed, his mind racing. Maybe he should call Carli. Either she or one of Katie's sisters could come by and help out for a while. He knew they were suspicious of him, but maybe if he spent a little more time with them, that would pass. But in all, it seemed like too much work at a time when he felt he had almost no energy. Patti occurred to him, though he rejected that idea almost as soon as it appeared. Seeing her even once yesterday — never mind the attraction, which was, if anything, stronger than ever — had been risky enough. If they were seen together in public, it could only be bad. It was already bad enough.

Realizing that sleep wasn't going to happen anytime soon, he swore at himself, then sat up and swung his legs over the side of his bed. What was he being so stubborn about? He should just call Ruth, and she would be here in no time. They could talk about logistics, maybe try to find a new nanny, some solutions for the long term. He picked up the phone by his bed and punched in her number.

"Of course," she told him with no hint of recrimination. "I'll be right over."

"You're great. Thank you."

"I'm not great. I'm your mother. This is what mothers do."

24

Wes Farrell believed that the hierarchy imposed by the desk and the prearranged seating in front of it was the enemy of communication. So after his election, he'd furnished his office with some library tables against the walls, to which he'd added a couple of distressed tan leather sofas and six or eight folding chairs that found their resting places in various permutations, depending on who and how many guests were visiting. Adding to the relaxed tone was a dartboard by the door, a Nerf basketball net hanging off the bookshelves, a chessboard — with a game in progress — on one of the coffee tables, four baseball bats piled in a corner, and an ancient poster of Che Guevara tacked to the wall.

Fancy it was not.

This afternoon Wes had a couple of guests; he started off, trying to put them at ease, by ceremoniously unveiling today's T-shirt, which read "Indifferent to the whole apathy thing." Now, sitting on one of the library tables, he was buttoning up his dress shirt.

It wasn't a good sign that neither of his two guests broke a smile. Frank Dobbins, his chief investigator, sat back comfortably enough on one of the couches, but he was clearly marking time until Wes got down to the purpose of the meeting.

The second visitor, a DA investigator named Tom Scerbo, perched on the very front edge of one of the folding chairs. Scerbo, in his early thirties, wore a wary expression. He had never been summoned to Farrell's office, and clearly, in spite of the initial banter and the T-shirt moment they'd all shared, there was tension in the room, and now a small silence. Finally, he cleared his throat. "I don't mean to rush anybody, but are we all here because I'm in trouble?"

"Why? Do you think you should be?" Farrell asked.

"Not that I know of."

"Good. You're not, then," Farrell said. "But I did want to let you know in person that we're going to be taking another look at Alanos Tussaint."

His wariness increasing, Scerbo cocked his head. "What about him? There wasn't any case."

176

"Really? My understanding is that there was and then it disappeared."

"Right. Leaving us with nothing."

"Maybe. But I believe we may have something there to pursue, if we go about it a little differently." Farrell continued, matter-of-fact. "Bottom line is that we've got big problems at the jail with guards and excessive force, among a host of other issues, and I believe that Burt Cushing's in the middle of all of them. If that's so, this office should be building a case against him and these guys, not giving them a free pass over there. What do you think?"

"It's a noble idea, Wes," Scerbo said, "but we've had some difficulties executing it in the past, as you well know. Alanos Tussaint being a prime example. If you remember, we had a righteous witness to that beating . . ."

Wes nodded. "Luther Jones."

"Right. It was pretty straightforward. Luther saw the whole thing and told Homicide all about it. Homicide came to me about what kind of a deal they could give him and how they could hide him after he testified and got out of jail."

"That's what I understand, Luke, and it's why I invited you to be part of this. This is no reflection on your handling of that last case, but we may not be so far beyond it that we can't try to resurrect it."

Scerbo leveled his eyes at Wes. "You got another witness?"

"No. We're putting somebody else inside who's going to try to get back to Luther."

Scerbo was shaking his head in disagreement. "Even if you do, he's recanted once already. His testimony will be all but worthless."

Dobbins said, "Not if we can make the guard's threat to him part of the case. He's still the most likely place to start."

Scerbo wasn't buying it. "We can do anything we want with Luther Jones," he said, "but getting him to talk again is going to be some kind of magical trick. And I don't blame him. Those guards play for keeps. Luther had just seen a guard kill Alanos. He didn't have much doubt they'd do the same to him if he got . . . troublesome."

"Troublesome," Farrell said. "There's a good word."

"It is a good word," Scerbo replied. "Trouble is what these guys in the slammer want to avoid. And okay, Luther forgot that for a minute. He thought that he was a human being with rights, when in fact he was just another animal in the zoo. Cushing's the zookeeper, and he's got a long reach."

Farrell made a face. "I've got a long reach, too," he said. He looked from one investigator to the other. "Look, guys, as we all know, Luther's in for carjacking, firearm enhancement, second strike. He's looking at prison after his trial, so we've got leverage on him."

Scerbo said, "Prison is better than dead. We've got nothing while he's in jail."

"Trust me, Tom, we do have something. Frank and I have brought somebody on, and we're confident she can get to Luther. Under Cushing's nose."

"Okay," Scerbo said. "But even then, what?"

"Then we get Luther on board with us again. We keep him around in another jail — Alameda, Santa Clara, anywhere — and protected as a witness until he testifies about Alanos. Then get him in a program that lets him disappear."

Scerbo asked him, "You really think this will work?"

Farrell nodded. "I think it's as good a chance as we're likely to see. In any event, it's my call, and I'm making it."

Frank Dobbins dragged a British accent up from somewhere and said to Farrell, "Heavy is the head that wears the crown, sir."

"Bite me, Frank. Just bite me," replied Wes with a tired smile.

25

One floor above Farrell, Devin Juhle didn't have any problem with the hierarchy of the desk. He sat behind his and looked over the empty expanse at his two inspectors, who were pitching him on the idea of arresting Hal Chase for the murder of his wife, even in the absence of a body.

Juhle said, "But without a body, guys, and I know you know this, but it's hard to establish there's even been a homicide."

"And yet," Abby said, "here we are, Homicide inspectors, building a case that looks a hell of a lot like Katie is actually dead."

"Well, still," Juhle argued, "*corpus delicti* and all that. No body, no homicide. That's the way we do it."

"Aha!" JaMorris held up his index finger.

"Aha what?" Juhle asked.

"The body in *corpus delicti* isn't about the physical body of the dead person. It's about the body of evidence that proves the crime's been committed."

"Are you shitting me? Where'd you get that?" Juhle asked. "You going to law school at night or something?"

"I think it's true, Devin," Abby said.

"Even if it is, and I'm not so sure that Jambo's right on that, what's changed that we're now ready to go ahead?"

"The new thing is we've got the girlfriend," JaMorris said. "Plus, we know Hal's got nothing like an alibi. He could have left the house with Katie and the kids at four, five, six o'clock, driven to someplace secluded, done the deed, and driven back home."

"Everybody's been talking about the missing three hours, seven-thirty to ten-thirty," Abby added, "but it could have been as much as six hours. Then you plug in Patti Orosco and the affair and her several million dollars . . ."

JaMorris could barely contain his enthusiasm. "No jury's going to see her and not also see a motive."

"She really is something to see, Dev," Abby added. "I'm not a guy by a long shot, and she is one heck of a package."

"And then," JaMorris continued, "the jury learns about her fortune, and not one person on it, even in this town, will believe that he wouldn't have killed for her."

Juhle kept shaking his head. "We got nada. Equally plausible explanation: Katie finds out that she's losing her husband to a beautiful woman. She can't stand it and she runs away, maybe kills herself. If the jury has two explanations, they have to accept the one that leads to a 'not guilty' verdict. Your theory is compelling as hell, and I completely believe it, but I don't think Farrell will charge it — why would he, with no evidence? — so what's the point in pressing for a warrant? For that matter, what judge would sign off on it? We need more."

"How about if Farrell goes to the grand jury?" JaMorris suggested. "On what we've got, it'll indict Hal in a heartbeat."

"Same problem, guys," Juhle said. "Farrell has to think he can get a conviction at trial. Without that, he's not going forward, I promise you."

"But if Hal's indicted and locked up," Abby said, "then we can get some warrants and do some searches."

"First you need something beyond motive to open the door." Juhle pushed his chair back and settled into it. "While we're on this, what's with Glitsky's appearance? What the hell is that about?"

"It means our boy is lawyered up," JaMorris said.

"Glitsky doesn't have a private license that I know of, and I think I would have heard. Did he get in your way?"

"No," Abby said, "although he was surprised to see us."

"Did he identify himself to Patti as a police officer?"

"Not in front of us," JaMorris said.

"Although," Abby said, "if I remember, she called him Inspector Glitsky."

"That might be enough. If he's impersonating a police officer, he and I are going to have to have a discussion. He's talking to Hal, too?"

Abby nodded. "Apparently."

"It would be interesting to find out what he knows," Juhle said. "If he's on another track, what's he going on? And if he's pretending to still be a cop . . ." He let the comment hang.

"Whatever it is," JaMorris said, "it led him to Patti Orosco."

Juhle processed for a second. "She and Hal were definitely having an affair?"

"Until about a month ago," Abby said. "Total admission, in spite of what she knew it could mean to us. But she put the best possible spin on it."

Juhle asked her, "Who broke up with whom?"

"Hal ended it," Abby said.

"And how did Patti feel about that? Bitter? Pissed off? Hurt?"

The two inspectors shared a glance. Abby said, "None of the above, wouldn't you say, Jambo?"

Her partner nodded in agreement.

Abby went on, "She seemed completely okay with it. Hal wanted to go back and make things right with Katie, and for that to happen, she and Hal had to break up, and in some ways it was too bad, but she wished both of them the best."

"Really?" Juhle asked.

"That's her story."

"No scorned-women rhetoric?"

"Not remotely."

"That seems unlikely," Juhle said.

"We tend to agree," JaMorris said. "We talked about it after we left and agreed it was more like she was waiting a reasonable amount of time after Katie's disappearance before she and Hal could come out as a couple. If her heart was even a little broken, she was hiding it pretty well."

"So —"

Juhle was interrupted by the telephone on his desk. He listened for the better part of

185

two minutes, pulling over a yellow legal pad and taking a few notes. When he hung up, he came back to his two inspectors. "Somebody just found a woman's body, blood all over her head, on the Interior Park Belt out by Parnassus. You know where that is?"

JaMorris was already up and out of his chair. "Hal's neighborhood," he said.

Juhle nodded solemnly. "Close enough."

26

The steep sides of the canyon were thickly covered, mostly with old-growth eucalyptus, and this kept a great deal of the park permanently and deeply shaded. The ground cover was likewise dense with the barbs of blackberry bushes, a myriad of other low-lying shrubbery, and a good sprinkling of poison oak. Sometimes a daring hiker or jogger would take one of the slippery deer trails on the way to or from Mount Sutro, but for the most part, the Interior Park Belt remained a desolate place: dark, cold, wet, and generally forbidding.

JaMorris and Abby parked on Stanyan — Hal's street, about two blocks south of his house — and walked up to where the crime scene was marked by yellow tape, three black-and-white SFPD vehicles, a couple of news vans, an unnecessary ambulance, and the coroner's van. They showed their credentials to the pair of uniformed cops securing the scene, and then started uphill on a narrow trail of duff and mud to where another knot of officials huddled at a fork a hundred feet along.

The coroner's assistant, Angie Morena, took a step toward the Homicide inspectors and held up a hand, stopping them. "You're a little early. Crime Scene hasn't processed the path. Be careful where you walk." She pointed to a third spot where the indicated trail, half the width of the one they'd come up, split off to the right through the waist-high shrubbery.

"Who found her?" Abby asked.

"A neighbor kid," Morena answered, "playing in the woods. The little clearing back in there was one of his hiding places. It's a pretty good one."

Both inspectors looked over. The Crime Scene personnel photographing and measuring and looking for clues were visible over the low expanse of greenery, but the object of their attention could not be seen from the main trail.

JaMorris asked, "Any ID on her?"

"Not definite, but she's the right age and has on what Katie Chase was wearing the last time anybody saw her: jeans, a red pullover, tennis shoes. There's not much doubt."

Abby indicated the workers in the clearing. "How long before they're done?"

"You know as much as me. However long it takes. At least several hours."

"What if we brought around the husband?" Abby asked. "He's local, a couple of blocks."

Morena glanced back over at the crime scene. "Not to protocol," she said. "We ought to get her to the coroner's office first. You don't show the next of kin a body lying in a clearing."

"I know," JaMorris said, "but maybe it's time for some hardball. If he didn't do it, I'll apologize later. If he did, maybe this will shake him up and he'll give us something."

Fifteen minutes later, the two inspectors and a haggard-looking, stoop-shouldered Hal Chase broke through the cordon of police cars. By now four television vans clogged the street where the trail led up into the shaded canopy. When they got to the trail, Hal stopped and took a deep breath, then looked up the path as though it were a gallows he had to ascend.

"All right," he said to no one. He stepped up on the curb and over the sidewalk and into the park. From when the inspectors had first shown up at his house through the length of the uphill walk, Hal had projected impatience. He wanted to know; he had to know. But now, as he moved up the path, the urgency was gone. If anything, he seemed reluctant to keep moving.

Or, Abby thought for the tenth time, maybe he was just a fine actor.

They followed him up to where Morena waited. The ever nattily attired Len Faro of the Crime Scene Unit had come out to join her, talking with what looked from the distance to be enthusiasm; maybe he'd found a clue, some fabric snagged on one of the blackberry brambles. He had a plastic bag in his hand; as they got closer, he squared to face the small party and then put both hand and bag in his pocket.

"This is Hal Chase," JaMorris said when they got up to the other two.

Morena had obviously prepped Faro. He nodded a perfunctory greeting, then added, "We're all finished in there, if you'd like to follow me. Watch out for the stickers."

The smaller trail went back into the dense undergrowth for about thirty feet, then turned slightly to the right before it opened into a cleared area perhaps ten feet in diameter. Faro, in the lead, blocked an early visual of the body on the ground, but when he got to the clearing, he stepped to one side. Directly behind him, Hal stopped and drew in a sharp breath.

In the shade, the light was not good, though it was a long way from true dusk. The body lay facing away from them. The cause of death appeared to be a single gunshot wound to the back of the head, as though she'd been walking and, shot from behind at close range, simply fell forward onto her face.

Hal moved up next to the body, on the side her face had turned — one step, then two. He went to a knee, stared at the profile, hung his head. "Oh, Jesus," he said.

Nobody else said anything.

After a small eternity, he straightened up and turned to face Abby and JaMorris. Even in the dim light, his eyes glistened. Nodding once, he managed to whisper, "Yes, it's my wife," before he pushed to one side of the trail and squeezed past the people who'd trooped up behind him. When he got back to the main intersection where they'd hooked up with Morena and Faro, he stopped again and drew another breath, an unconscious moan escaping. He put his hands in his pockets, turned left, and one foot after another, slowly walked downhill.

27

They held the funeral Mass at St. Ignatius the following Monday morning. It was a tense and brittle affair.

In the days since the discovery of Katie's body, the suspicions about her husband had coalesced into what seemed a nearly universal acceptance that he was her killer and it would be only a matter of time before the police arrested him. No one with inside knowledge was supposed to be talking about the investigation, which, in San Francisco, meant everybody was. Both major city newspapers got up to speed quickly on everything that Glitsky and the two Homicide inspectors had discovered: Katie's counseling, Hal's refusal to be a part of it, his inconclusive alibi, his affair with Patti Orosco. Perhaps most damning was the revelation that just after the birth of Ellen, Hal and Katie had taken out a life insurance policy that paid the surviving spouse five hundred thousand dollars should the other die, double that for accidental or violent death.

No one could deny that it was a huge amount of money, especially for a family struggling to cover everyday expenses. As a purely objective matter, it painted Hal in a terrible light, in spite of his explanation that because of his stepmother's experience with his father's pension and a generous insurance policy, the family culture believed in insurance. Indeed, Ruth told any reporter who asked that Hal's father's insurance and pension had allowed her to raise and educate two sons in relative peace and comfort.

The topic of Hal's guilt was ubiquitous, with the ever salacious *Courier* publishing a poll on the day before the funeral indicating that sixty-eight percent of its readers thought Hal had "probably" killed Katie.

The high-pressure system of the past week held steady, and the skies were clear, although the temperature had been dropping each day. When the service began at eleven o'clock, it was forty-two degrees.

Inside the cavernous space, it didn't seem much warmer. Adding significantly to the chill was the very apparent estrangement between the two sides of the family, which had become entrenched since the discovery of Katie's body. The Dunnes wanted nothing to do with the Chases. Katie's entire extended family — sixty or so people — waited outside in the cold until it was clear on which side of the church Hal would sit (the right). Following Curt Dunne's lead, they walked not up the center aisle but all the way around to the left, as far from Hal as they could get. Also in those left pews were Katie's six playgroup friends and their husbands, all of whom had spent significant amounts of social time chez Chase and now apparently viewed Hal as a pariah. Abby Foley and JaMorris Monroe were there too, since it was not unheard of for a murderer — even if it wasn't Hal — to be among the mourners at services.

The Chase contingent was significantly smaller and more spread out. With the exception of a decent show of solidarity from Hal's boss, the sheriff, his chief deputy, Adam Foster, and thirty of his colleagues among the guards, bailiffs, and other deputies, barely a dozen souls had taken their places in the right-hand pews. Hal, Ruth, Warren (back in town for the funeral), and the two children sat in front. A scattering of guys from Hal's earlier life — bowling and fishing and drinking buddies — had entered on their own and filled in empty bench space. Three rows behind Hal, Dismas and Frannie Hardy sat with Abe Glitsky. Despite Hardy's advice to the contrary, Patti Orosco showed up. Although she tried to keep a relatively low profile, she wore a stunning hooded brown leather and fox-fur parka that looked like it cost five thousand dollars if it cost a penny, which immediately sparked a feeding frenzy in the media, some of whose bolder members had to be removed from the church.

Since he was the spouse of the deceased, Hal's wishes trumped those of his wife's nuclear family. The tensest moment came at the end of the service, when Daniel and Curt Dunne seemed to want to fight Hal about who would be pallbearers — they and their friends, or Hal and Warren and the sheriff's people. Finally, Cushing took charge; he and Foster and two other deputies stepped forward with Hal and Warren and got the casket lifted into the waiting hearse.

28

Maria Solis-Martinez sat at a pitted gray metal desk in the jail's infirmary. For security purposes, it was an enclosed place surrounded by glass windows and entrances without doors that could be closed or locked.

The surroundings did little to calm Maria's nerves as she awaited the arrival of Luther Jones. She might have been hard-pressed to identify any single immediate cause of her concern, since there were so many possibilities: She was meeting a dangerous and threatening inmate; she was here under false pretenses, pretending to be a nurse-practitioner at the jail and attending to the routine minor complaints of the various inmates; she couldn't allow herself to fail; she was unarmed — as an investigator, she was used to carrying her weapon — and yet she intended to have the guard leave Luther Jones alone with her, unrestrained by handcuffs or foot shackles.

So her mouth was dry and her palms damp when Jones — mean and scary in person, in his jailhouse orange garb — appeared at the entry, a confused look crossing his face as he saw her. She realized she would have to act quickly and decisively if she didn't want to have the moment get away from her, so she pushed back from the desk and stood.

"Mr. Jones," she said as she came around and advanced on him. "I'm Maria Solis-Martinez, and I'm here to replace Ms. Bartlett. I know you're here for a routine diabetes monitoring, but there's something I need to talk to you about."

Matter-of-factly, as though she did this every day, she maneuvered him to the bed farthest from the entry where the burly redheaded guard stood. She showed nothing but was relieved when the guard strolled a few feet from the door and began an animated conversation with another guard, leaving her effectively alone with Mr. Jones. She stuck out her right hand and said, "You can call me Maria if I can call you Luther."

He just looked at her hand, then half-turned to the door as though planning to call the guard back. Instead, he whirled on her and said, "I don't know you. Whatchu want?"

Instinctively, she retreated a step. Just as instinctively, she regained that lost ground and moved forward into Jones's personal space, forcing herself to look directly up — and it was a good way up — into his eyes. Before she'd become a DA's investigator, she'd been a patrol officer and then a vice inspector with the regular police in L.A., so she'd had her share of experience interacting with criminals. Still, this was as up close and personal as she'd gotten with one in years.

But she had not lost the skill set. "Don't fuck with me, Luther," she snapped. "I'm here to help you out, and if you fuck with me even a little, I'll call the guard in that hallway and he'll have you back in your cell before you know what hit you. Are you hearing me? Answer up, now. Do you hear what I'm saying?"

Jones, all six-four and two hundred fifty pounds of him, broke eye contact and looked quickly to either side of her. "I hear you," he said, if not exactly meek, then at least with a veneer of respect.

"Good," she said. "Now, let's go sit down over by that bed, how's that sound?"

Her heart pounding, she marched back

around the bed, then turned and sat. Luther had followed her, and he took the other chair. She gave him a reasonable facsimile of a smile and said, "I wasn't kidding, what I said just now."

Maria and Farrell, Frank Dobbins, and Tom Scerbo had gone around and around on this. Trying to talk to a represented defendant outside the presence of his lawyer created serious problems. If this didn't work, and Luther's lawyer found out about it later, there would be all sorts of hell to pay: He would claim interference with the right to counsel, maybe ask for a dismissal of the charges against Luther or even complain to the state bar. But all four of them had decided no guts, no glory. "I'm here to see if I can help you," she said.

"Why you want to do that?"

"That's for me to know, Luther. What's important for you is to know that I have the authority to get you out of here without a trial and to dismiss the charges pending against you. You're looking at carjacking with use of a firearm and a strike, which is twenty or thirty years in prison, minimum. That's about right, isn't it?"

"You tell me."

"I'm telling you. And your lawyer already told you. You're looking at long, hard time.

You want to do that?"

"Against dyin', that's what I choose."

"Who said anything about dying?"

Jones sat back in his chair and crossed his enormous arms. "You're here about that Tussaint thing, ain't you? What are you, really? Fed? DEA? I snitch out around that Tussaint thing, I'm dead. I got the message already. Loud and clear. I ain't seen nothin'."

"Luther. Do you remember talking about the death of Alanos Tussaint to San Francisco Homicide inspectors?"

"Okay, I did that."

"You were very clear that you saw one of the jail guards, Adam Foster, pull Mr. Tussaint out of his bunk and slam his head against the wall."

"No. I never said that."

"Luther. It's on tape. We got your voice on tape saying that."

"I don't know nothing about no tape."

"Look, Luther. Everybody knows what happened. You tried to do the right thing, and they got to you. Now you've changed your mind. I get that."

"I don't know nothing about no guard or no tape."

"It's not too late, Luther. I work with the DA. I can get you out of here. It's not too late for you to make a deal. Everybody knew you were talking last time. That was our bad. But nobody knows I'm here now. Nobody but me and the DA. We get you out of here, you say what you got to say. You're gone."

Luther shrugged elaborately.

"Who talked to you after you talked to those inspectors, Luther? Was it Foster? Was it another guard?"

"It don't matter. They all the same. No, Foster's the worst. Then they all the same after him. Either way, it don't matter."

"It might matter, Luther. This time nobody's going to know if you say anything about Foster or Tussaint until you're long gone. As soon as we get your testimony again, we're going to get you out of here and into Witness Protection, the charges against you get dropped, and you get another chance to put your life together. Maybe this time you'll do it right."

Maria knew that Wes Farrell had said no such thing; she was making promises she had no authority to make and no power to keep. She could also sense that if she was going to get anything at all from this guy ever, she had to go for broke right now. "What do you say to that?" she concluded.

"I'm saying you could be tryin' to trick

me, see if I'm gonna snitch. Is one thing I'm sayin'."

"That's not it."

Luther's gaze was dead flat. "I'll think on it," he said. "And then how do I talk to you? I ask for the DA from down here, the word gets out, I in some shit."

Maria had her phony business card with her real cell number ready for him, and she passed the card across the table. "You got phone privileges. Use 'em. You call, I'll come running."

29

Glitsky stood at the back of the crowd of mourners shivering around the Colma grave site. Coming to the actual interment wasn't his idea of a good time, but he thought there was a slim chance that it might be unpredictably instructive, so the cop in him had said goodbye to Frannie and Hardy at St. Ignatius and tagged along. As had been the case at the church, the sides were strictly segregated, and as he had done earlier, Abe gravitated to Hal's side.

They hadn't quite gotten started. Glitsky was keeping his eye on the interaction between Hal and Patti Orosco — the word was long since out about their affair, and to Glitsky, they seemed skittish as thoroughbreds in their careful dance around each other — so he was surprised when he felt a tap on his arm and turned to face Burt Cushing.

"Abe Glitsky."

"You got me." Glitsky nodded amicably. "Sheriff." He touched his forehead in a casual salute. "Nice turnout of your people."

"They're a good crew, and Hal's among the best of them. He's a popular guy. You here officially? I thought you'd retired."

"I did." Glitsky enjoyed watching Cushing do the math for a minute before he helped him out. "You notice I'm over here on Hal's side, same as at the church. I'm working with his defense attorney."

"He's smart to have one on board already. They're going to try to string him up. I'm surprised he's still walking around a free man."

"Me, too. Though I don't think that's going to last too long."

"Me, neither." Cushing hesitated, then asked, "So who's the lawyer?"

"Dismas Hardy."

Cushing whistled. "Top-drawer guy. Last week I would've asked how Hal could afford him, but I guess that's not an issue anymore."

"Which, in itself," Glitsky replied, "is an issue."

"I hear you." The sheriff cast a quick glance over the assembly. "Little tense back there, wasn't it?"

"Little tense here, too," Glitsky said.

"Katie's side looks like they're ready to string him up right now. I'm halfway expecting it."

"Not with my guys here. No question who they're with."

"I see that." Over the past few days, Glitsky had followed the television updates and read every word of conjecture about the case; that had brought him up to speed on the progress of the Homicide inspectors, including some stuff he hadn't come upon in his own investigation. One of those stories had been Daniel Dunne's theory about Katie's purported threat to expose Hal for his role in the alleged cover-up of abuses by the jail guards. Obviously, Cushing had been made aware of that theory as well, and Glitsky thought it couldn't hurt to probe a little. "Are your guys taking a lot of heat on Katie's brother's idea?"

"Which one is that? I've heard so many these past few days."

"That Hal had to shut her up before she blew the whistle on him and the other guards."

Cushing chuckled without mirth. "The only problem with that, and the other stories like it, is there isn't one grain of truth behind them. My jail's a fucking model of restraint and due process, and any report to the contrary is irresponsible and unfounded drivel."

Glitsky hated profanity but also knew that once in a while someone's lapse into it could be useful. Despite Cushing's dismissive chuckle and all of his protestations notwithstanding, Glitsky knew that he'd hit a nerve.

"Say what you really mean," Glitsky told him.

"We get that shit all the time," Cushing said. "If these bleeding hearts knew what it was like being in the cages day in day out with those animals, unarmed and outnumbered. It's a miracle there's as little violence as there is. But hey, you're a cop. You know this. Sorry to go off."

Glitsky shrugged. "No worries. So if Hal did it, that wasn't why."

"Couldn't have been, but beyond that . . ."

"What?"

Cushing looked over to where Hal was placing some flowers on the casket. "I know the guy. I knew his dad, Pete, back when I was a probationary deputy. He's good people. Katie was good people." Sighing, he went on, "There's just no way he killed her. They might have been going through a rough patch, but they had a real connection. I know that, which is why I can't believe any of this."

"That's good to hear," Glitsky said. Then, realizing what else Cushing had perhaps inadvertently admitted, he asked, "You knew her, too? Katie?"

The sheriff's visage darkened, and for a startling moment Glitsky thought he caught a glimpse of what might have been a tear in the other man's eyes. "I know most of the spouses," he said at last. "Something like this happens to one of us, it's a loss to the whole family."

When the mourners got back to Hal's house, Glitsky found himself struck by the similarities between this gathering and his own return to his duplex after the funeral of his first wife, Flo, who'd died of cancer many years before. Like Hal, Abe had young children at the time. His living room and kitchen had been filled to overflowing, mostly with somber men in uniform. His father, Nat, had been the only tie to the past generation, as Ruth was. The food, in both cases, was a couple of Safeway party trays.

Abe found himself a bare stretch of living room wall and leaned back, hands in his pockets, trying to shake off his own ghosts. Suddenly — he hadn't really noticed her approach — Ruth was standing in front of him with a glass in her hand, the contents of which looked like Coke and smelled like rum. "How did this tradition of throwing a party after a funeral ever get started?" she asked him. "You see anybody here who looks like they want to party, Mr. Glitsky?"

"Not so much," Abe replied. "Maybe it puts off the finality of it all for another day. Then you go back to real life, or try. Meanwhile, it's a last opportunity to drink enough to forget."

"That's exactly it," she said, "and spoken like one who's been through it." She cast her eyes around the room. "Sometimes I think someone put a curse on this family. On me, really. I never would have believed I'd be doing this again so soon."

"So soon?"

"After Pete. Hal's father. He overdosed, you know. By mistake. They eventually admitted it was an accident, which turned out to be good for us, since we could collect the insurance. But it was awful, no matter what."

"I'm sorry, I didn't know about that. When did that happen?"

"Warren was five. He's twenty-two now. And I guess Hal must have been fifteen. So seventeen years." She took a pull of her drink. "But it's like it was yesterday, especially here, now . . . all these uniforms. It brings it all back. Nothing ever changes."

Glitsky didn't want to air out his own memories, so similar to hers. Instead, he said, "Sometimes it seems that way, but things do get better. It may be hard to keep believing that, but it happens. It happened to me."

"Well, you're not cursed."

"Ruth, you've got two healthy sons and two grandchildren. You can look ahead. There can be a future. You're not cursed."

This made her laugh, a bitter and shrill note that already seemed more than a bit fueled by alcohol. Lifting her glass, she drank again. "No? How many people do you know who have lost two family members? And now they're going to arrest Hal. It's obvious that's where they're going with all that. They already think he's guilty. Everybody does."

Glitsky heard himself say, "I don't," and realized that this was what he intuitively believed, even if he couldn't marshal the facts to support it.

She took his words at face value. "Thank you for that. But you're in the minority. Everybody else thinks he walked behind her up that path and turned right through the bushes and shot her while she walked, maybe while she was talking, pleading over her shoulder. And that's just not something Hal could do. I know my boy, and he never could have done that."

"If it comes to it, and it may not, I think a jury will agree with you. He's got a great lawyer, and this city doesn't like to convict, even with lots of evidence." Except, he thought, in cases of domestic violence, where the accusation alone was often enough to convict a male suspect. This wasn't something he wanted to share with her now, though. "And here, there's basically no evidence," he repeated. "So I'd keep a little hope."

"I am. The hard thing is I never thought they'd arrest him. I really thought, because he didn't do it, they'd never get to that."

"And they haven't yet. Let's not get ahead of ourselves."

"All right. You're right. I'm just . . . my brain . . ." She stopped in apparent confusion and tipped up her glass, finishing it. "At least I'll be here for the babies," she said. "There's one silver lining. They'll be in my life again. I suppose I should think of things like that."

"That's a good idea. At the very least, you'll get to share them."

She hesitated and cocked her head. "What

do you mean, share?"

"With the other grandparents. Katie's family."

She shook her head with a firm show of defiance. "That is not happening. I'm not sharing with those people. Hal's their natural father, and he's the only parent left, and he gets to make that decision, even if he's in jail. He won't let those children go and live with those awful Dunnes, not even for a day. I know he won't."

Glitsky knew that this could, in fact, become a pitched custody battle over the next several months, but now wasn't the time to try and convince a grieving, drunk woman about something she obviously didn't want to consider. "I hadn't thought of that," he said. "And speaking of Hal . . ." Glitsky pointed to the other room, then excused himself and made his way through the press of deputies to where Hal stood, holding a sleeping Ellen in his arms, at the kitchen counter. "How are you holding up?"

Hal gave him a perfunctory smile. "Minute to minute. It ought to be over soon, although I'm not sure I want it to be."

Glitsky knew what Hal was talking about; it reflected his own former anguish at the prospect of dealing with the world without Flo. Eventually, for Abe, life had returned to what felt something like normal, but it had taken a very long time, and while he was waiting, he never felt anything like a guarantee that it would arrive at all.

"I'm going to head out," Glitsky said. "Is there anything I can do for you?"

"Yeah," Hal said. "Find out who did it."

"I'm looking," Glitsky replied, then added, "I really am."

And found — again with some surprise — that he meant it.

30

Frannie Hardy swung her legs out on her side of the bed and said, "Well, that's how that's done."

Among the many advantages of not having children living with you anymore, Dismas Hardy counted high on the list the fact that you didn't have to schedule lovemaking for when they were either away from home or in a far corner of the house. With his workload allowing him the occasional morning off, he and Frannie had fallen into, if not a routine, at least an openness to the possibility that they did not always have to wake up and immediately rise from bed.

Hardy lay with his hands behind his head and a grin on his face. "I tend to agree. Could it be we're actually getting better?"

"We should, after all the practice lately. Do you want coffee in bed? Or will Your Majesty be down for breakfast?

"I'll do what you're doing."

Naked, her finger to her chin, Frannie struck a pose at the door to the bathroom. "Coffee. Downstairs. Five minutes."

Hardy took a satisfied breath and nodded. "Done."

Next to the bed, the telephone rang.

"First amended response," he said to Frannie. "Maybe ten minutes." He picked up. "It's not yet nine o'clock, so this better be important."

"Why aren't you at work?"

"Because I'm at home, Wes. As should be obvious, since you called here."

"That's really not a very civilized way to answer the phone."

"Yes, well, no civilized person makes phone calls between nine at night and nine in the morning. So we're even."

"Who made that up? The nine-to-nine rule."

"Alexander Graham Bell. It was the first thing he invented after the phone itself, and a damn good invention it is. What's so important?"

"What's important is that this is a courtesy call that I probably shouldn't be making to you, as Hal Chase's attorney, but I've got a soft spot in my heart for my former partners. My sources are correct — he has retained you? Right?"

"Indeed."

"That's what I heard. So although I couldn't tell anyone about a grand jury proceeding because it's secret, I thought you might want to make an appointment to be with your client by noon or so. That way, if you got a phone call saying that — oh, I don't know — he happened to be indicted, you could surrender him to us as soon as you get the word."

Hardy sat up against his headboard. "This is a mistake, Wes. You get some new evidence I don't know about?"

"We'll get all evidence to you at the appropriate time, Diz, but in the meanwhile, Mr. Chase will need to be in custody."

"What's changed since yesterday?"

"I can't comment on that, but no doubt you've noticed the clamor — citywide, I might add — that we do something."

"Clamor isn't evidence, Wes. And you don't want to do just something, you want to do the right thing."

"That's going to be up to the grand jury. If there's not enough to indict him, they won't do it."

Hardy barked out a one-note laugh, and although Farrell couldn't see him to appreciate the gesture, he also rolled his eyes. "Oh, please, spare me." Both men knew that the grand jury was a prosecutor's blunt instrument whose primary function was to issue indictments against suspects, and since those suspects were not allowed to have an attorney with them in the room, the result of a proceeding was nearly absolute in its inevitability. "Seriously, Wes, if you've got nothing new, you might want to hold off until you get something that a jury in this city is going to believe. As you know, that's a pretty high bar. And I'm telling you, as your friend, I seriously don't think Hal did this. At the very least, there are too many unexplored questions that you ought to get some answers for."

"I think, hypothetically, of course, that a grand jury could decide we have enough answers to warrant a trial, Diz. And if they did, I would agree with it."

"You're making a mistake. Really."

"I hope that's not true — I don't think it is. And if it is, it won't be my first one. Come on, Diz, you saw this coming as soon as they found her body. I'm doing you a favor with this heads-up, and you know it. How about a little gratitude among old friends?"

"All right, I'm grateful, but —"

"Quit while you're ahead, Diz. And have yourself a nice day."

■ ■ ■ ■

"I know the grand jury has a low standard for indictments," Glitsky was saying, "but isn't this below even that threshold?"

The three of them were at the Hardys' dining room table. Glitsky had come straight from dropping the kids off at school. Frannie had gotten dressed, while Hardy remained in gray sweats.

"In theory, you're right. But what the grand jury really likes is a narrative, and even without much in the realm of physical evidence . . ."

"Much? How about none?"

"It's not none. They got the slug."

"They can't connect it to Hal's gun, though, can they?"

Hardy shrugged. "It's a hell of a narrative. Hal's got no alibi, and he and Katie are having problems enough that she's seeing a counselor, and a very pretty one at that." Hardy nodded over at his wife, who gave him a patient smile. "Katie's body's found less than a quarter mile from their house. He's been having an affair, cheating with a wealthy and beautiful woman, the wife's ex–best friend, who admits she'd marry him in a heartbeat. Oh, and did I mention that with

217

Katie's death, he's no longer a poverty-stricken deputy sheriff but a millionaire? You must admit, it has a certain je ne sais quoi, which, as we know, is French for 'holy shit.' Have I left anything out?"

"Well." Frannie cleared her throat and whispered after a small silence, "This is not good."

Hardy nodded. "To say the least, and now —"

Frannie held up her hand, stopping him. "No. Not what you're saying. I should have said something before now. Ever since they found her body, I . . ." She looked back and forth between the two men, let out a breath. "When I was still assuming — hoping — she was alive, it was all privileged, so I didn't . . ."

"It still is," Hardy said. "Privileged. That never goes away."

"I know. But she's dead now. So maybe betraying the privilege is technically unethical, but I don't believe it would be wrong. I mean, it can't matter to her anymore, can it? And that's my main concern, especially if it helps you discover who killed her. But I warn you. You might not want to hear it because it doesn't necessarily help Hal, either. It might even hurt him." She reached over and put her hand over her husband's.

"I didn't think his arrest would be so imminent. Now it looks like it could be any minute, doesn't it?"

Hardy nodded.

"What did she tell you?" Glitsky asked. "We're not in court, Frannie. Nobody's going to bust you on the privilege issue. I promise. If you know something that might be important, we need to hear it."

Frannie sighed, looked from one man to the other.

"What?" Hardy was brusque. "Tell us."

Another moment of silence. Frannie swallowed and came out with it. "She had an affair, too. Katie."

Glitsky and Hardy exchanged glances. "I don't believe that's made it into the record yet," Hardy said. "With whom?"

"I don't know. She never said."

"When was this?" Glitsky asked.

"A few months after her first baby was born."

Glitsky kept at it. "How long did it last?"

"I think a few months."

"Who broke it off?"

"I don't know."

Hardy stepped in. "Did Hal know about it?"

"No. Not as of last week, anyway." Fran took a small sip of her coffee and carefully placed the cup back in its saucer. "That's the other thing: I feel like I might have talked her into telling him. I made a big pitch for it in our last session, told her she should come clean, start over with trust and no secrets between them. Since they found her, I've been thinking what if she did? What if I talked her into it and she told him and that became the last straw?"

"I don't think so," Glitsky said.

"That's so good to hear," Frannie said, "but why do you think not?"

"Because he'd just been doing the same thing. Even if Katie told him, unless she rubbed it in his face somehow . . . would she likely have done that?"

"I can't see it. That's not how she was."

"Then I really don't see him reacting with outrage. He wouldn't have a leg to stand on. Not to say it doesn't happen, but . . ." Glitsky let the sentence hang.

Hardy's tone softened. "Strategically, it's not going to make much of a difference, whether Hal knew about it or not. From any kind of jury perspective, he doesn't need any more in the way of motive than the insurance and Patti Orosco. Besides, I agree with Abe. He wasn't going to decide to kill Katie because he found out she had an affair.

"But that doesn't mean it's not significant," he went on, "if only because it puts another player on the board. Somebody who was at one time close to Katie and who still might be. Or might have wanted her back, or might still want her back. And maybe because he couldn't, he had to kill her." He looked at his wife. "You're sure it was over as of a couple of years ago?"

"That's what she said."

"Well," Hardy said, "it's good to know about, in any event. And Frannie, I wouldn't beat myself up over what you told her. I assume you gave her similar advice in the past. Did she tend to take it most of the time?"

This brought a weary smile. "Not so much. One of her common themes was wondering out loud why she kept coming to me when she wasn't doing about nine-tenths of what I suggested."

"Why did she keep coming?" Glitsky asked.

"I think we just got along as people. She liked to have a chance to talk to another adult woman about her life once a week. That's the thing about what I do that's so frustrating sometimes. It's not so much therapy — I mean real psychiatric therapy, where your expectation is that you'll become more together and self-actualized and

221

maybe healed in some way — as it is problem solving."

"And what was her problem?" Glitsky asked.

"She wanted to be happier. She wanted to be a perfect mother and a full-time successful businessperson and a sexy and fun wife and a devoted daughter. It's the old cliché, guys. She wanted it all."

Hardy pushed himself back from the table. "And on that cheery note, I've got to get moving if I'm going to be surrendering the client sometime today."

31

Glitsky had made an appointment with the medical examiner of San Francisco, John Strout, who was ancient and had stayed on in his job long after his pension could have kicked in. Yet he showed no signs of slowing down. His acuity included what was lately a remarkable response to Glitsky's coming into a room, namely a comment on his retirement.

"How did you hear I was retired?" Abe asked.

Strout had a huge desk cluttered with ordnance and the tools of mayhem. For as long as he'd been the ME, Strout had, often quite illegally, assembled a collection of murder weapons that now graced a glassed-in cabinet against the side wall. If that didn't get your attention, he had a human skeleton perched on a medieval garroting device that he'd had shipped over from Madrid. Now, with Glitsky comfortable across from him, he sat back, idly tossing a hand grenade — rumored to be live — from hand to hand. "Hell, ain't it been like six months? Who ain't heard by now?"

"I could give you a list," Glitsky said.

"You still are, right?"

"I am."

"How you likin' it?"

"As you can see, John, I'm putting my foot back in the water. That answers that."

"All right, then, who are we going to be talking about?"

"Katie Chase."

Strout nodded as though he'd expected nothing else. "Damn straightforward. One shot, lower occipital, exit at the hairline."

"Anything on the slug?"

"Thirty-eight, brass jacket. Common as dirt."

This informed Abe that the murder weapon had been a revolver. It also explained the absence of a casing at the scene.

Strout went right on. "There were powder burns in her hair and on her scalp. It was close. Two to three inches. Who are you working for on this if you're off the force?"

"Dismas Hardy."

Strout's eyebrows went up. "Defense work?"

Glitsky smiled. "I know. It kind of crept

up on me, too. Is there anything you want to tell me that might be useful in court?"

"It's going to court? The husband?"

"Rumor has it that the grand jury's indicting him today."

Strout gave the grenade a spin on his desktop. "You met him, the husband?"

"Several times. We're pals by now."

"How tall is he?"

Glitsky cocked his head to one side. "That's an interesting question, John. Why do you ask?"

"You tell me first."

Glitsky thought about it. "Six feet even, give or take."

Strout nodded.

"You're being a little enigmatic, John. You enjoying yourself?"

"Always." Strout reached for the grenade again. "This is as nonscientific as it gets, but my instinct tells me the shooter wasn't that tall. Here's why: We got a clean trajectory back to front. There's a clear canal from entry low in the back to exit high in the front. Pretty good angle."

The corners of Glitsky's mouth turned down. "You been to the scene?"

"Nope. But I saw the pictures."

"Maybe not close enough," Glitsky said. "It was uphill."

"This would have been pretty steep uphill, Abe. Maybe thirty-five or forty degrees, almost too steep to walk without feeling like you're climbing. If it's less than that angle, the shooter probably wasn't six feet tall, although I'd never testify to that on the stand. Katie was sixty-eight and a half inches — that's five eight and a half. Pretty tall. Now, she could have had her head tucked in, any number of other variables. But I don't think that was it, either."

"Why not?"

"Because of where some sharp-eyed Crime Scene person found the slug."

"And where was that?"

"About nine feet off the ground in a eucalyptus tree."

"You're kidding me."

"Scout's honor. These guys comb an area, they don't mess around. Plus, they got lucky, which never hurts. Anyway, if Hardy's looking for something to argue about, and I assume that's what you're talking to me for, he could do worse than start with a short shooter. At least plant a seed, mount some posters, do a little show-and-tell."

"I'll mention it to him. You got anything else, defense-wise?"

"You want to give me a hint?"

"They found some of her blood in her

kitchen. Hal thinks she slipped cutting something. You got any ideas about that?"

Strout leaned back in his chair. Something about the question evidently pleased him. "Could have been. I wondered about that. Something cut two fingers of her right hand. Not deep, but it would have bled."

"What was that?"

"I don't know. Could have been self-inflicted, or maybe somebody getting her attention?"

"Wouldn't the gun have done that all by itself? If you've got a gun, you don't need a knife."

The damn grenade still in one hand, Strout spread his arms. "Hmm. All too true, Abe," he said. "All too true."

It was all well and good for Dismas and Abe to say that Frannie's advice to Katie "probably" had nothing to do with her death. Since both men were laboring under the assumption that Hal was innocent of the crime, any talk of his motivation was moot. If he didn't do it, then it didn't matter what reasons he might have had.

But her irresponsibility — whatever the result had been — left Frannie with a sick feeling in the pit of her stomach.

She had schmoozed with Abe for a while

until Diz had come down in his business suit, then she'd followed them out and waved goodbye as they'd driven off separately. The temperature had climbed a few degrees since yesterday, and it was pleasant walking to her office with the prevailing breeze at her back.

Now Frannie sat in her recliner with a small stack of her notes on Katie's visits, twenty months' worth. Katie's first visit had been triggered by her second pregnancy and by what she'd called an "emotional breakdown" over the fact that she was letting Ellen be raised by a nanny and the two grandmothers.

She was toying with the idea of quitting work to stay home and be a full-time mom, and she wanted to talk out all the myriad issues and implications, many of which Frannie had been able to relate to. (With a stab of chagrin, Frannie punched some numbers into her calculator and realized that while she was listening to Katie's problems, many to do with how tight the Chases' money and budgeting would be, she had billed her about ten thousand dollars.)

Only now, nearly two years after the event, did Frannie see what struck her as the most obvious truth in the world: that Katie may well have started to see her because of an emotional breakdown, but that crisis was probably caused not as much by her concerns over becoming a stay-at-home mom as by the fact that she was involved in an affair.

It had just begun, or she'd just ended it, or maybe she was smack in the middle of it and feeling guilty. It would not have been the first time that clients had started seeing Frannie because they were misbehaving in their private lives. She believed that basically people started going to counseling for two reasons: confession or absolution, sometimes both. She had always thought that Katie was an exception to that rule, but now she wasn't so sure.

Charged with adrenaline at the realization, she rose out of her chair, went over to where her coat hung on one of the pegs behind the door, got her phone, and punched in one of her favorite numbers. "Abe," she said, "sorry to bother you, but I've been thinking about what we all were talking about this morning. I know you and Diz don't think it mattered if Katie told Hal about her affair, but Diz said it put somebody else in the picture, and that could be a good thing for Hal if we could find out who it is. It's just occurred to me that I think I

229

know when that whole thing started. I mean, within a few weeks. And if you've got that, you've got a reasonable window where you can check her phone records, maybe her computer use, something that might identify him, don't you? How does that sound?"

32

Before the indictment came down, Hardy called Hal at his home and broke the bad news, suggesting that they meet where Hal could have his last good lunch for a long time to come and where they could talk some strategy. Meanwhile, Hardy told Hal he should get his logistics in order on who would be taking care of the kids. Hardy kept open the very remote possibility that Glitsky's investigation and his own access to the prosecution's discovery might lead to an early and positive conclusion, but the smarter move was to prepare for the long haul.

What he didn't tell his client — and probably didn't need to — was that a murder trial, especially one with sensational elements such as Patti Orosco and a million dollars of life insurance, could not be expected to begin in under a year, and that it could easily be two.

Hardy also did not add that even in the liberal enclave that was San Francisco, any husband accused of murdering his wife who made it all the way to a jury trial would almost certainly get convicted of something — second-degree murder, manslaughter — that would involve significant prison time. Hardy knew but again did not say that Hal's life as he'd known it was probably over.

They met at Original Joe's at Washington Square, one of Hardy's favorite locations in the city, going back to when it had been the home of the outstanding Fior d'Italia. He'd remained loyal to the physical locale — what wasn't to like about Washington Square? — when it had been a rather hoity-toity high-end steak house called DiMaggio's. Now that Original Joe's had relocated there from its earlier longtime home in the Tenderloin District, Hardy felt that the bones of the building had reclaimed its heart. When Hal suggested the place for his last lunch outside, Hardy's opinion of him shot up a few degrees, despite the questions about Hal's connection to his wife's murder.

They got a table against a window. Hal wore civilian clothes: brown slacks, a black dress shirt, a well-tailored charcoal sport coat. They ordered a split of carbonara for an appetizer, a couple of veal dishes, and a

232

bottle of Chianti.

Hal paused in the middle of buttering his sourdough. "How much of a done deal is this thing? The indictment."

"The DA called me personally first thing this morning. I'd say it's going to happen, or I wouldn't have called you. If it doesn't, worst case we get a nice lunch."

"I didn't kill her, you know."

Hardy nodded. "I'm going with that. How are things at home?"

"As well as can be expected. Except Katie's family is already circling. They're going to want to get time with the kids. But Ruth's a tiger, and I think, being their dad, I get the final say. Isn't that true?"

Hardy temporized. "Depends on how hard they want to fight. They're the biological grandparents, they've got rights they can assert, and they probably would get a good listen, at least for some visitation. While you're in limbo — and before we get a verdict, that's where you are — it might be best to contact them and allow them some visitation and hope that'll keep them from trying to litigate for full custody."

"Ruth's going to love that."

"It doesn't have to be her decision. In fact, it probably shouldn't be."

"Good luck keeping her out of that loop."

"I'll talk to her," Hardy said. "She'll have to come around."

Hal shook his head. "Not her specialty, I assure you. But she's the best I've got, and she's absolutely on board for as long as it takes. And she's not going to want to share. She's already bonding with both kids, I can see it. It's like a second chance for her, and she's not going to blow it this time."

"You're saying she blew it last time? You mean raising you?"

Hal shrugged. "I don't blame her. It wasn't easy for any of us after my dad died. I basically came off the rails, and Ruth didn't have much energy for me, especially with Warren and all of his problems. She just did her own thing and let me do mine, and that's probably not the best way to raise a happy, productive kid. Which I was not. And look where it's taken me."

"Being a deputy's not the worst thing you could be."

"It's a job. It's got benefits. I'm not complaining, but . . ."

"But you are."

"Well. It's dangerous work. People don't talk about that, if they realize it at all. Also, the pay sucks. It's not the kind of job you dream about for when you grow up. I always thought I wanted something more, you know? I didn't know what — maybe a lawyer, maybe a real cop, an inspector. But after Dad . . . nothing seemed worth the effort. I'm not blaming Ruth. I mean, she physically took care of me and got me through school, but she was emotionally checked out. And now she wants back in. I'm taking that as a good sign."

Their wine arrived, and Hardy sipped and pronounced it fine. The waiter poured the two glasses, and when he was gone, Hal picked up where he'd left off. "Ruth and the Dunnes and the kids, all that's going to play out the way it does," he said. "What happens today?"

Hardy killed a second or two with his wine. "Today," he said, "if the indictment comes in, you get booked, and after that I think you probably know the drill a little better than I do. The one bit of somewhat good news is they're putting you in AdSeg."

"That's good? It's isolation."

"It won't be for you."

"No? How's it not gonna be?"

"You'll know your guards. They'll talk to you, I bet."

This seemed to resonate as a probable truth, and Hal nodded. Then he had another question. "Are they going first degree?"

"The indictment doesn't allege degree. I

don't think premeditation will be their theory of trial, but we won't know until we get there."

"How about bail?"

"They're probably going to allege murder for financial gain — the insurance. That's a special circumstance, and there'll be no bail."

"Can you argue that I'm not going anywhere?"

"Sure, and I will. But it won't do any good. No judge is going to let you out."

"What about my insurance money? I could put some of that up."

Hardy shook his head. "Even if they don't allege specials and some judge sets bail, you're not going to get any of that insurance money until they find you not guilty. The main thing is, a case with this profile, there'll be no bail at any price. Period."

"So I stay in jail? When? Until the trial?" Hal sat back in his seat and turned his head to stare out the window. He whispered, mostly to himself, "What a fucking nightmare."

"It is. There's no denying it."

"What do we do?"

"The big decision is how fast we want things to move ahead."

"You mean to trial?"

"Yep. And you should know the conventional wisdom is that we want to put it off as long as we can."

"I don't. Not if I'm in jail the whole time."

"Well." Hardy paused, grateful that the waiter had returned with their food. He knew that the next few minutes were going to be uncomfortable if not downright ugly, and he wanted to give the tension a moment to dissipate before he started in again on some of the harsh realities his client was facing.

They waited silently while they both took extra Parmesan grated over their carbonara. The waiter refilled their glasses. Then they took their first bites and reached for their glasses. Hal drank his wine down halfway.

At last, Hardy talked. "I want to be clear, Hal. I'm not arguing this either way. It's completely and absolutely your decision, how you want to proceed. But there are a lot of good reasons to want to go slow. You want to hear some of them?"

"Why not?" Hal's hold on civility was slipping.

Hardy paused, then started in. "First, this is a red-hot case. Coming down here, I swung by the Hall, and they've pretty much blocked off all of Bryant Street to accommodate the news vans, like fifteen of them.

Which means somebody leaked the grand jury news to the media. Emotions are going to be running high, everybody's going to know or think they know all the facts, there's going to be political pressure on everybody from the DA to the mayor to bring you to trial and see justice done. Justice in this case means they find you guilty."

"The jury doesn't have to buy in to any of that."

"No, they don't, in theory. But they're humans, and they do. Fact of life, get over it. And then we've got the purely logistical considerations. Do we want to stay here in the city or go for a change of venue because of all the publicity? We need time to consider that, maybe do some polling. If we go slow, we get more time to prepare. In this case, more time to assign more help and maybe find out who actually did it. The prosecution might lose track of their witnesses —"

"*What* witnesses?" Hal interrupted, exploding. "Do they even have one witness? And what would that person be a witness to?"

"Okay." Hardy put up a restraining hand. Diners at a few of the nearby tables were looking over at them. "Easy now. The two Homicide cops, at least. The coroner, the

238

Crime Scene people, the lab folks, maybe Katie's friends or family. Believe me, they'll have witnesses. Over time, those witnesses might move away, or forget their testimony, or mix it up with another case, or even die. Lots of things can happen over time.

"But" — and here Hardy paused for emphasis — "the main thing that going slow gets us is keeping you away from a verdict, which might come back not guilty. Juries are nothing if not unpredictable, and it might not. You want to keep even the remotest possibility of a verdict as far away from the here and now as you can. Once you're found guilty, you're in a different world, and it's a world of hurt." Hardy pointed down at Hal's plate. "Eat something. It's too good to let it get cold."

Hal absently picked up his fork and began to twirl his pasta. He brought it to his mouth, chewed, and swallowed. "What about going fast?" he asked. "And what is fast, by the way? How soon can we get this trial started?"

"Sixty days from your arraignment."

"Okay, how is that better? I'm thinking off the bat that I want to go that way."

"Maybe you do," Hardy replied. "We know that the DA's got a weak case on evidence alone, and we don't give them much time to find anything else."

"There isn't going to be anything else. Not that implicates me."

"Of course." Hardy had to admire Hal's consistency. "But beyond any evidentiary issues, they barely have time to work out their theory of the case. If they want non-cop expert witnesses — don't ask about what — they'll have a hard time rounding them up on short notice. Same goes for lab results. Even if they've completed the work on everything they collected. At the very least, it puts a ton of pressure on everybody to get everything done, and that makes for mistakes. For you, if you get off, you're out of jail that much sooner."

Hal started to say something, then held up while a busboy cleared their plates and the waiter set down their entrées. When they'd both moved off, he said, "Bottom line, everything I'm hearing sounds like the smart approach is to push forward. No?"

Hardy bought some time with a bite of veal, a sip of wine. "It doesn't give us much time to investigate alternatives, or hire our own experts and check lab work they've done. That's one major drawback. The other one — the main one, really — is that if the jury does come in with a guilty verdict, everything's different from then on out."

"Different how?"

"Instead of being a suspect and presumed innocent, once the foreman says 'guilty,' you're a convicted felon. Your rights are different, many of them gone, and pretty much forever. Even if we come up with new evidence afterward, unless it's a total slam-dunk, like DNA or a confession, nobody's going to be in a hurry to get you out of prison. Any appeal, on any grounds at all, will take its own sweet time working through the system. I've seen it take years. One of my own clients" — Hardy held up his hand as if taking an oath — "honest to God, four years. He eventually got out. But four years! Gone out of his life. I don't want to see that happen to you. I'd rather put off the verdict as long as I possibly can and hope we find the actual killer or else something pretty damn exculpatory."

Hal chewed his meat, thinking about it. "Meanwhile, I'm in a cell."

"True. As I say, it's your call."

Hal put down his fork. "Do you think they could really convict me?"

"If they can indict you? I'd have to say yes."

"That is just so wrong."

"It is." Hardy went to cut another bite of his lunch when his cell phone rang. He saw the number and said, "I need to get this. Hey, Abe, talk to me." He listened, said, "When?" Listened some more, then punched off, holstered his phone, and looked across at his client, his face clamped down. "The indictment just came in. We've got till three-thirty to get to the jail."

33

On his bunk, Luther Jones sneaked another look at the false business card that Maria Solis-Martinez had given him. The card said she was Maria Castro with the Yerba Buena Medical Group. It said she was an LVN, whatever that was. He felt that just having that card was a risk, but he couldn't make himself throw it away.

That phone number might be his way out of here.

Ever since his meeting a few days before with Maria, Luther had been perplexed and on edge. Every bone in his body warned him that he was being set up and that as soon as he rolled over on Adam Foster as the man who killed Alanos Tussaint, he himself would meet with an unfortunate jailhouse accident.

But he'd been over it and over it, and it still didn't make sense.

What he couldn't figure out was why

Adam Foster would go to the trouble. Did he mean to test Luther? Make sure that even in the face of temptation, he wasn't going to talk? Why would Foster want to do that? Did he doubt that Luther would keep quiet? Luther didn't want him thinking that even for a minute.

Luther was worried enough that Adam Foster knew his name, knew his cell number, made it a point to come by every single day on his rounds and give him a cold nod with a colder smile, as though saying, "I'm watching every move you make." Luther knew that Foster was indeed aware of everything he did, either on his own or through the deputies.

Which probably meant, since Foster had spies everywhere and knew everything, that he also knew the truth about Maria. He definitely knew that she'd come to see Luther. The question was what Foster believed about her.

It seemed that Foster could believe one of three choices: Maria Castro was a nurse of some kind who was helping out at the infirmary. If Foster believed that, there was no danger to Luther.

Second choice, Maria was with the DA's office. In that case, Luther thought, he would already be dead.

The third choice was that Maria was — somehow — a snitch for Foster. This last one didn't make any sense to Luther. Why would he bring in an outside party to double-check his own work? There was no need. Foster had delivered his message, his death threat to Luther if he talked, with absolute clarity. Luther could think of no reason on earth for Foster to want to test him. If he thought Luther needed testing, he would kill him. Simple as that.

So choices two or three resulted in Luther being dead.

And then it followed — didn't it? — that since Luther wasn't dead, the first choice must be the right one. Hard though it might be for Luther to imagine, Foster seemed to believe in Maria's phony cover as a nurse. If that were true, and Maria was what she said she was, a DA with a real offer that would get him out from under the watchful, never-blinking eye of Adam Foster, why wasn't Luther taking her up on it?

He wished he could ask his defense attorney, Kaz Eames. The problem there was that Luther didn't trust Kaz, and with reason. He had a strong hunch about how things had gone wrong the first time he'd gone for the DA's deal, and he didn't want a replay of those events.

When he'd first told his defense attorney, Kaz, that he had seen Adam Foster beat Alanos, Kaz had arranged an interview with Homicide. At that meeting, the cops had taped his statement and he'd shown them some of his cards. The next step should have been a formal offer of immunity from the assistant DA, Tom Scerbo, in exchange for Luther's statement, and he was waiting in his cell for that offer when instead, Adam Foster had shown up with a couple of his goons. That team had been most persuasive — talking to Luther with his head in his cell's toilet — in outlining all the reasons why he did not want to testify about what he'd seen.

They'd convinced him.

The last time somebody had a big mouth, it hadn't been him, and he was pretty sure it wasn't Scerbo. That left Kaz. So Luther was through confiding in the fucking guy who could have gotten him killed.

Still, he knew he had valuable information. As an eyewitness to a jailhouse murder committed by the chief deputy himself, he could definitely trade his testimony for some kind of deal. Of course, the word of a jailhouse snitch, particularly one who'd already recanted once, wasn't worth much. But Luther knew more than he'd told anyone:

246

He knew why Foster had killed Tussaint —
that the whole thing was related to corruption in the jail. The dope, the selling of
privileges, the gambling and enforcement of
gambling debts, the whole rotten enterprise.
If he told the cops what he knew — names,
dates, connections, payoffs — and they dug
around, they should be able to find proof.

All this was potentially lethal stuff, and
there was no way he was telling Kaz any of
it. Kaz, though, was the only lawyer he had.
His only chance.

Unless he wanted to risk playing the hand
himself, call Maria on the number listed on
her phony business card, and hope she
could put things together fast enough to get
him out.

It was the only play he had.

If he just had the balls to make the call.

34

Glitsky drove out past Hal Chase's home, and kept driving for another two blocks, until he came to the Interior Park Belt. Parking there, he got out and stood staring at the large canopy of eucalyptus in front of him. The trail that Katie's killer must have taken had been pretty seriously trampled — the cops, the curious — in the days since her body had been found, so it was no trouble to follow it back up into the deeper shade.

Sure enough, a hundred or so feet up, a tributary trail cut off to the right through the low underbrush. The little path might originally have been challenging to pick up when the body was there, but after all the intervening foot traffic, it might as well have been lit by neon. It was also — and it seemed this must usually be the case — wet.

Glitsky picked his way through the low brambles until he came to the clearing where the body must have fallen. Here he stopped, turned, looked behind him.

John Strout, the medical examiner, had told him that the shooter might have been short in stature, and Glitsky had countered that he'd heard the trail was a relatively steep uphill climb. Standing there, he realized that it came nowhere near to reaching the thirty-five- or forty-degree threshold that Strout had talked about. In fact, by San Francisco standards, it would hardly be considered steep at all. The pitch of the canyon steepened significantly on the other side of the clearing, but here at the opening, the first steps in, it was all but flat.

So the brass-jacketed slug had entered at the base of Katie's brain and exited at the hairline. Strout's admittedly nonscientific pronouncement about the bullet's path seemed right, although, as he'd noted, there were several possible explanations: Katie might have had her head down as she walked, the shooter might have tripped and panicked and shot from below Katie's neck. There were any number of other possible scenarios, and he was keenly aware that, for an experienced Homicide inspector, all in all, this was an exercise in stupidity. There were at least a dozen quick-to-hand variables that could produce the kind of path that the bullet had taken on its way through Katie's brain and into one of the surrounding eucalyptus trees. This was something he shouldn't be wasting a minute on.

Except for one thing . . .

And that thing — Strout's mentioning it as more a likelihood than a possibility — Glitsky should ignore only at his peril. John Strout was an objective guy with vast experience. He dealt in science and numbers, angles and percentages and lab results at the microscopic level. He did not guess very often, and he never guessed when he testified. For him to tell Glitsky that he might want to consider the possibility that the shooter was shorter than Hal's six feet was remarkably out of character. Strout was speaking in an unguarded fashion to an ex-cop and longtime acquaintance about an instinctive feeling, nothing that he could mention or ever would consider mentioning in court.

Nevertheless, he had said it. It was, Glitsky thought, what the good doctor believed. He couldn't prove it, probably wouldn't even try.

But there it was.

Back at Hal's house about a half hour later, Glitsky sat at Katie's computer in the master bedroom upstairs. Below, he was vaguely aware of the constant faint hum of activity of Ruth and the children, punctuated rather too frequently in his opinion by explosions of young toddler pique and impatient snappish adult response. Ruth, Ellen, and even to some extent baby Will working out the kinks in their relationships.

He wasn't paying attention to that, though. He was here, at Frannie Hardy's suggestion, to try to get a line on Katie Chase's love affair, which was quite possibly going on or had just ended in the months surrounding March 2010. The computer had been turned over weeks before by the officers in Missing Persons, who had Hal's permission. They had since downloaded and returned it. But they had been looking for more recent activity that might have had to do with her disappearance, and probably they hadn't paid too much attention to three-year-old records. Fortunately for Glitsky, Hal had given them the computer's password, which Hal and Katie had shared, and the officers had left the sheet of binder paper containing Hal's notes, including that password, in the middle drawer of the desk on which the computer sat. As an added bonus, Katie was clearly not paranoid about her security and used the same password for her Facebook account.

But after nearly an hour of checking emails, her Facebook, and other random documents, Glitsky had come away with exactly nothing that looked even remotely promising. Her Facebook wall for those months after Ellen's birth had been filled almost exclusively with pictures of the new baby, dozens if not hundreds of them, and of the babies of the women who "liked" her photos. Her emails were mostly to her sisters and brother and some coworkers, and none of them contained any hints about her lover, or any indication that she and Hal were having problems. To all outward appearances, they were the glowing new parents.

Even if he was unlucky finding specific information, Glitsky considered himself lucky to have so much no-hassle access. When he decided to give up on the computer for the day, he went looking for her telephone records. Again, the super-organized, type-A Katie made things easy for him. She had three wooden file cabinets along the wall beside the computer desk, and in them she kept all their household records, in alphabetical order, for at least the past five years and what might have been their entire marriage. Glitsky pulled out the physical telephone bills for the first half of 2010 and, using the reverse-number feature on her computer, once again found nothing suspicious, much less damning. Certainly no string of calls to any one number. The outgoing calls from both this home number and from her cell phone — the same account — were again limited almost entirely to her family members, to her employer's office, and to the jail where her husband worked. The greatest number of the calls was likely there.

Glitsky sensed the early onset of dusk and saw that he'd have to leave for the day. He had to pick up his own children and needed to hustle if he was going to make it.

Downstairs, things had calmed down. Will was in his high chair and Ruth was feeding him while Ellen was the picture of intense concentration, her tongue sticking out of her mouth as she sat at the table across from her grandmother, drawing silently on an Etch A Sketch.

"How are you doing?" Glitsky asked.

Ruth turned. "Very good. I was born for this. Ellie and I are getting along splendidly, aren't we, sweetie?"

The child raised her head from her creation. "Ellen," she said, "not Ellie."

Ruth rolled her eyes for Glitsky's benefit. "Ellen then," she said.

Ellen said, "What?" and went back to her drawing.

Then, as if suddenly remembering why Glitsky was there, Ruth cocked her head. "Did you find anything?"

"Zero."

"Maybe I'd have heard something or seen something. Were you looking for something specific?"

Glitsky didn't want to burden Ruth with the supposition that her daughter-in-law had been involved in an affair. As far as he knew, even Hal didn't know that. Not yet, anyway. He shook his head. "Just anything that might jump out, and nothing did."

She sighed. "Tragic," she said. "Just so tragic."

"It is." Glitsky let out a breath. "I'm off to pick up my kids at school. Can I get you anything?"

"I know you're trying," she said, "but all I really need is to get my good son back. He did not" — she glanced at Ellen — "you know. About Katie. And no jury is going to find that he did."

"I hope you're right," he said. "Call if you need anything or think of something I should look into."

"I will."

"Bye, then."

"Bye." Then, "Ellie, say goodbye to Mr. Glitsky. There's a good girl."

But Ellen was immersed in her Etch A Sketch and didn't look up.

Glitsky said, "That's all right. She's got a lot to deal with right now. I'll see you."

When his hand was on the front doorknob, he heard the girl's voice in indignation: "Hey!"

"Don't you 'hey' me! You're not the boss around here, young lady. I'm the boss."

"That's mine! It's mine! Give it back!"

"When I want to, and not before, Ellie."

"It's Ellen."

"It's whatever I want it to be. Now settle down and be a good girl for once."

Glitsky pulled the door closed gently behind him.

35

At the jail, his former colleagues were giving Hal Chase every courtesy, breaking a lot of the rules to do it, but what the hell. He was still one of them. As soon as they got him in the elevator after he'd been booked, they took off his handcuffs. They couldn't let him remain in his civilian clothes, but at least the jail jumpsuit fit him.

The cell on the seventh floor was the same as all the others: ten feet by twelve, with a bare porcelain toilet, a sink, and a bed that was not much more than a mattress laid down over a rectangle of concrete. Someone, though, whether for him or for another segregated VIP guest in the past, had scrounged up a well-used comfortable leather armchair and a small wooden table with a wooden chair to go with it. The bed had a pillow. A makeshift shelf held twenty or so paperback books. The big problem everywhere in the jail was heat — the ambient temperature was around sixty-six degrees — so they'd provided him with two extra blankets and a red and green afghan he could throw over his shoulders. His dinner tray was loaded with double rations of meat loaf, gravy, green beans, mashed potatoes, pepper and salt, six slices of bread with packets of real butter. Milk and two chocolate chip cookies for dessert.

In spite of the terrific Italian lunch he'd had with Hardy at Original Joe's only five hours before, Hal ate it all, making conversation the whole time with Paul Landry, one of his buds from the shift. There were inmates on either side of him, but he couldn't see them and vice versa, and for the most part, he was unaware of their presence.

It was going to be a long haul, he knew, but he was confident he could handle it. He'd been coming to work in this same jail for half a dozen years; even if he was on the wrong side of the bars, he didn't feel particularly uncomfortable or threatened.

Or at least, he didn't feel threatened until he was settling down in his leather chair after dinner with Nelson DeMille's novel *Night Fall* — Hal was a big John Corey fan — and somebody knocked on the bars. He looked up to see his chief deputy, Adam

Foster, looking down at him. Closing the book, he got right to his feet and saluted.

Foster returned the greeting. "You mind if I come in?"

"I don't think I get to choose."

"True that," Foster said, not without humor. In a minute, he'd unlocked the door and come inside, then closed the door behind him, two big men in a small place. Hal sat himself on the mattress and motioned to the leather chair, which Foster settled into. "So, how are we treating you? You comfortable?"

Hal gestured at his surroundings. "Presidential suite. No complaints. The food's better than I make at home."

"Still, the situation sucks."

"No argument there. I didn't kill Katie, Adam."

"Nobody here thinks you did, Hal. You got any ideas who might have?"

The inmate shook his head. "If I did, I would have told somebody, I promise."

"You don't think your girlfriend . . . ?"

"No."

"Just sayin'. You could point at her, make 'em look that way."

"I don't want to do that. Besides, it wouldn't do any good. It could never come out, 'cause she didn't do it, either."

"You're sure?"

"No question."

"What's your lawyer say?"

"Not too much. He seems to think it's a good idea to put off going to trial for as long as I can. But nice as the accommodations are here, I don't think I want to hang out in this room for a year or more."

"No. You probably don't." Foster cast his eyes about the small space. He blew out a breath in apparent frustration. He lowered his voice so it couldn't carry to any of the adjoining cells. "And do I have this right? Your lawyer is working with Glitsky?"

Hal nodded, then also spoke more softly. "They're old friends. He's been an inspector half his life. Maybe he'll find something."

"Yeah. Well, the thing is . . ."

Hal waited him out for a moment before asking, "What?"

Foster took his time, choosing his words with care. "He talked to Burt at your place, you know. After the burial. He seemed kind of interested in this story your wife's brother was telling."

"Daniel's a jerk."

"Maybe, but still. Glitsky's at the goddamn grave site asking Burt about stuff he's heard about what's going on here at the jail, as though maybe he thought it had something to do with your wife's death."

"How could that be?"

"I was hoping maybe you could tell me."

Hal shook his head. "That's just trying to pin another so-called motive on me, as if they need another one. I was shutting her up because she was going to blow the whistle on what I'd told her about some things that happened here? I'm sure. What would that get me? Beyond that, what would telling her get me?"

"Plus, you know that nothing's happened here. We — you and me — were in San Bruno when Tussaint fell down."

"No. I know that. I never said anything else."

"That's the funny thing, Hal. You see what I'm saying? It sounded to Burt like maybe you'd gone and told your wife some stories about your work, stuff that's gone down here."

"I didn't do that."

"Somehow Glitsky was on to it."

"I don't know what that's about." Even in the chill room, Hal felt a film of sweat blossom around his forehead. "I never mentioned anything to Glitsky. I swear to God."

Suddenly, Adam Foster had moved himself up to the front edge of the leather chair. He had his elbows on his knees, his hands clasped between his legs. "That's the way we want to keep it, Hal. You understand me?"

"I've always understood that, Adam."

"How do you think your brother-in-law got the idea?"

"I told you. He's a jerk. He's a lawyer, too, you know. Maybe he heard the rumors we're always dealing with and decided to play with them."

"Well, that makes Burt nervous. Me? It just makes me unhappy."

"There's nothing to it. Nothing that came from me."

"You never talked to your wife about what goes on at work?"

"Not that kind of stuff." Hal swallowed, his throat suddenly parched. He got up, crossed two steps over to the sink, ran some water over his hands, splashed his face, cupped a mouthful, then wiped his face with the small hand towel. He turned back to his interrogator, sat down on the bed again, cleared his throat. "Adam. I swear to God. That's all I can say."

"Okay." Foster reached out and touched Hal's knee. Gave him a tight smile. "Just crossing my i's and dotting my t's, you know?"

"Sure."

"Okay, then." Foster started to get up, checked himself, settled back down. "One other thing. I mean, it goes without saying, but I'll feel better if I just come out with it so there's no . . . misunderstanding."

"I'm listening."

"If they convict you — not saying they will, but it's always a possibility — you're going to be looking at some serious prison time. You know that and I know it. In the face of that, you might be tempted to cut some kind of deal with the DA, maybe trade some testimony for a sentencing break. You know what I'm saying?"

"I'd never do that. That's not who I am, Adam. You ought to know that."

Foster shrugged. "That's who you are now, Hal. But people go through changes, get some different ideas. Think about saving their own skins. And all I'm telling you is that this would be unwise." He held up a hand as Hal started to object. "No, no. I know you're not thinking anything like that now. But the temptation might come along, and it would be a bad idea if you couldn't resist it. A long time in prison is better than some alternatives. I know you know what I mean."

"I do. Of course I do."

That same parody of a smile. "Otherwise"

— Foster stood up, prompting Hal to do the same — "you need anything up here, we're going to take care of you. You're one of us, Hal, and we're not going to forget, so long as you don't forget, either. And that's not likely, is it?"

"No. Not gonna happen."

The smile brightened. Foster punched Hal's shoulder. "We good?"

"Good."

Foster took a last look around the cell, lowered his voice. "Anything, just let somebody know, and we'll make it happen. You hear me?"

"Loud and clear, Adam. Loud and clear."

36

Dismas Hardy swung by Glitsky's on the way to work. Catching Abe in an apron over his nice slacks and shirt, Hardy followed him around to the kitchen and said, "I know people who would pay good money to see you this way. It's fetching."

"I'm making spaghetti sauce. You wear an apron or you get all splattered with tomato. Speaking of which, you want to stand back. Garlic pops, too." Glitsky stirred at the stove.

"Smells like fish," Hardy said.

"Anchovies. Secret ingredient. Garlic, onions, a can of anchovies with its oil. Can't miss."

"A whole can?"

"Sometimes two. You can't use too much. It disappears when you cook it."

"Where to?"

"Where to what?"

"Where to does it disappear?"

"I don't know. It just goes away. Take a look. No sign of it already."

Hardy leaned over and looked into the pot. "Wow," he said. "Magic."

Glitsky agreed. "It is. Even more magical is that there's no fish taste in the sauce."

"How does that work?"

"No one knows. It just turns into something else."

"Transmogrifies," Hardy said.

"That's what I meant to say, transmogrifies. Transmogrifying anchovies. Dave Barry would say that's a good name for a rock band."

Hardy shook his head. "Too many syllables. I don't think there's ever been an eight-syllable band name. Although come to think of it, the Fabulous Thunderbirds has seven."

"I never heard of them."

"They were real. Maybe still are. I don't know. The Trailer Park Troubadours. Nope, that's still seven."

"Are they real, too?"

"Absolutely."

"How come I never heard of them, either?"

"Because unlike your best friend, you don't have your finger on the pulse of musical culture. Hey, how about Crosby, Stills,

265

Nash and Young, Reeves and Taylor?" Hardy counted on his fingers. "That's ten syllables!"

"Hallelujah!" Glitsky said with modulated enthusiasm. "A new record." He finished cutting up an onion and scooped it up and into the pot, gave everything another stir. "Except who are Reeves and Taylor?"

"They were in the band. Second album."

"How do you know this stuff?"

"I remember everything," Hardy said. "It's a curse. Like too good a sense of smell, which Frannie has. She can smell a dead mouse behind the trash compactor from fifty feet. Anchovies even if they've transmogrified. Also if I've had onions for lunch."

"Curses abound," Glitsky said. "Maybe we should talk about the curse of not killing your wife and people thinking you did."

"We will, but finish your sauce first. Do you have anything in this kitchen as retro as coffee and something to brew it in?"

Hardy sipped and put the cup down on the coffee table. He had his yellow legal pad on his lap. "What I've been trying to get some traction on is this whole question of evidence. I know the grand jury can and often does indict a ham sandwich, but the evidence is so light here that I can barely see where they're coming from."

"They're coming from motive."

"Motive is good," Hardy said. "But it's not evidence."

Glitsky persisted. "True, but there's a lot of motive. A surfeit, as you might say."

"Even a surfeit should not suffice. And that," Hardy went on, "is why I want to talk to you about the things we do have that we can talk about."

"Like what?"

"Like, for example, the murder weapon."

"We don't have the murder weapon."

"Okay, but what do we know about it?"

"Caliber. Thirty-eight."

"Anything else?"

Glitsky considered a moment. "Revolver."

"Does that do anything for you?"

"Not much. Though it can't be the same as Hal's duty weapon, which is a forty automatic. And there's no record he's ever had another gun."

Both men knew that although California law required everyone purchasing a gun to fill out paperwork regardless of whether it was bought from a dealer or a private party, that hadn't always been the case. There were thousands of handguns for which there was a record of the first purchaser from a dealer, but the weapon had changed hands between private individuals up to a dozen times since the original purchase and was, in effect, untraceable.

"So the theory," Hardy said, "must be that he got the murder weapon a long time ago from a private party or he bought it on the street."

"So what?"

Hardy shook his head in frustration. "I don't know, goddammit." He reached for his coffee.

"Strout says the shooter might have been shorter than Mr. Chase."

Hardy swallowed. "What?"

"With all the caveats you'd expect. But I think he really believes it."

Hardy chewed on that. "Maybe I can build a whole defense on negative evidence," he said. "Hal was too tall. Missing Persons didn't check him for GSR." Gunshot residue. "Granted, they wouldn't have had any reason at the time, but the fact is, they didn't. And if Hal made up his alibi, wouldn't he have come up with a stronger one? Plus, why would he admit to his affair with Patti? Could he have been so stupid as to buy all this life insurance and think he could get away with murder?" He looked across at Glitsky. "Anything on Katie's affair?"

"Nothing. She was nothing if not discreet." Glitsky ran down the lack of results from yesterday's search. "If anything," he concluded, "from the phone records, anyway, I came away feeling they were connected at the hip — Hal and Katie. They were talking seven, eight, ten times a day after their daughter was born. A couple of first-time parents working it out together."

Hardy cogitated, hand to his chin. "Okay," he said. "Back to evidence. You find anything reasonable on anybody else? How about Patti?"

Glitsky shrugged. "Possible motive, of course, but here we go again. On the other hand, she probably knew pretty close to exactly what time Hal was leaving for the airport. She walks in and startles Katie, who cuts herself. Or maybe, even though she's looking at a gun, there's a tussle, and Katie gets nicked with her knife. Doesn't matter. Patti walks her outside —"

"And two blocks uphill in the dark?"

"Puts her in her trunk," Glitsky said, "at gunpoint. Drives her to the spot."

Hardy's eyes lit up briefly. "There you go. What kind of car does she have? Could you finagle a way to have her open her trunk? Katie's hand might still have been bleeding."

"I could try. But if you want to talk long shots . . ."

"That's where we're at, Abe. At this point, I'd take anything. How tall is Patti?"

Glitsky shrugged. "Normal, I'd say. Five-five, five-six. You see her and you're not thinking how tall she is."

"I barely got a look at the funeral," Hardy said. "I need to spend more time with this woman."

"Careful what you wish for," Glitsky replied. "She is some kind of distracting, let me tell you. The other problem, from our perspective, is that she's about it as far as active alternative suspects are concerned. And if she actually did do it all by herself, we're looking at close to the perfect crime. Plus . . ."

"What?"

"I hate to say it, but she's got to know that if she kills Katie to get Hal all to herself, there's the little flaw that in all probability, Hal's going to be the prime suspect and find himself where he is now, in jail, going to trial. And maybe never getting out. So what's that get her?"

"Maybe she thought he'd have an alibi, or that his alibi would hold up."

"Wouldn't you think, if she was contemplating murder, she would have made sure?

270

This is also the reason I don't believe they were in it together. They would have at the very least alibied each other, don't you think?"

"Unless it was just her and she wasn't doing it to get him back as her lover, but to punish him for dumping her." Hardy tipped up his coffee cup. "As always, we're back to no evidence."

"That ought to be good news for your client."

"That's the theory. Strangely enough, it doesn't feel like that."

37

Abby and JaMorris, with an indicted and arrested suspect, had been doing some grunt police work, interviewing Hal's neighbors. They had all been interviewed before by Missing Persons, but this time the two inspectors had a different agenda. They were focused on narrowing down the time Hal had left to go to the airport on that Wednesday night. If they could expand that window and prove that he'd had more time to commit the murder, it would be all to the good.

But their strategy backfired. Ray and Jeannette Rice, a middle-aged couple who lived three houses downhill from the Chases, had been taking a walk around the block on the night before Thanksgiving. They not only saw Hal exit his front door sometime very close to seven-thirty to go to his car parked in the driveway, they wished him a happy Thanksgiving, and he wished them the same. No, he hadn't been in any particular hurry. No, he hadn't seemed upset, had in fact volunteered that he was off to the airport to pick up his brother. He invited them to come by the next day for a cocktail.

Lieutenant Devin Juhle, head of Homicide, sitting behind the desk in his office, frowned. "The truth may set you free, but first it will make you miserable. Hal never mentioned this to Missing Persons?"

"It's not in the record if he did," JaMorris replied.

"And Hal never brought it up on his own?" Juhle asked. "He should have, since it helps him."

"Other things on his mind," Abby said.

Juhle sat back in his chair. "Naturally, you taped your interview with these Rices? They're sure it was close to seven-thirty?"

JaMorris said, "It would be better if he'd left around six or even before, but given that his kids had to be asleep first, we always figured that what Chase told us about when he left was close enough to the truth."

"He leaves the house at seven-thirty, and then what?" Juhle asked.

Abby took it up. "Drives around the block once or twice, pulls back into his driveway. Plenty of time."

Juhle chewed at his cheek.

273

"That's always been pretty much the timetable," JaMorris said. "It doesn't really hurt us."

"I'm not so much concerned about the time," Juhle replied, "although it's a bit of an issue. I'm worried about Mr. Chase wishing them a happy Thanksgiving and inviting them over for drinks if he's already got this plot to kill his wife in motion."

"He's a con man," Abby said. "Scott Peterson all over again."

Juhle still didn't like it, but there wasn't anything he could do. "Well," he said. "Get it typed up and run it by me when you get the transcript. I'll see how bad the damage is. Meanwhile, anything new on Glitsky?"

Abby nodded. "He was at the funeral on Monday, went over to Chase's afterward."

"What's he doing in this?"

Abby and JaMorris exchanged a glance, and Abby said, "He's working for Chase. Looking for the other dude." This unknown and unnamed person, they all knew, was the linchpin of the oft-favored SODDI defense: "Some other dude did it." Quite frequently, that other dude didn't exist, but juries could still be persuaded that he did.

"Is he impeding your investigation?"

"No," JaMorris said. "There isn't any other dude."

"Good point. But he's going to try to muddy the waters, isn't he?"

Abby said, "Dismas Hardy will, that's for sure."

"Abe's a good cop," Juhle said, "and I just hate to see him over on the dark side. Maybe I ought to give him a call."

JaMorris looked at Abby. She looked back at her partner. "Couldn't hurt," they said in unison.

Maria T. Solis-Martinez got the call from Luther Jones at around six o'clock. She contemplated having him pulled out of the jail immediately for the follow-up interview. She had already made plans, just in case, to have him housed in the Santa Clara county jail under an assumed name as soon as he decided to cooperate. It was clear from her phone conversation that Luther was coming on board and, as they had hoped, claimed to have even more information than he had let on initially.

They would need to get his new statement on tape and be ready to follow up immediately on anything he gave them. But her main job was to get him safely out of the jail and into some kind of living situation where he could remain anonymous and protected. So it was a matter of logistics, getting Luther sprung more or less surreptitiously from the jail and settled into his new home. She didn't want to go near him again until she had her own guys ready to get him down to Santa Clara and be sure that Santa Clara would take him once they arrived.

Maria was a little uncomfortable with the delay. She knew that jail phone calls were taped, and Luther hadn't been entirely discreet on the phone. In the end, it was more important that the move go smoothly. A few hours' delay seemed inevitable, but she could live with it.

What she didn't know was that, within twenty minutes of the call, Chief Deputy Adam Foster was fully aware that Luther Jones had made a connection with somebody in law enforcement, probably in the DA's office. With one call to his contact at the phone company, he quickly got the name and billing address to the number that Luther had called. He didn't know how much this woman knew in addition to what was in the phone call, but even that was too much.

As the lieutenant who coordinated the efforts of the Homicide detail, Devin Juhle knew that your most important task was to protect your people. You backed them up in their investigations. Where possible, you eliminated obstacles, whether political, administrative, or personal. You also tried to keep them from error, which Juhle felt he had done in the Chase matter by counseling Abby and JaMorris to proceed methodically, in light of the dearth of physical evidence against Hal. Though Juhle thought Hal Chase probably had killed Katie, he wasn't inclined to pressure his troops to make an arrest with insufficient evidence if the political climate became such that the grand jury could get involved and issue an indictment first, which is what had happened.

In terms of Gliksky's friendship with Dismas Hardy and his involvement in the Hal Chase matter, Juhle had more respect and empathy for him than he let on to his inspectors, which was why he had tolerated his presence up to this point. After all, both men had "San Francisco Police Person of the Year" on their résumés. Beyond that, Glitsky had been shot in the line of duty, so by Juhle's reckoning, he automatically deserved — and got — all the slack Juhle could conjure up. There was also the simple fact that Glitsky, as the lieutenant when Juhle was an inspector, had several times walked a very fine line about Juhle's own informal partnership (and friendship) with another mostly defense guy, Wyatt Hunt, a private investigator.

To the objective eye, Juhle might have seemed more than once to be working at cross-purposes with regard to his duties as a Homicide inspector. His arguments to Glitsky had always been that he was just trying to get to the truth of things, that Hunt had convinced him to look for alternatives to the man or woman they had arrested. He was making sure that the Homicide detail got it right so they wouldn't be embarrassed.

Now it looked like Glitsky was doing essentially the same thing. And it was Juhle's job — protecting his people — to sound out his old boss on his direction and his progress. He'd put it off long enough. He got the number out of his Rolodex, then pulled the phone on his desk over in front of him. Lifting the receiver, he paused for a second or two, then punched in the numbers.

"Glitsky."

"Abe, it's Devin Juhle."

A dry chuckle. "I was wondering when you were going to call. How are you?"

"Fine. We've got Hal Chase in jail, as you know. You mind if I ask you what you're doing around that?"

"Trying to find out who killed Katie."

"Not Hal, huh?"

"No. I don't think so. But listen, I'll be easy to convince otherwise if you've got some evidence I'm not aware of."

"I hear you're working with Hardy. He'll have everything the DA's got as soon as he asks for it."

"Well, that's the DA."

"Yes."

"I'm assuming Abby and Jambo are still looking."

"They're in the field, yes. Talking to people. Tightening up the case."

A pause. "From where I'm sitting, Dev, it needs considerable tightening."

"No comment. As you know, the grand jury made that call. Do you know anything I don't that you want to talk about?"

"You called me, Dev. If I had something that freed Hal, you'd know about it already."

"Anything else?"

"That's a pretty wide-open question. The good news from our perspective is that I've got nothing on Hal. The bad news is that I'm pretty much the same with anyone else. Hardy and I were talking about evidence this morning, and it's a barren landscape out there."

"So what are you working on?"

"You want the truth, Dev, I'm down to the dregs. There's a rumor that Katie had an affair a couple of years ago. Had you heard about that?"

"That's what her brother said. He mentioned it to my guys."

"Did he know who it was with?"

"I don't know. They didn't pursue it as any kind of lead. It didn't connect much to Hal that we know of. Plus, this was, as you say, two years ago. You think it's really got something to do with now?"

"I don't have any idea. All I know is it's an unanswered question. Otherwise, all I've got is Patti Orosco, and she just doesn't sing for me."

"Maybe that's because Hal did it."

"Well, either him," Glitsky said, "or somebody else."

38

It was a small thing, but Glitsky now understood from Juhle's information that Katie's brother was apparently the only person besides Frannie Hardy who might know something about Katie's affair. And though Juhle was likely correct that pursuing the identity of Katie's former lover would prove to be a dead end, it was the sole option that presented itself.

Glitsky called the number Hardy's office had provided, identified himself ambiguously as an investigator, and midway through Wednesday afternoon, found himself sitting across from Daniel Dunne in the man's impressive office.

Katie's brother got right down to it. "Why do you look familiar to me?"

"I was at your sister's funeral."

"Hal's side."

"Of the church, yes. I'm still investigating her murder."

"That's what you said on the phone. Even though you've arrested him? I don't have any doubt, I'll tell you that."

Because he did not want to identify himself as a police officer, Glitsky kept his response general. "It would be helpful if there were more physical evidence. Being a lawyer, you probably know that a grand jury has a lower standard of proof than a trial jury. They can indict, but before the court can convict, more will be needed. You told the other inspectors that Hal and Katie were having problems with their relationship. I wondered if you could enlarge on that a bit."

"You mean Patti Orosco?"

"Not so much," Glitsky said. "She and Hal both say that he'd broken up with her."

"Well, what's he going to say? Of course they're not going to admit anything. But you notice she was at the funeral? They're still together, you watch. They're just biding their time."

Glitsky wasn't going to fight him. He said, "Nevertheless, one of the things you mentioned to the other inspectors was that your sister also had an affair."

Daniel's brow clouded. "What has that got to do with anything?"

"I don't know. I thought you might be able to tell me. If Hal found out, especially recently, it might have played a role in driving him to do what he did. Did your sister tell you anything about that, maybe mentioning it to Hal?"

"No. I don't see her doing that."

"All right. Do you know who this person was? Her lover."

"I don't see why that would matter. But no, I don't."

"It would matter because anyone who had been intimate with your sister might still have a connection with her. For the trial, it would be better if we knew all the players so we don't get surprised. Katie never mentioned who it was?"

"I don't think so. Actually, I'm sure she never did. But you know, I don't see what this is going to get you, Inspector. Honestly. She made a mistake. She felt awful about it and put it behind her. Whoever it was — her lover, I mean — I have a hard time seeing him coming back into the picture after all this time so he could kill her. Does that make any sense to you at all? Really?"

39

Bundled up against the wind and the chill off the bay, Burt Cushing and Adam Foster walked along the Embarcadero, where there was no chance of being bugged. Foster was the taller of the two by at least six inches, but in their body language, there was no question who was in command — Burt Cushing — and he was shaking his head back and forth, back and forth. "No," he said. "No no no."

"I don't see what alternative we have, sir."

"There are always alternatives, especially in light of the heat we've attracted over the past few weeks. We can't afford any more attention at the jail until some of this has blown over. The deniability just won't be there."

"So what do we do about Luther Jones?"

"Frankly, I'm more worried about Hal Chase."

Adam Foster waved that off. "I talked to

him last night. He's a good soldier."

"He may be, but he's not under fire yet."

"Hal's not going to talk."

"Hal already did talk, didn't he? To Katie."

"Katie's not saying much, either, is she? But Luther is. Or will. Unless we step in."

Cushing walked on a few steps. "It can't be at the jail, Adam. That's what I'm saying. The jail is off-limits."

"All right. It doesn't have to be at the jail. There are other alternatives. I'm asking for some direction here, sir. Luther Jones called this woman. Something is going to happen, and soon, if we don't stop it."

"I'm worried about Wes Farrell. I hear from our people over there that he's starting to feel like he's got to do something."

"Farrell's a clown," Foster said.

"He may be," Cushing agreed, "but I hear that, for whatever reason, he's gotten behind this thing — Luther and this woman. We got too much connection to the jail, and the plain fact is now we're on the radar. Which means even a clown like Farrell can't ignore it anymore."

"So what do you propose we do? We've got to do something. And sooner rather than later."

"I hear you, Adam. Do you think I don't understand that? What I'm saying, my main point, is that whatever it is, it can't get back to anything at the jail."

"All right," Foster said evenly, checking his temper. "You know there's never been a problem getting it done, whatever it is, wherever it is. Just tell me how you want it to happen, and that's what will go down."

"I know that." Cushing put a hand on Foster's sleeve. "I'm not doubting you. And I think I'm beginning to see a way something could work."

Foster gave him a solemn nod. "Just give me the word."

Cushing nodded back. "All right," he said. "Bear with me here for a minute, but this is how I see it . . ."

On their way back from dinner at Farallon on date night, a Wednesday-evening tradition over the better part of their marriage, Dismas and Frannie turned in to a cul-de-sac north of Lake, and Frannie said, "I don't believe it. There's never a spot this close."

Hardy pulled into the parking space that yawned open directly in front of the Glitskys' duplex. "The power of positive thinking," he said. "I imagined a spot right here, and lo."

She gave him a look. "Lo yourself."

They were expected. Glitsky had called while they were eating, and when Hardy had called back as they'd left the restaurant, it turned out that Abe wanted to run a few things by Frannie as well as Diz.

". . . so I thought it made sense to ask you, too, Fran." Glitsky had pulled a kitchen chair into the adjoining living room and now straddled it backward. "Did she ever give you a name, a description, anything on this guy?"

Frannie sat next to Dismas on the love seat. In the past few months, Treya had taken up knitting — knitting? — and she sat on her rocking chair across the room, her needles clicking away, though she didn't appear to be paying attention to them.

"She barely admitted the basic fact of it," Frannie said. "She couldn't believe she'd done something so out of character."

Hardy canted forward slightly. "Not that I don't appreciate your dedication, Abe, but even if you find out who this guy is, so what?"

"I know. That's the song I've been hearing all day. Daniel Dunne asked me the same thing. Devin Juhle, too."

Hardy's eyebrows went up. "You talked to Devin Juhle?"

"Sure. We're old pals, after all. He called me."

"What did he want?"

"He wanted to know what we knew. So I told him. Nothing. No, correct that. I told him about the affair, but it wasn't news to him. He'd already heard it from Daniel Dunne."

"How did Daniel get it?" Frannie asked.

"Katie told him. Evidently, they were close." Glitsky shrugged. "He didn't know who it was, either."

"Not to break into another chorus of the same old song, but say you find out who it was, then what?" Hardy asked.

"Then I go talk to him, at least. The lover. See what he's been up to lately. Maybe he'll want to talk about Katie and tell us something we don't know. Maybe it's somewhat suspicious that he's heard about her death and hasn't come forward."

Hardy nodded appreciatively. "I like the way you're starting to think. Defense mode."

Glitsky shrugged. "I'm just still assuming it's not Hal. On your very clear instructions. And if it's not Hal, the real killer is out there, and that's who I'm trying to find. If I wind up helping with Hal's defense, that's incidental."

Hardy held up a palm. "No, really," he

said. "I'm convinced."

Treya stopped moving the needles and looked up. "So, the guy, if he's married or prominent, and Katie was thinking about exposing him to Hal, as Frannie says . . ."

"That's a motive," Glitsky said.

"Everybody's got a motive," Hardy replied. "We need somebody with a gun."

"Yeah, but there's something about this guy, or the affair," Glitsky persisted. "Something that's nagging at me, that didn't fit."

"Such as?" Frannie asked.

"If I knew that" — Glitsky gave her a tepid smile — "then I'd know what it was."

"Maybe something on her computer?" Frannie suggested.

"Nothing I recognized," Glitsky said. "Mostly pictures of kids and other moms and her sisters and their kids. I'm pretty sure our timing was off on that, anyway."

"Timing on what?" Hardy asked.

Glitsky told him about Frannie's theory that Katie had started coming to counseling somewhere near the time that the affair had begun, about three months after the birth of the couple's first child. Glitsky had reached the opinion that the affair must have begun much later.

"Why do you say that?" Hardy asked.

"Because while I was there, I also checked

their phone records, and three months after Ellen was born, Katie was talking to Hal on the phone ten times a day."

Frannie sat back into the love seat, her face a bit scrunched up in confusion. "When was this?" she asked. "These calls to Hal."

Glitsky pondered a moment. "Early 2010. January, February, somewhere in there. When she started seeing you."

"And she was talking to Hal ten times a day?"

"Unless she knew somebody else at the jail."

"I don't know about that," Frannie said. "But I'd be shocked to hear that she was talking to Hal. That was one of the main reasons she started seeing me. She and Hal couldn't communicate. She felt guilty and worthless all the time; he was mad and frustrated about Ellen and money. They'd pretty much given up trying."

"Maybe that was later, too," Glitsky said. "All I know is that in January and February — you can check it out — she was calling him at the jail every hour."

"Or" — Treya came out with it first — "she was calling her lover at the jail."

40

Maria T. Solis-Martinez already loved her new job. She also knew that even though she was hardworking, diligent, and smart, she was extremely lucky to have it, simply because in today's world, professional jobs with good pay and pension plans were incredibly hard to come by.

For a Hispanic single woman, she felt, this was especially true. It wasn't just the men's network that permeated the workforce. In her everyday life, even working out of her apartment in the Mission District, she always made it a point to dress professionally when she went out, and she was not unaware of the nasty looks and derogatory comments she got from her own people, both legal and undocumented. Not to all, but to far too many of them, she was a sellout, a traitor, even a snob. When, really, all she wanted to do was live a normal American life someday — own a nice apartment (or even a house!), get married to a good man, have children, and pursue a career that rewarded her brains and satisfied her ambitions.

Given all that and the fact that she was now on track, she felt she had to work harder than everybody else, put in longer hours, keep her nose clean, and it would all come about. She had worked hard as a cop in L.A. and would work hard as a DA investigator. It was a good life, and now that she'd managed to come to the attention of the district attorney himself, she was positioned for the next step in her steady advancement, whatever that would be.

Frank Dobbins had given her some paperwork jobs that she could do on her computer at home while she waited for Luther Jones's phone call on the special assignment. She was currently working four cases: a murder case from six years ago, reopened due to new DNA evidence; the mysterious disappearance of $248,000 over the past two years from the city attorney's general fund; a fraudulent environmental reporting claim against a large commercial construction company supposedly clearing a site by Candlestick Park for a proposed development project; and Luther Jones. Tomorrow morning, she was going to bring in Luther and hit a home run in her first big-league at bat.

Career aside, she loved where she lived. Even though she'd put in twelve hours of work today, by the time she shut down her computer at close to nine o'clock, her heart lifted as she walked out her front door into the fragrant evening. The afternoon wind had abated to a fitful breeze, and the smells — coffee, salt water, rotting flowers, gasoline — made her feel alive, part of something important and even beautiful.

It didn't take her five minutes to get to Hog & Rocks, a great restaurant two blocks down the street from her home. She lucked into a seat at the bar and ordered one of their signature Manhattans and then chose, from the "ham and oysters" menu, six Hog Island Sweetwaters and some outrageously great Iberian ham.

A handsome thirtysomething hipster in a plaid jacket hit on her a little bit. He seemed like a nice enough guy, and she contemplated the possibilities for a few minutes. After all, it wasn't every day that she ran across a straight guy in San Francisco who evinced interest in her, but — a plaid coat, really? — she politely steered the conversation around to her (nonexistent) boyfriend, whom she'd be leaving to meet any minute.

Another Manhattan later, she paid her bill and picked her way out through the milling indoor crowd. On the sidewalk at the front door, the last knot of diners awaited their turn. This was, she thought, why you lived in the city. Ten o'clock, and life still buzzing all around you. The place wouldn't shut down until well after midnight, and though she wasn't in the mood to take advantage of the nightlife now, it was wonderful to know that it was there almost anytime the mood struck.

Two blocks up, she stopped to fish out her keys at the door that opened into her apartment's lobby. She'd just gotten them out of her purse when a guy who must have been walking behind her came to a stop a couple of steps back.

"Maria?"

The breeze had faded away, and the night had become still. There was plenty of light from the lobby and the streetlamps. She could hear salsa music from another bar a block back and around the corner, where she'd passed a group of partiers. Even with her police training and a well-tuned awareness of the specific dangers for a woman walking alone at night, she was relaxed after the Manhattans and lulled by the nearby foot traffic. It never occurred to her to be afraid.

She turned around.

The second good-looking guy of the night. Maybe, she thought, she should take the hint and see where it went. She smiled at him. "Yes? Do I know you?"

Too late, she saw his hand start up. She may have registered the flash of metal reflecting some of the ambient light for the half second it took for the gun to be in her face.

She never heard the shot.

41

In the attorney's visiting room at the jail, Hal Chase slid down in his chair, his arms crossed over his chest. It was a few minutes after nine A.M. He was, of course, in his orange jumpsuit. He hadn't shaved yet, and his stubble was dark. His hair looked like he'd combed it with a towel. Having slept poorly, he squinted at Hardy through bloodshot eyes. His voice was phlegmy and weary, not much more than a whisper. "I don't understand what you're trying to say."

"I'm asking if you and Katie talked a lot when you were at work."

"When?"

"Any time."

"Why do you want to know that?"

"I'm collecting information," Hardy said. "Let's go with that for now."

"I don't know what you mean by a lot. Once or twice a day? Lunchtime?"

"More than that."

Hal closed his eyes. Hardy saw his chest rise and fall. When he opened them, he said, "No."

"There wasn't a period of time when you had to talk a lot? Maybe right after you had your first child?"

Hal shook his head. "We're not encouraged to take or make private calls at work. To get to a phone, you have to come off the tier. If it's incoming, a deputy has to get you and cover your station while you're on the phone. If it's outgoing, you've got to find a deputy. Either way, it's a major disturbance. I might have called her, or she might have called me, a couple of times with emergencies, or what seemed like emergencies. Ellen once swallowed a good part of a bottle of Tylenol. Katie called me then, and I met her at the hospital."

"No," Hardy said. "It wasn't like that. It was like ten times a day."

Hal almost laughed. "No way. No fucking way." He straightened up a little. "You want to tell me what this is about?"

Hardy told him about Glitsky and the phone records. When he finished, Hal had slumped back down, his visage closed and tight. "Son of a bitch," he said. "This was just after Ellen?"

"Apparently."

"That was our worst time. I mean, absolutely the worst. We couldn't say two words without fighting. That's when she started seeing your wife, wasn't it?"

"Pretty much," Hardy said.

"Yeah, well, if I was going to kill her, you know, that's when I would have done it. But I wanted her to get happy again. So who was she calling?"

Hardy shrugged and looked at him for a long moment. Then, "I was hoping you could tell me. Why did you just say 'son of a bitch'?"

"You're saying she had a thing with somebody here. Somebody I work with."

"I'm not saying anything, Hal. I'm asking if you ever suspected anything like that. Then or now."

Hal blew out heavily. "We never socialized with anybody from here. I mean never. Katie didn't want anything to do with . . . anyone from here. Somehow I made the cut. But the rest of the guys? To Katie, they were a lower life-form." He took a beat. "You know this happened?"

"I know the phone calls happened."

"Did she tell your wife something? Something Katie told her?"

Hardy hesitated, then came out with it. "It came up, but only recently."

Hal pulled himself upright, righteously angry, the volume way up. "She was fucking somebody here at the jail? She admitted that?"

"She told Frannie she was seeing somebody. She didn't say he was from here, but we've got the phone calls. They may be unconnected. We don't know." Hardy leaned in and lowered his voice. "I've got to ask you something else. I need you to tell me everything you know about this Alanos Tussaint matter."

If Hardy had hauled off and slugged him, Hal wouldn't have shown more surprise. His eyes darted around the room. "I don't know anything about that."

Hardy waited until Hal's gaze settled, then locked in to it. "Well, Hal, that's just patently untrue."

"It isn't. It's the goddamn whole truth."

"Hal." Hardy drew in a breath. "Listen to me. Daniel Dunne told the Homicide inspectors that your motive for killing Katie was that she was threatening to expose your role in the cover-up around Tussaint, if not his actual murder. So how did Daniel know about it — how did he even imagine it? — if he didn't hear it from Katie? And she had to have heard it either from you —"

"Or from somebody else who works here,"

Hal said, "who was making up shit on me."

Hardy acknowledged the point with a nod. "All right. So which was it? And if it's the second case, who would have done that?"

Hal uncrossed his arms, got to his feet, and walked over to the glass block wall. Hardy remained in his seat, watching and waiting. At last, Hal turned and came back to the table, where he rested his weight on his palms. "First thing," he said, "is that I never laid eyes on Alanos Tussaint. I had nothing to do with him getting killed. I'd barely heard about it when Burt Cushing had me and a few other guards up to his office and told us that if anybody asked, all of us had spent the entire afternoon the day before — one o'clock to five o'clock — transporting inmates down to San Bruno and bringing some back. He told six of us, including Adam Foster. Did we have any questions?"

"Did you?"

"Nope."

"But you told Katie?"

Hal looked over his shoulder, then came back to Hardy. "The whole thing was getting out of control. It was, like, the third or fourth time this year, covering up for Foster. Yes, I told Katie about it. I also told her that I was thinking of trying to get transferred out to Evictions, not that they don't have problems, but at least I'd be out of the jail. Then maybe, down the line a ways, I could leave the department altogether, maybe get into another line of work."

"How did Katie feel about that?"

"She thought it was a great idea. Couldn't be too soon."

"Did she threaten to tell anyone else about this or your role in it?"

"Why would she do that?"

"Her brother said she'd do it to ruin you if you left her."

"No. She wouldn't have."

"I'm just telling you what we're hearing."

"Well, that's Daniel, and he doesn't know. The thing that bothered her wasn't the cover-ups so much as what we were covering up for, the actual stuff going on here."

Hardy found himself lowering his voice. "Which is what?"

"Uh-uh," Hal said. "We're not going there. That's got nothing to do with me."

"I hate to tell you, Hal, but yes, it does. I need to know."

Hal shook his head. "With all respect, counselor, you don't need to know anything about that, whatever it is. You can believe me or not, I'm not involved in any of it. I come in and do my job, and so do most of the rest of the guys. We hear about some of this stuff, but we keep our mouths shut, and usually, it's under control and doesn't hurt anybody."

"Except when it's not and it does."

Another shrug. "Shit happens. It's a closed system."

"Katie wasn't in the system, and she knew what was happening."

"I guess you could say that."

"Okay. So maybe she had trouble dealing with the idea that people were getting killed here in the jail and nobody was doing anything about it. Maybe she wasn't going to threaten you with exposure, but she brought it up to somebody else, let him know what she knew."

"The guy she was calling."

Hardy pulled at the knot of his tie. "Did she know Burt Cushing personally, Hal?"

"No. Not really. I mean . . ."

Hardy could see it all falling together in Hal's mind, as it was in his own. "You mean she only knew him as your boss? Department picnics, like that?"

"Not exactly. He had a problem getting medicine for his daughter's acne a few years ago, and she met with him and the daughter a few times and . . ." Hal stopped. "Son of a bitch," he said.

His jaw set, Hardy nodded. "Right," he said.

42

Wes Farrell had been awake since he'd gotten the call from Homicide at around one o'clock that morning, telling him that Maria — sweet, ambitious, smart Maria — had been killed in an apparent robbery. They'd taken her purse; police found it in the gutter around the corner with her driver's license but no credit cards or cash. Even though there was a reasonable amount of foot traffic on Nineteenth Street — 911 fielded seven calls in the immediate aftermath — there had been no witnesses to the crime. People heard the shot and came running, but the perpetrator had fled, leaving no signs.

Wes wasn't particularly tired, but he couldn't seem to get his brain to focus. He'd canceled all of his morning meetings. In a minute, he was planning to draw the blinds in his office and lie down, but until he found the energy to commit to even that, he passed the time by mindlessly pumping a Nerf basketball at the basket hanging from a bookshelf. He'd been doing the same thing, over and over, for the past twenty minutes.

Treya's familiar knock, almost inaudible, startled him back to where he was. Before he had a chance to say anything, she opened the door a crack, swung into the office, and closed the door behind her.

"You're awake," she said. "I thought you might be sleeping."

"No. But I'm a zombie."

"Are you still not seeing anybody?"

"Like who?"

"Dismas Hardy's out here. He says it's important."

"Of course he does." Farrell realized that he was still holding the Nerf ball, so he took another shot at the basket and missed. "Oh, hell, Treya, he's here, just let him in."

Hardy hadn't gotten two steps into the room before he stopped and looked his former law partner up and down. "What's happened?"

Farrell almost couldn't get the words out. "One of my investigators got killed last night. Maria Solis-Martinez. Excellent kid. Sweet as sugar. It makes me sick to my stomach."

"Something to do with work?"

"No. Random robbery. Shot her in the face, grabbed her purse, and ran, the asshole. Did I once say I didn't believe in the death penalty? I get my hands on who did this to her, I'll shoot him myself."

"I'm sorry, Wes."

"Yeah. I'm sorry, too." He drew a deep breath, shook his head in dismay, raised his hand as though he was going to say something else, then let it fall. "Treya said you had something important?"

"It might be. I think so. It's why I came right up."

"Up from where?"

"The jail. Hal Chase."

"The jail, the jail, the fucking jail. And Hal Chase. I already told you it was out of my hands, Diz. The grand jury has spoken, and I'm not in the mood to argue about it. If you don't like the case against him, get him an early trial date and convince a jury to acquit him, but meanwhile . . ." Farrell's anger finally caught up with him, and he raised his voice. "Meanwhile, I've got a few things on my plate here, and I'm having just a little trouble trying to deal with any of them. Is that clear enough for you?"

Hardy waited a long three-count, then took a seat on the coffee table. "I'm not here

306

to argue about the grand jury."

Wes, who looked wrung out by his little explosion, inclined his head toward Hardy and sat on the arm of a stuffed chair. "Didn't you just say you were here to talk about the grand jury? Your man's indictment?"

"No," Hardy said. "That's probably what you expected to hear, so you actually thought you heard it, but all I said was I'd come up here from visiting Hal Chase in jail."

"Jesus Christ, you can wear a guy down, Diz, you know that?"

"That's not my intention, especially right now. I'm sorry about your investigator. I can come back another time, no sweat. But you need to hear what I've got, and the sooner the better."

"All right. What?"

Hardy started from the beginning: the bare fact of Katie's affair, corroborated independently by Daniel. On to Glitsky's discovery of the telephone records and the dozens of calls to the jail, where her husband not only did not receive those calls but where his use of the telephone was severely discouraged. Hardy concluded with a few words about Burt Cushing's daughter and her acne problems, which had put the sheriff into close contact with Katie Chase, at about the time she was conducting an affair and speaking to someone at the jail numerous times a day. In conclusion, he said, "It turns out the number she was calling wasn't Hal's, on the tier, but Burt Cushing's main office number."

By the time he'd finished, Farrell had slid down off the arm and into the chair. "I already know the answer," he said, "but have you come across anything like evidence that they were having this affair?"

"Just the phone calls."

"Lots of people talk to each other on the phone. That doesn't mean they're having sex."

"Granted. But ten times a day?"

"Did they meet somewhere that might have a record of it? Photos of them checking in together at some motel? Witnesses?"

Hardy didn't bother answering, just shook his head.

"So why are you telling me this?" Farrell asked.

"Because you need to know it."

"No, I don't. How long has it been since this alleged affair ended?"

"Couple of years."

"And you think, I gather, that it's relevant to her murder?"

Hardy stared across at his friend.

Eventually, Farrell raised a hand and, with his thumb and forefinger, pressed at his eyes, left them there for a moment, then brought the hand down and stared at the ceiling. "You know this investigator of mine, Maria?" he asked. "You know what I said about her death being unrelated to her work? I lied." He took a deep breath. "She'd just volunteered to reopen the investigation into Alanos Tussaint's death. You know about that?"

"A little hearsay."

Farrell filled him in on the rest: Luther Jones's recanted testimony, the possibility that he was close to cutting a deal to testify again.

"Which I guess won't be happening now, will it?"

Farrell seemed almost glassy-eyed. "I think I need to call in the FBI, although that's pretty much admitting that I've lost control of the situation, if I ever had any. Did I actually campaign for this job?"

Hardy hesitated. "Hal told me that this was the third or fourth time this year."

"For what, exactly?"

"For Cushing pulling in a handful of guys — Hal was one of them — and giving them the story they were to tell if anybody came

309

around asking questions about accidents that happened in the jail. He didn't know about the accidents themselves, hadn't been in the vicinity at all —"

"But of course he would say that."

Hardy shrugged. "The point is, Katie knew about them, too. And she wanted to be important, wanted to do something worthwhile with her life, not just be a stay-at-home mom."

"How do you know that?"

"She was one of Frannie's clients. Self-esteem was one of her big issues."

Farrell cocked his head. "Are you shitting me? Your wife's client?"

"Cross my heart."

Farrell shook his head in disbelief. "So you're saying that when Katie finds out about these alleged murders in the jail, maybe she calls her former lover and asks about them and threatens to expose what's been going on?"

"Yep. Maybe."

"Did she talk about any of this stuff with Frannie? Specifically? Did she say she was going to threaten somebody — this former lover of hers, maybe the sheriff himself — who worked at the jail?"

"No. Not that I know of."

"But you're saying maybe she did, and

then maybe because she did that, he had a motive to kill her? To shut her up?"

Hardy held his ground. "Not impossible," he said.

"Maybe not in the ultimate cosmic sense," Farrell replied, "but so unlikely that it is beneath contemplation. Truly. If that's going to be part of your working theory on your client's defense, you ought to cut a plea right now and call it a day, Diz. I'm serious." Farrell all but collapsed into his easy chair. He shook his head wearily. "What am I ragging on you about? I'm getting a pretty clear picture of what's going on here. Do I think part of it might have extended out to Katie's death? Could have. Do I think it also has something to do with Maria? Goddamn, I hope not. There is no evidence at all either way, which is a big problem when you have law enforcement officers like Hal Chase turning to crime. I just don't know how to go about any of this, except calling in the feds, which is something I really don't want to do."

"On that note," Hardy said, "I do have an idea."

He didn't get to tell Farrell his idea just yet. The telephone rang, and Wes shook his head — more interruptions, more exhaustion — then picked up the receiver. "Yes," he said. "Yes. All right. Yes, I hear you."

He hung up. His shoulders all but collapsed. "Luther Jones is dead. Heroin OD in the jail."

43

Glitsky had told everybody who wanted to listen that Patti Orosco just didn't sing for him as a valid suspect in the murder of Katie Chase. Nevertheless, with the client now in jail, the clock was ticking, and he owed it to the integrity of his investigation to pursue all leads until he was satisfied that they led nowhere. In actual fact, he hadn't pushed hard for answers to any difficult questions from the beautiful millionaire.

After examining his conscience on the matter, he realized there were three reasons for his prejudice in favor of Patti: In his heart, Glitsky didn't quite believe it, but he knew Hal might have killed his wife; second, he couldn't get any connection established between Katie's two-year-old affair and her recent death; finally, Patti was so darn sweet, cooperative, and pretty.

By admitting to her affair with Hal as soon as Abe and the Homicide cops had started circling around it, she'd taken away their big "Aha!" moment. She knew how bad it looked, how it cast them both in a less than flattering light, but what could she do? It was the truth, she said. They had been driven into each other's arms by Hal's emotionally disturbed wife. They were deeply in love, but in spite of that, a month before Katie's death, they'd ultimately decided to end their deception and do the right thing. Though the breakup hadn't been her idea, and it was still extraordinarily painful for her day to day, her nobler self had prevailed. Surely all the inspectors could understand.

She was a good person caught in a bad situation, and all she wanted was Hal to be all right. She herself was getting by — strong, sad, selfless, and truthful.

As a preemptive strike against the thought that she might be a suspect in Katie's murder, her attitude and admissions were inordinately effective. But seen in an objective light, uncolored by her sweet personality and physical beauty, her behavior could also be read as brazen, brilliant, and manipulative in the extreme. When Abe had called to make this appointment, she'd told him that she'd make the time for her "favorite almost-policeman." With a little laugh.

It was a bit too familiar.

Could she really be manipulating him, playing him for a sucker?

The possibility, and the fact that it had taken him so long to acknowledge it, had Glitsky's back up as he searched for a parking space near her home. He didn't like being fooled, but that he had not even considered her planning and perfectly executing a scam on him before today was something that galled him.

If it was a scam, he reminded himself.

Maybe it wasn't. Maybe she was all she seemed to be.

Though most people weren't.

He had argued with Hardy that if Patti had killed Katie to get Hal all to herself, that left Hal hanging out in the breeze as the prime suspect, which wouldn't have been to her advantage. Likewise, if they'd planned the crime together, he would certainly have arranged it so their respective alibis were bulletproof.

Those arguments left out one other contingency. Patti, a woman cruelly and recently scorned (regardless of the spin she put on it), might very well have been jealous of Katie and, because he had dumped her, hated Hal.

Killing Katie might have been a cold-blooded, carefully planned, perfectly executed murder, and Glitsky had been so charmed and bamboozled that he hadn't ever considered that as a viable possibility. Now that thought — that she was playing him like every other man in her life and probably many of the women — wouldn't go away. He heard the pumping of angry blood in his ears.

It didn't help that the eventual parking spot Glitsky found was at the corner of Van Ness, two long, steep downhill blocks from her place. By the time he rang her bell, he was breathing hard. He could feel the tightness in his jawline, his lips compressed, the scar through them no doubt in high relief. He dragged a hand over his forehead to remove the sheen of sweat.

She came into view at the top of the stairs behind the glass front door. She all but skipped down to open her door. Again she was barefoot — Abe realized that except at the funeral, he'd never seen her wearing anything on her feet — and she wore a black Japanese-looking outfit, silk pants and a matching short tunic buttoned to her throat. Her navel gleamed with a demurely visible diamond.

Stunning.

Opening the door, she favored him with

her generous and sincere smile. Immediately, her expression changed to one of concern as she read the obvious signs of his exertion. "Are you all right?"

"Fine. That's just a bit of a climb."

"I know. The parking here is murder. When you called, I should have told you to park in front of my garage. I'm sorry. I always forget to tell people."

"It's okay," Glitsky said. "I can use the exercise."

"Can't we all?" She half turned away, then turned back and gave him another smile. "Fourteen more steps to the top. You good?"

Glitsky couldn't help it. He felt his face break into a tight smile. "Lead on."

The tunic ended just above her waist, and the pants clung to her body. As he followed her up the steps, the shape of her ass made Glitsky wonder briefly if all of his rationalization about not having pushed her enough in his investigation was a flimsy excuse to spend time in her company again.

She led him into the living room and insisted that Abe sit in one of her comfortable chairs while she got him some water with ice and a wedge of lemon. Handing him the glass, she settled herself across from him sideways on her couch, one leg tucked under the other knee, her arm extended over the back of the sofa.

"Comfy?" she asked.

"Perfect, thank you."

"Before we start, can I ask you a question?"

"Sure."

"Are you married?"

A chuckle bubbled up out of Glitsky's chest. "Pardon me?"

She pointed. "I see you've got a ring on. But you could be wearing that to discourage women from hitting on you."

Still chuckling, Glitsky said, "No." He held up his ring hand. "That's a bona fide wedding ring. Why do you ask?"

"Just a pet theory of mine. All the good ones are already married. Witness you. Witness Hal."

"Well, I . . . Thank you, I guess."

"You're welcome."

"And thanks for agreeing to talk to me again." Lord, he thought, disgusted with himself, was he flirting with her?

"Of course," she said. "However I can help." And then, as though the thought had just occurred to her, "I can't believe they've got Hal in jail. I'm going down to see him later today. Do you know anything about where they're keeping him?"

"Away from everybody else," Glitsky said.

"You don't have to worry about him being safe. They don't put former guards in with inmates."

"That's a relief. It was . . . I thought . . ." She shrugged. "I didn't know."

"He'll be fine." Glitsky sipped at his water. "I wanted to talk to you a little bit about Katie, if you don't mind."

"Oh. Okay."

This was clearly not the direction she was expecting. Glitsky, knowing that he was on a true fishing expedition, felt compelled to explain if he didn't want to lose her. "We've eliminated Hal as a suspect," he began, "and, frankly, most of the inner circle of their acquaintances. It's time to widen the net, and the more we know about Katie, the further along we'll be." This was, as one of Glitsky's old professors used to say, vague enough to be true, and it seemed to work: Patti nodded in acquiescence, all co-operation again. Glitsky went on. "She was your best friend?"

"Since college, yes."

"And you saw her and Hal with some regularity?"

"A couple of times a month, at least. Which was much less than before."

"Because you had come into all this money?"

"I think so. Especially after Katie stopped working, when they were struggling. I think they felt what had happened to me was unfair. And I guess in a way, it was. In any case, things became . . . awkward."

"You say they felt it was unfair. So it was both of them?"

She thought for a short moment. "No. I didn't mean 'they.' Hal never turned sour on me. Although he had to be cool about it. He couldn't get too enthusiastic. About me, I mean." She brushed a wisp of hair back from her forehead. "I think Katie might have stopped seeing me if she'd been on her own. Except there wasn't any reason to other than . . . my situation. We never had a fight or anything, but she felt guilty. That was her whole life the last year or two. She felt guilty about everything. Not being nice to me, not trusting Hal with the kids, not working, not being a good enough mom, not making enough money. Everything."

"That sounds tiring."

"It wasn't good," Patti said. "It really wasn't good."

"Do you think the way she was acting might have particularly alienated anyone?"

"Enough that they'd want to kill her? I can't imagine that."

"But somebody did kill her."

"I know. I'm not forgetting that." She nodded, blinking her suddenly tearful eyes a couple of times. "I still can't get used to it. It's completely surreal. I mean, there was no reason for something that final and desperate."

Glitsky sat back, pausing. "All right. So let me ask you this. When you were together with Hal, can you remember anything he said that, when you think about it now, raises a flag? Was anything bothering him?"

This brought a kind of winsome chuckle. "Well, being with me bothered him. It bothered both of us."

Glitsky nodded. "Anything else?"

She frowned out at her view. "All the issues with child care, I guess. But that was more a hassle than anything."

"You mean that Katie wouldn't use babysitters?"

"That's not completely true. She'd let her mom or one of her sisters come by when she went out by herself. But when she'd get back, it would turn out that everything they did was wrong — they didn't get the right food, or enough of it, or they watched the wrong video, or God forbid they got off schedule . . ." She stopped, turned her face toward him. "It was so stupid. Katie knew it was stupid. It was one of the reasons she was going to counseling. And that was with her own family. Imagine how she was with everybody else."

"You mean Ruth? Hal's mom?"

"Hal's stepmother, not mom," she corrected him. "She didn't raise Hal as a baby, only his brother, and look how Warren's turning out. So, no, thank you. Ruth was not in the babysitter pool."

Glitsky, having witnessed a small sampling of Ruth's child-rearing skills, thought that Katie's lack of enthusiasm for her mother-in-law's babysitting help was probably well placed. But he was not here to pursue phantoms among the larger circle of Hal's and Katie's families and acquaintances. He was here to lull Patti Orosco into a false sense of security so that he could question her about Katie's murder with her defenses down. "All right," he said. "Moving on. Maybe his work?"

She shook her head. "He didn't talk about that too much. It was a job. I gather there were politics and other kinds of the usual BS, but it wasn't like he was a complaining guy. Honestly, this kind of stuff — the families and his job and kids and all that — wasn't what we talked about most of the time."

"No. I can see that." Glitsky picked up his

glass, drank some water, put it down, and then reached into his back pocket for a small notebook. "How do you feel about helping me with a little investigatory housekeeping?"

"Fine." She smiled. "I'll help you any way I can."

"Do you mind talking again about the night of Katie's death?" He indicated the notebook. "Written reports are my life."

"No problem. Shoot."

"The movie you went to?"

"Life of Pi."

"And where was it playing again?"

"The AMC down on Van Ness."

"You drove? Walked?"

She had to think for a beat. "I walked there. I took a cab back."

"Do you recall the cab company?"

She closed her eyes, thought, shook her head. "I don't think so." Then, "Is this about my alibi? Am I a suspect?"

"It would be nice," Glitsky said, "if we had some clear corroboration, that's all. You don't by any chance have the ticket stub, do you? Or maybe you met somebody there who could verify your presence?"

She brought her feet down and came around to face him, a hurt look on her face. "So I am a suspect. You're working for Hal, and you want to find somebody else who might have killed Katie."

"I am working for Hal's lawyer, but as to whether you're a suspect, there is an entire universe of suspects. My goal is to eliminate as many as I can, beginning with those who are most likely innocent." He gave her his good-cop smile. "I'd love it if you had your stub or ran into somebody you knew in the lobby."

She sat back, collected herself. "I didn't meet anybody. And I looked for the ticket stub last time. I don't have it."

"Okay." Glitsky let things cool down for a second, then said, "You're not going to like this one, either. Do you now or have you ever owned a firearm?"

She sighed deeply. "Yes. A Smith and Wesson. Registered. A three-fifty-seven Magnum. I haven't shot it in about five years. I don't know why I still have it. It's in my closet in a gun safe I bought at the same time I got the gun. Do you want me to go get it?"

"Sure," Glitsky said. "Better, maybe, is if you could show me where it is."

"You mean so I don't get it and come out and shoot you with it?"

Glitsky tried an apologetic smile. "That's one of the reasons."

"Unbelievable," she said.

They got up and walked to her bedroom at the back of the house. She'd made the bed. The room smelled like sandalwood. Everything was neat, organized, and tasteful. On her dresser, she had a framed color snapshot of Hal Chase. "I've never denied I love the man," she said when she realized Glitsky had seen it, "but I wouldn't kill for anybody."

The gun came as advertised. Since a .357 Magnum revolver would shoot a .38 Special round, Glitsky knew that it might be the murder weapon. On the other hand, the fact that she would so blithely hand it over to him seemed to radically diminish that possibility. If she had killed someone with that weapon, in all probability, she would have disposed of it soon thereafter. It was clean, oiled, and unloaded, with no scent of gunpowder. When Patti put the gun away and closed the safe, she turned around, looking up at Abe. "Is that it?" she asked. "Are we done?"

"I have one more question. What kind of car do you drive?"

"A BMW M3. Do you want to see that, too? What's my car got to do with anything?"

"Ms. Orosco. Patti. Please understand. It's

325

not what I think. It's what I've got the evidence to support. To get Hal off, I need something from you, from any potential suspect, that makes it possible that you killed Katie. Or something that completely eliminates you as a suspect, that makes it impossible that you killed her. I haven't seen that yet. If you can think of anything, no matter how small or seemingly insignificant, it would make my day. Truly."

"You mean my car doesn't do me any good, either?"

"Not by itself, no. Have you had it cleaned recently?"

"Only a few days ago. I got it detailed. It's a great car. I like to keep it perfect. But let me guess, that's the wrong answer, too."

Glitsky shrugged, and she led him back not to the living room, but to the top of the staircase, obviously bringing the interview to an end. She turned and faced him. "You know," she said, "I had an affair with Hal. I'm not so proud of that. But I'm a good person. And you've sat and talked to me a couple of times, and I've been honest and forthcoming with you, and you still think I'm capable of killing somebody who was a friend of mine?"

Glitsky had seen enough as a cop to believe in his heart that everybody was capable of killing someone, given the right set of circumstances. He said, "It's not that I think it. It's that I can't prove you didn't."

"You think I could, though. Kill somebody. I can tell. You look right at me, and you can't see who I am at all." She shook her head, touched his arm, brushed a tear from her eye, and shook her head again. "I feel so sorry for you," she said. "I really do."

44

Much more worn down by his interview with Patti Orosco than he'd expected to be, Glitsky was more than surly when he sat down in Hardy's office at a few minutes before noon. "Well," he said with sarcasm, "I really appreciate your calling me as soon as you knew this was about Cushing. Except if you had, then I wouldn't have gotten to go out and ruin Patti Orosco's day, which was a really good time. So thanks."

"Hey, we thought it might have been Cushing last night."

"But you *knew* it this morning."

"Excuse me all to hell, but it's not a hundred percent. I wasn't as sure as I am now until I talked to Hal, and afterward, I needed to talk to Wes more than I needed to tell you. It's not necessarily about Cushing anyway."

Glitsky cocked his head. "What part's not about him? I just listened to you for ten minutes, and all of it seemed to be about him. Farrell really thinks Cushing killed his investigator?"

"Not Cushing but one of his guys. If Hal's right, it's probably Foster."

"The chief deputy. I know him. And I don't use the word 'prick' or that's what I'd call him. What's Homicide say?"

"Not much, not yet. Murder in the commission of a robbery, so far. I guess they're writing off Luther Jones as a coincidence. Me, personally, I'm going to write that off as un-fucking-likely."

"Because she'd just started on the Tussaint thing?"

"It's quite a large coincidence, Abe. Too large to ignore. And combine that with the new information that it looks like it was Cushing who hooked up with Katie Chase. It's starting to resemble a case, you must admit."

"Farrell isn't tempted to let Hal go, is he?"

Hardy shook his head. "No chance. Too many headlines already. He'd look like a trigger-happy idiot, to say nothing of the fact that he'd have to talk about his new favorite suspects, which would pretty much tip them off. And there's no new evidence on Katie's murder. So Hal sits where he is. Oh, and P.S.: He isn't talking about covering up anything, and he's denying whatever he might have told me. The jail is a well-run and orderly place, and Burt Cushing is a saint."

Glitsky said at last, "This murder last night. Thirty-eight?"

"Nope. Forty. Common law enforcement service weapon." Hardy nodded. "I know, there are a million of them. But still."

"So what's Wes going to do?"

"He was thinking about calling in the FBI and going after the big boys themselves — Cushing and Foster — but he doesn't want to give up the jurisdiction, which is basically admitting that he's no good at his job. Plus, he liked this girl Maria, so it's personal. He wants to take these bastards down. But if he calls the FBI, what's he going to tell them? He thinks the sheriff is a bad, bad man? He's got nothing, and with Luther Jones dead, even less nothing than he had before."

"How did you get involved?"

"Hal. The cases are now related, at least tangentially."

"Okay. And so?"

"So I told Wes we'd do what we could . . ."

"We?"

"You and me. Us."

"What is it exactly that you think I'm going to be doing, Diz? I'm an unlicensed private investigator working for a murder defendant. You may have met him. His name is Hal Chase. So now somehow I'm supposed to get involved in the murder of an undercover DA investigator and, oh, by the way, the investigation of an accidental overdose in the jail. Let's not even talk about the fact that the SFPD is going to be on both cases. I've got to think they'll take at least a superficial look at Luther Jones, especially under these circumstances. So I'm supposed to do what? Dress up like Superman and use my powers to break the cases?" Glitsky shook his head. "It's completely ridiculous. You're out of your mind."

"I like the Superman thing, but I have a better idea," Hardy said. "I've talked to Wes Farrell. If you want it, you're his newest investigator. And guess what your first three cases are."

Glitsky still balked. "This is way more than I signed up for. It's exactly what Treya didn't want me to do: get involved with dead people and the very bad people who made them dead. Anyway, I'm working for you. How can I work for the prosecution and the defense on the same case?"

"Simple," Hardy said. "Hal and I will waive confidentiality. You follow the evidence where it leads. The chips fall."

"You're still out of your mind," Glitsky said.

"Your friend Mr. Glitsky still thinks it might have been me." Patti Orosco sat on one of the dozen hard wooden chairs in the jail's public visiting room, looking through the booth's window at Hal, talking through the speaker in the glass. Correctly guessing that she would be conspicuous among the other visitors in her black Japanese suit, she had changed into jeans with a white collared shirt and a green pullover sweater.

"He's not my friend," Hal said. "He finds something that gets me out of here, he can be my friend. Till then, he's just a guy working for my lawyer."

"What about your lawyer?" she asked. "What's he doing?"

"Hardy? Same as Glitsky, I suppose. Trying to get traction with another theory. Any other theory."

"Even me? Do they really think it could have been me?"

"We haven't talked about it, Patti. I know it wasn't you, if that's any consolation. If they're bothering you, I could tell them to back off."

"I don't know if you'll need to do that,

332

but it's just so frustrating. Wasting time talking to me when there's somebody else . . ."

"What do they want from you?"

"To come up with something that proves I was where I said I was that night. It makes me wish I'd done something else, some little thing, but I just went to the movies, watched the movie, probably bought popcorn, since I always do. Nothing memorable at all."

"I'm in the same boat," Hal said. "I tell myself, if I'd just talked to the bartender, if I'd just stopped for gas. If, if, if . . . but here I am."

They stared at each other through the glass.

"I miss you," she said.

"I miss you, too."

"What are we going to do about us, Hal? Is there even going to be an us?"

"I don't know."

"Do you want there to be?"

Hal scanned the area around them. Bleak and bleaker. "As long as I'm here, that seems a little moot, doesn't it?"

"Not to me. Do you have any sense of how long they're going to keep you?"

Hal started to give her the short version of what Hardy had told him. He'd stay under arrest, no bail, until the trial, which might be coming up sooner rather than later, since that gave the prosecution less time to assemble its case, which appeared to be fatally flawed for lack of physical evidence. "But maybe not so fatally that they won't convict me anyway."

"Have they gotten anything at all? Hardy, I mean, and Glitsky."

"If they're still questioning you, I've got to think not. Except, oh . . ." Hal's effort at a wry smile crumbled under its own weight. "I don't know if this is good or bad or neither, but it seems they've dug up something that ought to make you and me feel a little better, at least."

"What's that?"

"Evidently, Katie was fooling around, too."

Patti sat back. "You're kidding me. When?"

"A couple of years ago, just after Ellen was born."

Patti was silent for a few seconds. "What does that mean?"

"I don't know. Other than I can stop beating myself up so badly over us. So can you."

"I haven't been," she said. "I'd do it again. Wouldn't you, too, if you were honest?"

He nodded. "It just makes me look so guilty. Of killing her, I mean."

"But you didn't, so . . ."

"So without you and me as a couple, I'm

not in here, not yet, at least. If we hadn't admitted it . . ." He met her eyes, then lowered his gaze. "I don't know."

"It would have come out, Hal. Just like Katie's has come out. Then you're a liar on top of all the other suspicion."

"Better than a killer." He waved away the thought. "It doesn't matter. It's done."

Patti looked down, her hands in her lap. "Do you know who it was? With Katie? Might it matter?"

"Hardy's got an idea who it is, and it might matter," he said. "It's probably better if we don't talk about it until we're sure."

"So he, this guy, might have still been seeing her?"

"Not impossible."

"If he was," she said, "that could be important."

"Yes. Hardy doesn't want to say it and get my hopes up, but it could be the ball game." He leaned in toward the speaker. "But we don't know anything for sure, and in any event, we need to nail it down. At least it's something."

"You'll tell me the minute you know something? Promise?"

He nodded. "The minute," he said.

To the casual observer, Nat Glitsky was an

old white man with wispy white hair, iceberg-blue eyes, and a somewhat shuffling gait. His clothes didn't fit him because he bought the sizes that had always worked, even though he'd shortened up and thinned out considerably over the past few years. Now he checked in at five-eight or -nine, one-forty-five. Even a short conversation with this octogenarian, however, revealed a feisty and opinionated personality, a wide-ranging intellect (he'd all but memorized the Torah), and a soft-spoken gentleness that seemed to belie his other attributes.

Abe had left Hardy's office not knowing whether to be amused or outraged by his friend's apparently serious suggestion that he join the district attorney's Investigations Division as an inspector. The irony was that he would have taken that job in a heartbeat if Wes had offered it only a few weeks ago. Maybe, because it was Hardy's idea, he felt pressured, even coerced. But he could not deny that he was starting to care a lot about this case, following his own rhythm. It had somehow gotten into his bloodstream. He had something to prove about himself: He was still a more than competent investigator. After he'd spent a lifetime following strict procedures and protocols, he found the freedom to investigate in his own way more than appealing.

But in a larger sense, Glitsky had to admit that Hardy's proposed strategy might produce the evidence that would free Hal Chase. It was bold and unorthodox, and it might bring down a corrupt sheriff and his henchmen in the bargain.

By the time he'd turned onto his father's block in the inner Richmond, Glitsky found that the idea appealed to him. For the better part of the last two weeks, he'd been working on this elusive murder case. He was in his element, he knew: what hc was born to do. And now his own efforts — the jail connection with Katie's lover — had unearthed what appeared to be the first legitimate clue that might lead him to the killer, or at least to a new line of questioning. Was he ready to abandon his search right when it appeared that it was getting him someplace? Right now it looked as though deciding not to pursue Burt Cushing would amount to just that, and he might as well drop out of the investigation altogether.

"So," Abe said when he'd finished laying out his situation, "there you have it."

Father and son were sitting in Nat's small sun-dappled living room, Abe in a rocker and Nat in a lounger across from him. Sadie, Nat's wife for nearly a decade, was out visiting some girlfriends.

"Got it. What's your question?"

"I don't think Hardy has any right to put me in that position."

"That's not a question."

"Close enough."

"Does he have that right? Sure, you two go way back. He can ask you anything. Then you can answer however you want."

"Of course. But you know what bothers me most? I have a hunch that if I'd come up with the idea, I'd think it was brilliant."

"So the idea itself is good?"

"The idea is the only place the sheriff and our client intersect. Hardy's theory is that the sheriff had this other investigator killed last night, made it look like a robbery gone wrong. He's also covering up at least one other murder in the jail. That's two people we're almost certain he's had killed. Maybe several more. It's not that great a stretch to think he might have had Hal's wife killed as well."

"Why would he have done that?"

"Because she'd called to threaten him with what she knew."

"Why would she do that? Wouldn't she have known that he'd come to shut her up?"

"Maybe she thought she had influence over him, that he was still in love with her.

338

Maybe she called to warn him that it had to stop. That if it didn't, she'd have to tell somebody."

"A busybody, this woman?"

Abe shrugged. "Mostly confused and unhappy. A buttinsky, we used to say."

"And she butted in at the wrong time to the wrong guy?"

"That's the theory. Here's the problem. We have no proof the sheriff did anything. Katie's murder has virtually no trail. So we're stuck. Unless we connect him to Hal, which now it looks like we might be able to do. The thing is, if he sees anybody coming, he smells it a million miles away. The only way investigating him works is if it looks like I am — or somebody in the same position is — investigating something else entirely. Of course, a little slip and . . . it might be fatal."

"So what's your problem?"

"I don't know, Dad. Something about having a wife and two kids at home."

"What? You didn't have them before? I seem to remember you worked in the Homicide Department."

"Treya thought I was done with that."

"What were you doing these last two weeks?"

Abe made a face. "You think I should do

it, then?"

Nat held up his hand. "God forbid I tell you what you should do, Abraham. Nobody can make this decision but you."

"I know," Abe said. "I hate that part."

45

Since he was almost out to Frannie's office anyway, Abe decided to try his luck and see if she was in. He got her answering machine when he called, but he hadn't gotten far into the drive home when she called him back, saying she'd been with a client but was free for the next couple of hours if he wanted to come by.

"Diz fired me," he told her as he came into her office. "The good news is that Wes Farrell wants to hire me."

"Diz fired you? Really?"

"No. I'd be doing the same job for Wes. Diz just found a way to have somebody else pay me."

"What brought that about?"

Glitsky gave it to her in broad strokes: the likelihood that Burt Cushing had been Katie's lover, the connection between Hal, Cushing and the cover-up on the murder of Alanos Tussaint, Hal telling Katie about it, the shooting of Maria Solis-Martinez.

By the time he was done, Frannie was sitting on the love seat with her hand over her mouth. "You're telling me somebody shot this poor girl just last night? Because she was looking into this inmate getting killed in the jail?"

"That's our working assumption," he said, "although you should know there is absolutely no sign that we're right. It might have been what it was made to look like, a robbery. But why shoot somebody, and obviously shoot to kill, when you can just grab the purse and run? Not that it doesn't happen, but . . ."

"I don't see why that would work, Abe. Killing her wouldn't make whatever she was working on go away, would it? Why won't they assign her cases, and this particular case, to somebody else?"

"Because it's not about who gets the case. It's about what Luther Jones might have told her. Now, no matter who gets the case next, Luther is absolutely not talking, because he's dead, too. The message is that they don't control things just in the jail. If they can get to her, a cop, walking on the street, they can get to anybody."

"How do you think you're going to get to him? The Luther Jones investigation? Is that the idea?"

"Not exactly. We don't do anything with Luther Jones. Diz and Wes seem to believe that we can hide behind the smokescreen of the Katie Chase investigation, stir the pot at the jail, and force Cushing and Foster to make a wrong step."

"And then what?"

"Well, then it gets interesting. It depends on what they do when they find out they're under active investigation. They'll do something to obstruct it, and that'll be our opening."

"Except if the something they do is decide to kill more investigators."

A corner of Glitsky's mouth rose a quarter inch. "The consensus is that won't happen. In any event, this seems like a reasonably good bet."

"And now you're here." It was a question.

Abe nodded. "I thought we could talk a little more about Katie. You saw her every week for a couple of years. Maybe there's something, some things, in her file. Maybe she told you something she didn't know she knew. I thought if you didn't mind, maybe you and I could spend some time and take a run at finding it."

Glitsky expected a fairly serious and wide-ranging discussion with Treya when she heard he would be going back to work in the DA's Investigations Division. It would mean arranging the daily schedules the way they had been before he'd retired, among other things. Maybe their longtime nanny, Rita, would still be available; if not, they'd have to address that issue as well.

When he got to Wes Farrell's office at four-thirty, as requested, he realized he needn't have worried. Farrell had already called Treya in and sounded her out on the idea, painting the new assignment in the rosiest light. Abe, he had told her, with all of his experience, blah blah blah. He'd be taking over Maria's immediate caseload, but over time, he would move into his specialty, which was homicide. Abe had informally applied for the job before, and now he had it. It was a perfect fit, and Wes was glad Hardy had thought of it.

What did Treya think?

Treya had already aired most of her objections by the time Abe showed up, and she had discovered, to her surprise, that they weren't nearly as substantial as she had been thinking. The plain fact was that Abe hadn't been ready to quit when it had been decided that he needed to; he was bored spending all those hours reading and watching TV at home; he was ready for a new challenge.

She stood up at her desk when he appeared at the office door, came around, and gave him a chaste kiss on the cheek. "You know what this is about?"

"Generally," he said.

"And you want to do it?"

"I wanted to see if you were good with it first."

"The short answer is yes. I've already called Rita, and she's picking up the kids. We can talk about the long answer later tonight. Meanwhile, His Nibs is waiting."

She crossed to Farrell's door, knocked, and opened it for her husband.

After a short congratulatory meeting with Wes Farrell, Abe was on his way down to the office of Dr. Strout, the medical examiner, his mind racing.

He wasn't entirely sure that it was a reasonable strategy, but he did like the fact that he once again would be working as a legitimate cop. He would have a badge and his gun. He could make arrests. And this time, without the caveat that he couldn't pursue the most likely suspect, he could run a righteous murder investigation according to his own instincts, regardless of how Diz or Wes wanted him to proceed.

He also knew that Hardy and Farrell could have all the fine theories in the world about who killed Katie or Maria or Luther, or Alanos Tussaint, for that matter, and all of those theories would amount to nothing if he could not find physical evidence to support them. In the case of Katie's murder, he'd already put in a substantial amount of time and mental energy looking at people other than Hal who might have had means, motive, and opportunity. And he'd come up with nothing.

Now he had another murder victim — Maria — whose death was arguably related to Katie's. And Maria's was a murder that Hal definitely had not committed. If Glitsky was assuming that one person was responsible for all four of these murders — and this seemed to him at least a reasonable theory — then Hal was off the hook for Katie and, by extension, for Alanos Tussaint. As a working theory, it meant that whoever killed Tussaint had done the same to Maria and Katie and Luther. If this were the case, all the murders were somehow the work of only one pair of suspects: Burt Cushing and Adam Foster.

Glitsky thought it was a far more reasonable hypothesis than anything he'd been laboring under to date. It also might provide some new physical evidence, and that was what had him knocking on the medical examiner's door, catching the old man when he was getting ready to punch out for the day. "Won't take five minutes," Glitsky assured him.

"That's what they all say." But Strout ushered him in.

"Alanos Tussaint," Glitsky said without preamble.

Strout retrieved the name in about three seconds. "A month, maybe six weeks ago. Blunt force head trauma."

"Homicide?"

"My ruling was that it wasn't inconsistent with homicide. It also wasn't inconsistent with accidental slip-and-fall." He shrugged. "They found him in his cell. He had the top bunk. Could be he fell down and banged his temple on the corner of the bed, which is concrete. That's what the investigation went with."

"Okay, but let's go back a step. He fell down? What made him fall down?"

"I don't know for sure. He was loaded up with Oxy. But he'd also been in a fight with some other inmates. The guards broke it up and put him in the closest empty cell, and that's where he either passed out or slipped and fell."

"You believe that, John?"

Strout cocked his head, obviously wondering if he should take offense. "I believe he died of what I put on the death certificate, Abe. You know, whenever somebody dies over there, there's an investigation."

"Right."

"They had one in this case."

"I'm sure they did. But the guards there, they're all their brother's keepers, aren't they?"

"I've heard the same about guys on the regular force. I always think those rumors are just interoffice squabbling."

Glitsky nodded. "There's some of that. But sometimes it's not the case."

"You think this is one of those times?"

"This time we had an inmate tell a different story, then retract it."

"Well, inmates . . ." Strout gestured extravagantly and let the words hang in the air. It was no secret that jailhouse snitches were not the most trustworthy witnesses on the planet. Many would testify to almost anything in exchange for a slight improvement in their situations, the smallest reduction in their sentences. As a class, they were inherently unreliable, and everyone in law enforcement knew it.

"This inmate," Glitsky said, "was named Luther Jones. Ring a bell?"

Strout drew a frown. "That would be the Luther Jones on the slab in there?"

"The same. I just came from Farrell's office, and he told me that Luther called to set up an appointment to meet with a DA investigator yesterday and maybe retract his retraction of his testimony about Alanos Tussaint. She told Frank Dobbins about it. Her name was Maria Solis-Martinez."

Strout had no doubt spent a good portion of his afternoon performing an autopsy on the young woman. His face hardened further. "That was a damned heinous thing to do. I heard it was a robbery gone bad."

"You also heard Alanos Tussaint slipped and fell in an empty cell. There's always a story, John. Purse snatchers usually don't execute their victims with a shot to the face."

"You're saying somebody from the jail . . . ?"

"I'm not saying anything yet. I'm asking questions, trying to get a feel for things. What I know is that Luther told a DA inspector that Adam Foster had killed Tussaint."

"Adam Foster? Himself?"

Glitsky raised a hand. "Hear me out.

Luther then retracts that statement. Wes Farrell decides he believes the first version and sends Maria over to the jail to make a deal with Luther. A few days go by. Finally, Luther decides to play. He talks to her, and on that same night, Maria gets hit. Luther ODs the next morning."

Strout digested for a moment, then shook his head. "My, my, my."

"So far it's just a story," Abe said. "I'm nowhere near charging anybody yet. I don't have any evidence. Certainly nothing on Maria. Nothing on Katie Chase . . ."

"Katie Chase?"

"You remember her from the last time we spoke."

"She's in this?"

"Same threat to Foster."

"How's that?"

"Hal's his alibi for Tussaint. He told Katie it was a lie, and we think she called Cushing and threatened to talk."

"You are truly shitting me."

"I'm not, John. I wish I were." Glitsky let out a breath. "The logjam, of course, is that we don't have, and we're not likely to get, any new evidence on either Maria or Katie. You've already ruled on Tussaint, not inconsistent with homicide. I was just wondering if you might be persuaded to go back to your records on him, maybe take another look, see if anything new jumps out at you. And when you examine Luther, you might keep all these circumstances in mind. At least that might put some more evidence in play."

Strout's lips were tight with concentration. Eventually, he nodded. "If there's anything to find," he said, "I promise you, I'll find it."

46

CITYTALK
by JEFFREY ELLIOT

District Attorney Wes Farrell has wasted no time filling the vacancy in his Investigations Division caused by the murder of brand-new investigator Maria Solis-Martinez. Yesterday Farrell announced the hiring of Abe Glitsky, a longtime veteran of the Police Department, as assistant chief of inspectors and, most recently, head of the Homicide detail. Mr. Glitsky will be inheriting Ms. Solis-Martinez's caseload, but his first order of business, he said in an interview, will be an investigation into the killing of his predecessor, who was gunned down on Wednesday evening outside of her Mission District apartment's lobby. Her assailant fled with her purse, and investigators from the Homicide detail have described the crime as most likely a murder in the commission of a robbery.

Sources close to the investigation have said that Maria was developing information on a case involving a death originally ruled accidental in the San Francisco jail. Ms. Solis-Martinez was allegedly investigating the possibility that the death was not accidental but, in fact, connected to another homicide, that of Katie Chase, which happened outside the jail. The DA has indicted Ms. Chase's husband, a former jail guard, for that murder. Nevertheless, it appears the investigation has widened to include general allegations of corruption and wrongdoing in the jail.

No one in the District Attorney's office would comment on the record that the investigation had taken that turn. However, they would confirm that Glitsky, who previously worked as an investigator for Hal Chase's defense team, had obtained a waiver from his client so that any and all information in his possession, or garnered through future investigation, would be shared with police.

Dismas Hardy nearly spat out his breakfast coffee in shock and disbelief as he got to the end of the lead item in Elliot's column.

"What?" Frannie asked him.

He was already on his feet, pushing the

paper over in front of her. "Read that."

They had a wall-mounted landline telephone in the kitchen, and he punched in Glitsky's speed dial. It picked up on the second ring.

"What the hell are you doing?" Hardy asked in clipped tones. "What are you thinking?"

"Which one? Doing or thinking?"

"Either. Do you want to get yourself killed? Did you clear the interview with Wes?"

"No. I'm a grown-up, Diz. I can talk to the press if I want. Witnesses, too."

"What did you hope to accomplish? What do you think you did accomplish, other than put yourself right in their crosshairs and tell them we were coming?"

"That's not a problem."

"No? Well, it turned out to be a little problem for Maria Solis-Martinez and Luther Jones, didn't it?"

"Look, Diz. It's not like they don't get it. They see me in DA Investigations, they're going to know exactly what I'm doing. The best thing we can do is stir this up and see if we can put some pressure on the people around them. Foster's not going to crack. Not Cushing, either, but it's got to make people working with them nervous when they start to kill people, especially cops. So far, the heat's been all on us. Let's put some on them."

"Swell. And what about Hal?"

"What about him?"

"Well, he remains in jail, in Cushing and Foster's care or lack thereof. What about him?"

"He's in solitary under watch. Even Foster can't touch him."

"Except that you've basically given Hal yet another reason to have killed Katie. Because he was ordered to."

"One more reason to have killed Katie doesn't change this case at all."

"So you think Foster killed Katie. How'd you pick him out of all the possibilities? Why not Cushing or anybody else who works for him?"

"Foster did Tussaint. That's what Luther said the first time, and that's what I believe. Cushing can't have that many people under him ready to commit murder. I'm betting if Foster did one, he did the others, including Katie Chase."

"That would be nice, but have you even checked to see if he has an alibi for any of the other killings?"

"Diz, the man makes up alibis out of thin air, complete with corroborating witnesses."

"Maybe. But maybe he was with thirty members of his extended family and all his neighbors on Thanksgiving eve. Maybe last Wednesday was his bowling night. You ought to at least check those out."

"They're on my list. I promise."

"Jesus," Hardy said.

"Hey," Glitsky replied. "Didn't you tell me it wasn't Hal? Didn't you hire me to find the other dude? Well, I got him. It's Adam Foster. I don't see your problem. You ought to be doing cartwheels."

Hardy had barely hung up when his phone rang. It was Wes Farrell, in fine fettle himself. "I never figured Abe as such a loose cannon, Diz. I've got to fire him."

"You can't."

"Sure I can."

"Not the day after you hired him, Wes. You'd look like a fool."

"I already look like a fool for letting him run off like that. Now I'm going to be at war with Cushing and the mayor and probably half the judges in the building. Frank Dobbins, who, let us remember, is my own goddamn chief of investigations, is going to shit a brick. My idea was to go after this with a little finesse, and the first thing Abe does is go riding off the goddamn reservation. Christ, Diz. Stirring the pot might not even be a totally bad idea, but he can't do shit like that without talking to me first."

"He's already been on the case a couple of weeks, Wes. He's getting antsy for some results."

"What case? He's not on any case. I just brought him on."

"Hal Chase."

"Hal Chase? We've got no proven connection on that. It's just a theory."

"True. But it fits together as well as anything that's turned up in Hal's case, if not better. Now he starts digging, and I won't be surprised if he turns something up."

A silence descended on the line.

At last Farrell said, "You know, the really devious, nasty part of myself thinks that maybe you suggested I bring him back aboard so that he could undermine my case against Chase and nothing else."

"That would be the incorrect part of yourself, too. The grand jury jumped too soon on Mr. Chase, which I believe I mentioned to you at the time. He's going to wind up walking, you watch."

"If Abe has any exculpatory evidence on him. And you will recall that an explicit part of this deal your client signed off on was that Abe was going to hand over any evidence in the Chase case, regardless of where it pointed. I hope his next stop will be Frank Dobbins's office with that material in hand."

"I hope that, too, Wes. But he seems to be off on his own mission."

"I'm going to fire him."

"Suit yourself. You're the boss. But it's a bad idea."

"Shit."

"Yes, sir. I couldn't agree more."

47

Farrell was right about the big guns circling.
By the time Burt Cushing showed up for
the nine-thirty appointment in Farrell's office that he'd demanded, he had already
spoken to Mayor Leland Crawford, denying
the unfounded accusations in the strongest
possible terms, and getting, he said, the
mayor's vote of confidence.

"These are the most irresponsible accusations that I've ever heard in the course of
my twenty years of service to the city and
county of San Francisco, first as a supervi-
sor and then for the past six years as the
county sheriff." Cushing was pacing like a
caged animal between the couches and love
seats in Farrell's office. "You got a problem
with me or how I run my organization, you
come to me, we talk it over, see if there's
anything to it. Which in this case, there isn't.
This is pure slander. SFPD says nobody up
there is talking to Jeff Elliot. If you've got

somebody in your shop who's running amok, I hope you goddamn well get him under control."

In spite of his earlier anger at Glitsky's half-cocked decision to go public with his suspicions of Cushing, Farrell found himself surprisingly pleased that things between him and the sheriff were out in the open. He more than halfway believed that Cushing had played some role in Maria's execution, up to and including ordering it. So he wasn't inclined to apologize for Abe or anybody else. "Nobody in my office is freelancing, Burt. We'll be doing our investigation in a professional and straightforward manner, so I'm sure you won't have anything to worry about."

Cushing stopped pacing and pointed a finger. "You're not going to find anything in my shop."

"Well, then, you've got nothing to worry about, do you?"

"So you are behind this?"

"I'm behind asking Maria Solis-Martinez to look into the Tussaint business, if that's what you mean. And I think it's possible that the assignment led to her death. Which grieves me more than I can say."

"There was nothing in the Tussaint business, Wes. That was investigated by SFPD right after it happened, as you well know. Nobody found any sign of foul play."

"Luther Jones did."

For an instant, Cushing gaped, open-mouthed. "Luther Jones was a lowlife snitch who'd sell out his mother for a cigarette. He was a nonentity who lied to try to get something a little better for himself, Wes. That shit happens twenty times a day in the zoo." He spun around, worked up in a fury now, and came back to Wes. "Luther Jones. Give me a semi-fucking break."

Two could play the anger game, but when Farrell came down off the table, he wasn't playing. Getting right up into Cushing's face, he all but snarled, "You give me a break, Sheriff. Yeah, Luther Jones, who died of a heroin overdose in your jail and, as far as anyone can tell, never used heroin in his life. Luther called Maria on the day she was killed. He was going to deal and give up one of your thugs. And you knew it. So yeah, we're going to be looking into what's happening in that cesspool you run over there. You don't like it, you go fuck your-self."

Cushing's eyes narrowed. A muscle pulsed in his jawline. "You're making a huge mistake." He turned, yanked at the door-knob, and slammed the door behind him on his way out.

Besides his call from Dismas Hardy, Glitsky had also heard from Ruth Chase ("It makes all the sense in the world"), Patti Orosco ("I'm so glad to see that you have suspects who really might have done it besides me"), and Devin Juhle, who wasn't nearly as enthusiastic. The Homicide chief, who had a pretty good idea that Abe was the un-named source, didn't waste time asking him to confirm or deny. He just wanted to know if Abe had any support for his theories, particularly about Maria's killer, and if he did, would he please be so kind as to share his information with Abby and JaMorris, who had drawn Maria's murder and were again laboring under a dearth of evidence. Did the DA really have something, and if he didn't, what was this baloney doing in the paper?

Abe suggested that Juhle have his inspec-tors interview Adam Foster and get his alibi for the time of Maria's death. Juhle left it unclear whether he was going to follow up on that, but he told Glitsky that he'd try to hook up with him when he got downtown a little later.

With all the talking and explaining he'd done by phone from his home, by the time

Glitsky walked into the Investigations Division for the first time that Friday morning, it was almost ten o'clock. He expected an onslaught of profound silence, and even overt resentment, from the inspectors up here. As a lifelong cop, he knew exactly what he'd done and why he'd done it, but he didn't fool himself that it would endear him to his professional associates.

But he hadn't made it halfway across the bullpen on his way to Chief Inspector Frank Dobbins's office when the women at the desks nearest the door got to their feet and started to applaud. Chairs scraped against the floor as the other inspectors stood up and put their hands together. Glitsky stopped and looked from face to face, his own visage softening as he took in this rare display of support. Other people were coming out from the hall where Maria had kept her office. Dobbins came and stood in his doorway, clapping three times himself and nodding in welcome.

"About fucking time," someone said ambiguously, and Glitsky, back in character, frowned at the profanity.

Five minutes later, Tom Scerbo came back to Dobbins's office and dropped a manila file on the desk. "That's everything I've got on Tussaint, including the transcript of the first talk I had with Luther. It's also got the names of the five guards who swore they were out delivering inmates to San Bruno with Adam Foster. I only talked to two of them — Barani and Maye — and didn't have the heart to go through the motions with the other three."

"Not forthcoming?" Glitsky asked.

"Oh, to the contrary," Scerbo said. "They both knew the exact time they left the jail, the route they took, who sat where in the bus, who drove each way. Impressively well rehearsed, and of course the written records and logs all agree."

"Or they're telling the truth," Dobbins put in.

Scerbo was grim. "Of course. Or that."

Glitsky scanned the pages. "Hal Chase?"

Scerbo nodded. "One of the five."

"How about him being in jail now?" Glitsky asked.

Dobbins turned to him. "How about it?"

"Would he rat out Foster if we could do a deal and get him out?"

Scerbo shook his head. "No chance, Abe. First, these guys don't talk, period. Second, Chase is charged with one of the murders you're saying Foster did, so you're into 'I didn't do it, he did it.' It would never fly."

Glitsky nodded. "Okay. I'm open to suggestions from either of you. This Tussaint thing is the only one of the four murders — Marie, Katie, Luther, and Alanos — where we've got some reasonable chance to get some evidence working for us. And that was almost two months ago."

"It's a tough nut," Scerbo said. "Do you think Foster's good for Katie Chase?"

"Better than Hal. But I'm keeping my mind open," Glitsky said. "What about the other jail deaths this year? How many have there been?"

Dobbins clucked. "That number is open to interpretation. Does an overdose count? Suicide? Last April or May, somebody did a face-plant off his bed and broke his neck. No witnesses. That's the way they tend to go."

"To answer your question," Scerbo said, "let's go with three more that could use a little scrutiny. Which I'd be glad to give them."

"That would be good," Glitsky said. "Thanks."

The telephone rang on Dobbins's desk, and he reached over and grabbed it. "Dobbins . . . Yeah . . . Right, about fifteen minutes ago . . . I'll give him the word, he'll be right down." Hanging up, he said, "Mr. Farrell would like a word with you."

Glitsky looked from one inspector to the other. "Anybody want to bet he doesn't applaud when he sees me?"

48

Abby and JaMorris met Adam Foster in the main lobby of the jail as he arrived late for his shift. Both inspectors, trained to carefully observe, got the clear impression that he wasn't happy to see them. Their first clue was that, despite knowing them both at least by sight, he asked for their identification and looked them up and down with withering contempt. He directed them to follow him back to his workspace, which was the anteroom and reception area for Burt Cushing's office.

When they got there, Foster, still only marginally civil, indicated that the inspectors should take whatever seats they wanted. He walked over to the door with Cushing's name on it, knocked, and pushed it open. Evidently, no one was there. Foster turned and went to sit at his own desk, obviously gathering his patience and even slapping on a veneer of politeness.

"All right," he said. "What can I do for you?"

Abby Foley led off. "Mr. Foster, did you happen to get a look at Jeff Elliot's 'CityTalk' column this morning?"

"I did." Foster had his hands clasped on his empty desk. His knuckles shone white. "I got a couple of calls waking me up to tell me about it. Bunch of nonsense."

"You think it's nonsense?" JaMorris asked.

"What else could it be? I'm surprised they let the thing be published. Well, no, I'm not. Anybody wants a headline in this town, they lob some mud at this department. It gets old, but it's not like we haven't seen it before and won't again."

JaMorris nodded. "So you nix the idea that Maria Solis-Martinez is connected to the death of Alanos Tussaint in jail a couple of months ago?"

Foster dredged up a tired smile. "All of it. It's total bullshit."

"We ask," Abby persisted, "because we're on that case — Maria's — and we've got nothing remotely resembling a lead."

"I'm not surprised. How is some purse snatcher, probably tweeked out of his brain, supposedly connected to Mr. Tussaint? It doesn't even make sense."

"Well," JaMorris replied, "you must know

that at one point you were being investigated as the main suspect in the killing of Mr. Tussaint."

Foster played his response as if he'd heard a good joke. "Really?"

"Yes, really," JaMorris said.

"Okay," Foster said, "let's start with fundamentals. First, Mr. Tussaint wasn't murdered. He slipped and fell and banged his head and unfortunately died of his injury. The medical examiner made the call on the cause of death, then the SFPD — you guys! — did a thorough investigation, and that was your decision, not mine. How I'm somehow on the hook for killing a guy who wasn't even murdered, I don't know.

"On top of that, when did this accident of his occur? That came up in the investigation, too, and would you look at that? I happened to be on an assignment down in San Bruno. I've got five witnesses, all sworn officers, who were working down there with me and testified to that fact. So what do I think of the theory tying together this Maria person and Alanos Tussaint? Best case, it's some crazy person howling at the moon."

"And yet, coincidentally," Jambo said, "Luther Jones is suddenly dead in your jail as well."

The silence lingered. Abby interrupted it.

"So you did not know Ms. Solis-Martinez?"

"No. I couldn't have picked her out of a lineup." By now Foster had unclenched his hands and sat back in his chair, at ease. "Guys," he said, his voice all sincerity, "listen. My heart goes out to the poor woman. She was one of us, in law enforcement. She must have been in the wrong place at the wrong time, but you both know this happens every day. Now, I gather, if I'm a suspect in Tussaint, who wasn't even murdered, I might as well fit the bill for this other person, too. And that's why you're here, isn't it?"

With a sheepish smile, JaMorris conceded the point. "You know how it is, Deputy. We follow every lead, even if it's unlikely to take us anywhere."

Abby picked it up. "We figured we come down here today, do it the easy way. Ask you straight out what you were doing Wednesday night, and if it checks out, we cross you off and can forget about all these no-evidence theories."

Foster rubbed his hands together, palm to palm. "Wednesday? This past Wednesday? What time?"

"Ten-ish," Abby said without any hesitation.

Foster's hands went to his mouth, templed

at his lips. Suddenly, his eyes lit up. "I hate to ruin the fun," he said as he straightened in his chair, his hands back on his desk, "but Wednesday I was at a poker game with some of my buddies from, I don't know, seven or so until eleven, eleven-thirty."

"At your house?" Abby asked.

Foster shook his head. "No. Mike Maye's. One of my guys here." He went to reach for the telephone. "I could call him down if you want."

"How many other players were there?" JaMorris asked.

Foster cast his eyes to the ceiling, recalling, counting the names off on his fingers. "Mike, Steve, Eno, Jorge. Four. Five, with me."

"Do all of them work here?" Abby asked mildly.

The question didn't seem to raise a flag for Foster. "Mike and Eno, yeah. Eno Barani," he spelled it out. "Mike is May with an E. Steve and Jorge, Smith and Perez, are in Evictions."

JaMorris wrote it all down.

Again, Foster reached for the desk phone. "You sure you don't want me to call Mike Maye? Get a statement from him. Take five minutes."

The inspectors exchanged a glance.

"Sure," Abby said. "Save us another trip."

Foster picked up the phone and made the call. When he hung up, he said, "He'll be right down."

"Cool," Abby said. "Thank you." Then, back to her friendly conversational tone, "So this poker game, Sergeant: How'd you do?"

"Pretty good. I left with about two-fifteen."

JaMorris whistled at the number. "What's your buy-in? I've got a regular game where the buy-in's twenty, and I'm starting to think that's too low."

"Depends on the limit more than the buy-in," Foster said. "If you can't make it hurt to call, everybody's gonna call, right? And if you can't bluff, it's not poker. What's your limit?"

"Three," JaMorris said. "Dollars. Not three hundred dollars."

Foster shook his head. "Not near enough. We play a hundred buy-in and twenty-five limit. Three raises. Check and raise okay. It's a serious game." He broke a devilish grin. "Some hands get vicious, let me tell you."

JaMorris gave him an open smile. He reached for his wallet, extracted a business card, got up, and slid it across Foster's desk.

"If you let in new players," he said, "feel free to give me a call."

"I might just do that."

A sallow-faced, thin, balding man knocked on the doorframe. Foster told him to come in, and the two inspectors stood and introduced themselves, shaking hands all around. When they finished, Mike Maye asked how he could help.

Abby said, "We were hoping you could tell us what you were doing on Wednesday night. Two days ago."

Maye thought about it for a couple of seconds, cast a questioning glance at Foster, then turned back to Abby. "He didn't tell you?"

"We'd like to hear it from you, if you don't mind," she replied.

He shrugged. "There's not much to tell. I sat in a chair in my house for a few hours and watched my money disappear in a poker game. Most of it went to Adam here. I'm surprised he didn't tell you."

"He mentioned a little of it," JaMorris said. "Sounds like a good game."

"Better if you win," Maye said. "Which he did."

"What time did it break up?" Abby asked.

Another shrug. "I don't know, exactly. Oh no, wait. I know he called his wife on his cell at ten, told her he'd be a little late. I gave him some grief over it."

"Over what?" JaMorris asked.

"Having to call his old lady."

"You're not married?" Abby asked.

"Used to be," Maye replied. "Don't miss it so much."

JaMorris brought him back on topic. "So Sergeant Foster stayed till when?"

"Say eleven, somewhere in there. What's this about?"

JaMorris answered. "Somebody thought your boss was somewhere else."

"When?"

"Wednesday night," Abby answered. "Eight to eleven."

"Nope," Maye said, then broke a small rueful laugh. "I wish he had been, though." He turned to Foster. "No offense."

"None taken."

To the inspectors, Maye added, "If he'd left at ten when he was supposed to, I'd be sixty bucks richer, I'll tell you that."

"Everybody hates a sore loser, Mike," Foster said. "It's unbecoming."

Maye broke a lopsided grin. "Easy for him to say."

"All right, then." Foster pushed back his chair, stood up, and addressed the inspectors, who also got to their feet. "So?" he asked them. "Are we good?"

"Good," JaMorris said.

"Any more questions for Mike while he's here?"

"Not necessary," Abby said. "Thank you, Mike. And thank you, Sergeant. Sorry to put you through all this trouble."

"It's no trouble," he answered magnanimously. "As I told you, I'm used to it. It comes with the territory. You know your way out?"

"We can find it," JaMorris said. He pointed to Foster's desk, where his business card lay. "And I'm serious about that game."

"I'll keep it in mind."

They followed Mike Maye down the hall and left him as they turned off to the lobby. When they got outside the building, JaMorris said, "That was quite a performance."

"For all of us, I think. I loved the poker riff. I didn't know you played."

"I don't."

Abby broke a wide smile. "Well, aren't you just the pip." Then she added, "So Mike Maye isn't married. You get that?"

"It was hard to miss. And this means . . . ?"

"I'm not sure, except my gut says it's significant."

49

Glitsky sat at his empty desk in the DA Investigations Division on the third floor with the woefully thin Tussaint file open in front of him. He hated sitting there taking up space, but he was trying to decide what his next move should be. Without any leverage, how did he propose to break the story told by the San Bruno guards? Tussaint's murder had been two months ago. If any of their details about that day were murky, what else could be expected after all that time? But he was willing to bet that they wouldn't be too murky — by now they would probably be burnished to a high shine.

He looked up and saw the pair of Homicide inspectors coming into the lobby. He pushed back his chair and waited until they spotted him, then stood as they got closer. "Don't tell me, he confessed to it all," Glitsky said wryly.

"Close," JaMorris said. "He confessed to being Adam Foster. After that, it got a little squirrelly."

"But he talked to you?"

"Oh yeah," JaMorris said.

Abby backed up her partner. "He and Jambo are now buds. They're planning to get together for some poker any day now."

"Good to know," Glitsky said. "So you got him talking?"

JaMorris nodded. "I told him we thought the story was crazy. We're Homicide, after all, and you're not, and all we wanted was to cross him off as a suspect."

"We agreed that the 'CityTalk' column was ridiculous, of course," Abby said, "but we had no choice — Juhle ordered us to follow up. So if Sergeant Foster could tell us for the record what he was doing Wednesday night, we'd say adios and be out of his hair."

"He bought that?"

"He might not have, in the normal scheme of things, but after that article, I don't think he felt he had a lot of choice. And I think his arrogance got the better of him. He wanted to show off," Abby said. "I must admit, he was impressive."

"So he didn't shoot Maria?"

Abby shook her head. "He couldn't have.

He was playing poker all night at the home of his good friend and fellow guard Mike Maye."

"Why do I know that name?" Glitsky snapped his fingers, reached over, and flipped open the Tussaint file. "There you go. One of the San Bruno guards who alibied Foster last time."

"Wouldn't surprise me," JaMorris said. "Very believable dude. He never missed a beat. And oh, by the way, in case you were wondering, you can check Foster's cell phone records; old Adam called his home at ten o'clock sharp from Maye's house. The dutiful husband letting his wife know he would be late getting in."

Glitsky took that news in a growing gloomy silence. "Guy could give lessons," he said.

"No doubt," JaMorris replied. "Practice makes perfect."

Pulling around his chair, Glitsky sat back down and looked up at them. "I've been sitting here for half an hour trying to figure how I'm going to get at this guy, but I can't see where anybody's going to give him up." He fingered the file again. "How many other players were at this poker game?"

"Three." JaMorris pulled out his book and read the names.

"Eno Barani," Glitsky said when he'd finished, "is another one of the San Bruno guys. I don't know Smith or Perez."

"They're in Evictions," JaMorris said.

"Any idea why he would have used them instead of" — Abe checked the file again — "Chick Davis and Andy Biehl? Those are the last two of the original San Bruno guys."

"Maybe they were already tied up that night?" JaMorris said.

Deep in thought, Glitsky nodded. "So you're saying there really was a poker game?"

This stopped the conversation for a long moment. At last Abby spoke. "That's it."

Glitsky asked, "That's what?"

"Our opening," Abby replied.

"I'm listening."

"It's just a feeling, but I've been wondering why it seemed important to me that Mike Maye might be single." Abby's eyes were alight with excitement. "I'll bet you they're all single."

"Who?" JaMorris asked.

"Our poker guys. Maye, Barani, Smith, and Perez."

"And if they are?" Glitsky asked.

"If they are, they're more reliable than, say, Hal Chase, who finked to his wife and started all these problems. Wives are unreliable. Wives have moods, sometimes opinions." She smiled at the men. "Being a wife myself, I'm allowed to say these things."

"I'm feeling sexually harassed just hearing them," JaMorris said. "I'm going to file a grievance."

Glitsky asked Abby, "So you're saying what?"

"I'm saying that Foster and Cushing might have learned an important lesson about wives from Katie Chase. So now with these new guys, all single, Foster orders them where they've got to be and tells them how long they have to stay. There's no wife who's already planned dinner, or kids who have a soccer game or homework. No hassles. No contradictions. They go to Maye's bachelor pad and actually play poker. Maye calls Foster's home on Foster's cell phone at ten. The game breaks up at eleven. When everybody gets back to his own home, there's no wife around to hear about the night, no one to question what he did. It's perfect, or at least way more perfect than having another person in the loop who might be less than reliable. What do you think?"

JaMorris said, "You're probably right, but what does that get us? They're all solid witnesses, and nobody gives anything up.

380

How's that an opening for us?"

Glitsky was ahead of him. "Not Smith and Perez," he said. "The other guys." He checked the names in the file again. "From San Bruno. Biehl and Davis. Foster didn't use them for the poker alibi because they are married and they might say something to their wives."

"Are they? And are the other guys single?" JaMorris asked. "And still, so what?"

"So," Abby told him, "if I'm right, and we can find that out in about a minute online, we've got two wives we've never talked to who might be feeling stressed-out about now. Tussaint is back in the news big-time. If it were my husband and I knew he was covering up a murder, I'd be getting damn close to a breakdown."

"Okay, but even so," Glitsky said, "wives can't be made to testify against their husbands, so what does it get us?"

"Leverage," Abby said. "We're not talking about testifying in a trial, just finding out what actually happened, going back to the alibis and saying your wife's got a different story. Look at what Katie Chase did when she found out."

"We don't know for sure that she did anything," Glitsky said.

"We're pretty sure," JaMorris countered.

"Sure enough, anyway."

Glitsky, noncommittal, simply shrugged.

"All I'm saying," Abby continued, "is that one of these wives, or both of them, might be living in fear that their husbands are going to get found out. We let 'em know we're close, anything could happen."

Glitsky said, "Let's find out first if we've got these wives. If we do, I agree it's worth talking to them. What do we have to lose?"

50

As it turned out, it took them nearly a half hour to get their answers, but worth it because the answers were the right ones. Whether or not Abby's analysis of what it meant was correct, her theory was solid. Of the seven guards who had formed the backbone of Adam Foster's alibis, four of them — all the poker guys — were single. The other three — Chick Davis, Andy Biehl, and Hal Chase — were now or, in Hal's case, had been married. Given their first glimmer of hope, the inspectors divided up the spoils, with Abby and JaMorris on their way to interview Betsy Davis in the Mission and Glitsky taking Allison Biehl out in the Sunset. They elected not to make appointments with the wives; if either or both were at work or otherwise unavailable, they'd wait until the end of the workday and try again.

Surprise, everyone agreed, would give

them a very powerful advantage.

The high-pressure ridge that had kept the sky clear and the temperature low for the past couple of weeks had shifted, and as Glitsky crossed Van Ness on Geary, he saw a looming bank of fog piling up out in the Avenues. By the time he hit Arguello, he was in the soup. Slowing down, headlights on, he fairly hummed with adrenaline, gripping the steering wheel as he crept his way out to Nineteenth Avenue. After turning south through Golden Gate Park, he continued down to Quintara, took a right past the Sunset Reservoir, and finally pulled up to a nice side-by-side duplex with a tiny lawn and an Audi A5 in the driveway. He checked his watch and saw that it was 2:45.

Glitsky parked at the curb and climbed a small stoop to the right-hand door. A vacuum cleaner moaned inside. He rang the doorbell. The noise ceased and footsteps sounded and a female voice came through the door. "Yes? Who is it?"

Glitsky had positioned himself directly in front of the fish-eye. As a large black man with a scar through his lips, he was used to the default reception of mistrust or even fear. He wore a consciously neutral expression and held up his new badge near his face so that she could see it. "My name is

Abe Glitsky, and I'm with the DA Investigations office."

"Just a second." She turned the dead bolt and quickly opened the door as far as the chain would allow. She spoke through the crack. "Is Andy all right?"

"Andy's fine."

She put a hand over her heart. "Oh my God. You scared me to death. You're sure he's okay?"

"As far as I know. There's no reason to think he isn't. I'm sorry if I frightened you. I should have called first."

"No. That's all right. Now that you're here, it's fine." She let out a heavy sigh, patted her chest again, and swallowed. "I'm sorry," she said, "but could I take a look at your ID again?"

"Of course." Abe held his wallet and badge out at her eye level. "Feel free to take the number and call the DA downtown if you'd like. That's Wes Farrell's number, his office. I agree, you can't be too careful."

"Do you mind? I'll just be a minute."

"Not at all. Take your time."

She closed the door and threw the dead bolt again. Abe tried to summon all the patience he could muster, which, after the tortuous slow drive out, wasn't much. Taking small solace from the knowledge that jail guards were not encouraged to use the telephone at work, he hoped she would call the number he'd given her and not her husband. But this, he knew, was out of his control. He turned and watched the fog drift in front of him, sometimes thick enough to obscure the line of dwellings across the street.

He checked his watch again: 2:48. The slowest three minutes, Glitsky thought, in human history.

The dead bolt, the chain, and the door swung open. She handed him back his ID, a smile on her face. "I just spoke to your wife."

"She's the DA's secretary." The sides of his own mouth lifted. "It's the family business."

"After all that, what can I do for you? I'm sorry to be paranoid, but if I didn't check and Andy . . . Well, never mind. You're probably the same way."

"I probably am."

"Do you want to come in?"

"It might be more comfortable. Thank you."

"I've got to warn you, I've got a baby taking a nap in the back, and if she wakes up, I'll have to get her."

"That's fine," Glitsky said. "I've raised a

few myself. I get it."

Mrs. Biehl stepped back, opening the door all the way. He followed her into a small, very neat living room.

"Please," she said, gesturing to the couch. "Have a seat."

She was a petite brunette in her mid-twenties. She wore jeans and ballet slippers and a 49ers T-shirt tucked in, showing no sign of having recently borne a child. Sitting down across from him, her well-mannered preamble out of the way, she drew a deep breath — the first sign of true nerves, which Glitsky was happy to see — and gave him an obviously forced smile.

Glitsky took out a small pocket tape recorder that he showed to her with an apologetic look. "Do you mind if I tape our conversation?"

A moment's hesitation. "What's this about?" She pointed at the recorder. "Is that really necessary?"

"It keeps the record straight."

"This is official, then?"

Glitsky temporized. "I wouldn't want to misquote you."

"No, you wouldn't want to do that." She paused. "You need to tell me what this is about."

"It's relatively routine. We're following up

on an investigation into an incident that happened at the jail a couple of months ago. Your husband may have mentioned something about getting sent on a transportation detail bringing some inmates down to San Bruno with Adam Foster — the chief deputy — and a few of the other guards."

Mrs. Biehl's mouth formed a small O. She clasped her hands tightly in her lap. She inclined her head an inch or two. "Okay?"

"There has been some discrepancy about the details of this assignment, so we've reopened the investigation. As it turns out, the incident at the jail is quite a serious matter: actually, the murder of a man named Alanos Tussaint."

"A murder? They're calling that a murder now?"

"You're familiar with the incident?"

Quickly, she shook her head. "Just rumors," she said.

"Well, Mrs. Biehl, further investigation suggests that Mr. Tussaint might have died as a result of an assault at the jail."

"What does this have to do with Andy?"

"That's unclear at the moment. You might have read something about this in the paper already. We're just trying to make sure all the information we have is accurate, especially now that the press is asking questions.

In any event, as you may know, your husband has already said that he was with Sergeant Foster at San Bruno when this happened at the Bryant Street jail."

"If Andy says he was with Sergeant Foster, then that's where he was. I'm sure of that."

"He never discussed the incident with you?"

She pulled herself up straight and stared at him, not venturing a word.

"Mrs. Biehl?"

Another hesitation, then finally, "No."

"Never?"

This time she shook her head. "No." She was not a convincing liar, especially when she added with an air of petulance, "Why would he feel like he had to tell me about it? He was transporting an inmate. They transport inmates all the time."

"That's true," Glitsky said, "but they also keep records of who is assigned to them."

This was a wild shot across her bow, but it somehow found its mark and snapped her head back. She cast her eyes from Glitsky to the front door, then around the suddenly claustrophobic room.

Glitsky read the signs and decided to turn up the press. "Do you know Hal Chase?"

"I know who he is, yes."

"Do you know that he was supposedly on

that detail with your husband?"

"Not supposedly. He was with my husband."

"Was he? Have you and Andy talked about him the past couple of days?"

"He's in jail now. Which means he'll say anything."

"Is that what you think?"

"Everybody knows that."

"Okay, but why would he change his statement?"

"To help you build a case against Adam Foster. Then he goes into Witness Protection and they drop the charges that he killed his wife."

"Excuse me," Glitsky said. "If you think that's what's going on with Hal Chase, it sounds to me like you have discussed that San Bruno assignment with your husband, when earlier you told me you hadn't. So which is it? You talked about it or you didn't?"

"Okay. All right. It might have come up somehow."

"Somehow? In what context?"

By now her overt hostility was vying with her nerves. She looked again at the corners of the room, her mouth puckered in a tight kiss.

"Mrs. Biehl?"

"Hal Chase is making it all up!"

"Is he? All right. Then what about Chick Davis? He's not in jail, like Hal is. So what's Chick's motive? Is he making it all up, too?" Glitsky had nothing on Chick Davis except the name, but that was no longer the point. He had Allison Biehl on the run, and he needed to bring her to ground by any means necessary. "Now we've got your husband all by himself out there, lying to protect Foster and Burt Cushing, when all the other rats are jumping ship." Having already told one whopper, he decided to swing for the fences. "Let me put my cards on the table. We've already talked to your husband. If you can corroborate what he's told us, you'll be doing yourself a big favor. But it has to be now, before there's any chance that the two of you could get together and decide on your story. What did he tell you about Alanos Tussaint? Did your husband kill him, or was he just part of the alibi?"

Allison Biehl had her fists clenched against her stomach.

Glitsky had one more hunch and decided to play it. "I noticed the new car out there in your driveway, Mrs. Biehl. The Audi. That's a fine machine for somebody on a jail guard's salary, even more so if it's your second car. You know we've got auditors who get involved in a prosecution like this one. We know what's going on in the jail. We know there was money involved, and we know it led to this killing."

She raised her head, tears now streaming down her cheeks. "I knew it would come to this," she said. "Andy didn't kill anybody. Andy wouldn't ever kill anybody. I told him when it started happening to some of the other guys that it was only going to be a matter of time. It's not like they give you the chance to say no, you know? They tell you what you have to do, and then you just do it and hope it's something easy, like Andy got. There's no option. You do it or you're fired. You do it and take the payoffs. That's how it all works. It wasn't like this was Andy's idea or anything. They just picked him and then he was part of it. He really had no choice, no choice at all."

51

Outside the Biehl home, Glitsky called Dismas Hardy, who, as it turned out, was nearby. He had just arrived at the bar he co-owned, the Little Shamrock, where he was going to bartend from four to seven, as he liked to do from time to time. Hardy was interested and happy to hear about Glitsky's afternoon, but the details would have to wait; he was already jamming behind the bar. Maybe Abe could embellish the story when he showed up in person.

Either Hardy had lied or the crowd packing the bar had mysteriously disappeared by the time Glitsky grabbed one of the open stools down by the beer spigots and ordered an iced tea. After Glitsky gave him the broad-strokes account of his interview with Allison Biehl, Hardy took a sip from his beer and gave Abe a look of mild distress.

"What?" Glitsky asked.

"Nothing."

"Seems like something."

"No." Hardy sipped again, swallowed. "Nothing."

Glitsky shook his head, perplexed. "I don't get it. This is the second time today I tell you great news, and both times you're . . ."

"Surly, discontented, unhappy?"

"Yeah. That's a good start."

"And you have no idea why?"

"You're jealous 'cause I got all the answers first?"

"That's not it."

"Then how about you tell me what it is."

Hardy put down his beer, placed his palms on the bar between them, and leaned over. "I'm really glad you got the break, Abe. That's great news. But I'm just a little concerned. Let's just do a logic game for a minute and pretend that your theory about Katie Chase is right. Because of what she heard about Foster's alibi from Hal, she got perceived as a threat by somebody in the Sheriff's Department — Cushing or Foster, it doesn't matter. And their solution was to kill her. Doesn't that pretty well capture the highlights?"

"Close enough."

"Okay. Tell me, then. In what way was Katie's situation before she got killed any different from the one you just put Allison

Biehl in? At least, once you put the word out that she knows Foster's alibi is worthless, what will be the difference? Why won't she be in danger? Or her husband, for that matter? Just as an exercise in logic, mind you."

"Nobody's going to kill her, Diz."

"No? Why not, exactly? Because this time nobody will find out who's the weak link?"

"Among other reasons."

"Really? Well, this just in, as I hardly need to tell you, you can know who did something till you're blue in the face, and unless you've got some proof to take them down at trial, you got nothing. And these guys, Cushing and Foster and the rest of them, they're not dumb. They've got this control-your-witnesses thing down to an art form. How many deaths in the jail last year alone, and every one investigated by the SFPD, every one, Abe, and no charges? Who knows how long all of this has been going on?"

"But after today, we know it's going on. It's not just a theory."

Hardy pitched a glance at the ceiling. "There's never been any doubt that it's going on. It's never been just a theory."

"And now people are talking about it. And soon will be talking even more."

"Swell. How is this supposed to help us

prepare a case against any of them? With inadmissible hearsay from the wife of a witness who may or may not talk? No. The truth is that now they see you coming from a million miles away. And there is still no evidence. Even if Foster's alibi on Tussaint falls apart, so what? It doesn't mean he killed him. Nobody saw Foster kill him except Luther Jones, and he's not talking, not ever, regardless of what you've done."

Glitsky cupped his hands around his glass. "Correct me if I'm wrong," he said in a level tone, "but wasn't it you who said — it was yesterday, I believe — that nobody would come after Hal because the coincidence factor would be too great? Why doesn't that apply to Allison Biehl, too?"

"Okay." Hardy held up his hands. "Perhaps in my syllogistic zeal, I exaggerated about Allison. Perhaps she will be in no danger. Because she isn't a threat to anybody. Her husband sticks with his perjury about the alibi — and he will, because why wouldn't he? — and then Allison says you threatened or coerced or tricked her or something, and all of a sudden we're back at square one. Except everybody is warned about everything. How do you not see this?"

"I see it, Diz. But I see it playing out differently."

"You do? How's that?"

"I keep the pressure on, and something gives. It's already happened today, since 'CityTalk.' And now Allison. The logjam is breaking up."

Hardy blew out a long breath in frustration. "It might be. People might be getting nervous, but that's only going to make them more careful, not more reckless. Besides which, you know that the more you accuse without a show of proof — and I mean any proof — the less credibility you'll have. You give us another cockeyed theory, and people roll their eyes. Until finally, Wes has to bow to public pressure and lay you off because you're obsessed and you've stopped acting the way an inspector needs to."

"I am obsessed." Abe lowered his voice. "These guys are getting away with murder, Diz. Multiple murders. And I'm not supposed to break this nut open any way I can?"

"I hate to say it, but that's right. You're not just supposed to break it any way you can. You've got to break it the way you're supposed to, so a case can stick. Otherwise it's wasted effort. If anything, it'll help them, not us."

"So what about your client?"

"What about him?"

"Do you think he killed Katie?"

Hardy needed a moment to consider his answer. He suddenly remembered his beer. When he put it back down, he said, "The grand jury found enough to indict him, Abe. Even if most of what you think about Cushing and Foster is true, he's as good as any other suspect. Or, rather, because there's no physical evidence against him, as bad."

"Do you think he did it, Diz?"

"It's got nothing to do with what I think."

"Sure, but still. Simple question, yes or no."

At last Hardy nodded, barely whispering. "No."

"And I'm not supposed to do everything I can to get him off? Isn't that what you asked me to do, and what I'm doing now with Farrell?"

"You said it yourself. You're obsessed. What you need to do is find evidence. Nothing else. No more theories, no hearsay, just admissible evidence."

Glitsky found his temper flaring. "What do you think I got?"

Hardy shook his head. "Never admissible. Not in a million years."

"Diz. It's the first time we got a look at the truth here."

"Oh, and what's that? That Foster killed Tussaint?"

"And Maria, and Luther, and maybe Katie Chase, too."

"We don't know any of that. All we think we might know is that Foster's alibi might not hold up. That's a lot of maybe."

"It's a wedge. It's the first one."

"Yeah, if you could prove it. Can you do that? Because until you can . . ."

"I'm working from truth here, Diz. I know the truth."

"Spare me the truth, Abe. Get me something I can use."

In a cold fury, Glitsky stared across the bar at his friend. "You know what," he said in a clipped tone, "I don't need to talk about this anymore. I'm doing what I'm doing, I'm doing it my way, and I'm getting results. And I'm gonna keep doing it." He pushed his tea over to the bar's gutter and stood up. "Have yourself a nice day."

He walked out the front door.

52

The last person on the planet whom Abe wanted to see — except possibly Dismas Hardy or Wes Farrell — was Ruth Chase, but she had called him that morning, congratulating him on the 'CityTalk' column, and she called again just as he was starting his car to drive back downtown.

In his foul mood, he was tempted not to answer at all, but his sense of duty kicked in and he picked up. She hated to bother him, she said, but felt she needed some reassurance. She was worried about her son, languishing in jail. She was alone in Hal's house, watching the two children, a task for which Glitsky knew she was at best ill suited.

Admitting that he was around the corner and could spare a few minutes — and berating himself for his softheartedness as soon as he said it — he agreed to drop by and bring her up to date; they'd had a little bit of a breakthrough. As an unexpected bonus, he realized while driving up Stanyan, Ruth would probably see something positive in it, in contrast to Hardy's negative reaction. Small consolation.

In any event, five minutes after he left the Little Shamrock, he pulled up in front of Hal's home. Ruth greeted him at the front door like a long-lost friend and, after inviting him in, immediately began effusing again over that morning's 'CityTalk.' "It was amazing how you pulled all of those strings together. I don't see how anybody reading that could have any doubt about what's going on with the sheriff and his people downtown."

"I don't think people doubt it so much as they're stumped on how to go about proving any of it," Abe said.

"Wouldn't you think that once you know who you're looking at, you can focus your attention better on that one person and maybe find your proof? I know once Hal got arrested, they showed up with all kinds of warrants and Crime Scene and Forensics people. It was a circus my first couple of days here. Of course they didn't find anything, but that's because Hal's innocent. If he'd actually done it, they would have found something. After the column, that's how they ought to be treating the sheriff, wouldn't you think?"

"I couldn't agree more."

"So why aren't they?"

"Because on what we've got so far, no judge is going to sign a warrant, and you need a warrant. That's the bottleneck. You've got to have something to start with, not just a theory but something tangible. And that's been elusive, to say the least. Although I think today we may have seen the first hole in that particular dike."

"That's wonderful news!"

"It is. But as I say, even with probable cause, Cushing's got a ton of political clout. He and the mayor are allies, if not real friends, and so are half or more of the supervisors, probably. Anybody who goes after him — Wes Farrell, for example — is sticking his neck way out." Suddenly Glitsky glanced around the room. "I just noticed. Where are the kids?"

"They're fine," she said. "They're upstairs taking a nap." She looked over at the stairway, nodded, and sighed. "Do you mind if we sit down? Can I get you a drink? I'm going to have a little wine. It's been a long day."

"I'm good," Glitsky said. "I've just come from a bar. Any more tea and I'd float away.

But you go ahead."

She went into the kitchen. Glitsky lowered himself onto the couch and heard her open the refrigerator. In another moment she appeared with a glass of white wine. Crossing over to the reading chair, she sat. "I don't know whether it's me getting old or what, but the energy of those kids, especially Ellie . . . it's unbelievable. I don't remember my own boys being so exhausting, but I suppose I should have expected a few difficulties — not to speak ill of the dead, but given the way their mother was."

"How was that?"

"I think she and Hal were always in denial about it, but it was pretty clear to me and anybody who paid attention that she . . . Katie, I mean . . . had some issues with her mental health. You know she was in counseling?"

"I understood that was mostly about her marriage, not mental illness."

Ruth shrugged. "I suppose it was, to some extent, but it was also obvious that she wasn't completely right mentally."

"In what way?"

"I don't know the technical terms. Maybe bipolar, manic-depressive, whatever they call it nowadays, or ADHD. And I see much the same thing in Ellie. Whatever name you want to use, I'd call it hyperactivity, and she obviously got it from her mother." Ruth shook her head and sipped at her wine. "But that's under control. The children are doing as well as can be expected with their father in jail, and Warren — you met Warren — is coming back this weekend to help out some more. We'll get through this, especially if we can keep those damn busybody Dunnes away." She drank again. "But you mentioned that you'd had some kind of breakthrough. Did you mean in Hal's case? Can you tell me what it is?"

Still stinging from his argument with Hardy, Abe nevertheless realized that he didn't want to volunteer too much to Ruth Chase. Though a little bit of an enthusiastic reception over what he considered a major accomplishment in the investigation wouldn't be the worst thing in the world. So, carefully avoiding too much detail, he told her they had found a witness who would help Hal.

Ruth was a rapt and willing audience, a far cry from Hardy. And Glitsky knew that, even in the truncated version, it was a good story. "The bottom line," he concluded, "is Foster's alibi for the Tussaint murder may not hold. That's not proof that he killed him, but it's a good start. If I can get this in front of a judge, it might be enough to get a warrant. And as you say, once we start looking closely at any particular person, the odds go way up that we'll find something."

Sitting straight up on the front few inches of her chair, Ruth said, "All that sounds great, but I don't understand something."

"What's that?"

"It sounds to me, from what you learned today, that Foster must have killed this other man, Tussaint."

"I think he did, yes. But at the moment we don't have any witnesses saying they saw him do it. We don't have a murder weapon or a motive. We know where Foster wasn't that day — San Bruno — but we don't know where he was; if, for example, he was anywhere near Tussaint in the jail. There's no case to speak of."

"But he did kill him. Nobody doubts he did it, do they?"

Glitsky shook his head. "I don't. Not seriously."

"And he also killed this Maria woman?"

"Not so certain. Likely, maybe, but with no proof it was Foster, it might just as easily have been one of the other guards. Or none of them. Or a robber, even."

"You don't think it was any of those?"

"No."

"You think it was Foster."

Abe nodded. "I do. And I also think he's the guy doing the really dirty work."

"Why do you say that?"

"Because why would he and Cushing want anybody else involved? If it's only the two of them, they're cold-blooded, efficient, and keep their own secrets. It's a closed shop, and since it's been working for the past six years, why mess with it now?"

"So it's both of them?"

"That's my call."

"Which means this man Foster shot Katie, too, doesn't it? It has to mean that."

"Let's just say it would be consistent with what I think we already know."

This got Ruth pumped up enough to stand. "Well, Inspector, some judge has to be made to see this! Don't you think? Or the DA. Don't you work for the DA now? Didn't that column say you did? You work for Mr. Farrell, the very man who's charging Hal."

"Technically, yes, but . . ."

"If Mr. Farrell knew everything that you've been telling me, he'd never be able to keep Hal in jail, would he? He'd have to let him go. There wouldn't be any way they could convict him."

"Possibly not," Glitsky said. "But we have

no admissible evidence. At the moment, Hal is a suspect" — he held up his hand as Ruth opened her mouth to object — "as likely as Foster or anybody else. Much as there wasn't enough to arrest him, there's even less on someone else. We have to be patient and hope we can build a case. If it's any consolation, we're a step closer than we've been."

Something went out of her shoulders. "If you want to know the truth, Mr. Glitsky, that's not much consolation. I'm going to check on the kids and pour myself another glass of wine."

Glitsky watched her walk up the stairs. Slim yet curvy, she wasn't his idea of your average grandmother. He sat back on the couch. Outside, dusk gathered along with the fog at the windows. He wanted to be on his way and swore at himself for coming here with his ego-driven need to pass along his supposedly good news on her son's case. He realized that he should have waited until he had a result of some kind. Hal was still in jail, charged with murder, and Abe should have known that there would be precious little comfort for a mother dealing with those conditions for her son. He waited for her to come down, hoping he could find a way to spin his conclusions another half turn and leave on a more positive note.

When she reappeared, she gave him a quick thumbs-up with an indication toward the kids' bedroom, then grabbed her wineglass on the way back into the kitchen. Returning to her chair, she drank off some of the wine and said, "It's just Hal. I don't know how he's going to take all this. I mean, Katie first, then him getting arrested for killing her, and now, say what you will, he's one of the guys who lied to cover for Sergeant Foster. Don't you think some people, they get to a point where their life goes so far wrong that they can never get it back?"

Glitsky knew what she meant; to some extent, he thought the same thing. But he said to her, "Hal seems like a pretty strong guy to me."

"He is, but . . ." She sat back with a sigh and lifted her glass, took a drink, put it back down. "You know," she said, "I think it all goes back to his father's suicide."

"I thought that was ruled an accident."

"It was, but . . ." She took a deep breath and nodded. "The story we told Hal, everybody told him, was that it was an accident. I think Hal always knew it that wasn't true, or guessed it. Losing your dad is bad enough, but to lose him that way, you'd always feel like you'd been abandoned, wouldn't you?" Her next deep breath seemed to catch in her throat. "I don't know that he's ever really gotten over it, and now he's . . . Look where he is."

Ruth stared with an empty gaze across the room. She blinked once, twice, a third time, and to Glitsky's surprise, tears glistened in the corners of her eyes. "I'm just so afraid that these kinds of things — these tragedies — run in families, and they defeat people completely. And even though Hal is innocent, there's not going to be anything he's going to be able to do about it. But I know he didn't kill Katie. And we can't let this travesty continue. Someone has to stop this Foster person. And the sheriff."

"I believe that's going to happen, Ruth. It just may take a little more time." Abe leaned forward. "Are you all right? Is there somebody you can call to be with you here tonight?"

"That's all right," she said. She wiped the tears away from each cheek. "I'm a big girl. And Warren will be here tomorrow. We'll be fine."

53

Glitsky wasn't kidding when he'd told Hardy he was getting obsessed.

And why wouldn't he be?

He had made a career as a homicide investigator, and the idiots and sycophants within the city's bureaucracy had taken that away from him; more, they'd made him question his instincts and belief in himself. Many people, even now — including his friend Dismas Hardy — seemed to believe that he was following a false trail in this matter. He wanted — no, *needed* — to show them all that he still had what it took to do the job, had in fact never lost it.

The facts of the case cried out for obsession.

Ruth's wholly unexpected if subdued breakdown over Hal's life story had only added to Abe's sympathy for the man's plight. Here was a kid who had lost his mother, and then his father to suicide, followed by an unpleasant (to say the least) career choice, a challenging marriage, the murder of his wife, and his own incarceration.

From his car outside Hal's house, Abe called an understanding Treya and told her that he was going to be late getting home. He then placed another call. Fifteen minutes later, he pulled into the driveway in front of Jeff Elliot's home, a gingerbread Victorian just off Upper Market. Jeff's wife, Dorothy, greeted him cordially at the door and led him down the central hallway to a brightly lit office at the back of the house where Jeff sat in a leather recliner.

"The man of the hour," Jeff said. "I don't remember the last time the column got so much attention, Abe. It almost made me feel relevant for a minute there."

Glitsky took a seat. "I'm glad the reaction on your end was positive. I can't exactly say the same for mine."

"You're kidding. Who didn't like it?"

"Farrell. Diz. Especially Cushing, who I heard went to the mayor."

"I know." Elliot fairly beamed. "I got a call from my boss, who'd heard from him, too. Irresponsible journalism and all that. But I was quoting 'a source close to the investigation.' What was I supposed to do, ignore you?"

"Others have been known to."

"I'm sure. Mostly to their detriment, I'd bet."

"Sometimes that, too."

"So what's up?"

"What's up is I broke Foster's alibi for Tussaint."

Jeff looked at him with unfeigned admiration. "That was fast. And you're right, it's huge. What do you have?"

Glitsky took out his tape recorder, placed it on the recliner's arm, and hit the play button. Speaking over the opening minute of the interview, he brought the columnist up to date on the woman he was talking to, how he got connected to her, and how she fit into his investigation. Dorothy came down the hall and, leaning against the door, listened in as well. When the playback stopped, Abe picked up the recorder and hit the pause button. "What do you think?"

Somewhat to his surprise, and definitely to his disappointment, Jeff's countenance had darkened as the playback had gone on, and now he was all but frowning. "You got her, all right," he said, "but I can't use it. At least as it is."

"Sure you can. Why can't you?"

"Because it's too far removed, Abe. She

412

didn't tell me this. She told you. And you're telling me what she told you that her husband told her. Not gonna fly."

"Sure it will. I went and talked to her, and she told me her husband was told to lie. Don't you believe that?"

"Of course I believe it, Abe. But there's none of what the lawyers would call foundation. You could have hired an actress to say these words, and if I ran them, or even an account of them, where would I be?"

"You'd be breaking a monster story."

Elliot shook his head. "Not this way." He held up a calming hand. "And I absolutely believe you, but that's not the point."

"I've got her number, Jeff. You can call her."

"And then what? You really want me to tell her that the cop she talked to went to the press?"

Glitsky let out a breath and looked over to Dorothy, who was looking at her husband. "She's telling the truth. This is the break you've been waiting for, Jeff."

He nodded patiently. "I'm not denying that, and I'm delighted to see it, because it tells me where I might be able to bring some pressure. But I've got to get this, the basic information, from the horse's mouth. Not to worry, because from what you said on the tape here, it sounds like somebody's already got that. From one of the other guards. What's his name?"

"Davis. Chick Davis."

"That's it. That's how you got her to cave, when you said —"

"I know what I said."

"Right. That Chick Davis had already said they'd never gone down to San Bruno that day. Let's get Davis to come down and talk to me, and then I've got a source I can use and print."

"Except," Glitsky said, "that I made that up about Davis, to get her to talk."

"You lied to her?" Dorothy asked from the doorway.

Glitsky turned to her and shrugged. "I gave her some false information. She reacted to it by telling me the truth. It's not an unknown technique."

Again, Jeff lifted his hand. "Thus the issue with quoting people who told you they talked to other people. I'm sure Dorothy doesn't mean to criticize, Abe. I'm glad it worked. I just can't use it. That's the problem."

Glitsky brought both hands up to his forehead and ran them back over the top of his head. "This is too close. We can't let it slip away."

"Okay, look, hold on a minute," Jeff said. "You say you've got their number. Maybe all is not lost. You play Andy Biehl the tape, or maybe not even that. Just tell him you know what you know. This is his chance to save himself. You offer him some kind of deal. You already know the truth, and it's only a matter of time before it comes out. Or I call Foster in my role of ace reporter. I've got this information. I don't name the informant and — my own little lie — I think we'll be running with it. Would he care to comment?"

As it turned out, Foster didn't care to comment. As soon as Jeff identified himself on the phone, the chief deputy hung up on him.

Midnight, and Glitsky was still awake.

He'd gone to bed with Treya at ten-thirty and hadn't been able to get to sleep within the next twenty minutes; that was the limit of his endurance before he declared the effort hopeless and got up. Now he sat up in the living room by the picture window — still life with fog — with a book called *Consider the Fork* facedown on his lap. It was a good book, full of fascinating facts about how cooking utensils and pots and kitchens had evolved, but he'd given up after only a few pages, turned off the light, and tried not to think.

The not thinking wasn't going very well.

Eventually, he got up and walked in to check on Rachel and Zachary. They slept in the same room because that was how they felt most comfortable. Thank God for them, he thought as he pulled the blankets up first around one, then the other. He stood at their door, listening to them breathing, grateful that both were healthy and apparently well-balanced.

For an instant, his overactive brain flashed back to the Chase children, with all their difficulties, especially Ellen, or Ellie, as Ruth called her. He couldn't imagine dealing with that day to day with his own children — ADHD or hyperactivity or whatever it might be. Unbidden, Ruth's comment that Ellie's problems were "under control" slammed into his brainpan. He wondered if that meant Ruth had put Ellie on medication. He should tell Hardy to talk to Hal about his instructions for the kids, make sure things at his home didn't get lost in the shuffle.

Thinking about Hal brought him sharply up against a conflict he'd had to resolve in his own life. He was nearly fifteen years older than Treya. When they'd started talk-

416

ing about marriage, Abe hadn't wanted to start another family. He'd already raised three boys. He did not want to have children with Treya and then not live long enough to raise them. His relationship with his own father, Nat, was one of the touchstones of his life and always had been. He regularly talked to all of his grown-up boys and saw them with as much frequency as he could. The importance of fathers could not be overestimated; for a child to lose one had to be devastating.

Even more so, to lose a father to suicide.

As Glitsky looked at his son and daughter, he felt a pang. He had no control over it, and he knew it, but he vowed silently that if he could extend his life span at all by will or fortitude, by nutrition or exercise or attitude, he would do whatever it took.

Someday, Abe knew, Zachary would move into his own room down that short hallway, but for the past four years, his young son's future bedroom had been the family's computer room. Now Abe went there, closing the door behind him. Sitting at the ergonomic chair in the dark, he reached for the mouse and brought the screen to life. Going to Google with no plan in mind, he pulled up Jeff Elliot's column from that morning, which he reread and where he found nothing new — just the same tantalizing connections.

Searching "Hal Chase" provided him around a thousand hits, everything from the articles that had run in the local and national media, to blogs and discussion groups and all of the other permutations of online madness that seemed to attend any sensational story. He glanced at the first couple of websites at random, then realized that there was too much information to digest, and probably little if any that he didn't already know.

He should go back to bed and try to get some sleep.

Instead, he typed in "Katie Chase" and discovered nearly as many hits as he had for her husband. Glitsky made a mental note to check back with Frannie on Ruth's contention that Katie had been dealing with mental illness as opposed to emotional problems. He thought it unlikely, first because Frannie was a marriage and family counselor and not a licensed psychiatrist, and second because he hadn't heard it from any other source. If Katie suffered from mental illness that needed medication, Glitsky was fairly certain he would have known about it before today.

Of course, mothers-in-law had been

known to form and hold opinions without any basis in fact. Almost everybody in the world saw what they expected or wanted to see, believed what they wanted to believe.

The name "Ruth Chase" brought up several hundred more hits, but Glitsky knew it was a common enough name. Finding the various hits on Hal's stepmother among the other Ruth Chases would require more time and energy than Glitsky felt it warranted, especially since all of this Web surfing was mere curiosity, a mindless exercise fed by his insomnia.

However, at the bottom of the first page of the Ruth Chase hits, under "Searches related to Ruth Chase," he saw "Ruth Chase San Francisco" and clicked on that. Once again, several pages of hits turned up, but this time Abe could identify Hal's stepmother among the crowd. Somewhat to his surprise — although it shouldn't have been, since he knew she had a college-age son — she had a Facebook account. A blog site, the last entry from three years ago, gave her tag as WineBitch and seemed to be about investing in upscale wines and the wine auction market. There was a short article in the *San Mateo County Times* about the marriage of Ruth Johannson to Peter Chase in 1989, the second marriage for both and a new beginning for the couple, each of whom had lost a spouse to tragedy — Pete's first wife to a cerebral hemorrhage and Ruth's first husband to a tragic accident. There was a legal notice about her adoption of Hal in 1991.

Yawning now and finally beginning to fade, Glitsky clicked on another site that caught his eye and found himself looking at a short news article from the *San Francisco Chronicle* in 1995:

Deputy's Death Ruled Accidental
After an initial preliminary ruling of suicide, a police investigation into the death of a San Francisco jail guard has concluded that the drug and alcohol overdose death last Saturday was accidental. Peter Chase, 46, was taking medication for his insomnia and imbibed alcohol in a combination that proved lethal. When his wife, Ruth, returned from grocery shopping, she discovered her husband lying on the floor of their garage and called paramedics. Following the autopsy, police investigators noted that there was no sign of foul play, that Chase had no reason to take his own life and had been in good spirits when last seen by his wife. Investigators also found no evidence of marital or financial difficulties. Ruth

Chase expressed her gratitude to the investigating team for the revised ruling: "I'm just so relieved to have this ordeal behind us."

54

Adam Foster's feet pounded on the tread-mill. He didn't give a shit about the signs that told all the exercisers to be thoughtful of the other members and limit their time on a machine to twenty minutes. Fuck that and fuck them. He'd already gone a half hour and had barely gotten a good sweat going; he'd go at least that long again. The one thing you didn't want to do if you worked with clientele like his was to get soft. He wasn't about to let that happen.

As he jogged, his mind ran along, think-ing that all this recent media hoopla about Alanos Tussaint and the rest of it was a pain in the ass for sure but that it shouldn't really worry him. These things tended to go in cycles. He remembered, for example, when Wes Farrell had been running for DA and his main opponent, a liberal cretin named Ron Gabriel, had decided that conditions in the jail should be a main concern of the citizenry.

The incumbent DA, on his way out, hadn't been nearly hard enough in investigating allegations of impropriety in the lockup, and Ron Gabriel was going to make a Sheriff's Department cleanup a major priority in his administration. The poor inmates were being mistreated on a daily basis, and a city that prided itself on sensitivity to the plight of misunderstood and underserved individuals should not stand for it.

Adam Foster's take on Ron Gabriel? The guy didn't have a clue. First thing, most of the inmates lived the life of Riley, with more amenities than they had in their own rathole apartments, flophouses, crash pads, or whatever other cribs they might have called home. They got three square meals, and good ones, every day. Meat, spuds, gravy, bread, milk, green stuff if you wanted it. His fellow guards ate the same meals, and you never heard them complain.

On top of that, with a little cooperation, any reasonably motivated jailbird could get his hands on whatever else made his life good — drugs from weed to heroin to Oxy, alcohol, and television. Of course, none of that was free. There was even a charge for the choice bunk in each cell. But this stuff wasn't free on the outside, either. If Ron Gabriel or any of his ilk wanted to ask the average inmate how he or she liked the jail experience, Adam Foster bet eighty percent would say it was just fine.

What Burt Cushing always came back to was true: It was a well-oiled machine. The oil that made it all work so well was the money the inmates brought in on their books from peeps on the outside, then spent on the goods he and Burt provided.

Once in a while you'd get some greedy douche bag who thought he was a player and could ease in on some of the action, and that's where Adam came in, enforcing the status quo. He was their keeper, supplying protection so the majority would be safe while they were behind bars. Protection was a major commodity all over the world. Everybody understood that. It was only when some foolish or mentally challenged inmate, such as Alanos Tussaint, tried to upset the apple cart that action had to be taken.

Given the socioeconomic background of most of these animals and their marginal-at-best levels of sophistication, action had to be forceful, immediate, and unambiguous. No. Somebody stepped out of line, you whacked him back in, and if he still didn't get it, what happened was unfortunate but had to be done for the greater good. They always brought it on themselves. Always.

Now they were in another cycle where the call for reform hovered in the air. Foster was surprised to see it coming from Glitsky, who, as a longtime cop in the Hall, must have been aware of the basic realities. And from Farrell, who had been the soul of benignly tolerant laissez-faire for the first three years of his administration. What the hell had gotten into these guys?

Well, okay, Solis-Martinez.

Maybe they'd moved too fast on that, didn't think through the ramifications. But he wasn't about to whip himself over it. She'd put herself into a situation that had been settled. If you stir up a hornets' nest and don't expect to get stung, you're a dumb shit. And dumb shits have a tendency not to survive.

Despite the rants of that meddling Jeff Elliot, they had no chance to connect Foster or Burt to Maria Solis-Martinez. He'd done that job right. There was no evidence, and none, he knew, would ever turn up. Foster was a pro, and the truth was that random violence happened every night in the city. Glitsky and Farrell could believe what they wanted, but they'd never be able to prove a damn thing.

So, yeah, the next few weeks would probably be a hassle, but if there was one thing Foster had learned about his boss, it was Cushing's ability to deflect not only most general criticism but especially official opprobrium. In six years, through at least three cycles of the kind of witch hunt they were experiencing now, no one had ever laid a glove on them. Every investigation into alleged crimes committed inside the jail had come to nothing.

Foster had no doubt that even the Tussaint situation, which had bred its own unexpected and festering sore, would be settled in the coming days or weeks. The Luther Jones case was a nonstarter. This time Foster had been careful that nobody saw anything. He would bet they wouldn't be able to prove he was even in the jail when Luther OD'd. If there were alibi discrepancies for Tussaint — Foster was thinking of Hal Chase — he knew that an alibi problem, absent evidence of or an eyewitness to the crime, was all but useless. People mixed up dates and days and what they had done and when they had done it. The paperwork showed he'd been at Bruno. It would be a nonissue.

Right now he was more concerned about

a call he'd gotten this morning about Hal Chase. The woman said she had important information and needed to see him in person but wouldn't elaborate. She wouldn't give her name and wouldn't come to the office. He couldn't get her to say if it was about the Katie Chase murder or something else, and it was the something else that worried him.

Chances are it was bullshit. Somebody who'd had a dream or a clairvoyant moment or otherwise wanted to grab a piece of a high-profile case. There was also, truth be told, an unheralded and titillating but under-the-table upside to these regular flare-ups of infamy. For as long as his name, and sometimes his picture, was in the paper or on the news, Foster became — for a certain type of woman — catnip. Clean-cut, hard-looking, unyielding, he seemed to fill a specific niche: equal parts cowboy, outlaw, celebrity, killer. It shouldn't have been much of a surprise when he considered the amount of mail that inmates received was usually in direct correlation to the degree of their notoriety, but the few times it had happened to him, it always struck him as a pleasant bonus to his work, a reward of sorts for the way he did his job.

One way or the other, with all the shit that

was going down, he could ill afford not to follow this up. He told the woman he'd meet her after he finished his workout.

Though John Strout hated to admit it, occasionally he was not as absolutely rigorous as he could have been in the performance of his duties. As a doctor and a scientist, he knew that his job as medical examiner was to objectively analyze the bodies of the deceased and to make a definitive ruling on what had been the cause of death. Over the course of his forty-some years on the job, he had performed literally thousands of autopsies, and he took great pride in his work, knowing that he was often in a sense the last true voice of the victim, calling out from beyond the grave for justice.

The body, he knew, held its own truths, and his sacred duty was to tease out the oft-times hidden meaning behind those truths.

But sometimes — he hoped and believed that it was once only in a very great while — circumstances would conspire to impact his diligence and his objectivity. The van would pull up, and all at once he would have four bullet-riddled young bodies to autopsy, and he did not generally go looking for signs of congestive heart failure; or an elderly homeless man whose blood alcohol level of 4.6 would have been enough to kill him several times over — did it really matter that he was also fatally hypothermic? Or, as in a case like that of Alanos Tussaint, Strout would get a body that, frankly, nobody cared about, and a plausible story from a reliable source to go along with it, and he'd find the obvious cause of death and rule on it.

Now, on this gray Saturday midmorning, he was sitting in front of the computer at his desk, going over the results he'd signed off on with Tussaint. At first glance, nothing had been amiss. Blunt force head trauma was unquestionably the correct call. Since the body had long since been cremated, nobody was ever going to examine it and come to a different conclusion. But Strout had followed his own guidelines for conducting autopsies and had taken a couple dozen very clear full-color photographs of the body back and front, as well as of the fatal head wound, and he could blow them up on his computer screen to examine in larger-than-life detail.

He'd hardly begun to go through them when it became clear to him that he had not given sufficient attention to Tussaint's body as a whole. Strout knew that life in jail was not easy, and everyday interactions could result in lacerations and abrasions. These guys didn't tend to say "excuse me" when they got close to each other in line, or shackled and in transit, or passing in a hallway. They'd push each other around, get slammed into bars or walls; being physical was more or less their default setting.

Even against that backdrop, this time around, the pictures of Tussaint's injuries showed unmistakable signs of the deceased having been the focus of if not an outright beating then at least a substantial fight. And yes, both the guards' statements and the following investigation by SFPD inspectors had acknowledged that Tussaint had been in a fight just prior to his slip. That was how he'd come to be in an isolation cell. But how, Strout wondered, had he missed the similarities of the welting and the other bruising on the shoulders and upper back?

He probably hadn't paid enough attention to the full-body pictures because he'd been expecting a single sharp blow to the temple that had produced a concussion and massive internal cerebral bleeding, which had brought about Tussaint's death. But upon closer review of several of these bruises, he could make out the clear outline of the weapon that had caused them — straight and almost an inch thick. It read "nightstick" almost as clearly as if it had a caption under it.

Strout knew that the thick, black, heavy, rock-hard batons, a staple on the belt of most city policemen, were forbidden in the jail, but he'd stake his reputation that a nightstick had caused at least three of the injuries. They may not have contributed directly to Tussaint's death — Strout could not say when the man had sustained them in relation to the fatal head injury — but the fact that he hadn't focused on them as part of his investigation was, at the very least, an oversight.

He scrolled back to the extreme close-ups of the wound that had split the scalp and broken the temporal bone. Yes, he realized, this could have come from a slip-and-fall situation where Tussaint slammed his head against the concrete corner of a bed. But, Strout noted (with some very small satisfaction to balance his growing disgust with himself), while taking his pictures, he had peeled back the skin over the bone at the side of Tussaint's head to reveal the damage to the skull itself. This was a shallow furrowed indentation about four inches long — about what you'd expect (if you'd recently been looking at similar bruises) from a nightstick or some similar object, rather than the kind of sharp-edged break in the bone that a fall against the corner of a concrete bed might produce.

Strout sat back and pulled his eyes away from the computer screen. He reached for the hand grenade he kept on his desk and absently tossed it from hand to hand, his face etched in a deep frown. After perhaps a minute, he placed the grenade back on the desk and reached for his Rolodex, flipping through the names until he got to the one he wanted. He punched the numbers on his desk phone.

A woman's voice answered the phone with a simple "Hello," and the doctor said, "Good mornin'. This is John Strout over here at the morgue. I wonder if I might have a few words with Abe Glitsky. I'd say it's pretty important."

"He's changing his ruling?" Hardy asked. "Has Strout ever done that before?"

"Not exactly changing his ruling," Glitsky said. "Although he made it a point to remind me that he'd originally left it as 'Accidental death not inconsistent with homicide.' "

"That's way different than straight-up 'homicide.' "

"Yes, it is." In his own self-contained way,

432

Glitsky was obviously pumped up. "He just wanted everybody to know that in his opinion, it was a whole lot more homicide than accident, and he was respectfully suggesting that everybody take another look at the case. Anyway, I wanted you to be the first to know. You think Farrell's at home?"

"Saturday? Anybody's guess. Your wife might know, wouldn't you think?"

"Good call. Maybe I'll ask her."

"What do you want with Wes?"

"Well, if this is now a righteous homicide at the jail, I want the DA to take over the investigation."

"You want it." It wasn't a question.

"I can taste it," Abe said. "It's all unraveling over there. This Tussaint thing is going to take them down."

"Call Wes first," Hardy said. "Don't do anything dumb. Or should I say anything *else* dumb."

"I'll be the epitome of restraint," Glitsky said. "But only for fifteen seconds after Wes gives the okay. I will talk to Burt Cushing, I promise you that. I wonder how he'll take getting sweated."

"There. That's what I mean. You don't want to talk to anybody else about this. As you say, it's starting to unravel all on its own. This is when Wes really ought to call in the feds. Killing an inmate is a clear civil rights violation, a federal felony. They've got all the jurisdiction in the world, and they love this stuff. Plus, you lie to the FBI about any old thing, on that alone, you go to prison. They'll have tremendous leverage you don't have any part of. And there are how many liars on the San Bruno thing alone?"

"Six."

"There you go. One of them will talk."

"I wouldn't be so sure, Diz. If any of them admits they weren't in San Bruno, they're essentially confessing to covering up a murder. All of them could wind up going down for conspiracy or worse. I don't think Cushing or Foster is going to let them forget that."

"The feds offer immunity, and that goes away."

"Maybe, but maybe not. They don't need immunity if they never cop to the lie, so why would they? Here's another idea. How about your client?" Glitsky asked. "He's one of the six."

"On the advice of his attorney," Hardy said, "Hal won't be talking. Especially not to the feds. You want to know my real concern?"

"Sure."

"If it comes to it, they try to pin Tussaint on Hal. The bogus alibi, if it comes out, doesn't need to have been for Foster. Any one of the six would do, wouldn't it? And Hal's already up for murder. Why not stick him with another one?"

Glitsky was silent for so long that Hardy asked him if he was still there. "Just thinking," he said. "You might be right."

"I don't want to be," Hardy said, "but I don't think it's an impossible scenario."

"It still depends, though, on one of the five giving up on San Bruno. And if I were one of those guys, I'd never admit it. Ever. To anybody."

"No," Hardy said. "Neither would I."

55

Glitsky didn't know whether to blame it on the six months he'd spent being a civilian, or on his disgust with the ease with which law enforcement professionals could and did game the system, but he felt that the only progress made in any of these investigations had been because he'd followed his own path, not necessarily the rules of procedure about which he'd always been so punctilious, and which sworn officers were supposed to follow.

His 'CityTalk' interview, his chat with Allison Beale, his decision to go to Strout for a second look at the Tussaint autopsy: All of these moves had brought him new and important facts, as well as a sense that he was closing the net around Foster and Cushing; eventually, he felt, if he kept at it the way he was going, he'd get them, along with the evidence to put them away. If he personally kept up the pressure, one of the principals — Cushing, Foster, a guard, a guard's wife — would break.

He wanted to rattle some more cages. Play people off against one another. Make something happen.

So he didn't call Farrell when he hung up with Hardy. Hardy was right — when Farrell heard about Tussaint, he would almost undoubtedly call in the feds, which would be a clarion call to everyone in Cushing's realm to go into severe lockdown mode. Everybody would lawyer up and take the Fifth. Nobody was going to give up the truth about San Bruno. No witnesses would turn up to say they saw the Tussaint beating. Nobody was even going to point a finger at Hal. This was blue-collar-cop culture, where the code of silence was all but absolute.

Around one o'clock, Glitsky found himself knocking on Burt Cushing's front door, a beautiful house on Clay in outer Pacific Heights that Glitsky thought could have gone a long way toward supporting an investigation, not to say an indictment, for corruption. How a career civil servant who'd gone to City College and never earned a salary over a hundred and fifty thousand dollars could afford to live in this stately mansion was the sort of question that tended not to get asked of politicians.

The sheriff wore khakis, black cop shoes, and a blue pullover sweater. He greeted Glitsky with a firm handshake and some small talk as he led him though a lavishly furnished living room with a view to rival Patti Orosco's — Golden Gate Bridge, Marin headlands, sailboats on the bay — and into his dimly lit office down a short hallway to the left. In that room — floor-to-ceiling bookshelves, high-backed red leather chairs, latticed windows, a huge globe of the earth — he went around his desk and sat down, indicating that Glitsky should take one of the chairs.

"All right, Lieutenant," he began, and came out swinging. "I admire your balls, I'll give you that. Cutting into my weekend when you've got to know I have nothing to say to you. I only agreed you could come by because I assume Wes Farrell ordered you to apologize to me in person for that 'CityTalk' horseshit, and I would like things to run smoothly between our departments down at the Hall."

The opening was fine with Glitsky, who didn't want to pretend to be friends or even colleagues anymore. "That's not it, Sheriff. Not even close."

Cushing's nostrils flared. He put his palms

down on the top of his desk. "Well, then, I don't know what else you think is important enough to get in the way of the kickoff."

"I got a call this morning from John Strout," Glitsky said. "He no longer thinks that Tussaint's death was an accident."

"Really?"

"Really. You've got a handful of guards who have sworn that he was alone in his cell when he died. Now Strout's saying somebody killed him."

Cushing showed no sign of surprise or alarm. Shrugging elaborately, he said, "The old fool got it wrong the first time, then got it wrong again. So what?"

"I talked to another witness yesterday who said Adam Foster killed Tussaint. A credible witness. Not one likely to die of an overdose anytime soon, and that witness is on tape."

Cushing shot a flat hostile glance over the desk. "How many times I got to say this, Lieutenant: So the fuck what? Who's this witness?"

"No comment."

Cushing huffed out a small laugh. "Oh yeah. Very strong. Stop the presses. So Strout says he was killed. Who cares? He'd been in a fight. Everybody says there was a fight, the animals going at it like they do. If Strout thinks it's one of them instead of the fall that killed him, who gives a shit? The guy's just as dead either way. They want to do another investigation, be my guest." Shaking his head, he sounded almost apologetic. "Look, Lieutenant, I don't know any more about it. Are you about done?"

"Not quite. I thought we might talk a little about Katie Chase."

Cushing's eyes briefly went to the corner of the room. Then back to Glitsky. "What about her?"

"You told me you didn't have any special relationship with her."

"Right. I've been married twenty-five years. I've got three daughters." He pointed a finger. "Don't you fuck with my marriage, Lieutenant. I'm warning you."

"You've already threatened your marriage, Sheriff. And it's going to come out, just like all the rest of this is going to come out."

"There's nothing to come out."

"You deny talking to Katie Chase on the phone several times a day over a two-and-a-half- or three-month period a couple of years ago?"

"She helped my daughter with some medication. We talked a few times about that."

"I'm not talking a few times, Sheriff. I'm talking every day for a couple of months."

"No."

"No, you didn't? Katie's phone records indicate otherwise."

"Those records couldn't show anything."

"There are records, though. Is that what you're saying?"

Cushing made no reply.

"The answer is yes," Glitsky said. "There are records of her calling you at your office."

"Records don't show what you're talking about."

"So you admit there were calls and the records are correct." Glitsky sat back into the chair. "Listen to me, Sheriff. Nobody outside of you and your family is going to care about your infidelity, but those folks are going to care a lot, aren't they? And you know that it'll be a piece of cake to verify wherever you met and whatever you did once it's part of a homicide investigation. And it will be."

Cushing made a move to get up. "We're finished here."

Glitsky put out a hand, stopping him. "Not quite. I'm not talking about infidelity. I'm talking about homicide. I'm talking about Tussaint, and Maria, and Luther, and Katie Chase. I'm talking about Adam Foster."

"Good for you," Cushing said. "I'm not talking about any of it or any of them. Not here, not now, not ever. It's all a house of cards."

Glitsky shook his head. "What I'm telling you is that we and probably the feds are going after Foster for the homicides, at least on Tussaint and Luther and Maria, and the wider the investigation grows, the more likely it is that your infidelity will be part of the story."

"It's not part of the story, Lieutenant." Cushing pushed on his hands and got to his feet. "You can't prove a lick of it, and I've wasted enough of my day talking to you. So now I'm telling you to get your meddling ass out of my house. And I mean now. Before I call the real cops."

56

At eleven-fifteen that night, the phone rang next to Abe's bed. Jolted out of his slumber, he reached over to grab it before it rang again. "Glitsky."

"Abe, this is Abby Foley." It wasn't her half-apologetic late-night voice; she was all but breathless with excitement. "Sorry to wake you, but you might want to come down."

"Down where? The Hall? What time is it?"

"Late. We're out by the Lombard entrance to the Presidio. One of the parking lots just inside." She got herself collected for a half second before she blurted it out. "It looks like Adam Foster shot himself."

It didn't take Glitsky fifteen minutes to get dressed and make the drive through the dense fog. When he got to the lot, he parked next to a black-and-white squad car at the periphery and made his way over to where a good-sized knot of people had gathered by one of the lot's overhead lights. Across the asphalt, about as far away from where he stood as from where he'd parked, he could make out a set of klieg lights and another area of activity — undoubtedly the Crime Scene team — surrounding a dark-colored car. After nodding around at the group, Abe moved off a few paces with Abby and JaMorris.

"How'd you two get the call on this?" he asked.

"Pure luck," JaMorris said. "We were on call. We didn't know it was Foster till we checked the registration and then looked at the body. It's him."

"Suicide? Clearly?"

"Sure looks like it," Abby said. "One shot to the temple. Gun still in his hand."

"Who called it in?"

"One of the security guys here. We've already talked to him."

"What'd he know?"

"Not much," JaMorris said. "The car wasn't here at eight, then it was when he made his rounds again at nine. This is evidently a favored make-out spot, so he gave it some room until ten, when he thought he'd go over and move 'em along."

"So he didn't hear the shot?"

"No," Abby replied. "Windows closed.

Nothing out of the ordinary."

"Has Crime Scene told you anything else?"

"Not yet," JaMorris said. "Tell you the truth, we were waiting for you."

"Not that I don't love getting called out at midnight, but why was that?"

"After the 'CityTalk' thing," Abby said, "he seemed like he was your guy. We thought you'd want to be in on it from the get-go."

"I appreciate that," Glitsky said. "Let's go check it out."

Their timing was excellent. The techs had finished the preliminary work; they would tow the car down to the police lot and go over it in greater detail, but they had already photographed and swabbed, fingerprinted and measured, and now they were ready to have the body tagged and bagged and hauled off to the morgue, although for the moment it remained slumped against the driver's door.

Len Faro, the always well-dressed head of the CSI team, saw them coming and walked out to meet them. "Hey, Abe," he said with recognition. "You back on the job?"

"More or less," Glitsky replied. "The glamour keeps drawing me back." He cocked his head at the car, a Honda Civic. "Is this what it looks like?"

"Maybe more than most."

"Meaning?"

"Meaning, they tell me we got a note." Reaching into his trench coat, Faro extracted a Ziploc bag. In it was a small piece of paper torn from a spiral-top notepad. "I saw this sticking out of his coat pocket, and I lifted it," he said. "I don't want to take it out of the evidence bag before it goes to the lab, but you can see through the bag what he wrote."

He held it out, and Glitsky leaned over to read the words, written in pencil in a bold though barely legible cursive scrawl: "Hal Chase never killed anybody. I'm sorry I got him into this."

Abby Foley, leaning in closer for a better look, grabbed her partner's arm. "Jambo, look at this."

JaMorris stepped forward, squinted at the page, then straightened. He put a hand on Glitsky's shoulder. "I'd say you got to him, Lieutenant. Congratulations."

"Got to who?" Faro asked.

"Our victim here," JaMorris replied. "Abe was a step or two away from bringing him in."

"I guess he decided he wasn't coming in alive," Abby said.

"How close were you, Abe?" Faro asked.

"Obviously," JaMorris answered for him, "close enough."

Abe scowled. In his wildest dreams, he hadn't contemplated this kind of resolution. It had never occurred to him that Foster was the kind of guy who would kill himself; his first reaction after the dawning certainty was a gnawing hollowness in his gut. Viewed in a certain light, he knew that it was a clear win for him and for justice. But it felt so sudden, so incomplete, so unfinished; Foster had cheated Abe out of his victory.

In a second wave of guilt and nausea, he flashed back to his talk earlier that day with Burt Cushing, in which Abe had made his case against Foster abundantly clear, and equally clear the unspoken message: If Cushing gave up his defense of and collusion with his chief deputy, his family might never hear about his infidelities; all of his immediate problems in terms of the jail would be laid at Foster's feet, and the sheriff himself, though equally guilty under the law, would walk away clean.

Had Cushing called Foster today and cut him loose? Glitsky couldn't dismiss the possibility that however much this looked like a suicide, it was Burt Cushing cleaning up loose ends.

Glitsky swallowed against his rising bile,

chewed at his cheek. "You got anything else, Len?" he asked. "Before we take a look."

"As a matter of fact," Faro said, "I was just getting to it. We're having Christmas a little early." He pulled a Baggie from another pocket and held it up in the light. "Bullet. From the cushion behind the seat."

Abby said, "Let me guess. Thirty-eight?"

Faro shook the slug in its bag. He nodded. "Looks like. That would match the gun we found in his hand." Then added, "You really know this guy, don't you?"

Abby broke a smile. "We were just getting close. And talk about Christmas — you might want to check that slug and the gun against the Katie Chase evidence."

JaMorris turned to her. "You think?"

Abby shrugged. "Worth a try. How could it hurt?"

While they'd been speaking, the coroner's van had arrived, and the assistants were rolling their gurney over to Foster's car.

"Last chance to get a good look," Faro said.

Glitsky nodded. "Should we expect any other surprises?"

"Not so much. But if you see something you want to talk about, let me know. I'll be hanging around for a while."

"We're on it," Glitsky said.

They walked over to the Honda, the two Homicide inspectors trailing a step or two behind Abe, who opened the passenger door and knelt down on the asphalt. There wasn't much to see. CSI had taken the gun away. Foster, up against the other door, wore a herringbone sport coat over a canary-yellow dress shirt with the collar unbuttoned. A gold chain hung around his neck. There was a clean bullet hole in front of and a little above his right ear, with a line of blood flowing out of it down into his shirt. The rest of the blood and other matter had spattered the driver's-side window, leaving the front of Foster's body unsullied — the neatly pressed black slacks, black socks, alligator loafers.

Though the klieg lights lit up the area like daylight, Abby handed Abe a flashlight, and he ran it over the rug and flooring on both sides, the passenger seat, the dashboard. With the exception of the fingerprint powder, the interior of the car was pretty much spotless.

There was the bullet hole in the cushion behind his head.

Glitsky turned to the inspectors and handed the flashlight back to Abby. A little rickety, he got to his feet. The car had a showroom finish in the bright lights. Leaning over, he took a last look inside. "Do you see something?" Abby asked him.

"No," he said, "but I know I should. I always miss something the first time. You guys notice anything?"

"No."

"No."

Abe gave it a last glance, stem to stern. "Okay, then," he said. "What do you say we call it a night?"

57

CITYTALK
by JEFFREY ELLIOT

According to sources close to the investigation, progress has been made in the case of the murder of DA Investigator Maria Solis-Martinez, who had been working on a case involving purported improprieties over the past year at the San Francisco jail, including the deaths of several inmates.

In an earlier "CityTalk" column, an unnamed source made clear accusations against the Sheriff's Department under Sheriff Burt Cushing and his chief deputy, Adam Foster, citing a conspiracy linking Ms. Solis-Martinez's murder to the deaths in jail of inmates Alanos Tussaint and Luther Jones, as well as to the murder of Katie Chase, the wife of jail guard Hal Chase, who had been indicted and jailed for the crime.

The outcry from public officials was immediate and strident. Mayor Leland Crawford, four Superior Court judges and no fewer than six city supervisors called this newspaper to demand a retraction. Sheriff Cushing threatened a lawsuit against the *Chronicle.* One of the most specific allegations concerned the death of Alanos Tussaint, first ruled an accident as a result of the alibi of Chief Deputy Foster at the time of the death.

On Friday afternoon, DA investigators learned of gaps in Foster's alibi. The next morning, Medical Examiner John Strout confirmed additional findings suggesting that the Tussaint killing was not accidental.

On Saturday evening, perhaps feeling the noose tightening, Foster apparently shot himself in a Presidio parking lot. Investigators today confirmed that a note in his jacket pocket appeared to be an admission of responsibility for at least one of these deaths. Ballistics tests confirmed that the gun Foster allegedly used to kill himself — a .38 revolver found in his hand at the scene — also fired the bullet that killed Katie Chase.

When apprised of these developments late Sunday afternoon, Sheriff Cushing issued the following written statement from his office: "I am shocked and saddened beyond words to learn that Adam Foster, my trusted deputy and friend for more than twenty years, has evidently taken his own life. I am further shocked by what appears to be evidence pointing to his involvement in corruption at the jail. If these allegations are true, that conduct would be out of character with the man I knew and trusted for all these years. I have ordered an immediate, thorough, and transparent investigation into all aspects of our jail policies and procedures, with an emphasis on anything that might have been under the control of Chief Deputy Foster. The public demands and deserves the highest level of integrity from its law enforcement officers. I intend to ensure that that standard of excellence is met in the jail at all times."

Meanwhile, Wes Farrell has announced his own investigation into the running of the jail, and invited the federal authorities to consider opening their own parallel investigation. In light of the ballistics evidence directly linking Foster with the murder of Katie Chase, DA Wes Farrell has ordered Hal Chase released from jail and all charges relating to his wife's murder dropped. Asked about his reaction to this chain of events, my original source, who was primarily responsible for the DA's investigation into these incidents, declined to comment except to say that "the evidence speaks for itself."

The impromptu get-together at Hal's house that Monday night wasn't what Dismas Hardy would have called a great time. After all, Katie was only a couple of weeks dead, and nobody could forget that. Her shadow hung over the gathered guests like a shroud. But there was no question that the fresh air of pure relief had washed the house clean of its psychic overload. It didn't hurt that the fog had disappeared over the weekend, and the temperature had cracked seventy during the day. Downright balmy, by the city's standards for midsummer, much less for December.

The front door stayed open, and the food was an unintentional reprise of exactly what they'd had after Katie's funeral — a large deli tray and some salads, rolls, and condiments. A good-sized crowd, anchored by Hal's brother, Warren, Ruth, and Hal with his two kids — little Will in his arms and Ellen glued to his leg — the gathering was far larger than Hardy had expected. People were standing all around the living room and kitchen in conversational groupings.

There were other surprises: The dreaded "in-law" women — Carli Dunne and Katie's two sisters — were already there when Hardy and Frannie arrived; they'd apparently made peace with Hal right away. About a dozen guys near Hal's age — likely other guards from the jail — half of them with their wives, were standing in a little pack by the ice-filled beer cooler; an older couple Hardy hadn't met — neighbors? — chatted with a supermodel who Hardy figured had to be Patti Orosco. Another couple of guys, probably more guards, came in and headed over to say hi to Hal before hitting the beer.

Frannie sipped from her plastic cup of chardonnay. "I'm a little surprised by all the guys," she said. "You'd think a few of them would be laying low, wouldn't you? I mean, after 'CityTalk.' "

"Why do you say that?" Hardy asked.

Frannie lowered her voice. "Because it's obvious — isn't it? — that some of these guys must have known what was going on. I mean with the chief deputy. Right?"

"I don't know. Which ones?"

"I don't know that, not specifically."

"Specificity is what we like in the criminal biz."

"At least Hal, though. Don't you think?"

"Why do you say that?"

"Diz. Come on. I mean, at the very least, he told Katie about the whole San Bruno thing. We know that."

"We do?"

"Sure."

"How do we know that?"

"Because Katie's brother knew about it. Because Hal told her, and she blabbed to him."

"Maybe. But it could have happened other ways."

"You know it didn't. And that means Hal was in on it with Foster, or at least knew about what he was doing, backing up his alibi. So Hal's not out of the woods yet, especially if they do this investigation and really get to grilling him."

Hardy had been nursing his can of Bud, and now he took a pull at it. "Okay, say you're an investigator, the dogged and brilliant Abe Glitsky, even. You get Hal into a cozy little room and close the door and ask him about Foster and the San Bruno thing. You tell him we know that Foster didn't go to San Bruno that day because we know he was killing Tussaint at about that time. So we know his alibi's no good. What does Hal say to that?"

"First choice? He lawyers up, takes the

Fifth, and says absolutely nothing without immunity."

"But if he doesn't?" Hardy asked.

"Sure he does. He's got to. It's his only chance."

"Not true. He says, 'I was at San Bruno with the chief deputy. Prove I wasn't.' Which the prosecution, as we know, has to do."

"So they get one of the other guards and break him."

"How do they do that if he doesn't want to talk?"

"Okay," Frannie said, "if I'm Abe Glitsky, for example, I go to his wife."

Hardy was shaking his head. "When they get her alone in the interrogation room, she tells whoever will listen that Abe scared her, coerced her, threatened her. Her husband's a saint, and he never would have lied about something that important and illegal."

"So they do the audit Abe was talking about, and there's tons of extra money with no explanation for it."

"Tons? Look around you. This is Hal's house. Do you spot any insane displays of hidden wealth? Wasn't money one of the big problems between him and Katie? Even if he and a few of these other guys were making, let's go wild and say five grand in cash

457

a year, it's not going to change anybody's life."

"Somebody will be more ostentatious."

"The only one who's more ostentatious is Burt Cushing, and he's got twenty years of practice on how to make that dirty stuff go away and come back clean."

"What are you saying?"

"I'm saying the turnout here is a show of strength and solidarity. If nobody talks, nobody goes down."

"So what happened that day with Tussaint?"

"They can't prove Foster killed him."

"But we know he did kill him."

Hardy, enjoying himself now, grinned. "No, we don't. How do we know that?"

"How about the piece of paper in Foster's handwriting?"

"Not even close to a confession. I defy anybody to tell me what that means: 'Hal Chase didn't kill Katie.' Foster had the murder weapon, but it doesn't mean he used it on Katie. The note doesn't say he did. It doesn't even mention any of the other killings. It's a non-confession confession."

"But we know what it was, basically."

"Basically does not cut it. Basically is like almost. Which is, by definition, not good enough. Besides, you're leaving out one other crucial element."

"What's that?"

"It's so very San Francisco, I know you're going to love it."

Frannie sipped and thought a minute. "I give up."

"You can get it. Look at how Cushing is already spinning it. The guards who might have been involved, those poor guys . . ."

"Victims!"

"Bingo. If they did anything wrong, they were forced to because Foster threatened and harassed them and would have at least fired them, maybe killed them, if they made any trouble. I think Cushing in one interview or another used the phrase 'institutional terror,' which you must admit has a terrific ring. I'm thinking by the end of this, any guard they identify as under Foster's influence should get a medal if not some workers'-comp lifetime disability for the stress they had to endure."

"You are so cynical," Frannie said.

"People do say that, but . . ." Hardy tipped up his beer, leaned over, and kissed her cheek. "You watch."

Glitsky came through the open front door and made it a couple of steps into the room before Hal Chase saw him and said, "And here he is!" Much to his chagrin, for the second time in a week, Abe had to endure a spontaneous round of applause. He reacted to it as though he were being pelted with fruit, holding a hand up and ducking his head slightly, a sheepish grin creasing the contours of his face.

A minute or so later, Hardy sidled up, Frannie at his side. "Go ahead," he said, "hog all the glory."

Glitsky gave him a cold eye. "Please."

"No, really. All I did was put you on the case in the first place, give you direction and guidance, then get you hired where you had some authority. After which you take all the credit. But that's all right. I don't need the recognition. I can be magnanimous. Don't worry about it."

"Thanks, I'll try not to." Abe gave Hardy's wife a welcome hug. "Hey, Fran. Has he been like this all day?"

"All tonight, anyway. It's kind of sad, but he's bearing up."

"Magnanimous," Abe said.

"That's my man."

Hal broke up the banter by coming over to say hello. "Lieutenant," he said, "I just wanted to congratulate you and say thanks. Great job."

Glitsky made a dismissive gesture. "I appreciate that, but it's all because you picked the right lawyer, though he doesn't want to take the credit."

"Whoever takes the credit, thanks to both of you. I never thought I'd be out this soon. It's fantastic. I really can't thank you enough."

"What's the plan now?" Hardy asked. "Are you going back to work?"

Hal glanced around as though someone might be listening. "I thought I'd give that a few days, hang with my kids a little, see what shakes out downtown." After hesitating, he went on. "Tell you the truth, I'm kind of blown away by the whole thing. It never occurred to me that Adam could be part of it."

"More than part," Glitsky said.

"Yeah, well, that's one of my concerns." Venturing another look around, apparently satisfied that no one was paying attention, he stepped up closer to the trio and continued in a near whisper, "If Katie went directly to Cushing, the only play that makes sense is that Burt ordered Adam to take care of the actual dirty work. You know what I'm saying?"

"The thought has occurred to me," Glitsky replied.

"Unless she had" — Hal cleared his throat — "unless the direct connection was to Adam. Which it wasn't." He paused, then said, "I don't see how I can go back in to work. And I mean ever."

"What'll you do?" Frannie asked.

Radiating embarrassment, Hal said, "As it turns out, that's not going to be a problem. The insurance, you know? Plus, me and Patti . . . nothing's really in the way of that anymore, of us. It's almost enough to make me think I can hope again."

"I think you can definitely do that," Frannie said.

"Well, maybe. To tell you the truth, I'm feeling a little snakebit. I don't even believe I'm standing here in my living room. And the plain fact is that Cushing is still out there." He focused on Abe. "He's on your radar, right?"

Glitsky nodded, suddenly grim. "He's on everybody's radar. The question is, how do we get him?"

"Or," Hardy said, "should you even try to get him?"

"What do you mean?" Frannie asked. "Of course they should try to get him. This is murder we're talking about. Abe?"

"I hate to say it," Glitsky said, "but Diz isn't all wrong. Foster did Cushing a huge favor. All the troubles at the jail, all the rumors, all the cover-ups, everything, they all get laid at Foster's feet. He and he alone was the bad apple. On Saturday, after I went over and talked to Cushing, maybe he called Foster and told him it was all coming out, I don't know. But Foster must have understood that he was going to get caught, and he decided to kill himself instead.

"That clears the books. If Cushing's smart, and he is, he lays low for the rest of his term, shuts down his underground economy, and all at once there's no more impetus to clean things up at the jail. Because they're already clean."

Hal's face had hardened. "So you're saying Cushing orders Katie killed, and he walks? What about Wes Farrell? What about the feds?"

"Something could happen," Abe admitted. "I'm just saying, given the way the real world works, there's also a chance it might not."

Hal Chase rolled over and lay back on his bed. "Oh my God," he said.

Patti Orosco came up and kissed him. "Oh my God is right," she whispered, snuggling in against him. "I have so missed you, Hal

463

Chase. I don't want us to be apart anymore, okay?"

"We're not going to be."

"Promise?"

"Promise."

She pressed her naked body against his. "Do you think we were too loud?"

Hal chuckled. "It's possible."

"Is your mom going to hate me?"

"Never. You don't have to worry about my mom. She loves you."

"I don't know . . ."

"Believe me, after this weekend . . ."

"All I did was call and ask if she needed some help."

"Right, that's all. And then you came over and stayed the whole time. She and Warren couldn't have made it through the weekend without you, and you know it. She told me she'd about reached the end of her patience. If you hadn't called, she didn't know what they would have done."

"They would have found a way, I'm sure."

"Maybe, but because of you, they didn't have to, did they?"

"I wouldn't make too big a deal out of it, Hal, really. I was just being selfish."

"Selfish?"

"I hadn't seen Will or Ellen in forever. All of a sudden I get a chance to spend a whole uninterrupted weekend with them. Are you kidding me? Wild horses couldn't have stopped me. I love those guys." She poked gently at his side. "And you don't have to say they love me, too. I know they don't, not yet. But they will. I promise."

"I know they will. I mean, if you've already got Ruth on your side . . ." He drew in a breath. "Do you know how great it feels to have her actually like the woman I love? Do you know how long it's been since that's happened?"

Patti didn't answer right away. "Well," she finally said, "I'm glad of that. She's not the easiest person in the world, I admit, but I think we can get along. I'm going to try. I know that. And there are moments when she can be pretty great. Like when I lost my cell phone this weekend and was having a total meltdown about it, she was so patient and got me to retrace my steps."

"Yeah, but you didn't find your phone."

"My point is, she calmed me down and was so helpful and nice in a moment when I needed it."

"She said it was nothing."

"You weren't here. I was beside myself for a few minutes there, I assure you. I don't know where I could have lost the darn thing."

"That's why they call it lost," Hal said. "But the point is, you and Mom and even Warren got along. You know how miraculous that is?"

"This whole thing," she said, "feels like a miracle." She kissed him again.

"I know," he said. "It does. As I told Abe tonight, it's almost enough to give a guy reason to hope."

"Now you're calling him Abe? Do you like him?"

"I don't know, like, but I'm feeling pretty good about him. He's the reason this all worked out."

"I guess. But he thought it was possible that I killed Katie."

He kissed her. "He's a cop, babe. That's how he thinks. Early on, maybe even later on, he thought the same thing about me. It doesn't mean anything."

"Maybe not, but it felt awful."

"It's his job." Hal fell silent, then sighed.

"What?"

"Nothing."

"That deep breathing didn't sound like nothing."

Hal said, "I just wish they were going a little more after Cushing."

"For what?"

"For giving Adam Foster his orders,

466

maybe including the order to kill Katie."

"Do you think he did that?"

"I don't know. I think it's possible."

"And they're not going after him?"

"Abe thinks not."

"What's going to happen to him? The sheriff?"

"Nothing. He goes riding off into the sunset."

"That's just not right. They at least ought to find out what actually happened."

"You'd think so, but Abe says maybe not." He turned onto his side, propping his head in his hand. "You realize that I can't go back to work as long as Cushing's there."

"That's all right. You don't have to. I mean, money-wise."

"Right. But if I don't go back, isn't it telling him I suspect he ordered Katie's death? Maybe I even know it for sure. And if nobody else is investigating, doesn't that mean I'm the last threat to him?"

She met his eyes in the dim half-light. "I hate this," she said.

Hal reached over and pulled her to him. "I'm not so wild about it myself."

58

The discussion with Hal Chase wouldn't shake itself out of Glitsky's mind, and it was wreaking havoc with his imagination.

Be happy, he had told himself at the breakfast table as they got Rachel and Zachary ready for school.

Don't worry, be happy. On his drive downtown after the morning stop at school, he forced the Bobby McFerrin song into the front of his brainpan, following it up with the Beach Boys doing "Don't Worry Baby."

He was going to be happy. There was no reason not to be happy. Hal Chase was out of jail. Three homicides had been solved in one swell foop.

Abe was, after all, a hero.

Sometimes, he told himself, the universe just dropped a bunch of good stuff in your lap, and you found you could use all of it, and your problems went away. It had happened when he'd met Treya; when he'd come out of surgery after being shot; when he'd regained consciousness after his heart attack. And it had happened to him Saturday at about the same instant as the .38 bullet had creased its way through Adam Foster's evil and conniving brain.

By the time he got to his desk — no applause now — Glitsky had been reminding himself pretty continuously that he had been at the crime scene on Saturday night, along with the CSI team and his Homicide pals, and no one had thought for a moment that Foster's death had been anything but a suicide. Over the weekend, Abe had followed up with the forensic evidence as best he could, making sure Len Faro got a handwriting analysis from their local expert and ballistics results from the lab in near-record time. Glitsky had actually let out a whoop, scaring his wife and children in the backyard playground, when he'd gotten the news that the Foster bullet and the Katie Chase bullet had definitely come from the same weapon — the one in Adam Foster's hand.

And then Abe had gone to Hal's homecoming party on Monday night.

Cushing had ordered Foster to take care of Katie, just as he'd later ordered Foster to take care of Solis-Martinez. This was, after all, Foster's role whenever it became necessary. In the Chase matter, it would have been child's play for Foster or any one of Hal's fellow guards, just making small talk, to find out from Hal when he was going to pick up his brother at the airport.

But . . .

Glitsky left his desk, took the elevator down to the lobby, bought a bag of peanut M&M's from the shop, and left the Hall of Justice through the back door leading to the morgue on the right and the jail on the left. No doubt, Burt Cushing was less than a hundred yards away when he passed.

He'd given up on trying to be happy. Happiness wasn't happening. Not yet, anyway. Walking under the freeway, picking his way through the parking lots as he chewed his M&M's, he tried to banish the doubts from his mind. But they would not go away.

Just because everybody thought Foster was a suicide, did that mean it had to be the case? Was there anything that positively precluded any other interpretation? If not, might an experienced law enforcement person be able to make a murder look like a suicide? Glitsky knew the answer to that.

Glitsky admired the statement that Cushing had released about Foster's death, particularly how it neatly framed the discussion so as to divert all suspicion onto Adam Foster as a fait accompli. The chief deputy was so obviously guilty of at least one homicide that he was guilty by extension of everything else that had gone bad at the jail. It broke the sheriff's heart, but there it was.

This, of course, took Cushing off the hook for all of it. True, Foster's transgressions under the sheriff's nose might hurt his reputation as a competent administrator, but this was about the worst he would have to deal with — next to conviction for a murder or two, there was no comparison.

Somehow, Glitsky found he had turned uptown and was on Fifth near Mission. Close enough, he told himself, to drop in unannounced again on Jeff Elliot.

Who, it turned out, was in his cubicle, pecking away at his keyboard, eyes locked on his monitor.

Abe stood unmoving in the doorway, waiting until his presence made itself known. Jeff eventually felt it, looked up and brightened for a quick instant, saved his document, and pushed his wheelchair back from his desk. "Dr. Glitsky. Still basking, I presume."

"Mostly. It's been a good couple of days."

"And now you're here because you've got

another scoop you want to share with your humble reporter."

"Maybe."

Elliot straightened himself up. "You're kidding."

"I don't know. I'm not completely happy about the Foster verdict."

"There wasn't any verdict."

"Yeah, there was. There just wasn't a jury bringing it in. And I know it bothers you, too."

"What does?"

"That it turned out to be all Foster. Which conveniently leaves out Burt Cushing, who, you might remember, was the guy you wanted all along."

Elliot squinted down. He scratched at his beard, both sides. "I'm listening."

"It's a work in progress," Glitsky said, "and off the record at this stage. I just wanted a set of ears."

"You got 'em."

"This is what I'm thinking about. First, the gun. We don't know where it came from, period. Could have been Foster's, could have been Cushing's, could have been mine, for that matter." Glitsky held up a hand. "It wasn't. The question remains, if Foster knows he's going to kill himself, why not take his own trusty service weapon?"

"Because with the one he used, he confesses to the Chase murder?"

Abe raised his eyebrows. "Really? Pretty subtle. But let's go on." He came inside and lowered himself onto the cubicle's only chair. "Let's say Cushing calls Foster on Saturday and tells him the jig is up. Cushing himself is going to roll over on Foster. The evidence is piling up on Tussaint. His own guards are going to turn. Old Burt doesn't have a choice, and he's sorry, but that's the way it's got to go down." He waited. "You see my problem?"

"You don't think his reaction is to kill himself?"

"Do you?"

"Now that you say it, it is a bit of a reach," Jeff said.

"At least a reach," Glitsky said. "If it were me, I know I wouldn't kill myself. I'd go on the offense and try to take it to Cushing, cut some deal with some prosecutors, either that or kill him instead. But instead Foster shoots himself? Again, really? Why?"

"It must have seemed like a good idea at the time."

Ignoring that, Abe cocked his head. "I've got nothing that eliminates suicide. The whole thing was, pardon the word, perfectly executed. Cushing invites him down to this out-of-the-way place so they can speak freely without fear of being seen or recorded. He hops into the passenger seat in Foster's car, pulls a gun, and tosses Foster the notepad and tells him to write his note. The second he's done, before there's any more discussion, Cushing pops him, leaves the gun in his hand, and takes off."

Elliot digested this for a moment. "You're saying that Cushing killed Katie Chase, too."

"Very good, Jeff. Maybe his original plan was to do both Katie and Hal together, but then when Hal wasn't home . . ."

"Why wouldn't he have waited for him?"

"I don't know. Maybe Katie told him Hal was coming back with his brother, and that started to get too complicated. Besides, if he got rid of her, that alone plugged the potential leak. Plus, she knew him. She would have let him in, no problem." Abe shrugged. "I admit I don't have all the details worked out. But Cushing is every bit as plausible as Foster, maybe more."

"Except you don't have anything that proves it wasn't suicide?"

"That, in a nutshell, is it."

Elliot drummed his fingers on his wheelchair's arm. After a minute, he asked, "Where's the pencil? Where's the notepad that he wrote the note with?"

"Good," Glitsky said, but then shook his head. "He could have written it anywhere before he got in the car. So, no good."

"No, he couldn't have. I mean, yes, if it was suicide, he could have written the note at his home or anywhere, but not under your Cushing scenario. If it was Cushing, it had to have happened in the car."

"Neither proves anything. If Cushing took the pencil away, or if it wasn't there to begin with . . . it doesn't fly."

"All right." Elliot sighed, thought another second or two, brightened again. "How about GSR?" Gunshot residue. "If Foster didn't actually shoot the gun . . ."

This time Abe nodded. "That's a good call. I'll ask Crime Scene about it. But in that close an environment, probably everything's got GSR all over it. Anyway, the gun was in his hand, and that puts GSR on his hand whether he fired it or not."

Another small silence, both of them thinking. Finally, Elliot asked, "Do we know what Burt said he was doing Saturday night? I mean, a fund-raiser or something public . . ."

"It gets demoralizing, asking these guys for alibis. But I'll check if it was something public. What I'd really like is something to positively eliminate the suicide first. Otherwise, I'm just howling at the moon."

"Well, I wish you luck." Jeff rocked back and forth a little in his wheelchair. "It would be too sweet if we could bring all this back to that asshole and take him down, wouldn't it?"

"Yes, it would. I'll keep thinking on it."

"Somehow, Abe, I thought you might."

59

Due to the sense of urgency surrounding the ballistics test on the past Sunday morning, Len Faro had spent a good deal of time at the police lab in Hunters Point. Aside from being the snappiest dresser on the police force — today he was in about five grand worth of Brioni — he was punctilious about his evidence, especially the chain of evidence. In a perfect world — the one he tried to inhabit — once he took an item into custody, it remained under his constant guard, either in his personal possession or, eventually and more likely, in the city's evidence locker, until he needed to produce it again at trial. That way, when he was called to testify at court — and he always was — he could swear under oath that every item introduced as an exhibit had been under his personal and uninterrupted control from the moment it had been discovered until its appearance in the courtroom. On the flip side, anything that did not meet these criteria would not be admitted. So no one was planting any bogus evidence on his watch, thank you.

It made Faro nervous enough for regular police officers, even those under his direct command, to have access to this stuff; today, with someone like Abe Glitsky, with whom he had a long and cordial history but who no longer worked for the Police Department, he had his defenses on full alert. Not that he really thought Glitsky might plant or remove anything, but why take the chance?

So when Abe had stopped by to ask permission to review the evidence in the Chase and Foster matters, Faro had volunteered to drive him down — he had some stuff on a new case to drop off, anyway — and together they could see what Abe needed or thought he needed to see.

Now they sat at a large table in an air-conditioned room adjacent to the evidence locker. Both of them wore latex gloves. On the table were two medium cardboard boxes, and in front of the men was a good-sized pile of Ziploc bags of various sizes. Everything taken from the car and from the body of Adam Foster.

Glitsky's first close look had been at the

gun, followed by the slugs. He also examined the blown-up copies of photographs of the ballistics test, which, to his experienced eye, made the report's conclusion unambiguous. The same weapon had fired both bullets. Foster's fingerprints were the only ones on the weapon, and their positioning was absolutely consistent with the theory that he'd fired the gun himself. Further, Glitsky's understanding about gunshot residue turned out to be correct — Faro told him that they'd checked Foster's hands first thing, and there was plenty of the stuff on his right hand to verify that he'd been holding the gun and pulled the trigger.

Though he wasn't certain what, if anything, it might mean, Glitsky brought up Jeff Elliot's question about the pencil and paper; Faro and his techs had found neither in the car. The car was pretty darn spotless inside and out. Glitsky remembered the showroom shine he'd noticed and picked up a Baggie containing a business-card-sized bit of cardboard with the words "$1 Discount Off Your Next Carwash — Cable Car Washers. Good until . . ." An ink stamp had printed out the date "December 21."

"Where did this come from?" Glitsky asked.

Faro glanced at the card. "That little

covered cubbyhole between the front seats."

"Anything else in it? Coins, CDs, anything?"

"They'd be here if they were."

"I know, Len, just making sure."

"There is," Faro added, picking up another Baggie, "this little trash bag. Same carwash." He read the logo. " 'A clean car lasts longer.' I'm not sure of the veracity of that statement."

"Sounds like false advertising to me. Somebody ought to sue 'em." Abe stared at the card for a few more seconds. "Do we know when he got the wash?"

"Actually, we do. It was Saturday."

"How'd you get that?"

Faro wasn't entirely successful hiding the pleasure of his accomplishment. "I called them yesterday and asked them about that date. You get a week between washes if you want to save a buck. December twenty-first is next Saturday. So he got his wash on the fourteenth. Saturday."

"Nice work." Glitsky sat back. "So the guy gets his car washed when he's planning to go kill himself?"

Faro shrugged. "It could have been his Saturday routine. Wake up, get the car washed, save a buck. He didn't think about it."

Glitsky felt he had something and didn't want to let it go. "Okay, but I'll tell you what he did think about. He thought about getting dressed up."

Faro, who dressed to the nines every day, clearly hadn't viewed Foster's outfit as out of the ordinary. Glitsky realized that it quite possibly meant something important.

"What are you getting at?" Faro asked.

Up to now, Glitsky had kept the reason for his interest in looking at the evidence under wraps. The last thing he wanted was to let the rumor mill get wind of the idea that Foster might not have killed himself. And until he found something that verified his suspicions, he preferred, if possible, to keep them to himself.

That was becoming less feasible by the second. "I'm getting at wondering why Foster gets himself all dolled up if he's planning to shoot himself in the head."

"You think he was all dolled up?"

Glitsky's mouth twitched up in a quick smile. "Maybe not by your standards, Len, but the rest of the world, yeah. He was going out on the town. Until somebody stopped him."

Faro blinked in surprise. "You're saying you don't think he killed himself?"

"I'm thinking it more and more every

minute."

Obviously taken with the idea, Faro reached over and went through another small pile of Baggies. Lifting one of them, he held it up. It contained a condom. "That might explain this, too," he said. "Front pants pocket. And you want to hear something else? I talked to Strout yesterday. I didn't think anything other than it was a little unusual, but now . . ."

"What?"

"He had just shaved his balls."

"Just?"

"That day. Saturday."

This slowed Abe down to a dead stop, and he sat motionless until he remembered to breathe. "So he washes his car, shaves his balls, gets all dressed up, drives out to the Presidio, and shoots himself? How many ways does this not fit?"

Faro had no answer and turned his palms up. He didn't know.

Glitsky reached out for another of the Baggies, the one that held the alleged suicide note. He turned it over, checked the back, flipped it again. "This was in his coat pocket, you said?"

"Yep. Front left outside."

"How'd you find it so soon?"

"I saw the perforated top sticking out.

Grabbed it with my tweezers."

Glitsky flipped it another time, sighed, put it down in front of him. "What else we got?"

Faro threw a glance across the table. "Cell phone," he said.

"Now we're talking." Glitsky was pulling the Ziploc toward him. Removing the cell phone, he pushed the button to bring up the screen, and nothing happened. "It's dead."

"Perfect," Faro said. "I think I've got my charger out in my car. You want to take five while I go grab it?"

"More than anything. And wait another twenty or so while it charges, if it does after all this downtime. I love technology."

"Everybody does. We can use the extra time to think."

"My favorite." What other option did he have? "Go," he said.

As the door closed behind Faro, Glitsky stood up, stretched, walked out in the hall, found the restroom, and used it. When he got back to the table in the little room, he absently started going through the pile of Ziploc bags — the bullet, the gun, the condom, the carwash discount stub, what must have been Foster's set of keys.

Abe paused to count the keys, see if one of them jumped out at him as possibly significant, but he couldn't identify anything. Frustrated, he leaned against the hard back of his chair and cast an evil eye at the door. Where was Len? He checked his watch. He'd been gone eight minutes, not that Abe was counting.

Coming forward, he reached for the Baggie that held the alleged suicide note, checking it again. Nothing had changed, of course. He turned it over, looked at the blank side, sat back again, closed his eyes.

Time stopped.

He heard the door and opened his eyes, saw Faro shaking his head. "Sorry it took so long, but no luck. I must have left it back at the office. Maybe one of the guys here has one we can borrow." He got no reaction, Glitsky sitting slumped with no expression. "Abe?"

Glitsky had the sense that he'd somehow been away for a long time. Coming back into the present with Faro, he fought off a keen and disturbing sense of disorientation.

"Are you all right?" Faro asked.

"I think so." Abe let out a breath that he felt like he'd been holding, getting his bearings caught up to where he found himself. Shaking his head as though to clear out the cobwebs, he picked up the Baggie with the notepad page, held it out, and said, "Tell me again how you found this thing." When Faro finished identically repeating the story he'd told before, Glitsky sat with it a minute and then asked, "How far was it in the pocket?"

"Pretty much all the way. I just happened to notice the ragged top where it had been torn off."

"And the rest of the paper?" Glitsky glanced at it again, no creases. "It doesn't look like it got bent over or scrunched up."

"No. He just slipped it in the pocket."

"All the way down?"

"I think I just said that. What are you getting at?"

"When did he put it in the pocket?"

"What do you mean?"

"I mean, if he killed himself, he probably wrote this note someplace besides the car, maybe at his home, right? Since there was no pencil or the rest of the notepad in the car. Good so far?"

"Okay."

"On the other hand, if he was murdered after somebody made him write the note at gunpoint in the car, then what?"

"Then," Faro replied, "the next thing is the murderer tells him to put it in his pocket so we'd find it, just before he shoots him."

"Right. What if the murderer didn't do

that last part, wait for Foster to slide it into his pocket? What if it was a pretty uptight moment, as it must have been, and the exact second Foster finished writing, his killer popped him?"

"Okay. What would that get us?"

Glitsky put the Baggie down as if it had become radioactive. "Foster's writing the note. The notepad's on his lap. He finishes, and the gunshot splashes blood all over the driver's-side window. It also has to leave a mist of blood all over the body, to say nothing about the GSR, which is all over the place, too."

"Right. So?"

"So" — Glitsky gingerly picked up the Baggie again — "if this thing was in Foster's lap when he got shot, it's going to have blood and GSR all over it. If it was a suicide and all the way down in his pocket before the shot, it won't." Abe was on his feet and moving. "Let's go find us a tech and find out which it was."

60

"You think that's conclusive?" Hardy asked. Glitsky sat across from him in his office, where Faro had dropped him on the way back downtown.

"I don't see a flaw in it."

"Don't get me wrong, I think it's good, but let me play devil's advocate here for a minute."

"An hour, more likely. But go right ahead."

"Take the GSR first. As we know, it's notoriously transferrable. If it was on Foster's coat by the front pocket, when Faro took out the slip of paper, it could have picked up the stuff from whatever cloth it rubbed against. Probably would have, in fact."

"You're making my argument for, not yours against, Diz. As it turns out, the paper didn't have just trace amounts of GSR. It was loaded with the stuff. And if anything, putting the paper in the pocket would have transferred some of it to the coat's fabric, taken it off the paper. Therefore, it wasn't in the pocket at the time of the shot. Couldn't have been. It was in his lap or in his hands or on the seat. It's a sure bet that after the shot, Foster being dead and all, he didn't put it in his pocket. Same with the blood."

"Lots of blood?"

"Plenty. Invisible till we tested it at the lab, then everywhere. DNA is probably going to tell us it's Foster's blood, but so what? So the paper wasn't in his pocket when he got shot. It went in afterward. As you would say, conclusively. And that can only mean one thing."

Hardy rolled his chair back, put his feet on his desk, templed his hands at his mouth. "You're thinking Cushing."

Glitsky nodded. "You'll like this. Cushing called Foster on his cell phone about twenty minutes after I left his house on Saturday."

"You think that's when they set up the appointment?"

"I don't know, but I'd guess so. The timing certainly works."

"What was the hurry? I mean, why Saturday night?"

"Because I'd just finished drawing the

picture for Cushing at his house. So if he could get rid of Foster quick, before an investigation by us or the FBI got any further, then he could spin the story that everything was Foster's doing, exactly what he did. It's kind of elegant, you must admit. Make your decision, act on it. Done deal."

"If all this is true, Abe, he is one dangerous guy."

"I think we already knew that. And believe me, I'm going on that assumption."

"So what's your next step?"

"I've already made it. You know Foley and Monroe?"

Hardy nodded.

"I thought it would be worthwhile to spread the love among a few of us, so Cushing doesn't get the idea that this is just me and all he's got to do is arrange another accident. This is still Katie's homicide, too. So I'm letting the Homicide guys interview Cushing without giving away that we know Foster was a murder, so maybe his guard's down. We sweat him on the affair with Katie, find out — just curious — where he might have been on the night before Thanksgiving, what he says he was doing last Saturday night. Just grunt work on the details, which I don't want any part of. Assuming that it all works out, we shoot for a warrant to take his world apart."

"Good luck with that. You've got a judge who will sign off on it?"

"We'll find one. I think they'll get enough."

"Well, let's hope." Hardy swung his legs down. "Let me ask you something. What got you thinking Foster wasn't a suicide? I thought that was a slam dunk."

"You've hit upon my favorite part," Glitsky said, and launched into a recital of the elements around Foster's death that didn't make sense if he was planning to take his own life that night — getting the car washed, shaving his pubic area, dressing nicely, the condom.

When he'd finished, Hardy said, "So Foster was planning to hook up with somebody after his meet with Cushing?"

"That's what it looks like."

"You know who it was?"

"No idea. Looks like he was setting up a date with more or less a stranger for that night, but the main thing we needed from his phone was verification that Cushing had called him Saturday afternoon. Which is what we got."

"You didn't check all the numbers?"

Abe showed some impatience. "Twenty-four hours in a day, Diz. We had what we

490

wanted out of the phone. I needed to get Abby and Jambo moving."

Hardy held up a hand. "Easy, Tonto. No criticism implied or stated. I'm sure it makes no difference. After all, whoever it was, it looks like he stood her up."

"Yes, it does. And now I've got one for you."

"Shoot."

"Faro and I were talking about this and couldn't agree. If you're us, do you go public with Foster being a murder and not a suicide?"

Hardy thought for a moment. "I don't think so."

"Great minds," Glitsky said. "That was my call."

"Although," Hardy went on, "since Cushing's your target, I'm guessing he'll figure it out pretty quick. About the time your Homicide colleagues show up."

"True, but he might be lulled for a few minutes first and make a mistake."

"On the other hand, if he knows the murder he's committed has been exposed for what it is, he might panic and make a mistake. In either case," Hardy concluded, "handle with care."

"That's my plan."

"I mean it, Abe. I really mean it."

"Me, too."

Back at the Hall of Justice, Glitsky checked in with his boss, figuring at the very least that Wes Farrell deserved an update. When Farrell heard Glitsky's conclusion that Foster's death had not been a suicide, he stopped in the middle of his Nerf ball shot. "You are shitting me."

"No, sir. I don't think any other explanation is possible."

"And it's Cushing."

"He's a good bet. He's the only bet at the moment."

Farrell rubbed his cheek with the Nerf ball. "Who else knows about this?"

Glitsky cocked his head, rattled off the names: "Len Faro, Abby Foley and JaMorris Monroe, I assume Devin Juhle, Diz, Treya, and now you."

Farrell broke a wan smile. "It's good of you to include me on the list."

"Well, it was —"

But Farrell stopped him. "Doesn't matter, Abe. It's done. What's Homicide doing?"

"I think they were going to talk to the sheriff."

"You think they've done it yet?" Farrell checked his wristwatch. "You've got their numbers? Call them and stop them if you can." He strode by Glitsky and opened his office door. "Treya, if you please. Immediately." She nearly bolted out of her desk chair, came into the room, and shot a fast worried look at her husband as Farrell closed the door and whirled around.

"Abe," he said, "make that call. Treya, get Len Faro on the phone right now. Use the one on my desk. The message is that nobody's going to say one word to anyone else about Adam Foster. He's still deader than hell, and dead by his own hand." He was punching his own phone, then speaking into it. "Hello, Phyllis, this is your old friend Wes Farrell. I need to speak to Mr. Hardy as fast as you can get him on the phone. It's important."

Over the next five minutes, Abe, Treya, and Farrell got ahold of everyone who knew about the new theory, and each of them delivered the message that one and all were to put a lid on it. No one was to tell anyone else, and if they'd already done so . . .

No one had. Abby and JaMorris were coming back from an interview in another case and hadn't set off to go and double-team the sheriff. Juhle hadn't heard from his two inspectors, so he knew nothing about it. Faro hadn't mentioned a thing to anyone; nor had Hardy.

Satisfied that he had the basic news contained, Farrell at last leaned back against one of the library tables. "Okay," he said, "thanks to both of you for jumping in on those calls, but here's what's going down next around all this. As you might remember, I've already lost one of my investigators over this case. Besides that, after bowing to public pressure and other more subtle incentives, I've already persuaded the grand jury to issue one indictment for the murder of Katie Chase. That one didn't turn out so well, did it? And I'll be good and goddamned if I'm going to be coerced or hurried into another one.

"All we've got here is conjecture." He held a finger up, cutting off Abe's attempt to register an objection. "Conjecture that we're dealing with a murder here and not a suicide. I admit, the whole idea that somebody killed Foster and also Katie Chase is exciting and provocative. Maybe even true, who knows? But the main thing is, we're not going off half-cocked this time on any one suspect, even if our good Sheriff Cushing leads the pack. I mean it. We're not doing that. We're not letting the killer know that we even think there is a killer out there, much less who we think it is.

"Instead, I'm going to do what I should

have done in the first place, and that is invite in the FBI. They'll be so happy to launch a covert operation, maybe put a few agents secretly in the jail, whatever they want to do, including a little more sophisticated lab testing on the one piece of paper you're basing all this on. If they agree with your opinion, Abe, then they can subpoena everything they need — financials, phones, computer files, you name it — and nobody will have to know they're even around until they've got something strong enough to make a case, and then guess what? They make a righteous arrest. If it's one of the jail killings, it's a federal case. If not, it's ours. Meanwhile, I'm not going to put anybody else in harm's way. Especially if it does turn out to be Cushing, which, don't get me wrong, is what I think, too. He is one devious and cold-blooded mother-fucker, and I'd like nothing better than to take him down, but this time we're going by the book. Agreed?"

"I still think —" Glitsky started.

Farrell slammed a flat palm down on the table. "I said, 'Agreed?' Are you going to make me fire you before you've even put in a full week? Is that what you want?"

"No, sir."

"All right, then, let's do it my way this

time. How's that sound?"

Truth be told, it didn't sound too good to Abe, but he didn't think it was a fortuitous time to argue. In his opinion, the positive evidence that was all over the small sheet of notebook paper did not leave room for conjecture at all. In Hardy's words, it was conclusive. There was no possible way that Adam Foster had killed himself. This also meant that the same person who had murdered Katie Chase had killed him.

Abe felt he was this close.

"Even so," Treya said, "you've got to let it go. At least for now. You've come up with this last crucial bit that changes everything, and Wes recognizes that, but . . ."

"But he won't let me close the deal."

"He doesn't want you to get killed, Abe. How about that?"

"I'm not going to get killed." He lowered his voice. "That ship has sailed. Killing one cop more won't change anything."

"Famous last words."

"No, they're not. This is when I can get him. I can taste it."

The phone on her desk rang. Reaching over, she picked it up. "District Attorney's office, how can I help you? . . . Hello, Lieutenant . . . Yes, he's still here. I'm talking to him just now, as a matter of fact . . . Sure, just a second." Handing Abe the phone, she said, "Devin Juhle."

The Homicide chief said it was important. The summons was also a fine excuse to end the conversation with Treya, which wasn't really going Abe's way. He told her they could resume later but stopped short of telling her that he would let the whole thing go.

Though he understood that Wes was concerned for the safety of everyone involved, Abe planned to let none of it go. He couldn't shake the feeling that with the smallest push on his part, Cushing would make a mistake and the whole enterprise would come tumbling down. But he might have to go underground to make that happen.

Five minutes later, he knocked on his old office door on the fifth floor. The door was open, as usual, and somewhat to his surprise, Abby and JaMorris sat on the folding chairs in front of Juhle's large desk, both wearing a bit of the attitude of scolded schoolchildren. "Abe," Juhle said as he waved him in. "Thanks for coming on up. You mind getting the door?"

Glitsky pushed it closed and said, "What's up?"

Juhle scratched at the wood on the top of his desk. "Abby and Jambo and I have just been discussing this thing we're not supposed to talk about." He chuckled. "Which I guess right there is saying something."

"I think, among ourselves, it's not much of a problem," Glitsky said.

"In this case," Juhle replied, "I expect we'll be glad we did. Last I heard about this was Monday, with that column in the paper, Adam Foster killing himself, and Sheriff Cushing going on about how shocked he was that anything illegal had ever gone on at his jail. You all remember that?"

Nods all around.

"I thought you would. It turns out that Foster's gun is the same one that killed Katie Chase, and I'm thinking, like everybody else, 'Good, we got the bastard.' Or he got himself, but either way, it's three one-eighty-sevens" — the Penal Code section for murder — "off the books. At this point, I'm not thinking too much about the details. Obviously, the guy killed the Chase woman, then himself. What more was there to think about? Everybody with me so far?"

Abby Foley cleared her throat and spoke up. "Yes, sir."

"Good. Then I get this call from Wes Farrell a few minutes ago telling me to hold on, Foster wasn't a suicide after all. Abe's done some yeoman police work, and all of a sudden it's looking like a murder. And if it's one, it's pretty much got to be two: Foster and Chase. Then Farrell tells me the main suspect — although we're not going to talk about it — is Burt Cushing. So I go, 'Okay, I'll keep it to myself,' and then hang up. I know something's nagging at me, but I can't exactly put my finger on it, and since we've just been told we're not doing anything about these two cases for a while, I put it aside" — he now spoke directly to Abe — "figuring I'd catch up with these two when they checked in. Which I did."

"Okay," Glitsky said.

"Not okay, as it turns out, Abe. The three of us start talking, and about the first thing Jambo mentions is Katie Chase got killed on the night before Thanksgiving, which wasn't something I'd really thought about since it happened. But I hear that, and I'm like, 'Whoa, wait a minute. What time?' 'Seven, eight, somewhere in there.' And I say, 'The day before Thanksgiving? Absolutely?' They're both sure. I mean, this is one fact that's in no dispute whatsoever, right? Katie Chase is killed on Wednesday night, the day before Thanksgiving."

"Right," Glitsky said. "No question."

"Okay," Juhle said. "Here's the problem. You want to know where I was on the night before Thanksgiving? I was at Burt Cushing's yearly Thanksgiving party at his house. I was there from sometime around eight until maybe eleven, eleven-thirty. So was Cushing. So, in fact, was Adam Foster. And in case you were wondering, I promise you I'm not one of the sheriff's stooges, backing up his alibi. There must have been two dozen of us there, and you can check with any or all of them. They'll all tell you the same thing. The point is, if Katie Chase got shot that night, Burt Cushing flat-out didn't do it. And neither did Adam Foster. I hate to say it, Abe, but you're barking up the wrong tree."

61

Glitsky didn't feel like he could face a living soul.

He sat in his car in the waning daylight, caught in rush-hour traffic leaving the city. He didn't have a destination in mind. Badly shaken, he'd called Treya immediately after leaving Juhle's office and told her that he was going to be busy until late, checking on some evidence. No, he had promised her, it wasn't about Cushing. He wasn't looking into Cushing anymore. Wes was right, Abe was sorry. He'd get home when he could.

How could he have been so completely wrong?

Every single fact about Burt Cushing fit perfectly into his theory, except the tiny flaw that he was somewhere else when the first crime was committed. Abe had neglected to perform the most perfunctory police work — checking his suspect's alibi. Or, really, both Cushing's and Foster's alibis. That oversight had rendered all of his other efforts useless at best, pathetic at worst.

By the time he'd gotten down as far as Candlestick Point, he'd conjured up another theory that might still fit his facts: Another deputy might be the button man within the Sheriff's Department. He thought about Andy Biehl and his brand-new Audi. He considered Mike Maye of Foster's poker alibi. It could be any one of a dozen deputies, maybe a hundred.

He'd said it to placate Treya, but by the time he reached Burlingame, he had come to the decision that Wes Farrell was right. Whatever this was, it was too big for him to handle alone. Or even to be a part of. He'd just demonstrated how badly his investigative chops had deteriorated. He might not be a true menace, but neither was he much of a help.

Farrell was also right about keeping Abe out of harm's way. Chances were, if he could be this wrong about a case, he could be this wrong about his ability to defend himself. His instincts and skills had rusted to the point that anyone could walk straight up to him, wish him a Merry Christmas, and put a bullet through his eye before he'd had a chance to blink.

He was old, old, old. He might not have

loved retirement, but retirement was clearly where he belonged.

But God, it galled. It galled.

Now, with full dark having fallen, he sat again in the evidence room at the lab, the cardboard box with Adam Foster's stuff on the table next to him. He hoped something in that box would speak to him again. He had been wrong in the conclusion he'd reached about the sheriff, but no one could deny that his main insight and discovery — that Adam Foster was not a suicide but a murder — was the breakthrough moment in that case, as well as Katie Chase's.

And that moment had been his and his alone.

He belonged here. This was his world. For nearly forty years, his work and his passion had been bringing murderers to justice, and he was not about to abandon all of that now. He was who he was. He keenly felt the scorn of his unknown quarry and vowed anew that somehow he would bring it down.

Foster's cell phone was the most likely and obvious source of something Glitsky might have missed while he'd found what he expected. For nearly an hour, he went through Foster's deleted emails of the past month. Foster was on LinkedIn and had a couple of hundred connections; he was asked for connections, endorsements. But it seemed that he mostly accepted people who wanted to connect with him and didn't do much afterward. Glitsky could relate, since he treated the social networking app the same way.

There were also several dozen administrative emails either up or down the chain of command at the jail. A flurry of messages in early November about Alanos Tussaint segued into an equal number about Luther Jones. Glitsky knew that these would probably be helpful to the FBI if they took over the investigation; they could follow up on Foster's home computer. Aside from that, Adam Foster had a few friends, almost all of them male, and there was the usual assortment of purportedly funny attachments that pretty much identified him as the redneck asshole Glitsky had always considered him.

Finally, Glitsky got to Saturday morning and Foster's cell phone. The only calls from unknowns were from the same number. Glitsky assumed that would be the number of the woman Foster had presumably made his date with on the night of the killing.

Thinking what an idiot she must be, Glitsky got out his own cell phone — he did not want to add or subtract anything on Foster's phone — and punched in the numbers on his keypad, then pressed the call button.

He was holding the phone to his ear, listening to the ring. The phone eventually kicked over to the recorded message, and he felt the room come up at him.

"Hi," the voice said. "This is Patti Orosco. You know what to do."

He couldn't undo it. He'd left his name and phone number on Patti Orosco's telephone, and knew she would call him back before long.

In his car driving home, he decided that the wisest course of action was to pretend that he was a concerned servant of the people and following up on things with Patti and Hal and the gang. He would tell her that maybe they could make an appointment and get together to do a little debriefing. He would lie to her about this being the normal routine following a murder investigation. He would remember not to refer in any way to the murder, as opposed to the suicide, of Adam Foster.

First and above all, he would get her alibi for Saturday night.

When he got home at 8:45, Treya had

already put both kids to bed. In their years together, tension had only rarely invaded their home, but tonight it entered draped on Abe's shoulders and spread out to cover every inch of the duplex. Glitsky, seeking comfort where he could, opened the number one forbidden food item in the house of a heart attack victim — a can of Spam — and fried it as patties with three eggs. Treya started to say something — about the job, about Spam, his health, retiring again — but Abe's excessive politeness drove her to a frigid kiss good night, then to their bedroom, where she turned off the lights and closed the door after her.

Glitsky washed and dried his dishes. Sitting in the living room under his reading light, he didn't so much as pick up a book.

The silence in the home felt like a physical presence.

At 9:23, he punched Hal Chase's number into his cell phone. If nothing else, he told himself, he wanted to make sure Hardy's ex-client was alive. Hal picked up on the second ring, and the two men said their hellos. Glitsky apologized for calling so late.

"No worries. We're just sitting up talking, having some wine."

"You and your mom?"

"No. Patti and me. Mom and Warren both

left today. And no offense, but not a minute too soon, if you know what I mean. I'm so ready to get back to real life."

"Are you going back to work?"

"Maybe not. I mean real life outside of work. My kids. Patti."

"I'm glad for you. Listen, that's part of the reason I called. I tried reaching Patti earlier to follow up on a few things — just routine bookkeeping — and I couldn't reach her on her cell phone."

"No, you wouldn't have," Hal said. "She lost it on Saturday."

"Ah."

"It's a drag, but I'm sure it'll turn up. She probably just put it down someplace and forgot, what with all the chaos this weekend."

"Chaos?"

"She was over here, helping out. Mom was at the end of her rope, and Warren . . . well, you know Warren. So Patti volunteered to lend a hand and wound up staying the weekend." Glitsky could hear that Hal said the next for her benefit. "This is what we call a good woman. Patti plus Warren plus Mom equals let the good times roll."

Abe heard Patti's laugh, heard her say, "Better times if Mom goes to a movie."

"When was that? This movie?" Abe asked.

"Saturday night. Mom was driving everybody nuts, so they sent her to a movie. Evidently, it made for a better night. But what is it you wanted to talk to Patti about?"

"Actually, it's you, too." Abe was riffing blindly, since he'd just heard that Patti Orosco apparently had an alibi and a witness — Warren — on Saturday night.

Which meant . . . what?

He all but stammered, "I just wanted to personally follow up how you're doing with the whole Adam Foster thing."

"Still in a little shock," Hal said. "But not really surprised. On the other hand, the son of a bitch got me out of jail. I'll probably get it all worked out someday. Maybe I'll go to the counseling you and I were talking about. Get so I can put it all someplace. It would be nice to have some of it make sense, but I think that might take awhile."

Abe heard Patti comment in the background and asked, "What did she say?"

"She said," Hal replied, " 'tell that mean Mr. Glitsky I don't care what he thinks. I could never kill anybody.' "

Glitsky was paddling upstream alone in a kayak. Dense jungle hung over the water, and the hanging vines and foliage swiped at his face with regularity. He had both hands on the oar and couldn't wipe any of the stuff away. A helicopter's rotor sounded behind him, coming up low and fast, and he shored the kayak, coming up on the muddy bank. He ran up the steep and slippery trail as the helicopter got louder. Finally, he got some traction and forced himself up through the waist-high brambles, pushing them aside. They were following him on the main trail, but a smaller path broke off to his right. He took it and broke into a jog but almost immediately tripped on a log across the path. Except, turning, he saw it was not a log but a body . . . a woman's body.

With a terrified yell, he sat upright.

Treya woke and put her arms around him, holding him. "It's okay. You're all right. It was just a dream."

Glitsky gripped his chest with his right hand. His breath was coming in gulps. He felt his wife's hand moving up and down over his back, her lips brushing his shoulder, shushing him as if he were a baby.

Closing his eyes, he let his body settle, his breathing slow down, forcing one deep breath, then another. He moved his right hand to cover Treya's, gave it a small squeeze. "Sorry I woke you up."

"It's okay." She kissed his shoulder again. "Bad one?"

He nodded. "I'm going to get up for a minute."

"All right. If you need me, come and get me."

"I will."

He padded into the kitchen, ran cold water into his hands and drank some of it, then splashed the rest of it onto his face. Closing his eyes, he let his weight settle on his hands, braced on either side of the sink. He summoned back the scenes from his dream, climbing the muddy trail, breaking to the right, pushing through the brambles.

Breaking right.

Opening his eyes, he could barely make out his reflection in the window over the sink, more a shadow within the shadows than a mirror image. He couldn't see any of his specific features: the shape of his head more like an apparition, the guy from his dream.

The dream, coalescing into something tangible. A memory.

He had it.

62

There was no question what Abe should do.

There was also no question that he wasn't going to do it.

What he had done: He had called Wes Farrell at his home at six-thirty A.M.; by seven-thirty, at the Hall of Justice, he had included Devin Juhle, along with Abby and Jambo, and he had shared all the information he had. He then gathered a number of relevant facts, for a change. Certain he wasn't giving anything away, he'd spoken on another pretext with Hal first thing in the morning and followed up on what he'd learned from him. With all the resources at their disposal, Homicide could undoubtedly move the case along to its conclusion, or at least to an arrest, much more quickly and efficiently than he could. Abe knew that Abby and JaMorris had already gotten their first search warrant and that several others would be forthcoming before long.

He was finished. He had done his work and should just butt out.

He didn't care.

He had amends to make with these people, all of whom he had led down the primrose lane over the past weeks, pursuing a theory that turned out not to have been based on the facts.

There was also his reputation.

This time he wasn't taking any chances. He still had some critical questions to which he'd much prefer to have answers before he dropped another theory in everyone's laps. He was confident that he could get them.

Alone.

Though it was now late morning, the fog clung as heavy as ever.

Glitsky parked within a block of the address on Upper Ashbury. To his surprise — although he should have expected it — the house was not just beautiful but large and elegant: a dark brown two-story bungalow set a bit farther back from the street than most of its neighbors. Its surrounding shrubbery was well kept, perfectly trimmed. A colorful array of flowers trimmed the walkway up through the lawn. A brace of large ceramic urns graced the steps leading up to the wide wraparound porch. The front door was paneled glass.

Glitsky stood in his heavy jacket on the welcome mat and took a breath. He carried two small tape recorders: one that would remain hidden in his jacket pocket and another that he would put out for the world to see.

Turning the hidden one on, he pushed the doorbell.

A deep gong resounded through the house, and through the panes, he made out a woman's shapely figure as she emerged into the entryway. The door swung open, and she greeted him with an easy smile. He'd called, and she'd been expecting him.

"Good morning."

"Good morning, Ruth." He kept his tone cordial, low-key. "May I come in?"

"Of course. It's a little brisk for conversation out here, wouldn't you agree?" She stepped back, holding the door open, and Abe stepped over the threshold into the house, a seemingly casual but legally critical moment — no assertion of authority, no sign of coercion, a "consensual encounter." He could ask her anything he wanted, and her answers would be admissible. "I've got a little fire going in the library, come this way," she said.

She turned and walked in front of him.

Her above-the-knee skirt and low heels showcased her legs, and the clinging sweater, with three buttons undone, her cleavage — the package much more put together than he'd seen at Hal's with the kids. Chattering easily over her shoulder, she went on, "I know they don't want us to burn real fires anymore, but really, how silly, don't you think? Why have fireplaces if you can't burn wood? It doesn't make any sense. In any event" — she turned and led him into a cozy book-lined room on their left — "here we are." Two nicely upholstered wing chairs sat before the low fire, a small coffee table between them, and she motioned Abe into one. "Can I get you anything?"

"Thanks. I'm fine." He motioned for her to take the other chair.

As she sat, she said, "I must confess, I'm a little bit curious as to what could be so important that you had to see me today. I was under the impression that you'd pretty much cleared everything up. Of course, I'm completely at your disposal if it will help Hal in any way, but I did wonder."

Looking over at her, Glitsky had a moment of doubt. Not about what Ruth Chase had done but about his own personal strategy, his decision to confront her alone. He knew it was possible that Abby and Jambo had already completed some of the searches he'd outlined for them that morning, and that they might even have enough evidence and a cooperative judge to sign off on an arrest warrant. They could be here as his backup, ensure everyone's safety, and formally take her into custody.

Abe also knew that if the inspectors came with their warrant, any chance to talk to this woman would be gone. Once she knew the game was up, she'd go quiet, far too cunning to waive her rights and talk to police. It had to be now, informal, a voluntary chat. Though Abe had no doubt about her guilt, there lurked in his mind an uneasy concern that she might find a way to escape. He had to keep that from happening.

He had to get her talking.

He took out his tape recorder. "Do you mind?"

"Do I have a choice?"

"Of course." He gave her his closest approximation of an apologetic smile. "Just to keep the record straight. And I'm a lousy stenographer." He began by saying in as casual a tone as he could muster, "As it turns out, there are a few outstanding and unanswered questions I was hoping you could help me out with."

"If I'm able to. Of course."

"Do you remember at Katie's funeral, you and I had a discussion about Hal, and I told you I didn't think he was guilty after all?"

She nodded. "That was one of the first hopeful moments I'd had since his arrest. I was so grateful for it."

"I remember. I also remember you told me in some detail that you couldn't imagine Hal walking up that path behind her with the gun at her head. You said you couldn't imagine him pushing her onto that path off to the right through the bushes and shooting her. Do you remember saying that?"

Ruth smiled uncertainly, her brow furrowing slightly. "I do, yes. As I said, I was grateful you were being so open-minded about Hal. I remember it distinctly."

"So do I." Abe let a silence build. "I'd pretty much forgotten about it until last night. Then it came back to me and got me wondering how you knew about that right turn."

Ruth shot him another questioning smile. "I . . . I don't really know. I think maybe Hal must have told me about it when he found her."

"I don't think that was it," Abe said. "I talked to Hal this morning and asked if he remembered telling you about him being taken to see Katie's body, and he said you wouldn't even let him start. You told him it made you sick just thinking about it. You didn't want to hear any details at all. Do you remember telling him that?"

"Not really. He must've started and . . ." She stopped. "It might have been one of the other guards who was there."

"And how would they have known?"

"Maybe Hal told one of them."

"He says he didn't, though. Thinking about it made him sick, too. He says he didn't tell anybody."

Ruth, her lips tight, let out a breath through her nose. "This has all been so upsetting. At this point, I'm not sure what I knew or how I knew it. Do you know what, Abe? It's almost lunchtime. I'm going to make myself a drink. Can I get you something?"

"No, thank you. I'm fine."

Abe watched her stand and then disappear into the hallway. In fact, it wasn't almost lunchtime, and when she returned, she wasn't drinking wine but a nearly full glass of clear liquid on ice.

"So," she began as soon as she'd sat back down, "about where they found Katie's body. Maybe I saw or read something."

"You looked at pictures and articles even though you didn't want to know any details because they made you sick?"

"Maybe I did. I don't really remember. What does it matter?"

"Maybe it doesn't, Ruth. Except that it led me to another question. About Pete's death, Hal's father, your second husband."

Ruth's gentle smile vanished. "This is getting rather far afield, isn't it, Lieutenant?"

"I don't think so. I know that Pete died of an overdose of barbiturates and alcohol. You take barbiturates, don't you?"

"Not barbiturates. Just some amitriptyline to help me sleep."

"When they prescribe that kind of drug, they tell you not to mix it with alcohol, don't they? And there was an awful lot of both in Pete's system when he died, wasn't there?"

She waved that off. "Pete didn't pay much attention to that kind of stuff. Besides, I already told you that while it was kind of the coroner and the investigators to help us by calling it an accident, I've always believed Pete killed himself."

"Well, however he died, you ended up with a million dollars." He saw her straighten and decided to tone it down a bit — too much of a press might shut her up, and he needed to keep her talking. "Tell you what," he said, "let's get back to the

518

matter at hand. Katie's murder."

Ruth finished her drink with a gulp. "Mr. Glitsky . . . Abe," she said, "I thought we were getting along so well together. Just tell me what it is you want to know."

"I want to know why Katie turned against you. Why she was keeping you from the kids. Katie got curious for some reason — maybe she noticed that Ellen acted different every time you babysat for her, suspected that maybe her little girl had been drugged — and sometime around the day, maybe the same day, she was killed, she looked you up on her computer, just like I did. But then she took it a step further, the step I should have taken when I first came upon it."

Shaking her head in apparent bewilderment, her voice dripping with disdain, Ruth asked, "And what, pray tell, was that?"

"She found the article in the *San Mateo County Times* on Ron Johannson, your first husband, who also died in a tragic accident. He drowned, didn't he? Another secret you chose not to share with Katie and Hal. You kept a lot from them, didn't you?"

"I kept what I needed to keep," she said.

"I know," Abe said. "Quite the keeper, aren't you?"

She shrugged. "Some secrets need to be

kept. No one needs to know them."

"Except," Abe said, "that Katie found out, didn't she? And realized that coincidentally, in Ron's case, there was also some question of accident versus suicide, but the death got ruled accidental, and once again you made almost a million dollars."

"Ron's death was an accident. This is all ridiculous. You have no proof of anything you're insinuating about me." Again she got to her feet. "And I'm having another drink."

Again Glitsky waited patiently, and again, when Ruth returned, her glass was nearly full. "So?" she began almost brightly. "Where were we? Oh yes. You don't have any proof of a single thing you're saying."

"Katie didn't need proof, did she?" Abe asked. "She just needed to know in her own mind that you were a sick and dangerous person. But I'm guessing there will be something in those files when we go through them again, as we're already doing. Although I think we're not really going to need it. Proof about your husbands, I mean."

"I don't —"

Glitsky held up a hand. "Let me ask you this, Ruth. Did you know that most cell phones today keep not only a record of

520

whom you call but where the call was made?"

"What does that have to —"

Abe cut her off once more. "On Saturday morning, you told Warren and Patti that you were having a bad day, so they took Will and Ellen out to the playground in the park, where they stayed for about two hours, didn't they?"

Ruth sat back in her chair, hands clasped in her lap. "You tell me."

"I will. They did. This is when Patti discovered that she'd lost her cell phone. But she hadn't lost it. You had taken it. And it was with you when you stayed back in the house, all alone. And where you placed two calls to Adam Foster while Patti and Warren were at the playground. No one else besides you could have placed those calls, Ruth. You called him and arranged to meet him that night."

"No, I didn't."

Glitsky knew he might have been giving her answers to questions that, better prepared, she could counter later in a courtroom. He didn't care. He wasn't finished yet, not by a long shot, and he wanted her to know what he had come to understand about her, what he had uncovered that would bring her down.

He leaned toward her again. "The other thing you thought you knew, Ruth, is that even with a serial number, Pete's gun couldn't be connected to him. But service weapons don't belong to individual officers. They belong to the city and county. When you quit or retire, your gun comes back. If you die on the job, though, sometimes — especially back then — they forget to ask for it. If it's an old revolver like Pete's, it's retired, but it's still on the books."

This brought a bit of a rise. "Pete didn't even have a service weapon," Ruth said. "Guards can't carry guns in the jail."

"That's right, they can't. So you thought that his gun was just something he acquired on the street, like a lot of cops do. An old throwaway with no history and a serial number that couldn't be traced to him. But as we discovered this morning, it wasn't an old throwaway. It was his service piece. You didn't turn it in after Pete's death. So maybe you'd like to try to explain to me how that gun, the gun that killed Katie and Adam Foster, with a serial number registered on the city and county books as belonging to your husband, Pete, got in Adam Foster's hand."

Ruth Chase sat dead still for a long moment, unblinking. Finally, turning her head toward Abe, her voice impossibly calm, she said, "Maybe Pete gave it to Adam Foster." Perhaps realizing how absurd that sounded, she relaxed back into the cushions. "That fool girl," she said, her voice changing. "What did she want me to do? Go, 'Oh, you're right, it was so wrong of me to kill my husbands. Maybe I'll just forget about the money and start over again somewhere else'? What did she think was going to happen? So she called that day, and I asked her to wait a little, give me a chance to explain in person. It wasn't what it seemed to be."

"But it was exactly that, Ruth, wasn't it?"

She didn't answer, staring into the empty space in front of her. "She actually thought I should get into counseling, tell somebody, and it would all be fine. And she couldn't let me see the children anymore, but I'd understand that. I mean, with my history, she couldn't let me near them, could she? That would be irresponsible. But she wasn't going to turn me in. Although she told me she wouldn't be surprised if I decided to do that on my own. I'd feel so much better. What a fool she was. What a complete and utter fool."

"So you killed her?"

She looked him straight in the eye. "And the world is a better place for it."

"What about Hal?"

"What about him?"

"You were going to let him go down for killing Katie?"

She shook her head. "It was never going to come to that. I knew he didn't kill her, you see? There was no evidence. He had a good lawyer. He would walk. I never worried about it." She took a breath and straightened her back. A bit unsteadily, she got to her feet. "What do we do now, me and you?" she asked. She broke an ice-cold smile. "Usually, it's the guy who says it, but I suppose a blow job is out of the question."

Glitsky looked up at her. "You think this is funny?"

"Fucking hysterical," she said. "Really. So what now?"

Glitsky stood up. "Now we are driving downtown."

"Oh, please, spare me this shit."

"Please turn around and place your hands behind your back."

"You're going to handcuff me?"

Glitsky already had his cuffs out. "Please do as I ask."

"What if I don't?"

"Then I'd be required to use force. Neither of us wants that. Please turn around."

Ruth threw a glance toward the ceiling. "I

need another drink," she said. "And then I need to use the bathroom. Can we put off the handcuffs that long? You can come in with me if you're so nervous about it."

Without another word, she headed for the door, got to the hallway, and turned left toward the back of the house. Abe, skittish, grabbed his tape recorder and turned it off before he drew his gun. Carrying it at his side, he followed a few steps behind her. In the kitchen, out of her arm's reach, he stood in the doorway and watched while she poured more vodka into her glass and took one deep swallow, then a second.

Abe took a step forward. "All right," he said, "that's enough."

She chortled, met his gaze, and lifted the glass again.

"Ruth! Stop! Now!"

She tipped the glass back, emptying it, then placed it on the counter. "Might as well make a party out of it," she said. "And now the bathroom."

He was not going to let her dictate what she did next. She was a suspect, and he knew the protocol for an arrest, and that did not include either her taking that last drink or her using the bathroom. He knew that he needed to get her locked into the backseat of his car without any more compromise.

"Turn around. Hands behind your back," he said. "You can use the restrooms downtown."

She sighed, her shoulders sagged, and for an instant she looked like what she was — a pathetic old woman. There was no need for him to be gratuitously cruel to her. She raised her eyes and looked at him. "Really, Abe," she said, "I have to pee. Please. I won't be a problem. I promise."

"All right. Move," he said.

"Thank you."

She passed by him again, and five or six steps later, she turned in to a door they'd passed on the way up the hallway. Abe closed the gap between them.

She abruptly turned. "Should I leave the door open?"

"Not necessary," Abe said. "But don't lock it."

She went in, closed the door. He heard her tinkle and the toilet flush. Then he heard a rinse in the sink, long enough for him to touch the door with the butt of his gun. "All right."

She came out drying her face. "Now I want to call my attorney. You tricked me into talking to you."

Glitsky realized that if his goal had been

to break her spirit, he had failed. But he had wrung from her a confession, every word of which was recorded. Twice. He decided to let her make the call, then he stood five feet in front of her while she evidently spoke to a secretary, left a message, and hung up.

"All right," Glitsky said, "turn around, hands behind you."

When he had the handcuffs on her, Abe held her, truly unsteady by now, by the upper arm and walked with her out the front door, down the path to the sidewalk, and over to the city police vehicle that he'd driven down in. Opening the back door, without a word, he helped her get in, then closed the door behind her.

He hit the ignition and turned to see her settled against the door, her eyes closed, to all appearances sound asleep. He put the car into gear and pulled out into the street.

The fog remained impermeable, and thick traffic was backed up crossing Van Ness and then again at Market. In the next twenty minutes, Abe checked the rearview mirror continuously and asked Ruth several times how she was doing. She remained motionless, eyes closed, slumping against the door. She refused to answer or acknowledge him in any way. It took him nearly ten minutes more to cover the two blocks on Bryant from Fifth Street to Seventh Street, then another five to get to the parking lot.

When he came around to open the door Ruth was leaning on, she collapsed, almost falling out on the pavement. As he grabbed at the dead-weight and lifted her back inside, it occurred to him that she was faking it, but then he recognized the pallor and, hand to her forehead, felt the clammy coldness of her skin.

He tapped at her cheek with his palm, spoke her name.

Straightening, he pulled out his cell phone and punched 911. When he got through to the dispatcher, he said, "This is Lieutenant Abe Glitsky with the DA Investigations Division. I have a prisoner in custody in the back of the Bryant Street jail parking lot, and she is unconscious and unresponsive. I need paramedics immediately."

63

CityTalk
by JEFFREY ELLIOT

The long and winding road that has been the investigation into the death of Katie Chase came to an abrupt ending yesterday with the suicide of Ruth Chase, the victim's mother-in-law. Following a lengthy tape-recorded interrogation by Abraham Glitsky, the former head of San Francisco's Homicide detail, who had become the lead investigator in the case, the elder Mrs. Chase confessed to four murders: her two former husbands; Katie Chase; and Chief Deputy Adam Foster, whose death by gunshot last Saturday was previously considered a suicide.

During the interrogation, Mrs. Chase apparently decided to end her life rather than face prosecution and probable imprisonment. According to police, she was able to consume a massive dose of the prescription drug Elavil without being observed.

According to Ruth Chase's taped statement, Katie Chase had discovered that the deaths of both of Ruth's husbands, which had been ruled accidental, might have been murders. In each case, the elder Mrs. Chase had received substantial life insurance payments. When Katie Chase confronted her mother-in-law with her suspicions, supporting them with documents retrieved on Internet searches, Ruth Chase decided that she had to act. Knowing that Katie would be alone while her husband was driving to the airport on the day before Thanksgiving, Ruth confronted her daughter-in-law at gunpoint, somehow got her to a nearby park, and shot her.

Later, after her stepson, Hal, had been arrested and charged in his wife's death, Ruth Chase saw and took an opportunity, perhaps under the guise of a proposed sexual encounter, to meet with Mr. Foster, who was already a suspect in three other murders: Alanos Tussaint, Maria Solis-Martinez, and Luther Jones. Meeting with Mr. Foster in a Presidio parking lot, she shot him in his car and was successful in making it look like a suicide, complete with a handwritten suicide note.

Although Mrs. Chase's confession clears

Mr. Foster of any involvement in Katie Chase's death, it also leaves unresolved the investigations into those latter murders.

As Jeff Elliot had noted in "CityTalk," Ruth Chase's arrest and suicide essentially negated the solutions to the murders of Alanos Tussaint, Luther Jones, and Maria Solis-Martinez. Since Ruth had no possible connection to any of those individuals, and since she had confessed to shooting Adam Foster with her husband's old service revolver, there was no longer any reason to believe that the chief deputy had played a role in those other three deaths.

For Burt Cushing, this was unacceptable.

So on the Monday following Ruth's demise, after a weekend of feverish activity among the jail guards, and in cooperation with the Homicide Department, Sheriff Cushing stepped before the microphones in front of the mayor's office at City Hall. He carried an impressively thick manila folder. With His Honor Leland Crawford hovering behind him and making the flattering and supportive introductory remarks, he was flanked by SFPD Homicide chief Devin Juhle and by the city's medical examiner, John Strout. (Rather conspicuous in his absence was the district attorney, Wes Farrell, who had begged off because of a previous speaking engagement.)

When he got to the podium, Cushing's usual jovial political face was nowhere to be found; in its place was a stern and solemn law enforcement officer with some serious news to convey. "Ladies and gentlemen," he began, "we're going to take all the time we need to answer your questions regarding the results of the examination that is the subject of this press conference today, but first I'd like to present you with the conclusions that have been reached by a joint task force of the Sheriff's Department, working in tight partnership with the SFPD, especially with Devin Juhle here, who, as you all know, is the head of Homicide.

"A week ago Saturday, my chief deputy, Adam Foster . . ."

Cushing went on to reiterate the salient points: the apparent suicide with the damning note; the conclusion shared by all that Foster had murdered Katie Chase, Alanos Tussaint, and Maria Solis-Martinez; the startling confession of Ruth Chase regarding Foster and Katie, followed by the even more shocking fact of her own suicide, which, Cushing gratuitously noted, took place in the presence of Glitsky, "whose actions in that setting are even now the subject of a major investigation."

Cushing looked down at his notes, raised his eyes, and surveyed his audience, then started in again. "When I first heard about Ruth Chase's confession, the first thing that occurred to me was Adam Foster was innocent of the murders that had been attributed to him. My trusted lieutenant, even more than the other men under my command, had been like a son to me" — here he wiped a finger under his right eye — "and I did not want to believe him capable of those kinds of heinous acts.

"Nevertheless, upon reflection, I realized that my duty came first, far above my personal feelings. If Adam was indeed responsible for these crimes, it was my job to find out about it. I'll admit right here that my original intention in ordering a task force investigation was to find proof that Adam was innocent. To that end, we began a series of interviews and searches that, to my great sadness, revealed a long-term pattern of corruption and institutional malfeasance, at the center of which was Adam Foster."

He held up the manila folder. "In these pages are a collection of memoranda, emails, phone records, testimony of other jail guards, and personal notes that unequivocally document the bare fact of the matter: Chief Deputy Foster ran a large contraband smuggling ring into and out of the jail. Of course, Chief Deputy Foster could not have done all of this without the cooperation of several of his coworkers, many of whom worked under extreme duress and threats. Over the course of the past five days, we have identified most, if not all, of these accomplices, and we will be determining the proper disposition of these individual cases on an ongoing basis over the next several days, weeks, and months."

Cushing glanced at his notes, squared his jaw, and continued. "As to the main event — the allegations of the murders of Alanos Tussaint, Maria Solis-Martinez, and Luther Jones — it is my terrible duty to inform you that these, too, appear to be the work of Adam Foster. Several guards who had provided an alibi for Mr. Foster on the day of Mr. Tussaint's murder have come forward and, no longer under the sway of Mr. Foster's coercion, admitted their roles. Likewise, all of the so-called poker group members who had verified Mr. Foster's alibi on the night of Ms. Solis-Martinez's murder have recanted their earlier testimony. One of them, Michael Maye, has further testified that Mr. Foster admitted the killing to him.

All of these men lived under the constant threat of reprisal by Mr. Foster if they did not play along with his nefarious plans. Let me be clear: That behavior is not acceptable, especially for people in law enforcement, and the Sheriff's Department, again, will be dealing with these cases individually to restore public trust in the department."

Cushing drew himself up straight. "I would be remiss if I tried to deny my own responsibility for this scandal. As sheriff, I supervise the jail. The buck stops here. I should have seen or intuited what I did not see. I let a culture develop on my watch that is unacceptable in every respect, and if the citizens of this city, in their wisdom, choose to remove me from office, I will humbly do their bidding.

"But if, as I hope, the city can forgive me, I promise that in the future, I will earn your trust and your respect once again, and that this Sheriff's Department will again be a beacon of efficiency, organization, and most of all, compassion.

"Now I'll be happy to take your questions."

Over his petrale at Tadich, Abe was enduring Dismas Hardy's scorn over the events surrounding the death of Ruth Chase. From

Hardy's perspective, though he had gleaned essentially all the amusement he could from the situation (which was not especially funny), Diz wasn't quite ready to give up. "I think about what you would have done to one of your own troops, back when you were in management, if they'd arrested somebody and then stopped for a drink on the way downtown."

"We didn't stop for any drink. It was just her, at her house."

"Oh, much better."

Glitsky pushed the fish around on his plate. "You had to be there. I'm not defending it. I've already admitted to the universe at large that it was a huge mistake, but . . ."

"But you're saying it was okay this time."

"What do you want me to say? I never expected it, not in a million years. Nothing like that had ever happened before. She totally blindsided me."

"You're lucky she didn't have a gun in the bathroom closet. You wouldn't be here now."

"Possibly not. On the other hand, I might have shot her first. On the third hand, look at the bright side. I am here now. Plus, I probably saved the city half a mil on her trial. Maybe more."

"More. I promise."

"See? Win-win." Abe took a bite. "Anyway,

I'm done beating myself up over it. Do you know how many people that woman killed?"

"Sure. Katie, two husbands, and Foster. Three humans."

"More."

"Five? Six?"

Glitsky nodded. "At least six, maybe seven."

Hardy put his glass down. "What?"

"These four. Then one of her uncles who apparently raped her, a high school teacher, ditto, and a kid in juvie, never proved but probable. To say nothing about both her parents. And who knows how many others."

"Are you making this up?"

"No."

"Where'd you get this? If she was in juvie, the record's expunged."

"Right, but what do you think I've been up to the last week while they were deciding what they were going to do with me?"

"Polishing your résumé?"

"Funny. No. Being a trained investigator, I was investigating, following leads and checking out the truly depressing and scary childhood of Ruth Paley Johannson Chase."

"Hal didn't know about it?"

"Not much. He got me to Redwood City, and I took it from there. One of the DAs down there — Mary Patricia Whelan-Miille, who says she knows you, by the way — knew all about Ruth, off the record, of course. Said she was the bad seed all over again. You'll love this: She'd been following Katie's case all along and told me if she'd known Ruth Chase was Ruth Paley, she would have called and clued us in, maybe saved a few lives in the process."

"There's an upbeat story."

Glitsky nodded. "I'm an upbeat kind of guy."

"Oh yeah. People say that all the time." Hardy sipped some wine. "So, upbeat guy, what are you doing next?"

"Hanukkah, then Christmas. All the kids are blowing through town."

"Nice. After that?"

"I thought by then, the investigation will be finished, and I'll get a formal reprimand and then go back to working for Wes."

"The old Abe would have been bothered by a formal reprimand."

Abe shrugged. "Sticks and stones. Worst case, they let me go. Then I'll stop by Wyatt Hunt's place and check out the PI business, where you don't have to follow all those rules." A glint of humor appeared in his eyes. "If it comes to that, I thought maybe you would give me a reference."

"As an investigator?"

"Either way, with Wes or with Wyatt, I'm going to be an investigator. That's what I do, Diz. That's who I am."

"You're killing me," Hardy said. "After all the madness this past month, I would have thought you'd had enough."

Glitsky spread his palms and broke into what was, for him, a wide smile. "Apparently not."

ACKNOWLEDGMENTS

Though the actual writing of this novel was very much a solitary affair, I'm much indebted to those friends and acquaintances who bore with me through the artistic and creative angst that seemed to be a near constant companion as the pages of *The Keeper* piled up. Helping to lighten that load on a regular basis were: my assistant, Anita Boone, Tom Hedtke, Max Byrd, perennial best man Don Matheson, Chief Sommelier and Chevalier of the Brazen Serpent Frank Seidl, the Bistro 33 Friday-night gang, and my golfing instructor, Bob Zaro.

Deserving special mention is my friend and consultant on all things legal, Al Giannini. As in almost all of my other books, Al not only acted as a sounding board for the flow of this story as it developed; he also offered comments and insight on legal issues and law enforcement culture that played a large role in the book's completion. The other main contributor to this book has been my longtime friend and agent, Barney Karpfinger, whose taste and sensitivity as a reader and critic cannot be overstated. Barney played an active supporting role in every aspect of this book, from the original outline to the finished manuscript.

Several people have generously contributed to charitable organizations by purchasing the right to name a character in this book. These people and their respective organizations are: Joe Payson (the Olaf Wieghorst Museum, El Cajon, CA); Maria T. Solis-Martinez (the Anaheim Public Library Foundation); Dan Sillin (San Francisco CASA); Mary Patricia Whelan-Miille (Yolo County CASA); Tom Scerbo (Baby Basics/Children's Aid and Family Services); and Lyle P. Wiedeman (Men of Mystery, Writers of the Future).

For some critical medical and pharmaceutical issues, I'd like to thank John Chuck for the introduction to Frank Paloucek, PharmD, DABAT (Diplomate of the American Board of Applied Toxicology), Pharmacy Residency Director, University of Illinois, Chicago.

For everything having to do with social media — my Web page (www.johnlescroart

.com), blog, Twitter (www.twitter.com/john lescroart), and Facebook — I'm grateful to Dr. Andy Jones and his crack team of computer wizards at Eager Mondays. I truly love to hear from my readers, and I invite one and all to stop by any of the sites and join these lively, interesting, and fun conversations.

My two private editors, Doug Kelly and Peggy Nauts, continue to find and correct mistakes that keep trying to make their way into my books. Thanks to both for their keen eyes and critical intelligence.

I am proud to be published by Atria Books, so thank you very much to my publisher, Judith Curr, and my editor, Peter Borland, for giving me the opportunity to work with one of the best imprints in the world. Thanks also to the efforts of the publicity and marketing departments at Atria, especially the indefatigable David Brown.

Oh, and last but not even a little bit least — my children, Justine and Jack, are great joys in my life, and inform all of my books in ways both great and small. I'm so glad we are sharing this life together.

ABOUT THE AUTHOR

John Lescroart is the author of twenty-four previous novels (sixteen *New York Times* bestsellers), including *The 13th Juror, Damage, The Hunter,* and *The Ophelia Cut.* His books have sold more than 10 million copies and have been translated into twenty-two languages in seventy-five countries. He lives in Northern California.

The employees of Thorndike Press hope you have enjoyed this Large Print book. All our Thorndike, Wheeler, and Kennebec Large Print titles are designed for easy reading, and all our books are made to last. Other Thorndike Press Large Print books are available at your library, through selected bookstores, or directly from us.

For information about titles, please call:
(800) 223-1244

or visit our Web site at:
http://gale.cengage.com/thorndike

To share your comments, please write:
Publisher
Thorndike Press
10 Water St., Suite 310
Waterville, ME 04901